STRANGERS ON A BRIDGE

Louise Mangos

from tree to book
and back again...

www.book-cycle.org

RED DOG

UK

For Chris, for always believing in me

CHAPTER ONE
APRIL

I WOULDN'T NORMALLY exercise on the weekend, but several days of continuous spring rain had hampered my attempts to run by the *Aegerisee* near our home during the week. The lake had brimmed over onto my regular running paths, turbid waters frothy with alpine meltwater. The sun came out that morning, accompanied by a cloudless blue sky I wanted to dive into. Simon knew I was chomping at the bit. He let me go, encouraging me to run for everyone's peace of mind. He would go cycling later with a group of friends when I returned home for domestic duties.

I chose a woodland track from the lowlands near the town of Baar, and planned to run up through the Lorze Gorge beside the river, continuing along the valley to home. A local bus dropped me at the turn-off to the narrow limestone canyon, and I broke into a loping jog along the gravel lane, which dwindled to a packed earthen trail. Sunlight winked through trees fluorescent with new leaf shoots, and the forest canopy at this time of day shaded much of the track. The swollen river gushed at my side. Branches still dripped from days of dampness as the sun dried out the woodlands. I lengthened my stride, and breathed in the metallic aroma of sprouting wild garlic. The mundane troubles of juggling family time dissipated, and as I settled into my metronome rhythm, a feeling of peacefulness ensued.

The sun warmed my shoulders as I ran out from the shade of the forest. I focused on a small pine tree growing comically out of the mossy roof shingles of the old Tobel Bridge. Above me, two more bridges connected the widening funnel of the

Lorze Gorge at increasingly higher levels, resembling an Escher painting.

Before I entered the dim tunnel of the wooden bridge, I glanced upwards. A flash of movement caught my eye. My glance slid away, and darted back.

A figure stood on the edge of the upper bridge.

In a split second my brain registered the person's stance. I sucked in my breath, squinting to be sure I had seen correctly at such a distance.

Oh, no. Don't. Please, don't.

The figure stood midway between two of the immense concrete pillars rising out of the chasm, his fists clutching the handrail. His body swayed slightly as he looked out across the expanse to the other side of the gorge, the river roaring its white noise hundreds of feet below him. Birdsong trilled near me on the trail, strangely out of place in this alarming situation.

At first I was incredulous. How ridiculous to think this person was going to jump. But that body language, a certain hollowed stiffness to his shoulders and chest, even from a distance, radiated doom. Unsure how to react, but sure I didn't want to observe the worst, I slowed my pace to a walk, and finally stopped.

'*Haallo*!' I yelled over the noise of the river.

My voice took some time to reach him, the echo bouncing back and forth between the canyon walls. Seconds later his head jolted, awoken from his reverie.

'Hey! Hallo!' I called again, holding my arm out straight, palm raised like a marshal ordering traffic to halt at an intersection.

I backtracked a few metres on the trail, away from the shadow of the covered bridge, so he could see me more clearly. A path wove up through the woods on the right, connecting the valley to the route higher up. I abandoned my initial course and ran up the steep slope, having lost sight of the man somewhere above me. At the top I turned onto the pavement and hurried towards the main road onto the bridge, gulping painful breaths of chilly air. My heart pounded with panic and the effort of running up the hill.

The man had been out of my sight for more than a few minutes. I dreaded what I might find on my arrival, scenarios crowding in my mind, along with thoughts of how I might help this person. As I strode onto the bridge, I saw with relief he was still there on the pavement. I was now level with him, and no longer had to strain my neck looking upwards. Fear kept my eyes connected to the lone figure as I approached. If I looked away for even a second, he might leap stealthily over the edge. Holding my gaze on him would hopefully secure him to the bridge.

'Hallo...' I called more softly, my voice drowned by the sound of the rushing water in the Lorze below. I walked steadily along the pavement towards him. Despite my proximity, this time he didn't seem to have heard me.

'*Grüezi*, hallo,' I said again.

With a flick of his head, he leaned back again, bent his knees, and looked ahead.

'No!' The gunshot abruptness of my shout broke his concentration. My voice ricocheted off the concrete wall of the bridge. He stopped mid-sway, eyes wide.

My stomach clenched involuntarily as I glanced down into the gorge, when moments before I had been staring up out of it. I felt foolish, not knowing what to say. It seemed like a different world up here. As I approached within talking distance, I greeted him in my broken German, still breathing heavily.

'Um, good morning... Beautiful, hey?' I swept my arm about me.

What a stupid thing to say. My voice sounded different without the echo of space between us. The words sounded so absurd, and a nervous laugh escaped before I could stop it.

He looked at me angrily, but remained silent, perhaps vaguely surprised that someone had addressed him in a foreign language. Or surprised anyone had talked to him at all in this country where complete strangers rarely struck up a conversation beyond a cursory passing greeting. His cheeks flushed with indignation. I reeled at the wave of visual resentment. Then his eyes settled on my face, and his features softened.

'Do you speak English?' I asked. The man nodded; no smile, no greeting. He still leaned backwards, hands gripping the railing. *Please. Don't. Jump.*

He was a little taller than me, and a few years my senior. Sweat glistened on his brow. His steel-grey hair was raked back on his head as though he had been running his fingers through it repeatedly. His coat flapped open to reveal a smart navy suit, Hugo Boss maybe, and I looked down to the pavement expecting to see a briefcase at his feet. He looked away. I desperately needed him to turn back, keep eye contact. My hand hovered in front of me, wanting to pull the invisible rope joining us.

'I... I'm sorry, but I had this strange feeling you were considering jumping off the bridge.' A nervous laugh bubbled again in my throat, and I hoped my assessment had been false.

'I am,' he said.

CHAPTER TWO

IMMEASURABLE SECONDS OF silence followed the man's admission. My brain shut out external influences. A blink broke the rift in time. Sounds rushed back in – the swishing of an occasional passing vehicle, gushing water in the river below, the persistent tweeting of a bird, like the squeaky wheel of an old shopping trolley.

'Now you've stopped me,' he said. 'This is not good. You should go away. Go away.'

But the daggers in his eyes had retracted. I held his gaze, trying not to blink for fear of losing the connection. Many clichés entered my head. In desperation I chose one to release the tension.

'Can we talk? I know things must be bad. But maybe if you talk it through with someone…'

I shrugged, unsure how to continue. Perspiration cooled my body, and I shivered. Pulling the sleeves of my running shirt down to my wrists, I rubbed my upper arms. Wary of the abyss at my side, I took a step closer to the man. He didn't speak, but stood upright, and raised his hand as though to push me away. He turned briefly to look into the depths of the gorge, and I grabbed his arm firmly below the elbow, gently applying pressure. His gaze at first fixed on the hand on his arm, then rose again to my face. He studied my furrowed brow, and the forced curve of my smile.

'Please. Let's talk,' I said.

I had no magical formula for this, but I sensed my touch eased the tension in his body. My nails scraped the material of his coat as my grip on his arm tightened. He slumped down to sit on the pavement with his back to the bridge wall. I closed my eyes briefly and puffed air through my lips.

Step one achieved. No jump.

Traffic was sparse on a Sunday. One car slowed a little, but kept going. No one else was curious enough to stop. The regular swish and thump each time a vehicle drove over the concrete slabs echoed between the walls of the bridge. We must have looked like an odd pair. Me dressed in Lycra running pants and a bright-yellow running top, the man in his business attire, now looking a little dishevelled. The laces on his black brogues were undone. I stared at his feet, and wondered if he had intended to remove his shoes before he jumped.

'Can I help?' I asked, crouching down. The man looked at me imploringly, hands flopped over his knees. The strain of anguish had reddened the whites of his eyes, making his irises shine a striking green.

'I don't know,' he said uncertainly.

'Well, let's start with your name,' I said, as though addressing a small child.

'Manfred,' he said.

There was no movement towards the traditional Swiss handshake. Still squatting, pins and needles fizzed in my feet. I kept one arm across my thigh, the other balanced on fingertips against the pavement.

'Mine's Alice, and I'm sorry, I don't speak very good German…'

'It's okay,' he said. 'I speak a little English.'

I snorted involuntarily. It was the standard *I speak a little English* introduction I had grown used to over the past few years living in Switzerland, usually made with very few grammatical mistakes. The tension broke, and relief flooded through me. *He would not jump.* I sensed my beatific smile softening my expression. Manfred looked into my eyes and held my gaze intently, absorbing the euphoria.

I turned to sit at his side, blood rushing back to my legs. His gaze followed my movement, a curious glint now in his eyes, and his lips parted slightly, revealing the costly perfection of Swiss orthodontics. Leaning back against the wall, the cold concrete pressed against my sweat-dampened running shirt. I extended my legs, thighs sucking up the chill of the pavement. Our elbows touched and he drew in his knees, preparing to stand. I laid my hand on his arm.

'You must not do this thing. Please…'

He looked at me, tears pooling briefly before he swiped at his eyes with the back of one hand.

'You stopped me.'

'Yes, I stopped you. I don't want you to jump, Manfred.'

'You…' He scrutinised me.

'It's messy,' I said.

Manfred's gaze travelled from my face, looking at the dishevelled hair I knew must be sprouting from its ponytail, down to my legs stretched in front of me.

'Taking your life,' I continued. 'It's messy. Not just the – you know…' I made a rising and dipping movement with my hand. 'Trust me, I've been there.'

'You… wanted to jump?' Curiosity animated Manfred's voice.

'Not jumping, no. God forbid. A failed attempt at overdose. A teenage stupidity after a heartbreak. But I wasn't going anywhere on a dozen paracetemol.'

I'd never told Simon this, and I bit my lip at the admission. I remembered the 'mess' I had caused: a hysterical mother, a bruised oesophagus, a cough that lasted weeks after the stomach pump, embarrassing counselling that all boiled down to adolescent drama.

'Whatever has happened to make you do this, people will always be sad. You will harm more individuals than yourself. Not just physically,' I continued.

Manfred hissed briefly through his teeth. '*Ja, guet,*' he said, the Swiss German 'good' drawn out to two syllables. *Gu-weht.* He stared at a point below my face. I knew he was watching the pulse tick at the base of my throat, the suprasternal notch. The place where Simon often placed his lips. I zipped my running shirt up to the collar.

His gaze shifted back to my face. A slip of a smile, and then a frown.

'I cannot live with myself any more. I cannot live with who I am, what I do. What I have done,' he said.

The back of my neck tingled.

'But it doesn't solve the problem for other people,' I interjected. 'It creates more. There must be another way to work out your... your problems. Your life is precious. Your life is sacred, and will be special to someone.'

His lips formed a small circle.

'My life is...'

'Precious. Valuable. Prized. A good thing, not to be thrown away,' I reiterated.

He smiled tentatively, siphoning my relief, feeding on my compassion. I felt my euphoria returned to me, delivered on a platter of... what? Gratitude? No, it was something else.

My mouth went dry.

CHAPTER THREE

HE SHIFTED HIS body. My hand moved on his arm as he lifted a finger to wipe the dampness from under his eye. I wanted to reach out and hold his hand, relieve his sadness. He reached into the breast pocket of his suit jacket and pulled out a pair of glasses. He pressed them onto his face, and the rectangular black rims gave him even more of an executive look. I wondered what dreadful mistake had led him to the bridge. The stereotype of a man on the brink of financial ruin.

'We have to get you out of here,' I said as I pushed myself off the pavement and knelt in front of him. 'Did you drive here? Do you have a car nearby?'

He shook his head, and looked down to the pavement.

'Do you have a phone on you? Is there someone we can call?' I asked more gently.

As he gazed up at me without answering, I looked down at his feet. I tied his shoelaces, feeling his eyes on me as I performed this task, putting him back together. Rocking onto my heels, I reached towards his hand, and stood slowly. Manfred stared at my wrist, hypnotised by the contact. His hand, at first limp in mine, strengthened its hold. Pressing my lips together into a flat smile, I dipped my head in encouragement, and pulled him to his feet.

I felt like brushing the dust from his jacket, handing him his non-existent briefcase like the caring wife, and sending him on his way to his high-powered job at some investment bank. But I knew he wasn't ready to be left on his own. I kept hold of his hand to encourage him along the pavement, if only to get him off the bridge. As we walked towards a distant bus stop, I relaxed as we left behind the chasm of this man's destiny. Manfred seemed to realise this too, gazing up into the bright sky. I was unsure whether the dampness between our palms was mine, or his.

'Where are you leading me? This was not my plan,' he said.

'It's okay. You'll be okay. Let's go.' I smiled again, encouragingly. 'Will you come with me to the bus stop? I don't think I should leave you alone, but are you okay with that?'

Manfred's lips tightened into a line. I knew I should keep him talking. But what the hell do you say to someone who's just tried to throw himself off a bridge?

I shivered now, both from my rapidly chilling body and the influence of the adrenalin wearing off. My upper chest whirred unhealthily, and I coughed.

'Come!' My tone was falsely boisterous, trying to convince a small child to share an unwanted excursion. 'It's not far to the bus. At least we can get out of this damned cold.'

Manfred frowned. In his smart suit and coat, he was unlikely to be feeling the deceptive spring chill with this blue sky and sunshine. Attempting to stop my trembling, I clenched my jaw, and had trouble speaking. It was hard to focus on the timetable once we reached the stop. The next bus to Zug was in over an hour's time. Apart from the fact that I didn't have enough money to get us there, I couldn't wait that long. I'd freeze.

'This way,' I said as we crossed the road to check the timetable for the bus going the other way, back to Aegeri, towards home. Ten minutes. *Thank God.*

As we waited, our hands fell apart. I fiddled pointlessly with my ponytail, tucking wild scraps of hair behind my ears. I rubbed my arms, occupying my fingers, trying to forget the connection of our palms. There was a steel bench, but I chose not to sit on the cold metal. Manfred stood within a pace of me, moving with me when I walked to the other end of the shelter. I was tempted to sidle up to him, absorb his body warmth. I had to remind myself he was still a stranger, despite what we had been through moments before. Instead I leaned against the glass wall to shield myself from the wind. Having held his hand for so long, I almost regretted the rift, but detected the return of some confidence in his demeanour.

'You're cold,' he said simply, but didn't offer me his coat or his jacket. I wasn't sure I would have taken it anyway. I wouldn't have wanted to infuse the post-sport odour of my body into the lining of his Hugo Boss.

I recalled the executives at the advertising agency where I used to work in London. They'd never been part of the group of employees who sought out my psychological counselling in the HR department. My experience there had extended only to office arguments, secretaries complaining they had been treated unfairly, and personality assessments. Studying a potential suicide scenario in college was one thing. Being faced with a true-life victim was something else altogether.

I wished Simon were there to allay my uncertainty. What might he do in my shoes? Even the company of my chatty running partner, Kathy, would have been welcome. I imagined she would have made light of the situation, distracting Manfred with her chirpy Northern-English accent. I wanted so desperately to bring this man out of his despair. I'd seen that look before, when I'd volunteered at the homeless shelter during college holidays. An intrinsic need to make people feel better, to ease their pain.

The whining of a large diesel motor interrupted my thoughts. We climbed on the bus, Manfred now complying without resistance. I used the last of the change in my money belt to purchase two tickets from the driver, quite certain Manfred wasn't carrying any money. I chose a seat near the middle and he sat beside me.

As the bus pulled away and picked up speed, we gazed out of the window. The vehicle turned in a wide arc, up towards the next village, every metre taking us away from the bridge. On the last hairpin bend before the valley disappeared from view, Manfred looked briefly back in the direction of the gorge, and nodded once, almost imperceptibly. He turned to stare at the road ahead, then surprised me out of my thoughts.

'What are you going to do?' he asked.

I honestly didn't know. I was making this up as I went along.

'I need to get a warm jacket or something,' I said. 'You shouldn't be on your own right now. We'll decide what to do after I get myself sorted at home, pick up my handbag, keys and stuff. We can use my car. I need my phone and then we can decide, Mister... um... Manfred.'

He seemed to accept this short-term first step and drifted back to gazing out of the window. I did the same, chewing my lip. I was impatient to see Simon.

'You *live* in Aegeri? You're not a tourist?' Manfred's delayed curiosity further reinforced my relief. It was as though he had joined me on the bus and asked whether the seat next to me was free. A passenger making polite conversation.

'My husband works for a small trading company whose financial offices are in South London. He was offered a posting at the head office in Zug a few years ago, so we moved out here. I'm afraid I haven't learned much German since I've been here. We were supposed to be here for two years, but they asked him to stay.'

'You like Switzerland?' Manfred asked with an edge to his voice, something between confused pride and disdain. I wondered again what had brought him to the bridge. Perhaps a failing in the machine that yielded Swiss bureaucracy.

'It's a beautiful country. It took me a while to get used to your... customs. But I love the rural alpine contrast to the city. I used to work in human resources at a busy advertising company, so this is a different world.'

I gazed out of the window at newly budding cherry trees blurring past, among fields strewn with the last of the spring crocuses.

'I think our language is difficult to learn for the *Ausländer*,' he said.

'It was hard for me at first,' I admitted, recalling a misunderstanding with our local electrician. 'Our family was considered somewhat of a novelty when we arrived in the village. I set up something I call the Chat Club, where mums of the boys' friends could improve their English.'

'You have good *Dialekt*. Easy to understand. Not like some American accents.'

'Thank you. And I can tell you learned your English from a British teacher.' I smiled, almost forgetting why we were there.

'Switzerland is a multilingual nation. We have four official languages, but you will see, English will become our *allgemeine* language.

'It feels like the idea of a universal language is a long way from reaching our little village. I was hoping to learn some German in return for my teaching efforts,' I continued. 'But I was outnumbered. It never seemed to happen. My kids learned really quickly, though. Starting with some not so pretty language in the playground at school.'

'Then they have learned two languages. High German in the classroom and Swiss German outside school,' he said.

I nodded, and remembered when I heard Swiss German for the first time, a more guttural dialect with a sing-song lilt, interspersed with much throaty rumbles and chewing of vowels.

'The language barrier was much more of a challenge for me. But the priority of the Chat Club is to practise speaking English. I barely have chance to improve my own German-language skills beyond sentences of greeting and consumer needs. My compulsion to help has not been reciprocated... returned.'

Heat rose to my face as I remembered the things I had done wrong at the beginning of our move to Switzerland, impeding my integration into the community. It had taken me a while to get my head round some of the country's pedantic customs.

I realised I'd been blabbing to Manfred, overly enthusiastic as a result of this rare opportunity to speak to someone socially in my own language outside the family. I folded my hands in my lap and looked at the passing houses as we entered the outskirts of the Aegeri Valley. As the bus drove past some woodland, the sudden darkness revealed the image of our two faces in the window, heads bobbing in unison with the movement of the vehicle. Manfred continued to look at me. I swallowed, and pulled my gaze away from his reflection to the front of the bus.

What was I getting myself into now? I felt a little lost in this situation. But it would have been unthinkable for me to have ignored this man and run on ahead up the valley. He was hurting enough to have wanted to take his life. I thought of all the times I'd seen people walk past someone needing help. A fallen man in the park who everyone thought was drunk but was in reality suffering from Parkinson's. Lifting a lady's shopping into the back of her car when I saw her press her hands into the small of her back. Bringing warm socks and a cup of soup to the hungry homeless. I'd had a compulsion to help where others would ignore since I was a child. It was what made me want to study psychology in college. But here was a scenario I was hardly trained to deal with.

'*End Haltestelle*,' announced the bus driver.

'Final stop, our stop,' I said, standing up. 'I live just outside the village. It's a pretty walk.'

Stepping from the bus, we headed away from the village centre, our increase in altitude affording an unimpeded view of the lake. Sunlight glinted off the water in shards.

'This is one of Leo's favourite views,' I said as Manfred turned enquiringly. 'My eldest son. He loves the view, but hates the fact that he has to walk to school every day.'

I was making light conversation, trying to separate Manfred's thoughts from earlier events. He said nothing, and his silence after our conversation on the bus felt awkward.

'It is incredibly beautiful,' I reiterated, then changed the subject. 'Do you live locally? Close by?'

He gave a slight shrug and a movement of his head that said neither yes nor no. His eyes, now clear and inquisitive, looked at the lake, and I could tell he was appreciating the view, as the ghost of a smile touched his mouth. I bit my lip and looked back towards the water.

When we arrived at the door of the old Zuger building of which our duplex apartment was a part, I hesitated. I knew the fundamental rule was not to leave Manfred alone, but I was cautious enough to not want this man inside my home. The main door was protected by an overhang. Against the outside wall stood a bench where the kids usually sat to take off their muddy boots or brush snow from them in winter.

'I need to get a few things. Just wait here. Take a seat. I'll be as quick as possible. I'll be right back.' I tried a cheerfulness that sounded empty. 'Okay?' I put my hand on his shoulder.

Manfred nodded uncertainly and sat on the bench. I could tell his confusion and confidence were fighting each other in waves. I took a breath, and knew I definitely wasn't equipped for this. I hoped more than anything that Simon would be at home to support me, to talk to this stranger who I had accepted as a personal responsibility. Together we would have a better chance of helping him.

But as I crossed the threshold to our apartment, I knew immediately no one was home.

CHAPTER FOUR

THE DOOR WAS unlocked, as always, security considerations not a priority in our safe Swiss world. The place offered the kind of muffled stillness where motes of dust were the only sparking movement through the strips of midday sunlight now streaming down the hallway. No breathing bodies.

A hurried note scribbled on the back of an envelope told me Simon had departed on a bike ride with his mates. He had dropped the boys with friends of theirs before heading out. The spidery scribble indicated he was mildly pissed off I hadn't been home when I said I would. My first reaction was guilt, then a flash of irritation as I imagined him hurrying the note, not stopping to consider I might have sustained an injury or had a problem on my run.

I unclipped my running belt and let it drop to the floor, prising off my running shoes. I was still cold, and wished I could stay in my warm, cosy house. I ran the tap at the kitchen sink and took several big gulps of water straight from the flowing spout to quench my thirst.

After grabbing a fleece jacket, I pulled the car keys off the hook. Picking up my mobile, I swore I wouldn't run without it again, despite its bulk and fragility.

I stabbed Simon's number on the keypad.

'Come on, *come on.*' The ringing tone went on and on, eventually switching to his voicemail.

'Honey, please call me as soon as you get this message.'

I imagined Simon pushing his cadence to the maximum along some winding alpine road, changing positions in the peloton as his turn came to draft the others, phone ringing unheard in the tool pouch under his seat. Placing the mobile in my pocket, I leaned over to pull off my socks and slipped my slightly sore feet into a comfortable pair of pumps.

I was wary and didn't want to taint my hands with a decision that might lead Manfred back down the path of self-destruction. I was no experienced psychologist, and had never really used my skills in the remedial sense. This man needed help I could not give. Above all, my lack of mastery of the language meant I didn't have a great deal of confidence when it came to approaching anyone in authority on this matter. And it was Sunday, the obligatory day of rest. Along with washing-hanging and lawnmowing bans, the police were also entitled to a day off. They might not be around to save lost souls on bridges. I wasn't sure who I would find to help.

I glanced in the hall mirror, registering my post-sport mussed look, and hurried down the stairs to the main door.

MANFRED WAS STILL sitting on the bench with his head lowered, but his body language had changed. My mood brightened as I noticed the squaring of his shoulders, the set jaw, and his hair neatly combed. He was cleaning his glasses with a tissue pulled from a packet lying next to him on the bench. His head was no longer poised in despair, but in a position of concentration, performing the simple task with an air of purpose. I had been expecting more empty looks and the shell of a wretched soul. The change in these few minutes was remarkable. Humility and purpose were evident, and I smiled broadly at his return to life.

'I cannot believe I am so *dumm*, so stupid,' he said, continuing to carefully polish a lens. 'What was I thinking?'

A huge wave of relief washed over me. Part of me still wanted to help, but part of me wanted to turn my back on this situation now I was home. I selfishly wanted my weekend back. I wanted a hot shower, and a cup of tea. I wanted to make up for my absence from our family Sunday when everyone came home.

As Manfred stood up, on impulse I put my arms around him and hugged him.

'Welcome back,' I said with relief.

As I felt the pressure of his arms gently hugging me back, with his palms on my shoulder blades, I cleared my throat and released him awkwardly.

'Is there somewhere I can take you? Would you like to use my phone to call someone?' I asked, reaching for the mobile in my pocket.

He shook his head slowly.

'No, I've no one to call. I don't know, but I think I'll go home.'

'Is there… someone at home who will help you?'

A muscle ticked above his jaw as he clenched his teeth and a small sigh escaped his lips.

'No, actually. On second thoughts, perhaps that is not such a good idea.'

I began to feel awkward about Manfred being in such close proximity to the house. His case needed to be reported; he should talk to someone.

'Will you drive with me in my car?'

He looked at me, green eyes shining behind his glasses, brows slightly raised in an expression of complete trust. He fell into step beside me as we walked to the garage where our Land Rover was parked. He waited while I started the car. After reversing out of the garage, I indicated he should get in.

'It's okay, you can leave the garage door open', I shouted through the open passenger window as he stood for a moment wondering what to do.

Manfred nodded once. He took off his coat and folded it carefully over his arm, then undid the middle button of his jacket before climbing into the car, as though sitting down to a meeting at a conference table. As I drove along our rough driveway, he glanced around the interior of the car, and I followed the direction of his scrutiny. A set of tangled headphones, an empty bottle of *Rivella*, one football shin pad and various sweet wrappers were scattered over and between the seats.

'Bit of a state,' I said. 'Two boys. Untidy boys.' Manfred nodded.

'I have a boy,' he said. *Oh.*

His expression revealed sadness, but not the despair I had seen on the bridge. I stared back at the road. He didn't elaborate, maintained a steady composure. I wasn't sure if I should ask something. I released the breath I had been holding.

'We need to find you someone to talk to,' I said tentatively. 'If you don't feel you can talk to anyone in your family, perhaps someone else, a doctor, a friend...?'

'When my English will be better I can talk to you,' Manfred stated.

The irony of the sudden grammatical error made me smile and without thinking I retorted, 'You mean, when my English *is* better...' I waved my hand apologetically as I realised how patronising I sounded, and when I looked at him, he was smiling. I wondered if he had made the mistake deliberately. He paused before saying:

'Yes. *Natürlich.* Sorry.'

'Where is home?' I asked.

'Home... was in the next canton, in Aargau. I don't think I can stay there. My wife is not... with me. She... she died.'

'Oh! I'm so sorry.'

'That was long ago,' he said with a matter-of-fact tone. 'My... my sister now looks after my boy. He is a student. But I don't have a very good relationship with my son.' He hesitated. 'They don't expect me back. I have broken that bridge.'

I was momentarily confused.

'Oh, you mean burned that bridge; that's the saying in English.'

I wondered if he had left his sister and son a note. And I found it ironic that a bridge had found its way into the conversation. He needed professional help straight away. I was hoping not everything would be closed on a Sunday.

'No, I will not stay there,' he said again as I glanced at his face. 'But it is okay, don't worry. You are helping. Thank you, Alice.'

It felt strange to hear him say my name for the first time. My hands gripped the wheel a little harder.

In the neighbouring village, I pulled into a parking space in front of Aegeri Sports, where we hired the boys' ski gear each winter.

'Wait here. I'll be a moment,' I told Manfred as I climbed out of the car.

The tiny sub office of the *Zuger Polizei* was situated between the sports shop and a tanning salon. But as this was Sunday, as expected, it was inevitably closed. The hours were marked on the police station's door like a grocer's: Monday, Wednesday and Friday afternoons between two and four, Saturday mornings from nine until eleven. It might as well have said *Citizens of Switzerland: criminal activity and social needs should be limited to these times.*

I glanced at Manfred, reflections of trees streaking light and dark across the windscreen, obscuring my view. He leaned forward, unsure what we were doing here as the police station's sign wasn't visible from where he sat. I looked away quickly, chewing my cheek. I realised I should have dialled 117 from home, but I hadn't been confident enough to explain my situation in German to the emergency services.

Anxiety tumbled my gut. Mostly because of Manfred's potential reaction if I turned him over to the police. I was sure he wouldn't be happy about that. I resigned myself to driving him to the hospital twenty minutes away in the valley.

That would mean twenty more minutes in the car with him.

CHAPTER FIVE

AS I CLIMBED back into the car Manfred looked at me
curiously. I started the engine and drove off without telling him
why we had stopped. He didn't notice the sign for the police
station as we pulled away.

'Manfred, you really need to talk to a medical professional, a
psychologist,' I said.

'But you are a mother too. You will know the problems
families have. You will understand. I was serious before when I
said I think you can help.'

'Is this only to do with your family? Your late wife? Your
son?' I asked gently.

I'd crossed the line, asked the question that had been in my
mind since I first saw him in his business suit on the bridge. Why
would he be dressed like that on a Sunday?

'There is a reason we met today, Alice. I realise that now.
There is a reason fate chose you to save me on that bridge. We
have a connection. I know you feel it.'

I forced my gaze forward for fear of giving a false message
with my eyes.

'I know you'd like to help,' he said after a moment.

'I can't help you, Manfred. I'm not a doctor or a nurse or a
person remotely qualified to help you in your situation,' I lied. 'I
can barely help my own kids when their team loses a game of
football.'

As the road curved down towards the valley, I shifted in my
seat when I realised our journey would take us over the Tobel
Bridge. At the next junction, I took the left fork without saying
anything to Manfred, retracing our bus journey back through the
other village, a minor detour from the main road to Zug. To
avoid the place Manfred had stood and contemplated his demise

only hours before. Despite seldom finding myself behind the wheel of our car, I felt I never wanted to set eyes on the Tobel Bridge again.

'Manfred, you need to talk to someone in your own language. There will be people at the hospital who can help you deal with the conflict going on in your mind and your heart. I cannot help you. I *cannot*.'

'You told me you'd thought about taking your life too, once. Do you think you would still do that if your husband and sons didn't want you to be a part of their lives anymore?'

'No, of course not!' I said spontaneously, thinking *what the hell kind of question is that?* 'I'm not the same person I was when I was a teenager.'

'But you don't know until you've been there,' said Manfred, looking away from me to the passing suburbs of Zug.

Why did I suddenly feel he had turned the tables, was interrogating me somehow? Testing me. Making me say things I couldn't qualify. My agitation increased as I realised he must be playing mind games with himself after a decision he couldn't unmake.

What would the scenario have been if I had arrived ten minutes later? I put my hand to my mouth.

Manfred put his hand on my arm, and my heart thumped.

'It's okay, Alice. It's okay,' he said, as though I was the one he had just rescued.

The clicking indicator echoed in the car as I turned towards the hospital. I shook my head, to try and shift the image of a body dressed in Hugo Boss, sprawled under the bridge, from my mind.

I drove past the visitors' car park and drew up next to an ambulance near the entrance to the emergency unit. I undid my seatbelt and was about to open the door, but Manfred hadn't moved.

'Please do this for me, Manfred. Please.'

I felt like I was bargaining with him to humour me. I couldn't help thinking I no longer had any control of this situation. He sighed, unclicked his seatbelt, opened the door and stood beside the car waiting for me as I took the key and grabbed my wallet from the console.

At the reception, the glass window framing the front desk displayed a disorganised array of notes. Post-its and mini-posters rendered the administrators almost invisible to visitors, furtively encouraging patients to take their emergencies elsewhere.

There was a row of plastic tube chairs lined up against the wall. The waiting area was empty.

'I don't need to be here, Alice,' he said. 'We're wasting these hard-working nurses' time.'

I rolled my eyes, something I did at least once every day with my kids.

'Did you forget where we've just come from?' I whispered.

His eyes widened, glistening behind his lenses, and his brows furled into an expression of hurt. I took his elbow as an apology and led him to one of the chairs, where he sat down and crossed an ankle over his knee.

The receptionist gave me the silent answer of a horseshoe smile when I asked if she spoke English. I sighed. I had no idea what the word for suicide was in German. I had visions of a macabre series of charades. I tried my halting German.

The nurse looked blankly at me until I mentioned the Töbelbrücke. At that point she meerkatted to attention with a sharp intake of breath. She knew the bridge. It was notorious.

'This man needs a psychiatrist, a psychologist, someone to talk to.'

The nurse explained that psychiatric help wouldn't be available on a Sunday, but she was now aware that Manfred genuinely needed care.

As he wasn't willing to cooperate, she asked me to fill in some details on a form. She slapped a pen down on top of a clipboard, and slid it across the counter. I reluctantly pulled the board towards me. The pen in my hand hovered over the form, my mind in a jumble, trying to comprehend the German words.

'What's your name, Manfred? Your surname?' I asked.

'Sir…?' Manfred immediately swapped his belligerence for confusion.

'Your surname, your *family* name,' I repeated.

'Guggenbuhl,' he said sullenly.

How the hell do I spell that?

'I'm sorry,' I explained to the nurse. 'It's difficult for me to do this, as it's not my mother tongue... I don't even know this man. Can you help him?'

She sighed, but to my relief took the clipboard away. She asked for my personal details in the event of a police follow-up. She looked at my details on the paper I pushed across the counter.

'If you have a mobile number, can we have that too?'

I nodded, scribbled down the number, and I was suddenly free to go. The last of my charity had long since expired. I wanted to go home.

Manfred stood up as I made to leave, but I seated him emphatically with a downward motion of my hand, the mistress trying to regain control of her dog.

'You're in better hands now,' I said sympathetically.

Manfred stared at my hands.

'I think you do know me. You are the key. My *Retterin*. My saviour. You can help me,' he said quietly.

'Someone here can help you much more than I can, Manfred.'

He held out his palm, and I suddenly felt bad about leaving him. I hesitated and shook his hand. Since our hug in the porch outside our building, I wasn't sure I should touch him again, not trusting either of our reactions.

The seal of a handshake put official finality on the departure. But as I was about to pull away, Manfred brought his other hand to the outside of mine.

'You will understand, Alice.'

As he smiled at me with what I assumed was gratitude, a flush tingled at my throat.

The yawn of space that opened between us as I turned to go was both cleansing and disturbing. Manfred smiled resignedly at me from his chair as I backed out of the sliding doors of the emergency room.

I walked back to the car, wondering what Simon would think about my experience, but more than anything anticipating a cup of tea and a hot shower.

SCALDING WATER POUNDED the back of my neck and shoulders. The crusted salt of dried sweat dissolved into the shower basin. I hung my head and let my arms flop, enjoying the release of tension, inhaling the whorls of steam rising up around me.

I wondered again what had driven Manfred to the point where he was ready to jump. I'd felt down at times. Dealing with the isolation of being an only child, that stupid mistake as a teenager when my attempted suicide was considered an attention-seeking exercise, a bout of postnatal blues, or the loneliness I'd felt when Simon started travelling, and the kids were still so young, and I had no one to talk to for weeks on end. But even under the worst of circumstances, such as those Manfred had hypothesised about, I couldn't do it. Because of the shame, the selfishness. All those hurt and confused souls wondering if it was their fault. The *mess* I had tried to convey to Manfred he would leave behind. I couldn't burden anybody with that. And jumping off that godforsaken bridge? It would be the worst possible scenario for me, with my inherent fear of heights. It was either the ultimate thrill or the ultimate nightmare. And neither was plausible in my world.

I closed my eyes, knowing I was wasting water, but unable to move from the ecstasy of cleansing. I smiled as I thought of Simon, who would soon be home from his ride. From the start we'd been the perfect fit, the perfect couple. Although we stood by our individual opinions, we both ultimately wished for the same things for the family, and were fulfilled by what life had to offer us. My forced independence in our foreign world had made our love stronger.

Simon would be preparing for another round of business trips over the next few months as his new project developed, but I felt balanced and content in my foreign space now. Although

I thought I could relate to Manfred's despair, I couldn't think of anything that would drive Simon and me apart, and I couldn't imagine what had happened within Manfred's family to lead him to that bridge.

CHAPTER SIX

I WAS STILL drying my hair as they came piling through the door, and the boisterous presence of cherished humanity made me smile. My family was home. I could sense their body heat spreading to various rooms; smells, noises and movements as familiar as my own. I headed downstairs and wandered into the kitchen where Oliver was making himself a jam sandwich.

'Hey, sorry, guys, I know I haven't been here all day, but I've had quite an experience,' I said, kissing the top of Oliver's head.

'This better be good,' Simon said, not unkindly, as he came through from the sitting room still in his bike gear. He reached into the fridge for a beer. 'Saracens are beating Sale. I missed the first half, and they're just about to restart.'

Simon's Sunday afternoons watching cable, his reward for the morning's workout, were only satisfying if a rugby match was airing.

'I stopped a man jumping off the Tobel Bridge this morning,' I said. 'He was about to commit suicide.'

Oliver gaped at me with his eyebrows raised, and a dollop of strawberry jam dropped onto the kitchen counter.

'Wow, that's a pretty impressive excuse,' said Simon. 'Where's the guy now? Floating down the Lorze?'

Behind Simon, Oliver giggled.

'Come on, I'm serious. This isn't a joke,' I said. 'It was scary. I kind of took him under my wing. Eventually took him to the hospital.'

I was about to say more, indignation fading at the lightness of Simon's comment. I could see in his eyes that he didn't want to discuss suicide in front of the children, but his words only emphasised how confused I felt at that moment. Had I done all I could to help?

Simon placed his beer bottle on the kitchen counter and put his arms around me.

'Are you okay, Al? I guess that messed up your Sunday,' he said quietly.

I nodded silently and leaned my head against his shoulder as he rubbed my back. I closed my eyes and breathed in his familiar musky smell.

'I'll put the kettle on, a nice cuppa will do it,' said Simon, sounding vaguely like my late mother. 'We wondered where you'd gone with the car,' he continued, taking a mug out of the cupboard and snapping open the caddy for a teabag. And then, as an afterthought: 'If you were at the Tobel Bridge, how come you came all the way back here to drive him to the hospital? How come you didn't just get on a bus down to town?'

Of course, this is what I should have done – I realised that now. My initial joy at regrouping with the family had turned from annoyance that Simon had no idea of the situation I'd found myself in, to a pang of guilt for the anguish I might cause him if he knew how much Manfred had latched on to me. I glanced at Oliver. It certainly wasn't a conversation to be had in front of the boys.

'I didn't have enough money for the ticket and would have had to wait ages for the bus down there. All I could think about was keeping warm, getting some dry clothes, but not leaving the poor sod alone,' I said, watching Simon pour boiling water into my mug. 'I made him wait outside in the porch.'

'The usual good Samaritan,' chirped Leo as he joined us in the kitchen, the main reason I'd been on the bridge already forgotten. 'We had to walk back from the Freys, Mum. *You* had the car,' he continued with a pubescent whine.

'Which doesn't happen often, young man. It wouldn't hurt you to walk home more – it's hardly a Himalayan expedition,' I replied in mock anger, ruffling his hair and lightly squeezing his shoulder.

We had reverted to the usual family banter. Simon would undoubtedly ask me later to elaborate, but for now I needed a little time to work out why I didn't feel good about the afternoon's outcome.

AFTER DINNER, I stood at the sink absently washing a pan. The kitchen at the rear of the house offered a view across the garden to the barn and a track to the farm on the right. I could see the car parked in the garage, engine ticking away after its day on the road. I remembered I'd left my mobile phone sitting on the dashboard.

Someone coming along the hallway broke into my thoughts. Seconds later, Oliver came in, cupping a handful of pencil shavings for the bin. I slid the cupboard under the sink open with my foot, my hands immersed in suds. Oliver attempted to deposit his stash, most of it fluttering to the floor. His fingers were dangerously smudged with pencil graphite.

I pointed to his hands 'Wash, please!'

Oliver dipped his hands into the sink, and before I could protest '*Not here*' he asked, 'Mum, why would someone want to kill themselves? What happened to that man that he wanted to die? Do you think he lost a pet or something?'

I smiled. My youngest child was growing up, but I still clung with maternal pleasure to his naivety.

Oliver had always been my little saviour. The family all knew how important my running was to me. I wasn't winning county competitions any more, but it was a part of my life not even motherhood could diminish. They could forgive a few dust balls under the furniture for the peace of mind my sport brought me. *It's my drug*, I used to say. *I need my fix*. Physically, it certainly was a fix, the feelgood effect of endorphins kicking in as I arrived home sweaty and pleasantly spent. After heated and fruitless discussions about homework, school problems, weekend activities or helping around the house, Oliver would occasionally bring my running shoes wordlessly to the kitchen, breaking the tension. The supplier bringing my elixir in a syringe.

At eleven years old, Oliver was too young to have experienced heartbreak, or the hormone imbalances that could lead to dark despondency. And a depression that made someone question the worth of their own life? Hard to explain to a child that it was probably all to do with chemicals. Despite the textbooks, I had a hard time understanding it myself.

'People who want to kill themselves have an illness in their heads, in their minds,' I said, drying a pan and clattering it into a cupboard. 'It's like a terrible sadness, and often there's no explanation, which makes the sadness harder to understand.'

Oliver cocked his head to one side, thinking. As he was about to ask another question, the phone rang. He left the kitchen distractedly, returning to his room. I answered the phone. A friend of Leo's needed to check up on a homework assignment due at school after the weekend. *Exasperating teenagers! It's a bit late to be rushing through it now.*

'*Leo!*' I shouted up the stairs, flipping the tea towel over my shoulder. 'Ben's on the phone!'

'I'll take it up here!' he shouted faintly.

I waited until I heard their voices connect in Swiss German on the bedroom extension before placing the kitchen phone back in its cradle. I hoped at least *he* had remembered the assignment.

I suddenly felt very tired. I gathered a bag of rubbish to take out to the communal bins and fetched my mobile phone from the dash of the car. I closed the garage door and walked slowly back to the house, continuing up the stairs of our duplex to start my evening ritual. Simon was at the computer in the office, fine-tuning some last-minute details of the presentation he was to give in London the following week. I could see my eldest son hunched over his messy desk, scratching his head with confused irritation. This gave away the fact that he had indeed forgotten the assignment.

'Just as well Ben called,' I said, leaning against his doorway. 'And turn on your desk light or you'll go blind, my love.'

As Leo mouthed the oft-spoken words in synch with me, I glanced around at the teenage chaos in the room. The usual end-of-weekend clear-up hadn't yet taken place. In the morning when the two boys deigned to get out of their pyjamas, every available article of clothing was hauled from their cupboards with dissatisfaction, the chosen uniform generally the one at the bottom of the pile. The scene resembled a jumble sale recently hit by a tornado. The phone rang again. I pointed silently but meaningfully at the disarray of clothes and backed out of Leo's room.

'No peace for the wicked.'

I sighed loudly as I headed towards our bedroom, leaving Leo twirling a pencil between his fingers and swivelling in his chair.

'It's probably Ben again, Mum. Can you tell him I'll call back in a few minutes? I just need to get my ideas down on paper.'

'*Ideas*?' I called back over my shoulder. 'I thought this thing was supposed to be *finished* by tomorrow.'

I reached for the phone.

'Hallo, Reed,' I announced, the upward intonation at the end of my surname really implying: *Speak now, Ben. I'm tired and it's late to be calling.*

Silence. A static crackle. Silence.

'Hello?' I asked, with a kinder and distinctly English accent. Sounded somehow long-distance. Perhaps it was my aunt who lived in the States.

'*Hellooo*,' I said persistently. Still nothing. I had no time for this. I put the phone down.

My contentedness at being home now transitioned to an aching head and dragging need to sleep. I went to the office and stood behind Simon, then put my arms over his shoulders and around his chest, smelling the musty bike-helmet aroma of his hair.

'Phew. Haven't you showered yet? Honey, I'm so pooped. I could never have imagined today's events would take so much out of me,' I said.

'Are you okay?' Simon asked kindly. 'Why don't you just go straight to bed? I'll see to the boys. Tell me all about it tomorrow, okay?'

I gratefully mumbled my thanks, having known he would suggest it, and went to brush my teeth.

Exhausted, I lay down in bed, closed my eyes and begged for the escape of sleep. It wouldn't come easily. When I heard Simon come in, shed his clothes and go through the usual nightly routine, my throat closed with the heat of gratefulness for this simple familiarity. As he shuffled under the covers, he laid his hand on my head and gently kissed my shoulder.

'I love you, Al,' he whispered.

And the lump in my throat finally gave way to tears. I let out great sobs, simultaneously attempting to suppress them to avoid being heard by the boys. My reaction was unexpected. As I turned onto my side, Simon gathered me to him, shushing me like a baby, pressing into my back in our usual spooning position.

'Crikey, Al. Hey. It's okay. It's okay now. It's the shock. That's it, get it all out. My poor baby.'

He crooned these soothing words as my breath returned raggedly to normality. My eyelids were hot and gritty.

As sleep finally grabbed me, I reflected on the irrationality of the emotions I was now experiencing. I couldn't stop wondering where Manfred was now. Who was looking after him? Were my tears for him, for his despair? Or for the relieved gratitude I felt at having been able to stop him from jumping.

CHAPTER SEVEN

'THE IRONY IS, when Kathy and I have run there before, we've often wondered about finding a body under the bridge.'

It was early the following day, and I hadn't slept well. I'd had a recurring dream about a body falling from the Tobel Bridge. The first time it bounced like a rag doll on the ground, and I woke with a start. The second time the body stretched into a marvellous swan dive and swept up through the forest like Superman, disappearing over the ridge of the canyon. The third time the falling image repeated itself over and over, never quite reaching the ground. After that I dared not go back to sleep.

Simon and I dodged each other through our breakfast routine like some ritual dance. He kissed my head and patted my backside as I paused to take the milk out of the fridge. A memory of how we couldn't keep our hands off each other at the beginning of our relationship sprang to mind, and I trailed my hand across his shoulder as he passed. His butter knife clattered into the sink, and the coffee machine whirred, clicked and trickled his morning pick-me-up into a minuscule cup. The kitchen filled with the delicious aroma of a rich Arabica blend, and my thoughts returned to the bridge.

'Kathy read about a woman who took her life last year in the local paper, and we were so glad it hadn't been us that found her. We'd run there a few days before. The paper said Tobel Bridge is a suicide hotspot,' I said.

'That would explain the flowers and candles I sometimes see clustered on the pavement there on my drive to work,' said Simon.

'Don't you think that's kind of weird? I think the relatives or loved ones should leave those trophies where the body lands, not up on the bridge. Surely the soul departs down below, at impact.'

I shuddered to think of witnessing a jump. To think of Manfred jumping.

'They need a wider audience to see their pain, Al. Better a string of commuters on their way to and from work than the occasional runner and mountain biker.'

'You have to wonder what goes through someone's mind when they jump, between take-off and the final lights-out. I wonder if anyone has ever regretted their decision in the moment it takes to fall?'

'Some people make stupid decisions every day,' said Simon, and I swallowed. 'But that one would be pretty final. No going back.'

He crunched into his toast. I shook my head, attempting to eliminate the thought of a jumper realising with horror they had made a terrible mistake in that split second before hitting the earth. I imagined them wanting desperately to turn back the clock, hoping an invisible force would lift them back onto the bridge, plant their feet securely on the tarmac. That could have been Manfred.

'There would be no chance of survival at that height,' I said absently, sipping my tea.

Simon licked a buttery finger and pushed his chair away from the table.

'Al, I'm not sure what you were thinking, but can you tell me again why you came home first? I feel like we have another case of a rescued mongrel here, not just a clinical experiment for a psychology assignment. You and your hare-brained SOS help routines. I thought we'd gone past your Florence Nightingale and Mother Teresa stage.'

I had relished his jovial mood this morning, and wanted to treasure the light feeling between us for a little longer. But as he said this, my stomach heaved. I hoped I hadn't made a huge mistake. I put my hand on his arm.

'I thought you might be home. This was beyond anything I've ever experienced at college or work. I thought a male influence would help. I wasn't sure I could talk our way onto the bus without the proper fare. We would have had to wait over an hour for the next bus down to Zug anyway. I was so cold by then, I knew I had to change clothes.'

Simon nodded nonchalantly, accepting my logic.

'Well, I'm very proud of you, Al, for saving that guy's life. He should be grateful. It's a terrible thing, suicide. But it's good there are professionals taking care of him now. I know you're concerned, but there's only so much you can do for someone with such an unstable disposition.'

He gave me a concerned smile.

ONCE THE KIDS and Simon had been packed off to school and work respectively, I thumbed through the local phone directory for the number of the police station where we'd stopped the day before.

'*Zuger Polizei.* Reto Schmid.'

The brevity and gruffness of the voice when he picked up on the second ring threw my confidence. I'd written down a few words in case I couldn't get the message across.

'*Sprechen Sie Englisch?*' I asked hopefully.

'*Ein bisschen*, but you can always practise your German, Fraulein,' he replied in German.

My heart sank. His tone, immediately patronising, was weighted with a message now familiar to my ears. *These bloody foreigners should learn to speak our language if they want to live in our community.* I ignored his comment and continued in English.

'My name is Alice Reed. I wanted to inform you of a suicide attempt yesterday.'

'*Ein... was?*'

'A suicide attempt. *Selbstmord Versuch.* Yesterday. On the Tobel Bridge.'

'Are you sure? Did you, how do you say, intervene?'

'Yes, I intervened. I took the man to the hospital in Zug. His name is Manfred Guggenbuhl. I just wanted to make sure someone knew, officially. I wanted… I wondered if you had heard anything about this man. If he's okay…'

'Someone knows at the hospital if you went there,' he said pointedly. 'If they make a report, usually they send this to my colleagues in Zug. I was not informed.'

'Well, I'm informing you now,' I said crossly, and heard a sniff on the other end of the line. 'I mean, I thought you might want to be vigilant, in case he tries again.'

'Vigilant?'

'*Aufmerksam*,' I explained.

'I know what the word vigilant means, Frau… Reed, *gell*? But are you suggesting the *Zuger Polizei* is not… vigilant?'

'No… I… You misunderstand. I'm sorry. I just hope… Herr Guggenbuhl is okay.'

CHAPTER EIGHT

KATHY AND I met the next day for our regular Tuesday run. A balmy breeze blew across the lake, a gentle *Föhn* from the south, threatening to strengthen as the day wore on. We ran slowly up the hill behind the house where the village road narrowed to a winding lane. I took a deep breath and my spirits lifted as I adjusted to Kathy's rhythm and pace. I could hear her struggling beside me on the steep sections, so I slowed down a little.

The road levelled out, following the contour of the valley and, as the trees thinned, we were afforded a magnificent view of the Aegeri Valley with the lake as its centrepiece. Towards the southeast lay the snow-capped Glarner Alps and to the west, through a gap in the hills, the magnificent Rigi rose like a giant anvil through a mauve haze.

We decided to continue to the Raten Pass on the easier forest trails skirting the valley. A few clouds scudded across a blue sky, casting the occasional shadow on the newly sprouting grass in the surrounding meadows. As we ran, we chatted about her son, Tommy, and my boys, and the improvement in the weather for running.

'You'll never guess what happened when I was running the Lorze route on Sunday, I saw a guy up on the Tobel Bridge about to jump off. I managed to stop him.'

'Holy cow, Al, that's pretty serious! How did you know he was going to jump? Must have been scary. Ironic that we'd only been talking about it last autumn. Remember that woman who chucked her dogs off first, then topped herself? We invented that new word, *canicide*. But this is no laughing matter. Jesus, what did you do?'

Kathy's curiosity had slowed us to little more than an exaggerated walk.

'I ran up that hellishly steep path next to the viaduct and managed to talk him out of the deed on the edge of the bridge. It was pretty weird to think that, if I'd been ten minutes later, I might have found him somewhere at the base of the bridge, maybe even floating in the river,' I said.

'Shit, Alice, I can't imagine. Did you call the police right away?'

'I didn't have my mobile phone with me. We went to the bus. I... We eventually went to the hospital and I left him there. They said someone would take care of him. I called the police yesterday, but it made me so mad they weren't very helpful. I wanted them to contact him, make sure he was okay, but they didn't seem to care.'

'Wow, Al. Hope the guy's okay now. You probably saved his life. Good girl!'

I wasn't convinced about being a *good girl*.

'I really hope they took care of him at the hospital, poor sod. Attempted suicide shouldn't be treated lightly, but I felt like no one was taking me seriously. Of course he didn't seem to want help, was probably more humiliated by his failure than anything.'

AS WE APPROACHED a thicket of trees next to a picnic spot near the pass, our mood was lightened by the haunting sound of a trio of alphorns. We stopped in our tracks at the beauty of the music.

'Can you believe it? I tell you, we're living in a fairy tale,' said Kath. 'It's not the first time I've felt so blessed to live in this country where we don't have to worry about locking our doors, we can run free in the mountains, and then get the occasional Heidi moment like this.'

I put my hand to my side and dug in my fingers to relieve a stitch that was threatening, before taking a moment to enjoy the evocative music, with the snowy Glarner Alps as the magnificent backdrop.

Three old men, dressed in traditional black wool jackets intricately embroidered with edelweiss, had carried their bulky instruments up the hill to this idyllic setting. The melancholic music drifted across the fields.

As the music came to an end, a long, hollow, three-pitch harmony fading to silence, I smiled and raised my hands to my mouth in a silent gesture of appreciation. Tears pricked at my eyes, and my throat wobbled with emotion. Kathy broke into a round of applause and one of the men beckoned her over to try the alphorn. After much honking and huffing, we were reduced to girlish giggles, and the musicians shared our amusement.

As they began packing their instruments away in their cases, Kathy said, 'Race you home,' though she knew I could beat her on any day. We started off at a jog.

'Speaking of races, when are we going to get you to run this elusive marathon then?' I asked.

Kathy snorted.

'I'm serious,' I continued. 'I know you said you didn't think you'd ever be able to set the distances in training, but I honestly think you can finish a marathon. It would be so much fun to train together.'

'Well, I *was* considering running Zürich next April,' she stated, as though it was something she had never stopped thinking about.

'Brilliant!' I said.

'But Al, a marathon! You have four under your belt. It will be my first. I'll be holding you back. You've had so much more experience than me. Jeez, you were county champion. How can I compete with that?'

'It's not a competition, Kathy. Well, only on a personal level. I'm keen to see if I can get anywhere near my previous personal best time. My PB. And I'm not thinking of April next year. I'm thinking about something closer. Perhaps one of the autumn races.'

She looked at me incredulously.

'*This* year? Oh, Al, I don't know,' she said hesitantly. 'I'll talk to Matt about it and let you know.'

'Come on. If you commit, you must sign up straight away. It'll give you the incentive to train if you know you have a place waiting for you. I'm going to sign up on Monday. You know Matt would be only too pleased for you to set yourself a big goal.'

'Wow,' she said. 'You're serious. Bossy, but serious.'

Earnest dedication to a training programme was needed for such an event, but a little voice told me to persuade her to make the commitment. Our breath now came easier as we loped downhill side by side.

'If we start a sixteen-week training programme before the school holidays, it'll be perfect timing for the October race. We can build a pyramid schedule, training up to a run around the Zug Lake six weeks before the race. That's about thirty-six kilometres. Perfect for the longest run. We can do a weekly speed session at the Zug Stadium track. It'll be great to keep each other motivated.'

She sighed. She knew I wasn't going to let it go. We were approaching the turn off to our home.

'Okay, look, I'll try. I'll sign up too, and hope I can keep up with you. I'm not going to come in for tea this time, Al. I have a lunch with the library committee at the international school, so have to get spruced up for them.'

My phone buzzed as Kathy unlocked her car. We hugged and I pulled it out of my belt as I walked towards the door. Simon must have forgotten something. I looked at the screen, a number I didn't recognise. Must be a wrong number. I clicked open the message.

Thank you.

I waved absently as Kathy drove off, with promises to stick to all our run dates as we prepared for our marathon.

Thank you.

I was confused, couldn't think who would want to thank me. And in English. Could this be Manfred? It made sense if it was. But my automatic relief that he was okay was short-lived as my heart skipped a beat.

How the hell did he get my mobile phone number?

CHAPTER NINE
MAY

LEO'S CLASS AT school had organised a public presentation about European cultures, and his teacher had asked whether some of the mothers from the Chat Club could help with an English-language exhibit. I was thrilled to be asked, for this was a tiny step closer to being accepted as part of the community.

I was helping Leo's teacher move a folding table in the foyer of the sports hall when the bell rang for the end of school. Children spilled out of the schoolhouse like marbles from a jar. Some of them dribbled into the exhibition and were joined by their parents later. Leo and a friend of his were in charge of one of the exhibits on the other side of the hall. He hadn't wanted to participate in the English project and had instead chosen an exhibit on Serbian culture with some friends.

'It's nothing to do with you specifically, Mum, but it's kind of embarrassing to be standing with your own mother at an exhibit all afternoon,' he said when we initially talked about the project.

I felt out of place, though. Parents stopped to talk easily to my best Chat Club 'student', Esther, and the other woman at our stand, but no one was prepared to speak to me in either English or German. I was still the foreigner here. When I caught Leo's eye across the hall, he looked away guiltily. He must have known it would have been easier for me if he were by my side. He wasn't aware I simply wanted to hold on to that mother-child connection before he grew into an adult.

As we cleared trestle tables and poster boards away at the end of the day, Leo's teacher caught up with me, and we crossed the courtyard together.

'Frau Reed, I didn't want to talk to you before because we were so busy with the exhibition, but I need to speak to you about Leo.'

My heart sank. Her tone didn't sound positive.

'I want to thank you so much for helping with this exhibition. Your input was invaluable.'

She hesitated. I knew immediately she had some bad news for me. The one-minute manager. Praise before the bad news.

'I don't know if you are aware, but Leo seems to have lost his way this year at school. His grades are way below the level for his transfer to *Gymnasium* and he does not seem happy to be at school. He and another boy are being very disruptive in class, and I am afraid they may have been picking on some of the younger students in the primary school during break. I wanted to wait until the end of the school year to see if things improved, but an incident this week means I have to speak to you. This is something the school cannot tolerate, and the school counsellor has asked me on more than one occasion whether we need to address the issue with you, the parents.'

'Wow, I knew he was behind on some assignments, but... no, I wasn't aware. I'm stunned.'

I knew I was distracted at the moment, with the Manfred incident and the decision to run a marathon later in the year. But I didn't think there were signs I had ignored. Or worse, could I be the cause? This was surely every mother's fear.

Taking a deep breath, I thanked the teacher for making me aware of the situation, and promised to address the issue.

SIMON AND I lay in bed reading, the silence a comfortable familiarity. I finished a chapter before closing the book and placing it on my stomach.

'Leo's teacher talked to me at school today. He's having a few problems with his work and... his social behaviour. I'm finding it very difficult to talk to him at the moment.'

Simon lowered his book and looked at me.

'Oh, really? What's up? It sounds like he's doing great when he talks to me. Is he getting poor grades?'

'His grades are pretty bad. He doesn't get his assignments in on time and he's doing the absolute bare minimum at the moment. Plus his teacher says he's been teasing some of the younger kids in the playground. She talked about getting the school counsellor in, to address bullying.'

I waited while Simon absorbed this.

'That's not so good, Al. I'll have a talk to him at the weekend. I'm sure it's something we can straighten out. Are you okay? I wouldn't worry. He just needs a bit of nudging in the right direction.'

'I'm fine. It's just a little weird, coming on the back of the suicide thing. I feel like a load of negatives are building up. I didn't get a very good feeling at the exhibition at school. It's still so hard to feel accepted by the community.'

'Then it's good you've decided to run this marathon. It'll be great for you to concentrate on a goal for yourself. And Kathy will be supporting you.'

I thought of Kathy and her lifestyle. Endless shopping and lunches with the executive wives. Running was really the only thing we had in common.

'I've got to get some sleep,' he said, pecking me on my cheek.

He rolled over onto his side and turned out his bedside light.

IT SEEMED I had been asleep but a moment when the telephone rang persistently on the bedside table. Normally a light sleeper, I dragged myself out of the somnolent depths before reaching across to the phone. The light blinking dully from the number display was enough to allow me to locate the handset in the darkness.

'Hallo', I mumbled sleepily. A static crackle. I was about to return the handset to its cradle when I heard a slow intake of breath. I pushed the phone tightly to the shell of my ear, thinking I had missed something, and heard a subsequent exhalation.

'Hello, who is this?' I asked, senses now alert.

'Mmm?' groaned Simon beside me, ever the comatose sleeper.

'Ssshh.' I pressed the receiver harder against my head, until all I could hear was my own ragged breath roaring from the mouthpiece to my ear. I cleared my throat, and heard a click and the drone of the dial tone.

'Wrong number,' mumbled Simon and sank back into slumber. I squinted at the caller-identity screen on the handset. It showed 'withheld' which didn't give me any clues. It could be a mobile phone.

Annoyed I had been fully awakened, I shuffled to the bathroom for a pee. The fluorescent light over the bathroom mirror blinded me. I gathered my nightie and sat on the toilet with my eyes half-closed, cursing the boys' inconsiderateness as my thighs hit porcelain so cold it felt wet. I reversed my crouch, put the seat down, sank back down and crossed my arms on my thighs, absently studying the ceramic tiles of the bathroom floor.

CHAPTER TEN

I SCROLLED BACK through my messages until I reached the one I assumed was from Manfred. I didn't have to go far as I rarely used my mobile phone. I opened the message and hovered over the choices available to me. I was about to begin keying a reply when I chose the CALL option.

'Alice!' He picked up on the first ring, and his voice made my earlobes tingle.

'Hi, Manfred, I just wanted to check in with you. Make sure you're doing okay. I've been thinking about you since Sunday…' I paused, hoping my statement didn't sound odd.

'What a coincidence! I wanted to contact you. I have to come to Aegeri at the end of the week. For some business. Will you meet me for coffee?'

'Umm…' I bit my lip. This was a far cry from the guy I'd found on the bridge three days before.

'It's okay. I wanted to thank you again. Maybe text messages don't come across in the right way. Please. One coffee.'

'Okay,' I said slowly. 'How about ten o'clock on Friday at the Lido Café? It's near the bus st…'

'I know where that café is. Perfect. We'll see each other then.'

As I pushed the END CALL button, I felt relieved. He sounded confident. Lively. Not like someone who would return to thoughts of taking his life.

AS I PULLED into a parking space in front of the café, Manfred strode towards me. He was wearing a charcoal-grey suit with a white shirt and smart maroon tie, and carried a leather attaché case under his arm. He was prepared for whatever his 'business' was in our quiet little alpine village, and he looked rather striking.

I felt a little sloppy in my fleece jacket over a T-shirt and a pair of patched jeans, and lifted my hand to my head to smooth my hair as I felt the heat rise to my throat.

I stepped out of the car and put out my palm for a handshake. He bypassed my hand and held my elbow, kissing me boldly three times on the cheeks in the traditional Swiss greeting between friends. I felt my face redden as he walked up the steps to the café and held the door open for me. I smiled my thanks and walked in.

The waitress recognised me and awarded me a curt nod. She glanced past me and beamed at Manfred, her eyes flicking over him in appreciation, and gave him a jovial *'Grüezi!'*

We took a table close to the window with a view towards the lake. I ordered a tea and Manfred an espresso.

'She doesn't seem so friendly with you,' Manfred whispered as the waitress walked away.

'No, I'm not her favourite person. She's the manageress here, and the mother of twins in Leo's class at school. They've been together all the way through primary school and she still holds a grudge for the things I did wrong when we first moved here. I walked the boys to school for months at first. I didn't realise it's taboo here. Part of the kids' education is learning independence. You'd never let kids so young make their own way to school in England. It's just not safe. Anyway, she reported me to the school director, and there were words. It's amazing how someone can keep hold of a bad feeling for so long, especially one arising from something so insignificant. I think it's more to do with the fact that I'm a foreigner. Anyway, it's the only decent café in the village with a good view, so I tolerate her grumpiness.'

The waitress returned with our order on a tray, and placed the cups on the table. Manfred said something to her in Swiss German. At first charmed by his attention, I caught the words *'Engel'* and *'Menschenliebe'* and her smile faltered as she glanced at me. I cringed inside to think Manfred was explaining my good turn the previous Sunday. I was sure this woman's imagination wouldn't stretch to thinking of me as an *'angel'* capable of *'human kindness*'. I concentrated on the cup in front of me, pressing as much flavour as possible out of the weak Swiss teabag.

'You didn't need to do that,' I said as she walked away. 'You're probably only making things worse for me.'

'People need to know about your goodness, Alice.'

I glanced at him, and he smiled. I wasn't sure whether he was joking, but I felt strangely flattered.

'What kind of business are you doing in the village?' I changed the subject, genuinely curious about his sudden return to confidence after wanting to take his life only days ago.

'I have a document I needed to sign. The lawyer needed to witness it. I… he lives in a house up the hill. It's done. I have everything I need. Everything is perfect.'

'That's good. I'm glad you're so positive.'

'You've made me realise how stupid my action was. I have rediscovered a purpose in life. That's why I wanted to thank you today.'

Manfred had already finished his espresso, but my tea was still too hot to drink. He gazed out of the window over my shoulder.

'I didn't want to hurt anyone,' he said, and I recalled my statement on the bridge about leaving a mess. 'I wouldn't have hurt them. My wi… wise sister. My boy.'

I frowned.

'They would have missed you.'

'You don't understand. You don't know why I was there. Last Sunday.'

Having been so curious for the past few days, I wasn't sure now whether I wanted to know.

'There was a knife,' Manfred continued, and I swallowed. 'For cutting bread. Sharp. Victorinox, good quality. Swiss.' He paused and I didn't know what to say.

'I never intended to hurt them. Would never have hurt them. But my son, that morning he was driving me crazy.'

I chewed my lip, but forced myself to maintain eye contact.

'So you see, there was already a mess in my life. I was leaving one behind, and the bridge was to solve that mess. But now I've met you, and you have made me see clearly. That's why I'm thanking you.'

My heart thumped. Manfred's arm lay next to his cup on the table, and I had the feeling he was going to reach for my hand. To keep both mine occupied, and wishing my tea would cool faster, I took a croissant from the wire breakfast basket on the table and tore off one end. The waitress would shortly clear the tables and prepare them for the lunch crowd. The bread helped ease the burning on my tongue but prevented conversation as buttery flakes filled my mouth. I sprinkled the crumbs from my fingers onto a serviette in front of me, filling the silence with meaningless distracting activity. Manfred watched my every move.

'Manfred, can I ask you where you got my mobile number?' I asked when I could finally speak again.

His face scrunched into an expression Leo might have used if I'd asked him the same question, as though I was supposed to know the answer. I raised my eyebrows. The pause had given him a couple of extra seconds to answer.

'At the hospital. I asked if I could have it. In case... you know, to thank you.'

I imagined him persuading the nurse to give him the number. That disarming smile. Those green eyes. Still, they shouldn't have given it to him. It didn't seem professional. Very un-Swiss.

'Have you tried calling on our landline at home?'

'No, is that preferable?'

'It's okay. I'm just glad you're okay. Who did you end up talking to at the hospital?'

He smiled and tipped his head, as though he hadn't understood the question.

'I hope they had a psychologist on duty,' I continued. 'Will you be having some therapy sessions? It's really important you continue to talk to somebody about what happened.'

'They have a good group of professionals at the cantonal hospital, yes. It's a smart new facility. Good to see the taxpayers' money going into something useful.'

'It's not just about the fact that you tried to take your life, Manfred. There is much more healing to be done. You have to start with yourself before you deal with your… family.'

'It's all about talking it out, isn't it, Alice? This is also good therapy. Talking to you.'

I smiled at him, and glanced at my watch.

'Oh, I'm afraid I have to go. The boys will be home from school soon and I need to prepare their lunch. I'm so glad to see you're feeling better. It's important to keep talking to the professionals. I'm not a very good practitioner.'

He looked at me with a quizzical smile. I reached into my bag for my purse, but he put his hand on my arm.

'Honestly, Alice, I'm okay. This is on me.'

He spoke as though I was being an overprotective mother, and I hoped he didn't think I was a prude. It was as though I was suffering more from his suicide attempt than him. I put on my fleece to cover my flustered state. He left a ten-franc note and a few coins to cover the bill and a tip.

'I came by bus,' he said as I unlocked the car outside the café. 'So I'll say goodbye here. Or I should say *Uf Widerluege.*'

And before I could say anything he kissed me again three times on the cheeks.

Uf Widerluege. Not *goodbye.* But *see you again.*

I hadn't asked him where he was going on the bus. I wondered what had really gone on in Manfred's house the morning before he went to the bridge. I felt so sorry for his confusion and conflict.

And then I thought what Simon would say.

That I was crazy to have even considered meeting with this man.

CHAPTER ELEVEN

'MUM, WHERE ARE you going?' Oliver asked. 'We're supposed to be driving to the sports store.'

I had taken a detour off the main road to Zug.

'Oli, we *are* going to the store. Just taking a diversion today.'

I sucked in my lower lip. Avoiding the bridge was like suppressing the memory of that Sunday. I hadn't driven the car anywhere outside the village since then. I made Oliver sit in the back. He complained at first, as he had only recently been allowed to ride up front, but relented when he found a long-lost electronic toy hidden in the depths of the rear seat pocket. He glanced out of the window briefly as we took the detour. After my laconic explanation, he went back to frantically clicking his game.

In the store, Oliver chose a new pair of shin pads and begged me to buy him a football shirt to add to the many in his collection. I was too weak to argue that he had enough football shirts. He climbed into the back of the car without prompting, happily clutching his bag. As I started the engine and began backing out of the parking space, he pulled his purchases out of the bag, absently looking at each item.

'Oh, yeah, Mum, I was supposed to tell you something earlier and I forgot. There was a man outside the school today when we came out for lunch. He said he knew you, and he wanted me to say hello from him.'

My eyes darted to the rear-view mirror, searching Oliver's face. He didn't seem concerned, merely recounting an observation.

'Who was it, Oli? Did he tell you his name?' I asked lightly.

Oliver answered slowly, stretching out his new shirt to look at the logo.

'That's the thing. I can't remember. I only remember he said to say hello to you.'

I took a deep breath.

'Can you remember what he looked like?'

'Um, a bit older than Dad, a bit taller maybe. He had kind of greyish hair.'

He sounded bored. Our eyes made brief contact in the mirror and he began shoving the shirt back in the shopping bag. His eyes glazed over as he looked out of the window.

'Can you remember what he was wearing? Did he have glasses?'

'Nah. Maybe. Don't know. Too many questions, Mum. He just said to say hello. It's no big deal, not like I had an important message to deliver, right?'

'Was his name Manfred?'

'Um… yeah, that was his name!'

'Was anyone with you?'

'What's with the twenty questions? Is this a test? Actually, I was with Sara. We walk halfway home together most days. But don't go thinking we're an item. That's totally not happening.'

'It's okay, Oli, I was just curious.'

'Anyway, Sara and I always split after the basketball court, and the guy had gone by then.'

Oliver pushed the bag to one side, picked up the electronic toy and continued his clicking. I dragged my eyes back to the road from the mirror, biting my lip. How had he recognised Oliver? Had he seen us together at some stage? I wondered what Manfred was still doing in our village and guessed he had more business appointments there. I shrugged and indicated to turn up the hill towards home.

Carrying the shopping from the garage to the house, my mobile beeped. I put the bags down and checked the message.

Thanks for coffee the other day. He hadn't signed it, but I knew it was Manfred. I hadn't put his number in my contacts because I didn't think I'd hear from him again.

I answered: *But you paid.*

He texted: *Thanks for everything that went with the coffee.*

I assumed he meant being able to talk to me. I wasn't sure what to reply. *You're welcome* seemed too gushy.

I texted simply: *That's okay.*

When he texted back: *We must do it again*, I didn't respond.

I picked up the shopping and paused to collect the post from the mailbox beside the door. In the parcel section underneath the letterbox lay a bunch of roughly picked marguerite daisies, stalks torn and bruised. Tied together with a stem of barley grass, it looked like a gift a child might leave. I often gave the farmer's wife a bag of the boys' outgrown clothes, and on more than one occasion had helped shoo the cattle back behind trampled fences. Their thanks often came in the form of a carton of fresh eggs from the farm.

'Were the cows out again this week?' I asked Oliver, knowing he and Leo were often enlisted to help put them back in the field. 'Looks like the farmer's kids have left us a gift.'

I took the marguerites with the post. Later that evening, as I began preparing dinner, I studied the flowers sitting in a glass of water on the bench in the kitchen and narrowed my eyes.

CHAPTER TWELVE

CLIMBING THE STAIRS to our bedroom that evening, I felt drained. Generally priding myself on self-control, I wondered what had shifted in my psyche because of recent events. But as I walked into the bedroom from the bathroom, Simon put down the book he had been reading, playfully pursed his lips and opened his arms to welcome me into a hug. I had been about to spill the beans about meeting Manfred and the coincidence of Oliver seeing him in the village, but filed the thought away for another time. Simon's suitcase was open in front of the wardrobe, displaying a few half-packed items. I didn't want to sour the mood by mentioning Manfred. Simon would be leaving in a couple of days for London and wouldn't be back until the following Saturday.

I shed my clothes, letting them pool at my feet, and crawled onto the bed, curling myself gratefully into his embrace. He kissed my hair and moved his hands to gently stroke my back and shoulders. I pressed my lips to his chest and felt his erection pressing against my thigh. I caressed him, and we began our familiar ritual of lovemaking, my passion rising as we touched each other tentatively where we knew the fires would ignite. Simon manoeuvred himself over me, sinking his hips to mine. I gasped with pleasure. He raised his face to the ceiling with eyes closed, exposing a day's blond stubble on his throat, revelling in the first slide into that special place. My hips rose to him as we moved together. I felt the familiar pressure clenching in my lower belly as Simon's movement became more urgent.

Then a loud beep. My mobile phone. I had left it in my jacket pocket hanging on the back of the door. It caused my already thumping heart to miss a beat. My eyes flew open. Simon stopped moving and looked at me with a frown.

'Ignore it, Al. Who the hell messages at this time of night? And since when did you become so reliant on your mobile? It can wait.'

'I know, it's okay,' I whispered.

But, of course, it wasn't okay. Of the few people I knew had my number, none of them would text at this time of night. But then again, it could be a wrong number... Simon resumed his slow lovemaking and closed his eyes again. I concentrated hard on recalling that rising sense of ecstasy, wanting to be right back in my passion. The phone beeped again. It was probably only a repetition of the same message, but I slammed my head back into the pillow.

'Gah!' I gasped.

The passion drained from me like water through a sluice gate, replaced with a feeling of self-loathing and frustration.

'Al. Honey, what's the matter? What's with the weirdness? If it's to do with your mobile, can't you ignore it?'

I shook my head, biting my lip as Simon pulled away. I remembered Manfred telling me he'd obtained my number from the hospital, and I couldn't think why he would text me now. Unless he was feeling desperate again.

'Al, you seem so preoccupied at the moment,' Simon continued gently. 'Maybe I can help ease your anxiety,' he added with a smile.

He reached for me again, but I put my hand against his chest.

My passion had gone, and with a sigh Simon lay on his back.

'I'm so sorry,' I whispered.

'Me too, Alice, me too,' he said as he patted my hip, rolled over, and turned out the light. 'I have a long day tomorrow. Let's get some sleep.'

I turned on my side, hugging my knees. When I heard Simon's regular soft snore, I climbed out of bed and took my mobile phone out of the jacket pocket. I clicked open the message:

I miss your wise words. And your arms around me.

I should never have hugged Manfred, should never have let him touch me. I thought perhaps I should block his number, for both our sakes. What would Simon think if he found out I'd met him?

But not knowing whether he would go back to that dark place without my support was somehow worse than knowing. I shivered. It was that same old concern of what might lie on my conscience if I chose to walk past the woman struggling with her shopping, the old man stumbling in the park, the man standing on the edge of the bridge.

I was compelled to know Manfred was going to be okay.

CHAPTER THIRTEEN

'I'M SORRY, *FRAULEIN*, I am not normally allowed to give information about the patients, but I can really say we have no record of Herr Guggenbuhl. I cannot tell you if he was referred to a specialist because his name is not in the system.'

The medical receptionist's hands lay unmoving on the keyboard of her computer, my eyes willing information out of her. The Post-it notes and papers had been removed from the area around the counter affording a clear view of the office. Manfred Guggenbuhl had become a ghost patient. There was no record of my bringing him in. I was sure I had signed a document relating to his admission. Perhaps my German was just too atrocious. Maybe they thought I was a tourist, and hadn't kept my details, even though I had given my address and telephone number. Surely it wasn't so unusual to hear English spoken in this canton with so many international corporations taking advantage of its tax-haven status.

'How about in the hospital patient records? Is there anything?' I asked, knowing I was repeating a question that had already been answered.

The nurse's hands remained immobile.

'The hospital's computer system is linked everywhere. When I type his name, any patient records from all departments will show. This name did not show anywhere. I'm sorry. I am also a little embarrassed to say that we had a few computer problems when the hospital opened,' admitted the woman.

That explained the Post-it notes, now absent from the glass between us.

'This man attempted suicide that day. He could still be a danger to himself. In any case, he would still need medical and psychological help. You do understand this, don't you? I can't believe his case would be treated so lightly, or ignored altogether.'

The nurse looked at me with sympathy, as though I was the one who'd required help. I sighed.

'I gave my contact details that day. Is it possible someone would have given them out? Mr Guggenbuhl has been calling me, and I'm not sure where he got my number.'

The receptionist looked taken aback.

'That would not have been allowed. Unless you gave it to him yourself? Perhaps you don't remember.'

'No, I didn't give him my number,' I said pointedly.

'I'm sorry, madam…'

I figured Manfred must have persuaded one of the other nurses to give him my number that day or maybe a few days later. They all seemed like a bunch of incompetents at the moment.

Outside the hospital entrance, I kicked a rubbish bin with frustration. A medic walking towards the door spontaneously sidestepped me with a shocked glance, but didn't say anything.

We lived in a country where everything worked, trains always ran on time, letters inevitably arrived in the mailbox the day after they had been posted, insurance pay-outs were implemented without question. And the average Joe who worked as a civil servant or council clerk knew exactly what everyone was doing at any given time in the hierarchical human ladder that made up Switzerland's complex functioning administration.

But it seemed they had all conspired to defeat me today. Most of all I felt sorry for Manfred, who had somehow slipped through the net to wander, lost in his misery, latching on to me of all people, a confused foreigner who had slipped through the other end of the system.

Two flukes in an otherwise perfect utopia.

I sat in the car and put my hand to my temple. My skin felt hot and my head had begun to pound. The frustration was beginning to build to an indefinable irritation, and I was losing faith in my ability to help Manfred resolve his issues.

CHAPTER FOURTEEN

WEAVING THROUGH THE trees along the Lorze Gorge, I stumble. The path morphs from packed dirt to cotton wool beneath my feet. I try to speed up, sense someone chasing me. I can't turn my head. There is a person... someone familiar. The person takes off, spreading great silver wings, flying. It's an angel. I twist my head, still can't quite catch the face. A face that is changing... Oh, it's Manfred. What are we running from together? I turn my head forward again, try to run harder. My feet sink deep into the cushioned softness and I can't gain purchase on the path. I'm getting nowhere. The next moment I am knocked over, the wind whipped from me, my face pressed down into the spongy earth. I can't breathe.

Waking out of the nightmare, I was at first confused to find I was looking at the ceiling of our bedroom. A great weight lifted from my chest as I gasped, filling my lungs full of air through an aching throat.

My eyes were smarting and sore, the place behind my sockets pounding to the rhythm of my heart, clumpy boots stepping across my brain. These, at least, were symptoms I recognised. I had a cold.

Simon had already left. I hadn't heard him. Unusual to have slept through his departure. I was further saddened by the fact that I wouldn't see him for a few days and that things between us were far from harmonious. I lacked energy, but knew I had to get the boys ready for school. I swung my heavy legs over the edge of the bed and padded to the bathroom. Checking the thermometer, I realised I had a mild fever. Even pressing the monitor to my ear caused discomfort. Every movement made my temples pound.

I winced with pain as I stepped gingerly down the stairs. In the kitchen I filled the kettle and took the cereal packet and two bowls out of the cupboard for the boys. Glancing at the clock on the oven, I saw it was later than I thought and hurried as best I could back upstairs to wake them. Oliver would be cross he hadn't been woken early enough. He hated to be late for anything, even school. Leo, on the other hand, would be grumpy he had been woken at all.

As I knocked quietly at the boys' doors, the phone rang. I returned to my bedroom and answered quickly, if only to stop the shrill noise from making my headache worse. I had assumed it would be Simon calling from the airport, making sure the household was up and about. I croaked a greeting.

'Hello?'

'You sound not good.'

Manfred. I really couldn't deal with talking to him just then, and wanted to get him off the line. I should probably have cut him off. But I felt I should say something.

'I'm not well, Manfred. I have a sore throat and a headache. It hurts to talk. I'm busy getting the boys ready for school. I'm still not sure how you got my numbers, but please, it's really best you don't call here.'

'I could come and care for you. Alice, you must not forget that I owe you my life. It is, how you say, my obligation to you.'

'Manfred, I…'

'I can make a good hot soup, a drink. You must take liquids if you are not well. Stay in bed. I can be there in a moment.'

'Please, Manfred, leave me alone!' My throat burned as I raised my voice. 'This is not the time. You're mistaken about my being able to help. Go to see a doctor. Find someone to talk to. I really don't feel I can help you.'

The phone slipped back into its cradle on a film of sweat. The product of my anxiety rather than my illness. It didn't take long for guilt to flood in on my frustration and misery.

Leo shuffled along the hallway, pyjamas in disarray and hair in a lopsided wedge only a pillow could design.

'Is everything okay, Mum? I heard you shouting. You don't sound like you're doing too good, you know.'

'No, I'm not well. I don't sound like I'm doing too *well*, Leo. It's late. You'd better hurry and get ready for school.'

'Not too sick for a grammar lesson,' he mumbled, shuffling to the bathroom.

I went to check on Oliver. He'd already perceived an edge of tension.

'It's okay, Mum, I'm getting up,' he said with forced cheerfulness. Of the two boys, Oliver was much less inclined to invite conflict. I was grateful.

'I'll see you downstairs,' I said, and went down to the kitchen to prepare myself a tisane.

I was at least relieved to know my silent caller hadn't been Manfred. There would be no reason for him to suddenly engage in conversation if he'd been the one making all those spooky calls before. But in my wretched state, I would have preferred to have the crackling static of a silent caller than to actually talk to Manfred now.

Then I felt really bad, wondering how harsh I'd sounded on the phone. He hadn't deserved that. There was always a worry the thread holding him to life was still delicate. Here was a sad human being who had fixed on the idea I could somehow help him.

Even though I'd already told him this was way beyond my psychological capabilities.

CHAPTER FIFTEEN
JUNE

MY INFLUENZA LASTED six days from start to finish. I had never felt so helpless before. It required superhuman effort to get out of bed for the first three mornings, and as soon as I had packed the kids out of the door, I crawled back to bed with a hot honey-lemon drink and handful of paracetamol. Simon called from London at lunchtime on the first day, sounding sympathetic when I explained I was ill. The battery in my mobile phone died and I chose not to charge it. I decided I could live without it, despite my earlier conviction that I should run with it in case of an emergency. The only person I truly needed to keep in contact with was Simon, and he could call me on our landline at the end of the day.

Midweek, after the boys had left one morning, the phone as I was making the beds. I glanced at the caller display. No ID. It could have been Simon. He knew I was ill, would expect me to answer. But I wasn't sure I wanted to talk to him either. Out of some perverse impulse to punish myself, I stood watching the phone to see how long it would ring. It clanged and jangled around my stuffy head, and when it finally stopped, the roaring silence was almost more disturbing. Long after I had walked away, I could still hear the phantom echo of ringing, matching the pulsing of my temple.

SIMON ARRIVED BACK from London at the weekend, and was perplexed to find me still ill. I had always been the stalwart of the family, able to function whatever my dilemma. Rendered helpless by the flu, my uselessness depressed me. He took over household duties, providing the boys with food, and tried unsuccessfully to delegate tasks to them. But he couldn't take any time off work. For the first time, I was really aware of how much work he had on at the moment. I wanted to talk about my own concerns over the past days, but they seemed so trivial compared to his workload. It was easy for me to keep quiet, keep the peace.

Simon took to sleeping on the fold-out sofa in our little home office with the excuse that he couldn't afford to fall ill in the middle of his current project at work. He brought me tea and soup and sat on the edge of the bed before going off to his quarantined space. But in my fevered state, I read far more into this separation, and irrationally wondered whether this was an excuse to distance himself from me, irrespective of whether I was contagious. He was behaving like a husband with a lover.

By the time he moved back to our bed halfway through the following week, I had become used to sleeping alone. My irrational anxiety at having him return to our marital bed was exacerbated by the fact that there was an unidentifiable thing between us I hadn't talked about: I'd met Manfred a couple of weeks before for a coffee to make sure he was doing okay and, rather than solving his problems, might simply have opened a new can of worms.

AN ANTI-CYCLONE settled over the Alps, and the beautiful spring days were set to last. The bilious strands of clogging phlegm finally diminished in my chest, and I was keen to get back into my running routine.

For my first run, I started out gently, cutting across the meadow dotted with young fruit trees to the north of the house. I took time to appreciate the view of our village below. The church spire commanded a matriarchal position, surrounded haphazardly by steeply gabled buildings, all rendered toy-like from this distance. Smoky wisps floated lazily upwards from the chimneys of the few homes still requiring heating during the clear nights.

As I jogged along the path, a prickling sensation crept up my neck. In that sure and certain human trait of premonition, I knew I was being watched. But when I looked around me, I couldn't see a soul. A breeze stroked the tips of the fresh new grass in the field, and a flurry of petals fell like snow from a row of cherry trees in the upper meadow.

As I rounded the barn in the upper field, I heard the occasional shake of a bell inside and thought it a shame the farmer hadn't let the cows out on this beautiful spring morning. I caught the flash of something in my peripheral vision. Next to the old plum tree at the end of the farm track. Was that a trouser leg, or the flap of a jacket? My gaze darted back to the spot, daring the movement to repeat itself. Like scouring the midnight sky for an evasive shooting star. My heart pounded and the breath stuck in my throat. One of the farm cats leapt across the track in front of me from the verge, and I squealed involuntarily. Its tail flicked back and forth as it trotted away, ears turned backwards, advertising irritation. I let out a rush of breath in relief and laughed at my ridiculous paranoia. Observed by a farm cat. Next I'd be suspecting the trees and the grass.

I shook my head and ran on up the hill. Adrenalin initially fuelled my progress, but I didn't get far before my chest began to feel tight and I knew I'd probably pushed my luck on my first time out after recovery. After several pauses, and one dizzy moment when I leaned over with my hands on my knees, I conceded it was time to head home and promised myself I would plan a gentler reintroduction to fitness by running an easier route next time.

CHAPTER SIXTEEN

I PUSHED OPEN the door of the police station and stepped inside, knowing I should have done this days ago. A young officer sat at a desk some distance behind the counter, studying a computer. His desk was surrounded with cardboard boxes full of files and books. The nametag on the royal-blue uniform shirt of the *Zuger Polizei* said *R. Schmid*. I remembered the name from the day I had called. He seemed surprised to see a visitor as he glanced up from the screen. His hand floated briefly above the keyboard with his palm raised, forbidding interruption while he finished typing slowly with one finger. My confidence began to wane as the seconds passed.

'*Grüeziwohl, was isch los?*'

I wasn't reassured by his unusually jocular informality. *What's up?* I wanted gruffness and officialdom.

'My name is Alice Reed,' I said in English. 'I called you a few weeks ago regarding a man I stopped jumping from the Tobel Bridge.'

'Ah, yes,' Schmid said. 'The lady who does not want to practise her German.'

He had that look on his face I had seen before. Taking a deep breath, I put on my friendliest tone.

'Do you remember my report about the man I saw on the Tobel Bridge?'

The policeman tipped his head on one side.

'This man, his name is Manfred Guggenbuhl. He wanted to jump. You know, suicide.'

I drew my hand comically across my throat. A flicker of amusement lit the policeman's face. I flushed.

'*Selbstmord,*' I reiterated, patting my handbag to reassure myself the dictionary was there should I need it.

Schmid compressed his lips and nodded slowly, bringing his hands together in a steeple of fingers, a gesture way beyond his years. If I couldn't make him believe I had prevented someone from committing suicide, how was I going to convince him I thought the man still needed help?

I haltingly explained the subsequent events, emphasising words I knew in German. The officer's expression, displaying initial displeasure that I hadn't tried to speak his language, soon faded to one of irritated boredom.

'Although I've asked him repeatedly, he hasn't told me he's sought help, and I'm concerned. It's important for people who have attempted suicide to have follow-up therapy and, through some strange mix-up at the hospital, I couldn't find out from them whether he has been assigned psychological help. Is there any way you could intervene? It's just that... my son has seen him in the village when I haven't been around, and although he told me he has business here, I'm not sure...'

I thought it strange Schmid hadn't stood up and approached the counter. The wild thought occurred to me that he was missing his trousers. More likely he wanted to finish his work without the interruption of some foreign woman.

'Shouldn't you be taking notes or something? Writing a report of my visit?'

He crossed his arms, and leaned back.

'I'm... I'm sorry,' I stammered. 'It just seems to be a lot to remember.'

'Well, Frau – Reed, *gell*? I cannot know yet what you are here to complain about. You are telling me this man did not jump, but neither did you call 117 on the day...'

'But I didn't have my phone with me.'

He carried on as if I hadn't spoken.

'...Instead you took him to your home, and you took him to the hospital, so he should certainly be thankful. And *you* called *him* to meet for coffee. Surely this is an invitation, how do you say, to engage? Has he been displaying behaviour that makes you believe he is still a danger to himself? Maybe the man who was outside the school is not the same person.'

'There's something else… We've been getting some silent calls at home. The two incidents are making me nervous.'

'What exactly are you here about, Frau Reed? Herr Guggenbuhl's well-being, or to report some fool making joke calls?'

Schmid leaned back in his chair and crossed his arms, a further sign I was getting a rejection. He continued.

'I took the liberty of learning a little about the gentleman in question after your telephone call. He has an unusual name, so I was curious.' Schmid was now openly patronising. 'He has an exemplary character, no record, and is well spoken of among his neighbours. He has recently moved to Aegeri and lives in an apartment in the same residence as the *Staatsanwalt*. It is natural he would be seen around the village. You must be very careful if you are to declare instability in a respected member of our community.'

My jaw dropped and I stood at the police desk dumbfounded. This information needed a replay button in my mind to allow me to compute.

'He lives here? But he lives in Aargau! He has family there…'

'This is a small community; people *talk* to each other, Frau Reed. The man you are concerned about has recently made his home here. He will pay his taxes here. Where he came from and his history are no business of anybody else. He has a right to move where he wants. I think you are being a little overexcited. Perhaps he has been trying to make a normal impression on people as a new resident and you have taken his politeness in the wrong way? If he was still… unwell, there would be evidence.'

The heat of tears prickled. I didn't want to humiliate myself any more. I turned to leave

and wandered back to my car. I climbed in and clutched the steering wheel for half a minute until my whitened knuckles began to ache.

BY THE TIME I arrived home, my humiliation about the scene in the police station had subsided. It worried me that Manfred had moved to the village, but those times he had wanted to talk to me were perhaps a simple courtesy of letting me know he'd become enchanted with the valley. Making a new break. Maybe he'd come here with his son. Judging from the policeman's comments, he must be feeling better.

As I passed the mailbox, the latest gift from the farmer was a small box of *Kirsch Stängeli*, tiny chocolate fingers filled with cherry *schnapps*. I thought perhaps the family was going a bit far with their kindness, but was grateful they hadn't shunned our presence in the community as everyone else seemed to be doing.

In the apartment, I went straight to the shower, having worked up an unpleasant sweat with my frustrating police encounter. I turned the water to as hot as I could stand and enjoyed the sensation of the heat on my shoulders and neck. I lathered my hair with shampoo and breathed in the whorls of steam to help ease the tightness in my lungs. I immediately felt better.

My mind turned to my running routine, and knew it wouldn't be long before I was back to my regular pace and distances. I made a mental note to be extra affectionate with Simon from now on. I would cook him a favourite meal, offer to give him a massage, try and reconnect where I thought we might have had a misunderstanding about my reactions and decisions regarding Manfred's attempt to take his life. With summer approaching, I wanted to broach the subject of fixing certain days of the week for marathon training. Tuesday afternoons for a long hill run, Thursdays at the track. If I alternated times, Simon might need to be available to look after the kids after school. I knew he was pleased I had formed a long-term goal to keep me occupied during his long working weeks.

I stepped out of the shower, towelling my hair. Squeaking a space clear on the fogged-up mirror, I pulled my fingers through damp locks. As I wrapped the towel round my torso, I heard the familiar creak of wood on the fourth stair and figured the boys must be home, or perhaps Simon, to surprise me for lunch. I smiled in anticipation of a complaint about the muggy bathroom, and threw open the door.

Steam swirled out after me as I walked barefoot into the hall and stood silently with my head on one side.

'Simon?' I called. 'Are you home?' Silence. 'Leo, Oli?'

I shrugged, figuring I must have been mistaken, and headed to the bedroom to open the window where condensation was blurring the glass from my shower. As I opened the wardrobe to pull out a pair of jeans, I heard the latch click on the door downstairs.

'Simon?' I called again, and looked over the banister to the empty hall. I must have left the door ajar, the breeze from the open bedroom window pushing it firmly closed.

CHAPTER SEVENTEEN

SIMON SAT AT the kitchen table sipping a beer and flicking through his latest edition of *The Economist*. I rattled around in the cupboard for a saucepan and ran cold water into it, preparing to peel some potatoes for dinner.

'I went to the police today,' I said.

Simon closed his magazine and sat back in his chair.

'You think they'll talk to your guy?'

Your guy? I narrowed my eyes. I wondered if Simon had ever taken me seriously about Manfred's psychological needs.

'I thought I should urge them to contact him. To make sure he's okay.'

'Is it worth kicking up a fuss about this? I trust your judgement, Al. But are you sure he needs your intervention? Don't forget you've misinterpreted the Swiss in the past. Remember the electrician incident? You've got to be sure if you're going to try and mix yourself up in someone else's life. He probably just wants to forget about it. Move on, like the rest of us.'

I set my jaw. I didn't like to be reminded of the *electrician incident*. When we first moved in we were having the wiring of a light fitting altered in the kitchen so the lamp would hang over the kitchen table. I'd thought the electrician was coming on to me. He'd put a hand on my shoulder and said something I didn't understand with an unusually broad smile. At that stage I understood practically no German, and hadn't realised he was trying to explain he was the father of one of the boys' pals at school, and that he'd be happy for our families to get together socially. Boy, had I got that wrong. Especially as this was not a typically Swiss request. I could have benefitted from a little help when it came to integrating. Instead, I ended up complaining to one of the mothers, who happened to be his sister-in-law, making the whole thing worse.

'The guy was imbalanced enough to attempt suicide,' Simon continued bringing me back to Manfred. 'You never know how someone like that is going to react, Al. Don't go interfering where someone else should be doing their job. You don't want any kind of repercussions from this guy finding out you've been meddling. I think you're worrying about nothing. It'll peter out. You'll see.'

'You're right. I don't think Manfred is a danger to himself.'

I bit my lip as soon as I had spoken. I remembered fragments of Manfred's unsettling conversation about the knife and tried to imagine his domestic situation. I wondered whether he had been cutting bread at the time, or if he had reached for it in response to some kind of sickening impulse. I remembered his eyes when he looked at me. I shook my head. I was relieved, at least, that Simon was being more pragmatic about things.

I was on the verge of speaking again, of telling him I'd instigated a meeting with Manfred. I knew Simon would be angry about my *meddling*. But it had happened, and I couldn't take it back. However, I didn't think it would change anything and I wanted to avoid giving him extra cause for concern just as his project at work was ramping up. I knew there was professional tension at the office, although he always made sure he didn't bring it home with him. I was eternally thankful for that. But the stress was there, and I shouldn't be adding to it.

Also, the length of time between my meeting with Manfred and telling Simon about it was making it even harder to admit what I'd done.

So I kept quiet. To end the conversation, I turned to carry our cups to the sink.

'Of course, it doesn't help that you showed him where we lived that day, Al. I wouldn't want to be proved wrong on this.'

Until now, I'd ignored the fact that the policeman had revealed that Manfred now lived somewhere close by. The cups rattled heavily on their saucers.

CHAPTER EIGHTEEN

AS I PULLED into the driveway after running errands the following day, I saw a police car parked outside the house and my hopes rose. I wondered if they'd talked to Manfred and had come to update me on their actions.

But then I thought maybe something had happened to Leo or Oliver. *Oh God, it must be Leo.* He must have finally gone over the top at school. Perhaps he had hurt some child. But the police… I felt sick that a parent might have intervened before talking to us.

Oh, Leo, I didn't think it would come to this.

As I walked into the house, Police Officer Schmid came out of the kitchen. Leo stood at the top of the stairs to the bedrooms, looking down at me. His eyes were wide, and he drew his hand across his throat in mock horror. The policeman couldn't see Leo from where he stood, and I was momentarily confused, looking from one to the other. Why was Leo at the top of the stairs?

'Ah, good afternoon, Frau Reed. Could you come in here for a moment, please?'

I followed Schmid into the kitchen, where Oliver sat at the table, fists clenched in front of him. Another policeman leaned against the kitchen sink.

'What's happened? What's going on, Oliver?' I asked.

He was upset, but not tearful.

'Mum, it was all Alex's fault. It wasn't me. I…' Schmid held up his hand to stop Oliver speaking.

'Your son has been caught, how do you say, doing shoplifting,' he said.

'Oh, no, Oliver…' My voice dropped in disbelief. *My good little boy?*

'Mum, listen, it wasn't me,' Oliver said adamantly.

I looked enquiringly at the policeman. It seemed strange he was in our house without me knowing, but maybe that was the way they did things here.

'He says he didn't do it. What has he been accused of stealing exactly?' I asked.

'It was a chocolate bar,' said Schmid. 'From the *Mölki*, the local dairy. Normally the shop owner would deal with this herself, this type of thing happens so rarely, but I think she wanted to make your son an example. But the truth is, Frau Reed, your son stole something, and then attempted to deceive us, telling us he hadn't stolen it. Frau Besmer and her assistant saw him do it with their own eyes. Two witnesses. We ignore his excuses now, Frau Reed. He is a thief and a liar. Of course we will not prosecute, he is too young, but his name will be retained on our records of this incident. We hope that you and your husband can deal with his discipline in a sensible manner. What he has done is against the law,' he concluded.

I winced to think of Oliver's name on some juvenile criminal list.

'Of course, Officer... Herr Schmid, we will talk to him,' I said.

I waited until Simon came home from work that evening to address the issue with Oliver. Once Leo had gone to his room to do some homework after dinner, we talked to Oliver at the kitchen table. He explained what had happened. It was a schoolboy prank turned bad.

'It was this bet. Alex and the others. We were messing around after school. They made me do it. Honest. I know it was wrong. But it was like they forced me.'

'The only people who can force you to do anything, Oliver, are your Mum and me,' Simon said with a little humour.

We talked about trust, telling the truth, and the need to ask himself if something was right before following the lead of others. We agreed we would go to the dairy early on Saturday, to apologise to the shopkeeper in person. I could tell Oliver felt wretchedly disappointed with himself. I was sure this was something that wouldn't be repeated.

'I want you to promise nothing like this will ever happen again,' I said.

'I promise, Mum, Dad.'

He gave us a hug, tears finally spilling over after the upheaval of his day. My concern as I hugged Oliver wasn't so much that he might repeat the misdemeanour. I was sure he wouldn't. It was that the reputation of my son was now tainted in the eyes of the police.

LOUISE MANGOS

CHAPTER NINETEEN
JULY

I'D BEEN RUNNING more frequently with Kathy now we had the marathon as our goal. There were some days when a weather inversion meant an early mist would settle in the valley around Zug. As Aegeri was often bathed in summer sun from early in the morning, she came to my place, and we would set off from home.

One morning, after a gentle run along part of the local Panoramaweg, a few fat drops fell bizarrely from an otherwise cloudless sky. A summer rain shower.

'Oh, crap, my washing would have been dry,' I said.

'Race you back,' she said. 'We can still rescue it.'

As we turned down our driveway, Kathy chortled.

'Looks like someone's already taken down your laundry.'

The umbrella washing line to the side of the house stood empty, turning slowly in the breeze.

'You've got the best neighbours,' she continued. 'Do you think I can hire them? Plenty of clothes to fold in my house.'

In the basket on the bench in our porch sat two neatly folded piles of laundry, plucked from the line before they had become dampened in the rain. No one had ever done that for me before. I took the basket wordlessly into the house, trying to work out which of my benevolent neighbours would have done such a thing. I would ask each of them later and thank them.

'Stay for a tea?' I asked.

'Of course, sweetie, the usual,' Kathy replied.

Placing the teapot on the low table, I flopped down on the sofa next to Kathy. She'd pulled on a fresh cotton T-shirt to replace her Lycra.

74

As the rain stopped, I flung the windows open to the rural summer sounds of the farmer mowing the paddock outside the house. The gentle putt-putting sound filtered into the living room with a dusting of pine pollen I would regret having to clean up later.

'I'm so glad we signed up to do this marathon,' I said.

Kathy nodded.

'It'll be good to concentrate on something other than shopping sprees and ladies pearl and twinset lunches. Which reminds me…' Kathy glanced at her watch. 'I must leave, although I really should stick around until your boys get here. I haven't seen them for so long. I don't know how you can stand having them coming home for lunch every day. I'm so happy Matt's company pays the international school fees and Tommy gets fed at the canteen.'

'You haven't seen my boys for ages. You'd be surprised how tall Leo is,' I said. 'It won't be long before he overtakes me, or Simon for that matter.'

'Well, you're both tall, Al, so it's a given they'll be giants of the next generation, especially with cooked lunches every day of the week.' Kathy winked at me.

I placed my mug on the table and pushed myself up off the sofa.

'It must be here somewhere,' I said absently. 'I had a photo of me with the boys, here…' I pointed towards the bookshelf. I picked up a framed photo of Simon and me on our wedding day, which had fallen over on its face. I propped it back up on its stand next to one of my athletics trophies.

'The photo was taken in front of the gates at Versailles on our trip last autumn. It shows Leo within inches of my nose in height. Even I was shocked when I saw it. Where is the damn thing? Oh, well. Tommy must be getting tall now. Matt's tall too.'

Kathy smiled. 'He seems to have stalled a bit… well, everywhere except his feet. At Christmas I bought him a new pair of Keds and then at Easter we had to go shopping again. His feet had grown another size. It's costing a fortune in…'

Kathy droned on, but I wasn't paying attention any more. *Where was that photo?* Someone must have moved it. I checked the back of the bookshelf to see whether it had fallen over. I suspected the boys had been throwing a football around the living room in my absence.

'I'll walk you to your car,' I said as Kathy gathered her things to leave.

As we came out of the house, an unusual silence surrounded us. The farmer had stopped his tractor-mower in the middle of the field. He sat at the wheel, hand on his chin, studying a *Braunvieh*, one of the unpretentiously named Brown Cows, which had lumbered away from the herd in a neighbouring paddock. The bells had momentarily quietened, and the herd was strangely still. The cow raised her pale muzzle to the sky, her chocolate-brown pelt gleaming, her fluffy ears waggling. She shuffled strangely on the spot, and a pinkish-brown wet bundle slithered to the grass. My eyes opened wide in wonder.

'Holy cow!' screeched Kathy, and we both laughed.

'You've just witnessed the miracle of birth, my dear. Easy as pie.'

We watched the new-born calf, now being sniffed and prodded by its mother as it lay on the grass. The birth membrane stretched as the young animal tentatively moved its limbs. The other cows gathered in a bizarre ritual circle around the calf, watching the proud mum with their doleful eyes.

'Blimey, I wish Tommy had been that simple to push out. We might have considered a sibling.' Kathy smiled.

When the farmer could see the calf was healthy and moving, he rushed back to the barn to fetch his flatbed truck. I knew he would remove the new-born, take it to the barn, and that I would be haunted by the heart-breaking moos of the orphan mother. I kept this news from Kathy.

'And here comes your number-two calf,' she said.

Oliver wandered down the driveway, swinging his schoolbag, deep in thought. He suddenly spotted the calf in the field and I smiled as he stopped to stare open-mouthed at the little creature now struggling onto its bandy legs.

The farmer drove back down from the barn and stopped in front of us on the way to the field.

'You must tell your young man not to get close,' he said.

I looked at Oliver who was hesitantly moving towards the group of cows to get a better look. Kathy reached into her bag for her car keys as the farmer continued.

'These old girls seem so docile and friendly now. But never get between a mother and her young, or there will be big trouble. *Hoi!*' he shouted to Oliver, who stepped back onto the driveway, pointing at the cows and babbling excitedly.

'A cow protecting her *Kalb* can kill a man,' concluded the farmer.

CHAPTER TWENTY

THE BOYS HAD long ago made it clear they were beyond bedtime cuddles, but I habitually looked in on them before I turned in. On more than one occasion I had gently removed the headphones from Leo's unruly hair while he slept, performing an elaborate manoeuvre to untangle the cable from around his face and arms.

On weeknights, they were both asleep well before I went to bed, but one night, as I looked in on Oliver, a barely audible sniff and a movement of the covers indicated he was still awake. I was about to close his door, thinking it was just a break in his sleep pattern, when he called to me.

'Mum? I can't sleep,' he stage-whispered.

'Are you okay? Can I get you a drink of water?'

Perching on the edge of his bed near his pillow, I began stroking the hair from his forehead. Oliver sighed and cleared his throat.

'Mum, remember that man I said was outside the school a couple of weeks ago?'

The regular combing of my fingers through his locks halted briefly before I continued, to avoid conveying any worry.

'Yes, sweetie, I remember. Have you seen him again?' I enquired, keeping my tone light.

'Not just saw him, Mum. He followed me up the road. I know you always told us not to speak to strangers, but he surprised me as he kind of bounced into step next to me. Then he started talking, like he knew who I was. It was weird, and he asked some strange questions.'

'Are you sure it was the same man?'

'Pretty sure, although he wasn't wearing the same clothes, and maybe his hair was different, longer than last time,' Oliver reflected.

'What kind of strange questions did he ask, Oli? Did that man touch you?'

'He put his hand on my shoulder, if that's what you mean. Kept it there while we walked'

Oliver eyed me warily as if he knew what I really meant.

'He yelled at Frau Biedermann's dogs when they ran up and down the fence barking as usual. That made me laugh, 'coz they've always made me jump. But it was like he *knew* I'm bothered by the dogs.'

'What was the weird thing he asked you, Oli?' I asked.

'He asked about you. Asked if I thought you were happy. Happy in the family. He asked me like there was something you *shouldn't* be happy about. Like he wanted me to rat on you or something. You know, like when you and Dad have a *discussion* about stuff.'

Whoa. I recognised my own use of the word 'discussion'. There had been the occasional tense conversation lately, mainly about preoccupations I wasn't sharing with Simon, but I didn't think we'd had any *discussions* Oliver would be aware of.

'You know you shouldn't talk to strangers.'

'I know, Mum, but he was walking with me. It's pretty hard to ignore someone who's practically carrying your schoolbag home for you.'

'Did he talk about anything else? Was anyone else with you? Last time you said Sara saw him too.'

I suddenly became concerned about Oliver walking home alone.

'I think he waited until Sara had gone up her road. Maybe he's lonely. He kind of made me feel strange, Mum, but you're making it sound scary. Why would he ask so many questions about you? What's up? You must know this person, right?'

I cleared my throat. I was on the verge of telling Oliver this man was probably the same one I had saved, but I thought it might conjure up scarier thoughts in his head.

'Oh, it's nothing, sweetie. He's just someone I know vaguely. I don't really want you talking to him, though. Can you do me a favour? For the rest of the week, can you come home by way of Sara's house? I know it's a bit of a diversion, but I'd feel happier if I knew you were with someone for that stretch of the walk.'

'Mu-um. That's a steep path she goes up. It'll put ten minutes on my walk. Come on!'

'Please, Oli, just for a few days, okay? And Oli, you don't need to tell your dad. He's so busy with his project right now, we don't need to bother him with this.'

A pulse ticked at my temples.

'All right.' Sullen, but sleepy.

The mundaneness of an undesired instruction replaced whatever demons had been playing in Oliver's head with regular fatigue, and I could tell he would be asleep within minutes. I kissed him on the forehead, ruffled his hair, drew up the duvet and pulled his door closed as he turned onto his side and sighed.

Something was niggling me from way back. From when Oliver first told me he'd seen Manfred outside the school weeks before. How had Manfred known who he was and where he'd be?

At the computer in the office I clicked open a new window and pulled up the phone directory on the screen, knowing the Swiss *Tel Search* would give me far more information than merely numbers and addresses. I typed *Staatsanwalt* and *Aegeri* into the search field, remembering the policeman had told me Manfred lived in the same residence as the public prosecutor. I noted down the address for a family Steinmann on a piece of paper, catching my breath as I recognised the street – *Alisbachweg*. Was that a coincidence? The name was uncanny. And it was a stone's throw from our street.

CHAPTER TWENTY-ONE

I DIDN'T WAIT for the weekend. I had a suspicion Manfred had either taken a holiday allowance, or perhaps even sick leave if he had indeed been placed under psychological care – which I doubted. But I was pretty certain he would be in his new home that day.

The houses in *Alisbachweg* were some of the most opulent in the village. They belonged to doctors, lawyers or CEOs of international corporations in Zug, of which there were many looking for ever-bigger and showier places to house their families in the vicinity of the unusually small global financial boomtown.

I found the Steinmanns' home easily. It was a four-storey whitewashed modern block with vast windows taking advantage of a view over the valley not dissimilar to our own at the farmhouse. I knew I couldn't see this house from our own, so although the proximity of the place to ours made me feel sick, there was a grain of relief in knowing we couldn't be seen from behind those metres of glass.

I checked the double mailbox at the bottom of the stairs leading to the residence. Manfred's name, *Guggenbuhl*, was handwritten on a card and stuck to the box. He must have been waiting for a proper tag to be engraved by his landlord. The wide stairs led up to the main entrance of the house, but a discreet path led around the side of the house and, as I approached, I saw his name again above the buzzer next to the door.

I rubbed my hands down my jeaned thighs and took a deep breath to try and calm my beating heart. I'd been so confident, but now I wasn't sure. I needed to know what was driving his decision to move into our community.

I reached up and pushed the button. I heard a three-tone electronic bell ring beyond the door, and before the lowest tone had even faded, the door swung open. Manfred wore a T-shirt and jeans, had a day's beard growth, and his thick hair was mussed as though he'd just got out of bed.

'Alice! You've come to visit!'

I suddenly had the feeling he'd been waiting for me, as though he'd known I was going to come here at this exact moment. My anger rose and I strode in without waiting to be invited.

I walked the length of the hallway, darker at the rear because his basement flat was built into the slope under the main house. I passed a kitchen and a small living room and, to the back, saw a bathroom with a towel on the floor, which brought Leo to mind. To the right was a bedroom with a mattress on the floor, neatly made with a duvet tucked around the edge of the wooden parquet.

'I'm still waiting for some furniture. A bed,' he said, and I inexplicably felt heat rise to my face.

I grabbed the handle of his bedroom door to close it firmly and put his personal space out of my sight.

'Manfred, this farce has to stop. I don't know what you think I can give you. Moving to the village… This is not a good idea. I'm not sure what you want from me. But I want you to stop calling me. And, especially, to stay away from my children.'

'Oh, come on, Alice. It was a harmless thing, to move here. Do not forget you're the one who showed me. That was the day I decided this is the perfect place for me.'

No, I could not forget that day. I wondered whether I would ever be allowed to forget it. My ponytail loosened from its scrunchy as I swung around. My hair flew about my face, emphasising my anger. I backed away from his bedroom door and retraced my steps to the kitchen. I looked around at his organised, single-living home. The Nespresso machine with capsules in a wire holder screwed to the wall. Mugs on the shelf. A microwave.

'You know we have a connection, Alice. Admit it. We have both been to the edge. Looked into the abyss of our lives.'

'Stop it, Manfred. My teenage error simply isn't the same as your decision as an adult. You cannot compare.' I wished I'd never told him. God, I hadn't even told Simon. I thought it was such an insignificant thing, and had only used it to persuade Manfred not to jump. 'This is… this is insane, Manfred. Please. I'm not sure what it is you want. But I cannot give it to you.'

'You can, Alice. You can give me the world. I know you have feelings for me too. That day on the bridge, and later when we met in the café. I've seen the passion in your eyes. We are like soulmates. I think you just need time.'

'What? No! Stop this!' My voice was rising dangerously in the small apartment. I leaned on the narrow granite table extending from the counter as part of his fitted kitchen. My palms pressed against the surface, as though pushing it between us like a shield.

Manfred came around the table, his head on one side. An arm reached for me, his hand cupped in what looked like a tender gesture, and for one horrible moment I thought I would go to him, was drawn somehow to the sick will of his obsession.

'You do know who lives upstairs, don't you, Alice? He is the public prosecutor for Zug. You know I could have your husband's permit revoked. He could lose his job. He would have to leave, and we could be together.'

'What are you saying? This is madness. You're crazy!' I yelled.

I stepped backwards, but he continued towards me and I suddenly saw the spark of something else in his eyes, of something evil. He came around behind me and, with one hand on my shoulder, placed the other over my open mouth.

'Goddammit, Alice. Stop shouting, will you?'

Even his tone was different, had an edge. I had to get away. I reached back and grabbed a coffee mug off one of the hooks and hurled it to the floor. The noise of the shattering porcelain broke the moment. He released me, and I ran towards the front door, hauling it open and breathing in great gulps of air.

I turned as I made my way briskly down the path.

'It's over, Manfred. This thing must finish.'

As I backed away, a face ghosted in the giant window of the main house upstairs. A woman. Frau Steinmann, perhaps.

I RAN ALL the way home, up the stairs, and, with my heart thumping, logged back on to the computer. It was all suddenly so clear to me.

One of the most fascinating units in my psychology courses at university had covered severe personality disorders and psychosis. At the time we touched on the clinical characteristics of stalkers, but I didn't recall ever studying the psychological consequences for victims of stalking. It was all very well knowing the cause, but the pervasive and intense personal suffering was something we never considered in a lecture theatre crammed with over a hundred invincible teenagers. Now I felt compelled to understand Manfred's motivations, and began clicking on stalker profiles on the Internet.

There seemed to be no typical profile for a stalker, but they fell into two identifiable groups. The most common group were the Simple Obsession Stalkers where some kind of romantic or personal relationship had already existed before the stalking began. The second type was the Love Obsession Stalker. This rare category of stalker developed a love obsession with someone they might not even know at all, someone they had no personal relationship with.

Someone like me.

I had somehow triggered Manfred's obsession by rescuing him on the bridge. It seemed he would most likely focus his entire attention on me, and was unlikely to be dangerous, merely mentally disturbed. I thought of Oliver initially telling me about the stranger outside the school. How many of us were involved here? I breathed deeply, reading on. A stalker's passivity could only be guaranteed if the victim appeared to play his or her assigned role. Manfred might want to establish a relationship with me, might absolutely believe he could even make me love him, but I couldn't face having to comply to guarantee his passivity.

I shuddered. To think I had thought he was a kind soul. Attractive even. I couldn't even begin to imagine the kind of help this twisted soul required.

CHAPTER TWENTY-TWO

SIMON AND I sat at the kitchen table, a cup of tea and a double espresso the only objects filling the space between us. I traced the pattern of the vine print on the tablecloth with my finger, trying to push this horrible feeling to the back of my mind, but knowing I had to say something to him.

Having observed Simon more closely over the past few days, I felt a rush of compassion as I realised how stressed he was about work. We had long ago agreed he would be the breadwinner. It was my job to keep the family and the household running smoothly.

It seemed petty to tell him I suspected Manfred of having attached himself to me in a way that wasn't normal. I should prove I was capable of dealing with this without disturbing the flow of Simon's business success. He already thought I'd invested too much of my emotion in the whole affair. But I had to voice my opinion to my husband, my best friend, to avoid it festering in my mind. I wanted his support, but not to pressure him into thinking *he* had to do something about it.

'Jesus, Al. Don't you think that's a bit far-fetched? I know he sent you a text message, but I think your imagination might be running away with you.' *God, he doesn't know the half of it.* 'Do you really think the guy Oli saw was the same man? Perhaps you should go back to the police. Tell them everything. If you truly think he's some kind of threat, they need to know, including those weird calls in the middle of the night.'

'I don't know any more. When you talk like that, it all seems so trivial. And you're right – I'm not even sure it was him making those calls. Maybe my mind is just playing tricks on me. The thing is, though, the guy has moved to the village. He's living here now. It's freaking me out.'

'You think he's moved here because of you? Come on, Al, don't you think that's taking it a bit far? We live in a beautiful village. Everyone wants to live here once they've seen the place. The moment we set eyes on it we chose this place over somewhere in Zug, nearer to my work. It sounds like he wasn't going home to Aargau, whatever the outcome of his actions in April. Don't be giving yourself delusions of grandeur now, honey. It's a coincidence. I mean, it's not like he's knocking on our door.'

I don't know what kept me silent. I didn't want to sever the last vestige of Simon's support by telling him I'd met Manfred at the café or been to his apartment. I wanted his easy chatter and our family routine. The boys were still upstairs, home from their sports, stinking up loos and sculpting hair in front of bathroom mirrors. I relished Simon's easy attitude, and couldn't imagine how he would react once he knew I had initiated a meeting with Manfred. Words stuck in my throat. I couldn't think how to start telling him. Casual voice? Worried voice?

'I think it's time to drop thoughts of this guy now,' Simon continued a little impatiently. 'He's not an aggressor. He's just a little lost.'

Simon's tone bordered on sarcasm. I could tell he was sick of this story.

'Well, you're not much help. What happened to your caveman's instinct to protect your wench?'

'You're a big girl now, Alice. You know what to do.' He paused. 'What do you think I can protect you from exactly?'

I bit my lip.

'I know there's ambiguity about stalking behaviour, but of all the countries in the world, I would have thought the Swiss would be all over something like this. You're right, I need to go back to the police. But I'm going because I have to make an official complaint. It would be great if you could support me in this. I get the feeling you don't believe me.'

'*Stalking*, Alice? Are you serious? It'll be pretty hard to prove this guy Manfred's actually doing anything wrong if he lives here now.'

I glanced at him. His comments made me feel suddenly uncertain.

A heavy set of teenage feet thumping down the stairs prevented any further conversation. Although I'd been unsure what Simon's reaction would be, I knew without a doubt the boys shouldn't know that their mother, in thinking she might be able to help a strange man, had effectively encouraged him to become part of their family life.

CHAPTER TWENTY-THREE

WITH A SINKING feeling I saw Schmid behind the desk as I pushed open the door of the police station. I was hoping to see a different police administrator. His eyelids fluttered. I must have been the last person he wanted to see that morning. At least he remembered me; that much was obvious.

'I'm here to make an official complaint now, Herr Schmid. About Herr Guggenbuhl. I think this man might be stalking us,' I said.

'I'm not sure I understand this word,' said the policeman.

'Wait!' I pulled my dictionary out of my handbag and flicked through. '*Pirschen*!' I proclaimed.

Schmid pursed his lips.

'It is the wrong time of year for this, Frau Reed. Did you see a gun?'

Momentarily confused, I realised I had found the literal translation in the dictionary.

'Yes… no… well… stalking is a word used for animals in the hunting season, but it is also used in English for a person who follows someone else, annoys them,' I said uncertainly. Schmid's reaction had flustered me.

'The word you are seeking, I think, is *Belauern,* but now I think about it I have also heard the word, how do you say, *stalking*. But it is not something that happens in this country.'

My composure crumbled, and I continued in a rush.

'What about my kids? He's approached my son. Oliver described him. I'm sure it's the same guy. Don't you have a policy for strangers watching kids on the streets, outside schools? Surely that's not *normal*? Please, you have to *do* something! This person needs help.'

My voice shook as I realised I could not know the extent of Manfred's intentions, especially after his menacing words at his apartment.

'We have no law that says someone cannot be in a public place in this country,' Schmid continued. 'This is all... how do you say... very soft, weak evidence, Frau Reed, and it is not possible for us to observe Herr Guggenbuhl unless he has threatened you, and it doesn't sound like he has *threatened* your boy. You are not even absolutely sure that the man outside the school was Herr Guggenbuhl.' He hissed this last phrase.

My shoulders slumped, and for the first time the police officer's face displayed some sympathy. He stood up and rooted through one of the boxes beside his desk. He showed me an official-looking tome with the word *Protokoll* on the cover. It would be futile to show me the text within its pages as I wouldn't understand a word.

'I see you are not convinced. If there was a problem, the rules we have in these situations are normally for problems or disputes between husbands and wives. There is nothing that defines problems between strangers. I have never heard about this before. Sometimes we have physical problems between people. This can involve a fight, and very rarely we have problems where someone may have been assaulted. But for the situation you are describing, we have no formula. I am sorry, Frau Reed. I cannot deny you might have issues with this man, but... Maybe your husband can talk to him?'

I sighed. I was living in a male-dominated society where women were discouraged from working, and had only been awarded the right to vote in the 1970s. His words simply proved I was powerless. I was a woman *and* a foreigner.

'My husband is a busy man. He has confidence that I can sort out the problem. He doesn't have time. Most of all I'm worried for this man. He once attempted suicide. I believe he is still unstable.'

I was now exasperated.

'When you make a complaint about someone in Switzerland, it is a very complicated process, Frau Reed. You effectively invited him to your house some weeks ago. Has anyone else seen him there since? And as for approaching your son, we cannot rely on the fantasies of an eleven-year-old boy.'

'Fantasies? I can't believe I'm hearing this!'

The policeman held up his hand.

'I will make a report, but I cannot create a file about a person's wish to kill himself when he is still alive today. If a report has been filed at the hospital, the *Stadtpolizei* in Zug will have talked to him.'

'Is it possible to find out whether they have contacted him? He needs to be under the care of a psychologist. Perhaps at least you could ensure that did happen.'

I could hear the whine in my voice. The words dead horses and flogging came to mind. I thought briefly about mentioning the knife, but knew Manfred's fleeting comment all those weeks ago would be even less believable now. To mention it would simply sound comical.

'Unfortunately, hospital patient information is confidential. With such sensitive subjects, records will not be published unless an enquiry is raised, and this I cannot do if the person has not committed a crime. I am afraid there is little I can help you with, Frau Reed. Your visit here today is noted, and of course, if anyone else should make similar reports, or he should threaten you in any way physically or verbally, then we would have a duty to approach this person and, how do you say, intervene.'

'He has approached one of my children more than once. My son is traumatised,' I exaggerated. 'I insist you do something. Surely the children should be protected? I can't walk my kids to and from school every day. You're the people who told us not to do that at the beginning.'

'So we must make a *Protokoll*,' he said with a sigh. 'But I have to stress to you, Frau Reed, that there is no legislation for this kind of behaviour in our country. It might be different where you come from. However, unless you can provide me with solid evidence, we cannot make a charge.'

He pulled his keyboard towards him a little abruptly. We were both on a short fuse.

'I've been studying the profiles of these people. People who stalk. Don't you think it's a little weird that this man has moved into our community, and so close to our home? Why are you finding it so hard to put two and two together? I have a little experience with psychological profiling. I have a degree...'

'As a policeman, we also have to study this kind of psychology. Don't think for a moment that we are not qualified to identify a certain type of person who breaks the law.'

He had interrupted me while he carried on typing slowly, peering at his computer screen. I took a breath, desperate for patience.

'As I was saying, I looked into the type of stalker you mentioned last time. They are called Simple Obsession Stalkers. The ex-husbands who... annoy their wives. But the police should know that the other kind of stalker, the Love Obsession Stalker, can be dangerous too, perhaps more unpredictable. You should have the same rules...'

'I understand what you are saying, Frau Reed, but I'm afraid the law states one thing, and we follow the law. There is also something else you should know, and may explain why your son has seen him around the school. Did you know Herr Guggenbuhl is now on the Board of Counsellors? He is increasing his respected profile in the village. If you accuse him of this *stalking*, you may be creating more tension in our community than you think.'

'I don't care if he's the fucking president of the confederation,' I growled. 'I want a report.'

Schmid stared long and hard at me before turning to his computer and typing silently.

'I have completed a *Protokoll*,' he said some minutes later, pointing to the computer screen. 'But I am afraid I cannot print it out for you. Our printer has been packed away. We are officially moving the office this week.'

'Can you please make sure I am sent a copy?'

'As you wish.'

He said it in a way that made me think he wouldn't send it at all.

CHAPTER TWENTY-FOUR

A FEW DAYS later I arrived home, arms laden with groceries. I pushed the door to the apartment open, and with horror realised I must have forgotten to lock it when I left that morning.

Ever wary, I carried the heavy shopping bags to the kitchen. My head tingled with a cold chill and I dropped the bags onto the kitchen table as I saw a bunch of carefully arranged wildflowers sitting in our water jug on the counter. My heart pounded and I put my hand to my throat, staring at the bouquet. My eyes darted to the window, expecting to see Manfred waiting outside for me to acknowledge his gift. My mind went back to the time I thought I'd seen someone near the farm.

I grabbed the bunch of flowers from the jug, water spilling off their stalks, and threw them to the tiled floor. I stamped on their delicate heads, the pink petals of wild geraniums and the vivid blue of campanula bells staining the ceramic tiles. The heels of my shoes ground the chlorophyll out of their stalks until the palette resembled a fibrous rainbow pulp.

And then I heard a thump on the stair. *Oh, my God, he's still here.* I reached for the jug, threw the water into the sink, and turned towards the door with it raised above my head.

'Hey, Al!' Simon stopped in his tracks. 'What do you think you're doing? I picked those for you! What are you *doing?*'

My mouth hung open, my eyes hot with the realisation that I had almost thrown the vase in my trembling hand at Simon's head.

'Those were for you – it's our anniversary, for fuck's sake!'

'Oh, my God, Simon, I'm so sorry.'

'I was going to surprise you. I planned an outing on the ferry on the lake. Thought we could have afternoon tea. I had something for you... Had you forgotten?'

'Shit, Simon, yes. Oh, I'm so sorry. I had no idea what date it was today.'

'Jesus, Alice. You are so distracted. That guy Manfred is occupying way too much of your thoughts. Did you think these were from him? Do you really think he'd come into our apartment? He can't anyway now because you keep the place locked all the time. This whole situation is out of control. You're reacting so badly. It has to stop now.'

Simon bent down and began the futile task of gathering the limp stalks together, no longer making eye contact with me.

I pressed my fingers to my temples, and squeezed my eyes tightly closed.

He picked up the floppy flowers and threw them into the sink, then turned and stormed out of the kitchen.

'Seeing as I've taken the afternoon off, I'm going for a bike ride,' he shouted as he headed up the stairs.

I stood staring at the empty kitchen doorway, arms hanging at my sides.

I figured I'd let him go, work out his anger on the bike. I had to find a way to make it up to him later.

But a challenging homework problem kept me with Oliver after dinner, and by the time I went upstairs for bed, Simon was deep into something for work on the computer in the office, and I knew not to disturb him. Instead I left an anniversary card I had made on his pillow.

I don't know if he read it; by the time he came to bed late that night, I was already asleep.

CRACKS WERE STARTING to widen in our relationship.

To stop myself dwelling on my failure to confront Simon, I ramped up the pace of my training schedule, ever aware of the commitment I had made with Kathy to run this marathon in autumn. I found it hard to believe almost three months had passed since my intervention with Manfred on the bridge on that first long run of spring.

To avoid the heat of the day, I regularly woke early to train. The cows were often still in the barn. I could hear the lazy shake of an occasional bell over the humming of the giant fans drying the hay in the attic space above them.

On one of these mornings, as I came running back down the track, I passed the small copse at the turnoff to the farm driveway. I backtracked to have a closer look at the gnarled trunk of an old plum tree. Its half-dead branches were covered in lichen and moss. The ground at the base of the tree, facing the house, had a well-trampled look, the area in front stunted from regular sitting or standing. A slight dip had formed where someone perpetually leaned against a fence post. I leant down, smoothing my hand over the patch of ground. It looked welcoming, inviting me to sit. And then I snatched my hand away.

Crouching on my heels, I looked back at our house. My hand flew to my mouth. I could see directly into our kitchen. From this distance I could make out the calendar and the clock on the wall. I could even see several pieces of Oli's artwork tacked on the far cupboard near the cooker. I also had a view down the road leading away from our driveway. An observer would know everyone's movements in and out of our home. I shuddered at the thought of having been so acutely scrutinised. The reality of it now so apparent.

Now that he lived in our village, I doubted Manfred would ever go back to his home in Aargau and rekindle a relationship with his son and his sister. Hopes were slim that he had confessed his suicide attempt and made it right with his family. In an ideal world he would ask them for forgiveness for his selfishness and wrap his sorrow around his son. But he was deceiving them, deceiving us all.

When I reached the apartment, I went straight to the computer without showering. I googled his name. It wasn't a name one would easily forget. An online phonebook revealed about three hundred Guggenbuhls in Switzerland and, aside from the brand-new entry in Aegeri, which hadn't been there a couple of weeks before, I saw that thirty others resided in the canton of Aargau. I figured he must still have a presence there. His family. His late wife's family. There was a Matthias Guggenbuhl in Wohlen, and an M & G Guggenbuhl in a place called Buttwil.

Oh, Leo would love the name of that place.

If this 'M' was Manfred, what did the 'G' stand for? His sister? His son? I looked on Google Maps. Buttwil was a little village just above the town of Muri, a place I knew Simon had cycled through many times as he and his buddies criss-crossed the great Reuss River Valley on their weekend outings. I spontaneously grabbed the phone and rang the number on the computer screen. I don't know what I would have done if someone had answered, and after the eighth ring I hung up.

I wondered where Manfred had worked before his suicide attempt, and whether his boss or the company had given him time off. Sickness leave? Had he been fired, made redundant? How could he still be spending all this time and energy on *me*? What expectations did he truly have?

CHAPTER TWENTY-FIVE

'I DON'T KNOW this man, but your meeting with the *Polizei* is not normal,' said Esther when I confided in her after the next Chat Club meeting about Manfred having approached the children outside the school. 'Every visit or telephone call to the police requires a writing report.'

My role as teacher over, I made no attempt to correct her grammar.

'He didn't give me a report, and I haven't received anything by post.'

'I do not understand. We Swiss are, how you say, addicted to administration. It is strange that you were not asked to sign anything.'

'You must think I'm being a bit paranoid about this man talking to Oliver. It might not mean anything. After so many years living in England I know I'm being cautious. When I was a kid we walked to school too, but things have changed drastically.'

'I admit it sounds surprising. I will ask Sara if she remembers this man. And I will ask friends I know on the school commission who he is and what they think.'

'I can't believe he's moved to our village, Esther. That's the thing that worries me most. In a matter of weeks he's integrated himself into a community it has taken me years to even feel a part of.'

Esther pressed her lips together in a display I hoped was sympathy. Everyone felt so safe in her country. I was sure anyone would find it hard to believe threats could exist in a rural alpine village. Her tone was cautious. I was, after all, a foreign woman questioning the system. It wasn't the first time I'd wished I felt more accepted by the locals, or could make a friend in the village. Esther was an acquaintance, the mother of a child in Oliver's class. Kathy didn't live in the same community, so I didn't see her as much as I would have liked. Back in England we probably wouldn't have formed the friendship we had, with little in common other than running.

'But if someone was suspiciously watching the kids, what are the laws here dealing with such cases?' I persisted.

'I am going to ask my brother about the law here. He is a legal assistant for a company in Zug. He may have access to information about these regulations. I cannot believe the police will not act on the report of a stranger talking to a child. I think you must also say it to the teacher of Oliver at school. With both our reports, maybe the school will do something.'

Esther placed her hand on my arm reassuringly before we parted ways, and a rush of warmth flooded through me at receiving this simple display of compassion from someone I wondered whether I might one day be able to call a new friend.

As I pulled out of the car park, the figure of a man caught my eye in the entrance of the Co-op, next to stacks of plant trays loaded up with geraniums and marigolds. The screech of tyres and a short chip on a car horn made me slam the brakes in shock. I hadn't seen a car driving round the bend. If either of us had been going any faster, my left front wing would now be crumpled. With a face bright-red with embarrassment, I lowered the window, put on my best apologetic look and shouted '*Entschuldigung*, sorry!' to the driver. As I put the Land Rover in gear, I glanced back to the shop. The man I was now sure had been Manfred had disappeared.

ON OUR WAY back from our regular Tuesday run the following week, I slowed down and drew in my breath as Kathy and I passed the old plum tree at the end of the farmer's driveway. There was no one there, but the air was static with the uncanny sensation that someone had been there recently.

'Hey, Al, what's the matter?'

'Do you remember the guy I stopped jumping off the Tobel Bridge?'

'Of course, how could I forget? It's the story of the year.'

'I suspect he's been hassling us – me – making kind of hoax calls. And following me.'

'Oh divine, a pervert.' Kathy laughed, shaking her head.

'It's not funny, Kath. He approached Oli the other day near the school, and I don't think it was an accident,' I said.

We entered the house together and I pulled the key from the inside pocket of my Lycra running pants. Kathy raised her eyebrows without comment.

While she was in the loo, I made us our regular post-run cup of tea. Was Kathy going to make light of the Manfred situation like everyone else? She had no idea how seriously I was taking this. I felt like I had no one to confide in. As she joined me in the living room, she studied my face.

'Just tell him to fuck off, Al. Do you really think it's the same guy?'

'I'm pretty sure. It started when he texted me after I rescued him. I called him to check on him, to make sure he was okay.'

It wasn't so much a lie. More that I had missed out a big chunk of the truth. Initially wanting to share my concerns, the unease I felt subsequent to unfolding events now seemed trivial in front of Kathy. I couldn't explain it. Every time I was about to relate my actions, about meeting him in the café and confronting him in his home, I could only imagine how stupid and unrealistic I might sound.

'When I had 'flu in spring, he called out of the blue. He made me feel odd, not that I wasn't feeling odd enough, but he told me he owed me his life. It's like he's trapped in this weird honour code. You know, when you save someone's life, there's a compulsory bond.'

'I can't believe you didn't tell me this before,' said Kath, voicing my own thoughts.

'I haven't been sure about it until recently. It's giving me the creeps.'

As if on cue, the phone started to ring. It still made me jump even after all this time. I squinted at the display on the shelf and saw the number was withheld. Kathy's eyes widened as I quickly lifted the handset and placed it straight back onto its stand, cutting the ringing tone.

'You think that was him? Jesus, Al. How often does this happen?'

'Aside from that one time when he spoke to me, there have been several calls before and since I was ill, and whoever it is doesn't say anything – it's always a withheld number. I can't be certain, but I'm pretty sure it's him.'

'Crikey, recognise his heavy breathing?' she asked humorously as I sipped the last of my cold tea.

I could tell she wanted to keep the conversation upbeat, couldn't entertain the fact that such things might happen in our safe little Swiss haven.

'You should keep a referee's whistle beside the phone. That'll soon stop him. Have you called the police?' she asked more soberly.

'I went to see them, but they weren't very helpful. The problem is, I don't have any concrete proof. But I think I should go to them again if I think he's been in the house.'

'*In the house?* When might he have come into the house? I hope you're keeping the door locked all the time now. It's always been open in the past. God, if you think he's been in here, you should really hassle the police. Are you sure…?'

Kathy reeled off the sensible solutions I *should* have tried. I bit my lip and looked at the shelf where the pictures of our family were lined up.

'Shit, the missing photo,' she said.

She stood to leave, looking around as if she might see a stranger walk into the room.

CHAPTER TWENTY-SIX
AUGUST

THE SCHOOL HOLIDAYS started and Simon arranged to take the boys to see the new *Transformers* film in Zürich on a day I said I had errands to run. I had agreed to drop them off at the Zug train station and pick them up later after they had grabbed a pizza following the film.

As we drove up the driveway, my heart thumped as I saw Manfred in the distance by the farm track. He was leaning against the lichen-covered trunk of the old plum tree. I opened my mouth to say something, but knew I shouldn't alarm the boys. They were animatedly discussing potential scenarios in the film they were about to see and weren't paying attention to the environment outside the car. Simon was distracted on his mobile phone, typing some confirmation of a meeting he'd forgotten the following week.

I bit my lip, on the verge of pointing out Manfred to Simon, but kept quiet because of the boys. Manfred's eyes trailed us as we turned onto the road down to the village. He was wearing an oversized sweatshirt, and his hair ruffled in the wind as he turned to stare after our car. I glanced at Simon, but he didn't even lift his head. Manfred's figure looked pathetic as it diminished in my rear-view mirror, his presence confirming my suspicions about his lookout point. None of the others had seen him.

After waving the boys off at the station, I drove into the canton of Aargau. I followed the Reuss River for half an hour until the country roads took me up an escarpment to the village of Buttwil. I had noted the address from the Internet, and found the street on the village plan next to the *Gemeindehaus*. I left the car in the post office parking lot and continued on foot.

As I approached the turnoff to *Franzenmatt*, I felt foolish at the spontaneity of my journey. Did I think Manfred's sister might be able to help me? Had he left a note when he departed that Sunday to go to the bridge? Had she attempted to look for him? In her shoes, I wouldn't want to talk to a total stranger. I slowed to a lazy stroll, my face flushing, but not with the physical activity. A trickle of sweat found a free channel next to the vertebrae of my spine.

The drab, undistinguished construction of number four was a brick-and-plaster detached house typical of the late 1970s, when concrete was cheap and Swiss architectural inspiration sadly lacking. The garden in front of the house had been bricked over with concrete interlocking pavers, and a row of straggly ornamental cedar bushes in large pots hid moulding water stains under the windows. To one side of the house stood an open carport, empty but for compost and rubbish bins. A smudge of oil on the concrete floor of the carport showed that a vehicle usually occupied the empty space.

I had come this far, so I strode up to the door and rang the bell. A stark jangle was audible in the unseen interior. I suspected no one was home, but I rang again, confidence rapidly waning at the thought that someone might actually come to the door. After half a minute, I turned to leave, nervous relief gradually replaced with disappointment that I would once again have achieved little in my endeavours to stop Manfred.

As I stepped onto the paved forecourt, a young man on a mountain bike sped in front of the fence separating the garden from the pavement. He pedalled in a sharp arc and turned abruptly into the driveway. We surprised each other equally.

'Oh!' I exclaimed, as he skidded around me, almost losing his balance.

'*Ops!*' he said simultaneously, braking hard and leaping off the bike at a run. He made a quip about not having seen me.

He leaned the bike against the wall in the carport and came towards me, rubbing his palms down his jeans. He wouldn't ordinarily have offered his hand in greeting – perhaps I was delivering a letter or package to the house – but his eyes narrowed and a smile played at his lips as he tipped his head on one side.

'*Es duet mer Leid.* I'm sorry, I know you, but I cannot recall from where,' he said in Swiss German.

I had never seen this young man before in my life.

'I'm sorry, do you speak English?' I asked, still baffled.

'Yes, I do, but how do I know you?' He was now equally confused.

'I think you must be mistaken. We've never met before. I was hoping to talk to a Ms Guggenbuhl, Mr Manfred Guggenbuhl's sister.'

The young man's head pulled back, a frown now at his brow.

'My father doesn't have a sister.'

He shook his head slowly. A lock of wavy dark hair swung over his brow.

'Oh! Your father? Your father is Manfred Guggenbuhl?' I asked, suddenly nervous, remembering Manfred saying *I have a boy.*

I certainly hadn't expected his *boy* to be a tall young adult. I had envisioned a lad not much older than Leo. And then I saw this handsome young man had the same green eyes as his father. I clenched my jaw as I registered my first sudden thought had been *if I were fifteen years younger and single…*

'I… I wanted to speak to your aunt. Would that be Ms G Guggenbuhl? I found your address in the phone book.'

I didn't want to speak to Manfred's *son.*

'Well, no, I have an aunt, but she is my mother's sister, Katrin Hegi. But G Guggenbuhl is my mother – Gertrude – Trudi.'

His mother?

'She's not here, she is at work. I'm sorry, but do I know you? My name is Gerhard, but everyone calls me Gerry.' He said it with the hard German 'G', like Gary, finally holding out his hand to shake. 'And you are?'

His mother? Manfred's wife?

'My name is Alice Reed, you don't know me…' Shaking his hand as I said this, I saw Gerry's eyes open wide with a look I couldn't fathom, almost horror or shock.

'I do know you…' he said, dropping my hand and putting his own to his mouth.

'No…'

I now felt confused. I wanted to talk to Manfred's sister. Now this lad was telling me his father didn't have a sister, but that his wife, Gerry's mother, was alive. Is that what he had just said? *Manfred's wife is alive?* Why would he have lied about her being dead? I was beginning to think I shouldn't have come.

'I think I have made a terrible mistake. I must go, I'm so sorry,' I said hurriedly.

'No, please, wait. Please. I need to check, to ask you something. But don't go away. I have something I want to show you.'

Gerry took out his keys and headed into the house, leaving the door open. Before he disappeared from view, he turned.

'Please, wait,' he said again rather bossily, sensing I was ready to dash away. But he was emphatic, and I wondered what it was he had to show me.

CHAPTER TWENTY-SEVEN

WITHIN A MINUTE he was back, holding something in his hand. As he came towards me, looking from his hands to me and back again, his expression seemed almost pained, or bitter. He thrust a picture frame at me and I gazed upon my own face and those of Leo and Oliver, standing at the gates of Versailles. I gasped, and the young man's face frowned in distress. For him, or for me, I couldn't tell.

'Where did you get this?' I asked, my eyes narrowing.

'It was in my father's things,' Gerry said with a look of disdain.

Waves of hostility were now coming off him.

'This is where I know you from. The photo.'

'Your father still comes back here?' I asked.

An invisible wall came up between us. Yet I was the one who should be angry. This confirmed that Manfred had taken the photo from my home.

'No, I took this from his things before he finally left. My mother and father agreed they never wanted to see each other again. But he still has a family here too, you know. Do not forget that.'

His anger was now directed at me. I was confused. What had I done? *He has a family here too?* I suddenly understood.

'You think these are his kids?' I asked.

Gerry glared at me, and shrugged.

'Oh, Gerry, no! Listen, it's a long story – can we sit here on the steps?'

I walked towards the porch, Gerry following uncertainly. We sat down, and he swept his hair back from his brow with one hand in a gesture not unlike his father's, before tucking both hands between his thighs. His bitterness had caused the whites of his eyes to redden, making his irises turn a striking green. Here was an attractive young man, only a few years older than Leo. How would he react to what I was about to tell him? I tilted the photo frame towards him.

'My husband, Simon, took this photo,' I said gently. 'These are our two sons, Leo and Oliver. Your father removed – stole – this photo from my home.'

Gerry's expression softened, the wall instantly lowered. But instead of sighing with relief, as I would have expected, he pressed his lips together, his mouth turning down at the corners.

'I know you think I should be relieved he doesn't have a secret family,' he said, 'but I have been wondering about you and those boys for a while now, I thought maybe there was a chance I had half-brothers.' He hesitated. 'I always wanted a sibling. My mother was not able to have any more children after me. Although after my father… anyway, I know now that you are not his other family. But why would my father have your photo?'

Gerry brushed invisible dust from his thighs.

'What time will your mother be home?' I asked, ignoring his question.

'She gets back late on Saturdays. It's not her normal job. She helps her sister, my Aunt Katrin, at her shop in Muri most weekends,' he answered.

'I think I should talk to your mother about… about your father.'

'It's okay,' he said confidently. 'I am curious to put the pieces of this story together. I know my father has not been… well. And if you wait for my mother, you may not be able to talk to her. She has blocked him from her life, moved on.'

He reached towards the picture frame, then withdrew his hand, realising it was with its rightful owner.

'At first he came here when my mother was at work and I was at the university,' he continued. 'Now I am on holiday and around more often, I thought I might catch him one day. But I think he has found somewhere else to live. In any case, my mother does not speak English, so you would have to tell me everything anyway so I could translate to her.'

'I must tell you about the day I first saw your father,' I began hesitantly, not wanting to shock Gerry.

There was a slim chance this young man could help me. I couldn't read him enough to know how he felt about his father, but the family connection must surely still exist. If I played my cards right, here was an opportunity to get Manfred off my back.

'Some months ago, I found your father on the Tobel Bridge in the canton of Zug where I live,' I continued. 'He told me he was planning to take his own life.'

I paused, looking at Gerry. Instead of shock, he rolled his eyes and placed his head in his hands, rubbing the sockets with his palms.

'Not again,' he whispered.

Again? Surprised, I continued.

'Since that day, your father believes I am some kind of saviour. He says he has to protect me. He falsely believes I have... feelings for him. He says he has feelings for me. He has been watching me.'

I stopped as Gerry sat up and looked at me.

'Watching you? This sounds familiar,' he said, and my stomach dropped. 'How exactly?'

'He is always around our house, and sometimes he follows me when I am out running. In my country we call this stalking. I have reported him to the police.'

Gerry shook his head.

'You are a runner?'

'Yes, I'm training for a marathon,' I said dismissively.

Gerry looked at me with admiration, but I ignored his silent invitation to elaborate.

'I want to get your father to stop. I know he is not very well... psychologically. He hasn't told me what made him go to the bridge that Sunday in April. I was hoping your aunt... I'm sorry, I mean your mother... could shed some light on his problems, find him some help.'

'We can't help my father. You are right that he is not well. He suffers from a *manisch-depressiv Erkrankung*, he is bipolar,' Gerry stated simply. 'Now he has another obsession to add to his list. There was this woman. A neighbour. But she moved away.'

He saw my shocked face as he talked so unsentimentally.

'By the time I was eighteen, my father had been through some bad times. He once tried to cut himself, saying it would be better for everyone if he took his life, left us alone. The neighbour I mentioned? She found him, talked him out of it.'

'Has your father been treated? Has he seen a doctor?' I asked.

'He had psychoanalysis, and the family was brought in to try and help. I became involved only when I had reached the age of eighteen. His doctor said he should continue to take the medications he had recommended. It seemed to be the only solution, but my father was very erratic and undisciplined in taking his pills, and reverted to his unpredictable behaviour. He could not hold on to a job. It became very frustrating for my mother, for me too. He would not listen to us during the happy times. They sometimes lasted months. It was as though he didn't remember he had been having those opposite moments, those moments of despair.'

Gerry paused, looking towards the road, as if he sensed his father might wander into our conversation at some point.

'During an argument, my mother told my father she wanted to leave him. It was the first time I saw him really angry, rather than simply very depressed. He broke some things and shouted at my mother. Waved our bread knife around like a sword. He wasn't sure how to talk to me, although he was lucid enough to see that it wasn't my fault. I think he loved me very much, and didn't know how to react. Still doesn't know how to react. So he left, and my mother never wants to hear his name mentioned again. She helped him through so many of his painful up-and-down years. She is happy not to have to work like that again, not to be tied to him.'

Gerry's eyes glazed over.

'He mentioned the knife to me,' I said. 'Do you think he intended to hurt you?'

'No… I don't know. He would probably use it on himself before one of us.'

'Do you pity your father?'

'Of course I do, but if he doesn't want to heal himself, then he cannot be healed.'

I didn't want to close the door on the possibility that Gerry could somehow stop Manfred stalking me.

'Did it make a difference when he took his medication?'

'Of course, but if he refuses, you cannot force it on him.'

'Do you still have any here, any of his prescriptions?'

'I can look, maybe in the bathroom cabinet.'

'Perhaps I can persuade him to take it again.'

'Good luck with that,' he snorted, but stood up anyway and walked into the house.

I pulled my T-shirt away from my chest, flapping it to move some air. The porch was a suntrap and I suddenly felt very hot. Gerry returned, holding a box of pills out to me. I took them from him.

'Your father can be healed, Gerry. Many things between you could be healed. Things might change forever, but people are quick to forgive. There is always room to build a family again.'

I was grabbing at straws.

'Really, there is no point. You have seen my father only over the past few months. He lost his latest job in spring, one of many. I have lived with him all my life until the last few months. I'm sorry he is bothering you, but I know what you are asking. We've tried to help him. I cannot see that he will change. And we are all very tired. We no longer want to be dragged down into his world. It is better that he has gone. Not for you, of course, but for us. Now we can lead normal lives. I know you must think I am callous saying this, but my mother smiles again, she has made a better life for herself, and although I admire her for having stayed with him for so long, I think she was unfairly trapped. I want to see her happy. He must not come back into our lives. He is not welcome.'

My throat closed with the memory of the warm relationship I had had with my own father prior to his death from a sudden heart attack ten years earlier. It wasn't long before my mother went to join him after being diagnosed with liver cancer, and it was a small consolation to think she hadn't been able to live without him. I went cold at the inconceivability of my own children ever speaking Gerry's words about me one day.

We had been sitting on the step for over an hour. I pushed the packet of pills into my handbag and glanced at my watch. I wanted to be home when Simon and the boys arrived. They'd said they would take the train and bus back from Zürich. I took my keys out and fiddled with them in my hand.

'Do you think he would have jumped from the Tobel Bridge?' I asked.

I needed to know if my presence had saved his life.

'I don't know. Maybe. *Wahrscheinlich*. Probably.'

A breeze brought a welcome respite from the warmth.

'I'd have thought he would be too weak to do something like that,' he continued. 'Like his attempt at cutting himself. But he made it to the bridge, and that itself is quite a journey.'

Gerry suddenly seemed unsure of himself. Perhaps I was reawakening an emotion he didn't want to feel. I looked at my watch again.

'I had better go. I'm sorry to have bothered you,' I said, unaccountably querulous that this boy would no longer help his father, forgetting I was not the one who had lived with this for years.

'I'm sorry that I cannot help you, Mrs Reed. I am happy you have your picture back,' Gerry said as he shook my hand. And, as an afterthought: 'You know, it might have been better for everyone if you had not been running in the Lorze Gorge that day.'

CHAPTER TWENTY-EIGHT
AUGUST

WE DECIDED NOT to go away during the school summer holidays. We already lived in a holiday paradise. And with Simon travelling so much, it was hard to find the right moment. Much as I would have loved to get away for a fortnight, get away from *him*, we agreed to take a trip abroad later in the autumn, during the boys' half-term break, when the climate in Switzerland was cooler and my training schedule would have eased up before the big race.

My afternoons were devoted to spending time with the boys. While Simon had to work, the three of us often went to the local Lido, a grassy park on the shores of Lake Aegeri, boasting a small shingle beach, a jetty and a diving platform. Arming ourselves almost daily with a picnic, blow-up pool toys for the boys and reading matter for me, we spent the days lazing in the sun and the water. The boys were happy to meet their school friends there, and I saw some of the women from the village.

And then *he* arrived.

This was my public domain, a communal space. I found it hard to believe he would risk exposure on a regular basis. But he made no attempt to conceal his presence. The first time I saw him, I pointed him out to Esther. He sat near a hedgerow at the back of the lawn, wearing a baseball cap and a pair of red-and-blue board shorts. He leaned on his elbows, exposing a tanned torso. It was the first time I had seen his body and I glanced away as though I had seen him naked. I thought he might turn his head, look away, embarrassed. But he just stared at us.

'He is not as I expected,' said Esther, and I knew immediately she didn't find him repulsive. 'Ignore him,' she continued.

'Don't give him the satisfaction of showing him that he annoys us.'

I kept a wary eye on Manfred, making sure he didn't go into the water when my kids were there. I couldn't relax. This was no longer the school-holiday atmosphere I'd been hoping for. Esther saw that I was preoccupied.

'Do you not think you are mistaken about this man?' she asked. 'He does not look harmful. He looks at us very little. I think maybe you are overreacting to this situation.'

I swallowed and remained silent. I didn't want to lose the one ally I thought I had in the community. His simple presence here was certainly not the proof the police needed for a report of harassment.

Sometime towards the end of the afternoon Manfred left. This was the one place in the village I thought I would be free from his scrutiny. But now he was making his intentions public.

HE APPEARED AGAIN a few days later. I was on my own with the boys. Simon was away again. Copenhagen, Amsterdam, London. I could no longer remember. I might have joked that he had a lover in every city. But with the current emotional climate at home, I knew with absolute certainty this sentiment should never be voiced.

Manfred had the audacity to raise his hand and wave from his place in the park, fingers slowly undulating as though placed on the keys of a piano. I shuddered at his boldness. The boys had run straight to the water, and were already swimming out to the diving platform. I hadn't yet unpacked the beach bag. Shaking with anger, I marched over to where he sat.

'You have to *leave us alone*,' I yelled, hands on hips.

I stared down at him sitting on his towel, my determination to remain passive and not engage completely forgotten. People around stopped talking and looked over to where I stood.

'This stalking is freaking us out. It's too much, and now you're here, at *our* Lido. You have got to *STOP!*'

In the silence that followed, people whispered to each other on the grass around us. One girl dragged her towel further away from where I stood. Perhaps if I raged enough, he would approach me physically, do something to justify police intervention. *Yes! Someone call the police!*

I looked around at the people gaping at me.

'*Er ist ein Stalker!* He follows me everywhere!' Eyes wild, I addressed the staring onlookers, arm stretched out towards Manfred.

But they weren't looking at Manfred. They were staring at me, wondering about this crazy lady speaking bad German. One woman turned to her colleague and said '*Der Arme!* Poor man! With a sinking feeling I recognised her. The electrician's wife. I could see it in all their eyes. They thought *I* was the crazy one. Manfred's elbows rested on his bent knees. I realised he looked horrifyingly normal. A harmless, innocent fellow trying to enjoy some lakeside sunshine. I walked back to our bags, and one of the women in the Chat Club averted her eyes as I passed. My face reddened as my anger subsided, replaced by embarrassment.

The boys came out of the water laughing, demanding towels, ignorant of what had just happened. They complained when I said we had to leave.

'But we only just got here,' moaned Oliver, as I dried him vigorously with the towel. 'Mum, stop it. I can do that. Why do we have to go now?'

I gave them some lame excuse, something I had forgotten to do at home. We had to leave the Lido.

LATER THAT NIGHT, the phone rang. I suspected it would be Simon, calling to check in on us. I was in the kitchen, and picked up the handset at exactly the same moment Leo picked up the extension in the bedroom. At first worried it might be Manfred, I smiled as I listened to Simon and Leo talking about summer-holiday activities, reflecting briefly that my eldest son found it so much easier to communicate with his father than with me. After several minutes, I heard Leo say:

'I'd better get ready for bed, Dad. I've been up late a few nights in a row, and you know Mum will be on my case if I start to get moody. Do you want to talk to her? I think she's downstairs.'

I was about to interrupt when Simon spoke.

'No, it's okay, Leo, I've still got some work to do. I'll call again in a couple of days. Give my love to Oli. Enjoy the summer while it lasts. Love you.'

'Love you too, Dad. Bye.'

There were two gentle clicks as each of them put their handsets down, and I stood holding the kitchen phone to my ear, listening to the hiss. My throat tightened, and I felt a desolate sadness. Of course he didn't want to talk to me, his distant, indifferent wife. Just like Leo didn't want to talk to me, his distant, confused mother.

What was happening to us?

CHAPTER TWENTY-NINE
SEPTEMBER

KATHY AND I met at the running track in the Zug Stadium for our weekly interval training session, a set of sprint sessions designed to try and increase our overall speed on our longer runs.

We were sitting in the covered stands at the edge of the track. I had a notebook open on the plastic seat between us, drawing out our pyramid schedule for the afternoon's session.

'Okay, we'll do three times four hundred metres, three times six hundred, three times eight hundred, back to six and then to four. All with a slow jog once round in between in order to warm down.'

'Jesus, Al, that's huge,' said Kath. 'I'm not sure I'll be able to do them all, and I'll be slower than you. You're a hard taskmaster. We won't even be seeing each other at the beginning of this race we're doing. You'll be in a different start block to me.'

'It's not so bad. It's surprising how much this is helping both our individual goals. You'll see. And as for the race, I'll be there at the end with a bottle of fizz for you.' I laughed.

We began a gentle warm-up lap, and as we rounded the western end of the track together, Kathy nudged my arm.

'Bit of a rugged dish spotted at eleven o'clock,' she said.

I turned to see a man sitting on the grassy bank beyond the chain-link fence. I drew in my breath sharply.

'Well, I didn't expect that reaction!' Kathy laughed, then dropped her smile when she saw my face. 'Are you okay?'

'It's *him*,' I hissed.

'You mean Manfred the bridge guy? Oh, Jesus, what are you going to do? Can you call the police?' she asked. 'He doesn't look particularly disturbed. I thought he'd be creepier somehow.'

I looked at him surreptitiously as we rounded the bend and ran away from him down the home straight. He was wearing a pair of jeans and some kind of wind jacket. His hair was unkempt, and his jaw displayed at least a week's growth of beard. To me he looked like he'd let himself go. But I could see why Kathy thought he was handsome.

If I'd been on my own, I would probably have given up and gone home. But Kathy wanted to continue regardless of his presence.

'Don't let a curious stranger put you off, girl. We've got a job to do.'

How the hell had he known I was here?

I felt his eyes burning into my back every time I rounded the end of the track and ran away from him. The more his presence set me on edge, the more I panicked about how he'd known I would be here today, twenty minutes' drive from my home in a different town. It was bad enough he had access to my phone numbers. Had he followed me here in a car, or had he known I was going to be here by some other means; like my diary?

The thought made my head hot, and a burst of adrenalin increased my speed. I pulled ahead of Kathy and finished the next session well ahead of her. As I walked over to the water fountain to quench my thirst, I saw Kathy's head turn back towards Manfred. He had said something to her. As she pulled up beside me, I raised my eyebrows.

'He asked if I could make sure not to wear you out. As if! It's obvious you can run faster than me. Do you think he was trying to wind me up? Doesn't he know sarcasm is the lowest form of wit?'

'I can't stay here with him watching us. I'm going to have to call it a day.'

'Oh, Al. This is our last chance to do this before your holiday next week, and after that it won't be long until the race.'

'I can't, Kath, I'm sorry. He's making me feel sick, just standing there watching. I can't. We'll have at least one more session before the race. After I get back from our holiday we can choose a different day.'

'Okay, hon. I'd stay on and do the rest of the splits by myself, but to be honest I'm not very motivated now.'

'He seems to know my routine too well,' I reflected. 'This thing is starting to get out of hand.'

'Maybe he's been following your moves more than you know.'

As we said goodbye and I drove away in the opposite direction to Kathy, I wondered just how much access he had to my life.

CHAPTER THIRTY

WALKING DOWN THE aisle to my seat, my gaze slid over the passengers, subconsciously scanning the 737 from port to starboard. I was sure I had covered my tracks in booking this holiday by keeping my movements, negotiations and payments secret. But there was no knowing when my glance might fall on that dreaded face, no knowing to what lengths Manfred might go to infiltrate the next two weeks of our lives.

Finding the boys and Simon already in the three seats on the right, I sank into my seat across the aisle from them and closed my eyes. The usual procedures were announced over the intercom in several languages and I fastened my seatbelt without opening my eyes.

As the plane taxied, roared and took off, I turned my head to look at my family. The aisle suddenly seemed very wide, the three men in my life cocooned in a row of dusty grey upholstery and static antimacassars. Leo stared out of the window. From the middle seat Simon craned around him to share the mesmerising image of the city of Zürich sinking away below us. Oliver watched me, and I smiled, happy I had my family to myself for a while. He reached across the aisle and, in an unusually adult gesture, squeezed my hand.

'We're going to have fun, Mum. I'm really excited. Aren't you?'

'Yes, darling, I'm so ready for this holiday,' I reassured him in return.

SEVEN HUNDRED METRES long and four hundred wide, it took all of fifteen minutes to circumnavigate our Maldivian atoll on foot, along powdery silver beaches surrounding lush vegetation. Bungalows nestled among the palm trees above the shoreline. The barefoot policy throughout the island needed no enforcing for the boys. Having spent so much time on the shores of an alpine lake, they were both strong swimmers. They adored the balmy turquoise waters, and the fascinating subaquatic world of the reef surrounding the atoll. A perfect contrast to the misty autumnal conditions of our alpine home.

As I buried my toes deep into the soft white beach, the cooler sand underneath refreshed and softened the soles of my feet like a balm. The sound of the sea gently tipping its waves onto the shore and the children's screeches of pleasure mingled to provide a feeling of blissful contentedness long missing. The palm leaves clattering in the ocean breeze sounded like rain, although not a cloud could be seen in the cornflower-blue sky. I lay back on the sunbed, the brightness of the sun burnished orange against my closed eyelids. The coiling tension I hadn't realised was a permanent part of my life began to slowly unwind inside me.

I hoped desperately Simon and I could rediscover the magic that seemed to have gone missing from our relationship lately. Here was a place I felt sure *he* wouldn't be some ghostly presence. I could have stayed on that remote island forever, relaxing in the knowledge that he could not possibly have followed us to this place.

Except, deep in my psyche, he was there.

After dinner each night, Simon and I went to the palm-roofed bar and chose evermore elaborate cocktails from the menu, silently competing with each other to see who could escape the need for superficial dialogue by being the first to weave our way off to bed. Before we could even consider rekindling some lost passion, we both fell into an alcohol-induced slumber.

I hadn't been aware that our relationship had become so threadbare. But neither was it obvious to me which of us was avoiding the elephant in the room, the irony being that the elephant was physically absent for the first time in five months. Our forays to the bar were a great way to avoid starting a discussion about unfinished business at home. We were far more comfortable making trivial conversation with other guests. If we did deign to speak to each other, it was easy to forget what had been said in the tropical light of morning.

One afternoon, after a relaxing treatment at the spa, I joined Simon and the boys at the pool. I heard their playful voices through the palm trees and foliage. I kicked my flip-flops off and threw my book and sarong onto a spare sunbed beside the pool. Turning, I jumped into the water in an attempt to join in the frolicking. I forgot I had my sunglasses on, fumbled and grabbed them before they sank to the bottom, then had to swim awkwardly back to the side to leave them on the edge of the pool. Trying to look unruffled, my miscalculated timing was comic.

Simon surfaced in front of the boys across the water, roaring like a sea monster, sending them into squeals of delight. These games reduced them to infancy, removing the shackled obligation of teenage coolness. I swam slowly towards the trio. But they all carried on their game as if I wasn't there. No one came to splash my face, push my head underwater or grab my legs from below. In the past I might have been teased into some kind of tomfoolery. I now felt unaccountably left out of this tight little circle, as though my reactions were too unpredictable. The boys were obviously thrilled to have Simon's undivided attention, and I knew I shouldn't start reading something more into these actions than was intended.

But there was no accounting for my recent irrationality.

Later that evening, the boys shuffled reluctantly off to bed and Simon and I once again sat at the sand-floored bar under the palm-frond roof in soft, comfortable armchairs. This brought on instant fatigue in me and made my gritty eyelids droop. I took a sip of the potent cocktail I had ordered and, before I even had time to consider what the reaction might be, reached across to touch Simon on the knee.

'What are you feeling about this horrid Manfred thing?' I asked.

Simon's face clouded.

'That very phrase seems to belittle the situation. I don't know, Al. The trouble is, you said you were going to do something about him. I know you've been to the cops, and I know the school is aware, but no one seems to be following up, and when I think the problem has all gone away, you seem sulky and distant, and I'm sure it's him who's affecting you. I thought you were stronger than that, had the gumption to act, or at least to talk to me when things started going pear-shaped. You've convinced yourself this guy is a stalker. He's a sick man who's been following you. I know your intentions were good, and I know you think I blame you...'

'Well, do you?' I asked.

Simon combed his cropped hair with his fingers.

'I shouldn't, but I do somehow. I can't turn this *blame* off. I know it's not directly your fault that this guy is still around, but I feel like I need to blame *someone*. A selfish part of me thinks natural selection should have taken its course that day. The idiot should have jumped. But I can see that shocks you.'

He looked at my raised eyebrows.

'I don't know, Al, I guess I'm just pissed off you're so preoccupied with him, and that maybe you're not telling me everything.'

He took a sip of his drink, looking at me pointedly. I'd had no idea he thought I was so absorbed with Manfred. What would he think if he knew I had met with Manfred, and that I had sought out his family?

'I haven't wanted to bother you with the trivialities. I'm hoping this thing will get sorted out, and soon. Simon, you know my priority is you and the family.'

I turned away, my face reddening. I'd ruined a romantic opportunity here. This was supposed to be the holiday of our dreams. I continued to make unfathomable decisions and I was tired of mentally kicking myself.

'I know, Al. I'm just not sure how trivial you think these *trivialities* are.'

He stood up unsteadily and turned towards the bar. There was no point in furthering a conversation fuelled with alcohol.

'I'm tired, Simon. I'm heading to bed.'
'Okay. I think I'll stay on at the bar a bit. I'll see you later.'

CHAPTER THIRTY-ONE

AT ABOUT 2.00 A.M. I woke to find the space in the bed next to me empty. I slipped a sundress on and went back to look for Simon. He was still sitting at the bar, one hand propping up his dishevelled head. He was nursing a glass of whisky, his index finger chasing an ice cube around the glass. He was stone drunk. The barman appeared to be listening to him, tolerating his presence while he polished the last of the glasses.

'Ah,' said Simon, slurring. 'Here is my lovely wife. Do you know my wife?'

The barman dipped his head, unsure whether he should answer.

'Yes, my lovely wife. She has a boyfriend, you know. Someone who spends more time with her than I do. I'm not a very good husband. Away all the time. She deserves someone who can look after her more. Someone who can watch out for her *all* the time.'

Simon was slurring, the wickedness of alcohol producing this acrimony.

'Stop it, Simon.'

I stood beside him.

'Yes, she seems to enjoy being *observed*. Doesn't seem to want to do much about stopping this affair. Oh, well, what am I? Just the breadwinner. Shit.'

His voice sadly patronising, Simon swerved dangerously on his barstool.

'I said stop it, Simon. You're not being fair. Come to bed. It's the alcohol talking. This gentleman has to close down the bar.'

I nodded to the barman and took Simon's arm as he half-slipped, half-hopped off the barstool and we made our way back to the bungalow.

As I walked and Simon wove slowly along the sandy path beside me, he flapped his hand on my arm in a misjudged gesture of attention. I was sure he had been about to hold my hand, but I wasn't about to oblige so readily after his cruel words.

'I'm sorry, Al,' he said, his vitriol depleted, his voice cracking in an uncommon display of uncertainty. 'I'm sorry. It's juss that, why won't you talk to me about it? You're so distant. I feel like I don't know you any more, can't work out wha's going on in your head. For all your training as a psychollologist, you're one helluva communicator, not. S'truly like you're with him more than you are with me, mephatorically, I mean metaphorically speaking.'

He snorted at his own verbal error, but the comical drunken slur couldn't even raise a laugh in my throat. I found it hard to believe that, of all the emotions Simon could have exhibited while under the influence of alcohol, jealousy had raised its ugly head. I could not hope to further this conversation tonight. Above all, Simon might not remember anything we attempted to resolve this evening. It was quite possible he would have forgotten the whole incident by the following day.

WE FILLED OUR two weeks with ocean activities, swimming, sailing, snorkelling, fishing and scuba diving. My tapered training involved the occasional run on the treadmill in the gym.

It was our last day in paradise. Leo sat on the end of the wooden jetty near the bungalows, gazing into the turquoise shallows. Hundreds of pipefish swarmed in unison around the pillars. I stepped onto the bleached wooden slats, and sat down a little awkwardly next to him, pulling my bikini bottoms down a little to protect my backside from the hot wood. I perched on the edge, looking down with him at the fish.

'Leo, it's almost time to go back to school. Have things improved?'

'I knew you were going to talk to me about school,' he said sullenly. 'Can't you drop it? It is half-term break after all. That's a *break*, Mum. Give *me* a break. How come you're getting on my case? It was just a couple of bad grades last term, that's all.'

'Well, that may not be all, Leo. I thought your dad talked to you about this. I saw your teacher at the school before the summer, and she told me you might be in some kind of trouble with another boy. Something about some teasing that might be going a bit far with the younger kids.'

'Bullying, Mum. That's what you mean. Why don't you just say what you mean? Those farmer kids are such mongs, and they're always taunting us. It's not like we just pick on *them*, you know.' His moroseness bordered on sarcasm.

'But Leo, you're four years older than them. You're almost fifteen. You're getting close to adulthood. Surely you can ignore a little badgering from some overexcited kids? I hope it isn't still going on. I don't want to be called in for a session with the school counsellor.'

'Oh, come on! It's not that bad.'

I continued to look at him, but his gaze didn't leave the water.

'It's total rubbish,' he said finally.

'Well, I won't go on about it now when we're having such a great time on holiday…'

'And that's another thing, Mum,' Leo cut in angrily. 'You act like it's all so perfect that we're away on this amazing island in the middle of nowhere, and you're all happy and smiley one minute to have us all together, and miserable as shit the next because you're being totally weird about *something*, I don't know what. The atmosphere at home is, like, impossible. Maybe it's because you and Dad can't keep things together.'

I drew in my breath, and Leo continued.

'What you've done is drag us to the end of the earth, with nothing, *nothing* for us to do except watch a few measly fish, and you think you want to sort *my* problems out? Try looking at yourself. Get your own problems sorted out first, Mum. It's a joke.'

I swallowed. Leo had never spoken to me like that before. Actually, no one had ever spoken to me like that before. Was this what going on fifteen was about? My heart beat heavily in my chest. I didn't want to cry in front of my eldest son, so I stayed quiet, waiting for the threat of tears to subside. I stood up from the edge of the jetty, my exposed skin sticking painfully to the wood.

'I'm sorry you feel that way, Leo. I am sorting some stuff out at the moment, but there are some things you don't need to be concerned about.'

Leo snorted again, and anger replaced my pain. I couldn't continue, or I would be shouting. I wanted to tell him never to speak to me like that again.

But the truth in his outburst kept me silent.

I jogged up and down the beach a few times and after cooling off in the water, gazed at the milky shallows off the atoll, blending to a deep turquoise near the reef. I felt as if I were playing a part in a movie. *Robinson Crusoe*, perhaps. Synonymous in location and emotion. No matter how many kilometres I put between me and the primary problem, it wasn't going away. And tomorrow, rather than being rescued from my desert island, I was terrified of flying home.

Simon was having a siesta, still sleeping off his hangover. I promised myself I would work to save the remnants of something that was going terribly wrong. Leo's paroxysm was long overdue. At least a frustration had been aired by both of us. Surely communication would be easier now. He could stew in his juices for the moment.

Simon's outburst at the bar, however, was a sentiment that might have been festering much longer. I couldn't wait for some policeman to *maybe* catch Manfred stalking my kids. My family was more important to me than anything in the world, and I needed to reinstate myself into the equation. I had to get the mammoth task of the marathon out of the way and then sort out this absurdity. Time to pack the bags, go home to Switzerland and figuratively climb a few Alps.

AS I OPENED the apartment door on our return from the airport, I looked upon a home where not a speck of dust had settled in the two weeks we had been away. Clothes that had been strewn on the floor in a frenzy of packing were now packed neatly away in wardrobes. Sinks and taps gleamed in the bathrooms and kitchen, and the dishwasher had been emptied.

As Simon flicked through the mail in the hallway, and the boys hauled their cases upstairs to their rooms, I stared dumbfounded at a vase of freshly cut flowers in the middle of the kitchen table, and bile burned at the back of my throat.

CHAPTER THIRTY-TWO
OCTOBER

IT WAS HARD to keep warm after the mugginess of the car. Simon dropped me off near the registration tent so I could collect my number before taking the boys into town for breakfast. He was a reluctant participant in the logistics for my race, but the boys wanted to soak up the atmosphere and be there to see me finish. I wasn't even sure I would see them again before the start of the race.

A combination of chilly morning air and nervousness made my chest whirr, wasting precious energy. This was a far cry from the tropical warmth of our Maldivian beach. I pinned my number to my shirt, took a free bottle of energy drink and walked briskly towards the starting area of the race.

An autumnal haze drifted over the town of Lausanne in a chilled chiffon swirl. The sun had risen, but cold seeped into my bones. My movements were restricted, surrounded by so many people. Nervousness started a flow of adrenalin to my limbs. I had the urge to leap up and down doing jumping jacks, and imagined sending those around me flying like bowling pins.

I regretted leaving my windbreaker in the car. A few of the runners were wearing black plastic bin liners with holes cut out for their arms and head, to be discarded at the side of the road when the race started. Anything to keep the body warm.

The wait was interminable, but the buzz of excitement was palpable, and as the giant clock over the banner ticked towards the start, the runners shuffled towards the front, packing themselves alarmingly close. An army of strangers united by the claustrophobia of a thin ribbon. I could at least absorb some warmth from the bodies of others. Various aromas assaulted me. The stringent menthol of deep-muscle cream, the mild body odour of well-worn Lycra tops, laundered for this special day, but unable to hide the signs of hard-working training programmes. The smells of nervous excitement.

I turned to survey the crowd of spectators. Joy spread in my chest as I saw Simon and the boys among the supporters. Simon's face was neutral as he watched the crowd. Oliver saw me and punched the air with his fist in front of his face for encouragement. I could even hear Leo shouting 'Go, Mum, go!' between the cheers of '*Allez allez*' from the other spectators. Simon's face remained cool as our eyes connected, but I knew he understood how much work I had put into this. I raised my hand briefly and gave them a nervous smile.

The MC stood on an elevated platform of scaffolding at the starting line. He announced the final minute before the start of the race and I immediately felt the need to visit the loo again. Had I drunk enough? Had I eaten enough? If only I could have forced more breakfast into my nervous stomach. Was I wearing the right clothes? Was that a fold I felt in my sock, or a piece of grit in my shoe?

'*Trois, deux, un…*' The starting pistol sent another shot of adrenalin coursing through my body, but despite the urge to leap out of the starting blocks, I was obliged to wait while the runners ahead spilled slowly over the starting line, a human concertina opening onto the wide, empty avenue.

We all picked up the movement as a unit, first one tentative foot in front of the other, then a fast walk, finally striding into a slow lope past the starting line as the beep of a thousand microchips started our individual times. Hands simultaneously clutched the start buttons of watches on wrists, and the irregular tweets of various heart monitors mingled with the heavy breathing of the runners. No more talking now. There was business to be run. All forty-two kilometres of it.

For the first five kilometres I stayed with a pack of runners whose metronome pace slapped a steady beat on the road. As the adrenalin wore off, runners began to settle into a more comfortable pace. The course began a gentle uphill rise along the Riviera, following a road referred to locally as the Corniche. We passed through a string of Vaudois villages, where châteaux of the wine domains dominated clusters of ancient stone buildings.

The route was framed either side by rows of vines stacked up along stone walls, all bursting with plump grapes ready for picking. As I squinted towards the lake on my right, I was glad of the peak on my cap as the sun burned the last of the mist away and glittered off the water of *Lac Léman*. The view was breath-taking, a beauty I could appreciate, seeing as I was only a quarter of the way through my race and still full of energy and hope.

It hadn't been my intention to choose the Lausanne marathon. I would rather have run a circuit marathon than an out-and-back race, and would ordinarily have chosen to run in Zürich or Lucerne. But I wanted to compete as far away from home as possible, without leaving the country. Away from Manfred.

Kathy was upset I'd changed my mind at the last minute. We had both originally chosen to run the Lucerne marathon, closer to home. Everything had been arranged. When I told her I'd signed up at the last minute for Lausanne, I could see the disappointment in her eyes, along with the thought that I was taking things a bit far to simply avoid Manfred. I was lucky Simon and the boys still wanted to support me.

Finally out on the road, I was happy to be on my own here.

IN THE INCREASING heat, I knew I had to take on liquids at the next refreshment stand. It couldn't come soon enough. We reached the turning point in La Tour-de-Peilz and began heading back the way we had come. The next drink station marked the beginning of a steep incline. The gentle slope on the way out had transformed into an Alp on the way back.

Runners began overtaking me in increasing numbers. I stopped mid-pace to gulp down an entire beaker of energy drink. It was too concentrated, a radioactive blue that didn't help the sensation of it sloshing around in my stomach. Now I needed water, but my stomach was already full of the sweet drink.

My footfalls felt like useless slaps to the tarmac, my engine no longer running smoothly. We had reached Corseaux, barely twenty-five kilometres into the race, still seventeen to go, and the devils of doubt began invading my psyche.

I eased off the pace even more as one of my hamstrings tightened. Massaging it helplessly as I jogged along, I felt slightly nauseous and panicked as different parts of me began a chain of physical protest. The pace monitor on my watch showed several minutes' deficit and I knew my personal goal was slipping away. My body cried out to stop, legs like solid concrete. This had happened to me before in previous races, but I couldn't believe I had reached the 'wall' so soon, that place where marathon runners are challenged by the devils of self-doubt and inability in their heads. The mind telling them it is madness to continue, overruling the heart that says this thing is still possible.

Pushing on, I knew I only had about five or six kilometres to go. I started feeling good again, a seed of hope blossoming in the knowledge that I was almost there. Although I could do nothing to increase my speed, I seemed to have made it through the wall. My legs clicked into a rhythm of their own, knowing if I changed anything, or had to stop, my whole body would just seize up.

As I jogged through the village of Lutry, I saw a runner coming head-on through the now straggling competitors. His style was of someone fresh on the road, who hadn't yet worked up a sweat. He wore a pair of training pants and a white cotton T-shirt, his kit not at all common to the marathon runner, and he had no number pinned to his chest. We were on a collision course.

My stomach dropped, and I thought I might throw up.

You have got to be kidding me.

'I think I can help you now.' Manfred smiled, and did an about-turn to run with me as I approached.

CHAPTER THIRTY-THREE

'GET. AWAY. FROM. ME,' I growled between breaths, with my teeth gritted and my jaw set, trying not to waste precious energy. 'What the hell do you think you're doing? How did you find out I was running here?'

My pace decreased, but I kept my eyes fixed on the route ahead.

'I know where you are all the time, Alice. You cannot fool me by signing up for two marathons. If I hadn't seen you today, I would have seen you next week in *Luzern*. I am here to help. The last five kilometres are the most difficult. I will help.'

'You are not helping. You're not even allowed on the course. Just go away.'

Hot tears pricked in my eyes. Up ahead I could see a race official wearing a reflective jacket at the side of the road, and I stopped in front of him.

'*Excusez-moi*, excuse me – this man, he's bothering me.'

The volunteer looked uncomprehendingly from me to Manfred, who had stepped away to an unthreatening distance.

'He is following me! *Il est fou!*' I said, dragging up some high-school French.

Manfred turned to the group and spoke.

'*Désolé, Messieurs, je n'avais aucune intention d'emmerder la dame, je suis un ami, je voulais l'encourager à l'arrivée…*'

'Jesus, of course you speak French!' I clenched my fists. 'Leave me *alone!*' I yelled.

I glanced desperately around, hoping to see someone in uniform with a more authoritative role. The thought of having to explain my situation in yet another foreign language made my eyes sting. I turned back to the yellow-jacketed official.

'Police! I want the police, can you…?'

I indicated the radio poking out of a breast pocket of his waist jacket. He touched the button on the top, looking from Manfred back to me, and shook his head.

'*Non*, Madame, it is not necessary. Do you like something to drink? It is only four kilometres to the finish. Can you finish?'

'Come on, Alice, you can do it. I'm here to help you finish,' Manfred added.

'Get out of my face!' I screeched, my throat hurting with the forced effort.

Delirium drove my anger past the irrational. My left calf had begun to cramp, my back was stiff, and my hips were suddenly sore.

'*You have got to leave me alone!*'

I raised my leaden arms, shoulders burning with the discomfort of making a movement out of the ordinary during the past three hours. I rammed the sides of my clenched fists into Manfred's chest. He stumbled backwards with the force, then lurched towards me and clutched both my wrists with a grip of iron. I was shocked by his sudden strength. He dug his thumbs into the soft spaces next to the contracted tendons on my arms. I squealed and stared into his eyes, blazing with madness. His eyebrows furrowed as he clenched his jaw and my exhausted heart ramped up its pounding. I was about to turn and scream at the official for help, when Manfred released me with a push and turned away to avoid confrontation with the official.

The rebound put me off balance and I stepped backwards into the unseen kerb. My foot landed unexpectedly on the raised pavement, and slid sideways. With a sickening crunch I was sure everyone heard, the whole weight of my body came down on my ankle at right angles to the road. I opened my mouth and finally let out a wail.

The noise had the desired effect. A spectator came over and shielded Manfred from me. He flapped both hands downwards in a dismissive gesture that looked like disgust and walked away, his mouth downturned. The volunteer took me by the arm.

'You will change your mind, Alice. You will come to me in the end,' Manfred called over his shoulder as he was obliged to retreat, unaware that my outcry was now more a scream of pain than frustration.

I was miles from home, surrounded by French-speaking strangers who could all have been called as witnesses to Manfred's obsessive behaviour if I had thought about it, but I barely had the energy to plonk myself down on the kerb and reach for my foot, which was already swelling alarmingly. My whole body protested at the abrupt change in stance and motion, and the intense throbbing pain in my ankle was a masochistic relief from the overall pain in the rest of my body. I was locked to the kerb and thought I might never move again.

To have come all this way and have to give up because of a stupid slip of the foot. All that hard work. All that time devoted to training for this day, this point in my life. I felt abject. I sobbed. Thoughts of Kathy's imminent disappointment ran through my head. I thought of Simon and the boys waiting, expecting me at a predicted time, with the certainty of a Swiss train arriving. Every minute that passed beyond my expected finish time would worry them. They would wonder what had happened. My body began to shake, going into the shock of the injury. I had to get to the finish. I looked down the road. Manfred had disappeared. I tried to get up, but it was too painful.

The volunteer insisted I stay still. I must not put my foot down. He reached down and carefully undid the laces of my shoe.

'Madame, we must take away shoe, foot...' He held his hands around an imaginary ball in front of my face and moved them apart to indicate swelling. I wondered if he was a doctor. If so, he was now in his element.

'You cannot run. I sorry. Not good.'

He carefully loosened all the laces on my shoe and splayed it open. Expertly clasping my ankle with unexpected gentleness, he worked my shoe off without moving it sideways. My freed foot felt momentarily, exquisitely relieved as I attempted to wriggle my toes. A sharp pain pierced the arch, travelling to the outer ligament, and I knew it had stretched, perhaps even torn.

And then the throbbing started. I put my face in my hands as the volunteer finally reached for the radio in his pocket. An abrupt conversation ensued between him and an unseen helper. I attempted to move, and he put his hand out, commanding me to stay.

'Wait, Madame,' he said. 'Maybe we lucky. Someone coming for you. Wait, please.'

Fresh tears now mingled with the dried salty crust of sweat residue on my face. I felt a terrible sense of failure. Someone patted an emergency Mylar blanket across my shoulders, and I held two corners next to my chest to avoid the flimsy sheet blowing away in the breeze, trying to preserve some warmth for my exhausted body. I realised I must let Simon know. The volunteer was happy to lend me his mobile phone now I had a genuine problem to address. I called Simon's number.

It rang for a long time before he answered with a curious 'Hello?' as he saw a number on his screen he didn't recognise.

'Simon, hi it's me,' I said, my throat closing with a fresh bout of tears. 'I've had a little accident, twisted my ankle.'

'God, are you okay?' He was genuinely worried, knowing how important it had been for me to finish this race.

'Well, I'm… yes, apart from my ankle, I'm okay. I might have to wait for a sweeper van to bring me in. I can't walk.'

'Jeez, Al, what happened?'

'I slipped on a kerb as I was taking a drink. It's okay. I'm okay. But you won't be able to get the car here. The whole road is cordoned off for the race. Hopefully I'll be there as soon as I can. I'm sorry,' I said miserably, my voice breaking with a sob.

'We'll wait, it's okay,' he said in a surprisingly sympathetic voice. 'Don't worry about us. Just take care of yourself, get something to drink and don't get cold. Is someone looking after you?'

I answered his questions in monotone, all the while aware that the real cause of my accident had been Manfred, not some unseen curb at the side of the road. The fact that Simon was showing such empathy made me want to cry all the more, but I had no more energy for tears.

While I waited for the sweeper truck, someone managed to find some hot fruit tea in a Styrofoam cup, and a Mars bar magically appeared from a spectator. I was finally helped onto the corrugated flatbed of the sweeper vehicle. I sat with my legs hanging off the back of the little truck, still clutching the Mylar blanket, my right shoe resting in my lap. As the vehicle pulled slowly away, the volunteer waved and smiled sympathetically. I was sure he was glad to be shot of me.

The vehicle rounded the last bend of the course near the Olympic Museum in Ouchy. Glancing over my shoulder, neck creaking with stiffness, I could see the huge, inflatable, orange archway of the finish line in the distance, yacht masts in the marina piercing the background beyond. How humiliating to be finishing in this way.

Suddenly the boys appeared at the side of the avenue, waving their arms, concerned faces bobbing along as they ran at the same speed as the vehicle. I kept my eyes on them as they flashed between the gaps in the horse chestnut trees lining the road. My throat closed and tears immediately sprang to my eyes. Leo was caught up in the enthusiasm of his younger brother, and I was momentarily warmed by his unbridled display. The driver hopped out to move the metal barrier aside and drove off the course to avoid passing through the finishers' archway.

I slid gingerly off the back of the truck, and Leo ran to me, throwing his arms round my neck. I clung to him, relishing this rare display of affection, and bit my lip to hold back a new flood of tears. Oliver's smile of moments before dropped, and he stared, horrified, at the dried sweat and tears on my tired face.

Simon gave me a perfunctory hug, ignoring the stale smell of my body. It was the first time he had touched me for weeks, his recent frustrations forgotten in this time of primal need. I was sad, angry, and a plethora of emotions I couldn't put a finger on. I didn't trust my voice, but answered Simon and the boys' questions with as few words as possible. *How? When? Where?*

Stopped for refreshment. Moved to the side. Tripped on the kerb. Twisted ankle.

I kept my face down. The truth was I couldn't raise my head for fear of catching a face in the crowd.

I wanted to lean into Simon's chest, but his half-hearted words of sympathy had evaporated in the worry of how we would get out of town in the heavy traffic. Instead I clutched the Mylar blanket as we made our way slowly back to the car.

'Are you okay, Mum? Does it really hurt? It will get better soon.'

Oliver touched my arm and I smiled, wanting to hide my suffering from him.

'Oliver, darling, of course Mum will be okay.'

I spoke in the third person, a common trait of all mothers lying to their children.

We stopped briefly to cut off the electronic chip tied to my shoe and, as I winced, the volunteer suggested I visit the medics' tent at the exit of the enclosure. She threw my chip into the collecting box inside the race barrier. I gazed past the box to the runners picking up their medals and souvenir 'finisher' T-shirts at the adjacent stalls, and turned back to watch my chip disappear into the box under an increasing pile. My chip with thirty-eight kilometres of effort registered. My chip for an incomplete marathon. The chip that would confirm my status on the result sheet as DNF, Did Not Finish.

I hobbled to the medics' tent, supported between Leo and Simon. A man indicated I should sit down and tutted as he examined my ankle.

'I give you something for pain and inflammation, but you must go direct to your *médecin* when you are home. Maybe he will not see you until tomorrow. He will need to scan this.'

The man laid a box of tablets on the ground next to him as he expertly bandaged my ankle.

'Keep this *élevé* as much as possible,' he said, holding my foot with one hand and raising the flattened palm of the other.

As he secured the bandage with an elastic clip, he glanced around at the mayhem in the tent. The floor was littered with paper cups, and the menthol smell of muscle relaxant masked the smell of sweat. The other helpers who had been busy dishing out electrolyte drinks to exhausted runners, and space blankets to those with blue lips, were now rushing to pack up as they had been instructed by the police to open the area to traffic again. In his hurry the medic handed me the whole box of tablets. I turned it over in my hand. *Co-Dafalgan.*

'Is okay,' he said. 'You eat something first, then take two of these. Not more than two every four hours. Take the pack to your doctor when you make appointment.'

I thanked the medic and we made our way slowly to the car, which Simon had parked some distance away. There was nothing more to say. My family could tell how disappointed I was not to finish the race. I couldn't speak anyway.

The vision of Manfred filled my head each time I closed my eyes, along with the question of where he had obtained prior access to the starting list of the marathon.

CHAPTER THIRTY-FOUR

FOUR OF US sat at a square table barely large enough to hold the array of glasses, cutlery and plates. The echoing resonance of the high ceiling raised competitive speech to rock-concert levels in the Mexican restaurant. I sat across from Simon, and Kathy sat opposite Matt. We all blatantly avoided any conversation about the races. Kathy had run the Lucerne marathon a week after mine and had earned herself a respectable time. She was still irked I had changed my plans at the last moment, even though I explained about Manfred. It hadn't made any different in the end. He'd still found out which race I was running.

I recounted the events of our recent holiday. We leaned in to be heard, clutching sweating bottles of beer spiked with slices of lime. Kathy's high-heel-clad feet possessively touched Matt's under the table, making space for my heavily bandaged ankle stretched besides Simon's own feet. Simon and I sat with our elbows on the table, not quite touching. I was glad of the warm, muggy atmosphere, as I had boldly worn a short-sleeved shirt to show off my fading tan.

The conversation lulled as our food arrived, the table increasingly crammed with burritos, taco salads and all the paraphernalia required to construct fajitas. As Matt loaded a small tortilla with a pile of shredded beef from the sizzling pan in front of him, he started a new thread of conversation from that of palm trees, coral reefs and sand castles.

'Whatever happened to that arsehole who started stalking you, Alice?' asked Matt. 'Kath told me about the sleazy dude. He'd soon have felt the rough end of my fist if I had anything to do with it.'

I squirmed in my seat, felt my face flush, and hunger drained from me to be replaced by a tight knot in my stomach. I glanced at Simon, who held his head slightly to one side, eyebrows raised, waiting for my answer. Matt looked from Simon to me, realising he had raised a hot point. Rather than backing down from the sliceable thick air between Simon and me, Matt launched deeper into the bag of vipers.

'Kath said Al thought he might have been nicking stuff from your house,' Matt continued. 'Jesus, I'd be mad as piss if something like that happened in our home.'

'It was only a photo, Matty,' Kathy interrupted, 'and that happened ages ago. He can't get into the house now, can he, Al?'

Kathy shot an apologetic look at me, realising she should have briefed her buffoon of a husband before heading out for the evening. I wanted the floor to open and swallow me up. Simon's expression changed from curiosity to irritation. The noise in the restaurant increased, pounding in my ears to the rhythm of my heart.

'It's being sorted, Matt. The police know, the school knows, he'll be out of our lives very shortly,' I stated, more confidently than I felt.

'He's been in our *house*?' Simon asked. 'What has been going on? Which photo exactly?' The questions flew at me. 'I think there are a few things you haven't told me. Do please explain.'

He spoke with the patronising voice of a parent grilling a recalcitrant child. I couldn't blame him.

'Matt's got it a little out of proportion. I'll explain later. God, it's so loud in here. I'm just popping to the loo,' I said as I stood up suddenly.

The wooden chair slid noisily backwards and my crutches crashed to the floor. The noise in the restaurant decreased briefly as a few people around us stopped their conversations and turned to stare. Matt picked up the crutches and handed them to me. Smiling vaguely in the direction of the surrounding tables, I hopped to the ladies' cloakroom.

I splashed water on my hot face, dried it on a paper towel and took a few deep breaths before heading back to the table with what I hoped was a calm, controlled look on my face. I wasn't hungry any more, but didn't want the others to sense my discomfort. I forced my food past the brick in my throat, keeping my face as neutral as possible.

AFTER WE FINISHED our meal, Kathy kept up a chirpy, falsetto conversation. Matt was completely oblivious to the depth of trouble he had stirred up, and Simon sat smouldering, silence sitting between us like a wet blanket.

We climbed into the car at the end of the evening, doors clunking on the strained space of our proximity. As we fastened our seatbelts, I could tell he was dying to explode. He stabbed the key into the ignition, missing on the first shot, and I closed my eyes in preparation for the onslaught, Marie-Antoinette waiting for the blade.

'What the hell is going on, Alice?' Simon's voice was dangerously raised in the confines of the car, anger coming off him like knives. His use of my full name betrayed the extent of his rage. 'There seems to be a lot you haven't told me. He's been in our *house*? Come on, this doesn't just involve you anymore. Jesus, it's our home he's somehow defiled. Why didn't you tell me the whole story? What possible motive did you have to keep this from me? Like some kind of intellectual deception.'

I felt like I was looking up at that guillotine.

'Well… I don't know for sure, Simon. There was a photo. It was on our sideboard in the living room. And I had this feeling when we came back from the Maldives that he'd been in the house. The flowers... I know you've always been confused as to why I brought him back to the house before taking him to the hospital, but I never imagined he would come into the house again later. I never invited him *in*, Simon.' I remembered our meeting at the café, that I'd never told Simon. 'I wanted to help him. I obviously hadn't thought the whole thing through.'

I pushed my hair back off my slick forehead.

'Simon, I'm so sorry. I don't know what to say. I thought initially I was helping. I thought he was clinging to me because I had given him something to believe in and live for. Then it was confirmed that he had a photo of us, so he must have been into the house and taken it.'

'How exactly? Who confirmed it?' Simon's eyes narrowed.

'His son. I went to see where he used to live. His son gave it back to me.'

'What on earth have you got yourself mixed up in, Alice? This sounds suspiciously ironic. What were you thinking? Stalking the stalker!'

'There are many things I didn't know back then. And some of my decisions I made were wrong. I wish I could turn back the clock. If I'd known then what I know now... I'm so sorry.' My voice sounded pathetic.

'Sorry, sorry, sorry. That's not going to make the problem go away, Alice. Something needs to be done about this,' Simon continued. 'Jesus! Look, I don't want to talk about this anymore tonight. I need to think about what's going on. We'll talk tomorrow evening after work when I've got my head round a few things.'

The menace in his voice frightened me. What did he need to get his head around exactly? This felt like a threat from the inside, something he was suddenly considering about *me*, not Manfred. I so wished I could turn back the clock.

The run. The bridge. That first glance up.

I should have let him jump.

CHAPTER THIRTY-FIVE

AS THE DOCTOR took the bandage off my ankle, his hands eased my foot to the floor. Even without any weight on it I could feel my pulse thumping through the swollen, yellowing injury. I could do nothing to control the tears that suddenly came in great gulping sobs, and the GP looked at me horrified.

He rocked back on his heels and pushed his glasses up the bridge of his nose.

'It is not so bad, Mrs Reed. Please don't cry. Are you in bad pain?' I shrugged. 'You will be running again within a few months. But you must understand it will take time. You still have a lifetime of running ahead of you.'

I sniffed loudly. He handed me a tissue from his desk.

'It… it's not this,' I said, waving my hand vaguely at my foot. 'Well, it is this… but it's not the fact I c… can't run.'

In reality, I was beginning to wish I could run away from it all.

And out came the whole sorry story. As I recounted everything to the family doctor I wondered why I hadn't thought to come to him before. He'd been our family doctor since we first moved to the village. I'd originally chosen him because he was the only doctor in the valley who spoke English. We didn't require his services very often, but he probably knew the boys' medical history better than me, speaking to them in his native Swiss German when they needed vaccinations or treatments for minor ailments.

It was likely his semi-professional status made it easier for me to talk. I hoped he wasn't going to suggest I see a psychologist. Although I knew it might have been at the back of Simon's mind.

'It sounds like you've been under a lot of pressure, what with this person's unusual behaviour, and now this injury.'

'The worst of it is… it's affecting my relationship with my husband. It's driving us apart somehow.'

'I can see this is very stressful for you. You have obvious symptoms of anxiety. Now you're not training for the race, I could give you something to calm you a little, help you sleep better at night. It's amazing how a solid night's sleep can make you see things differently in the day. But this would not be something long-term.'

I shook my head. I wouldn't stoop to medication. Then everyone might seriously consider me a headcase.

'Oh, I forgot, I was supposed to bring back the tablets the medics gave me at the race.'

'What did they give you?' the doctor asked.

'I think it was Co-Dafalgan.'

'That's a mild painkiller and anti-inflammatory, like paracetamol, for headaches, period pains, that kind of thing. If the date is still valid, there's no reason for you to bring them in. Are you still taking them for the pain?'

I shook my head.

'The swelling is down now. You only need to do some gentle massage and little movements to continue the healing process. I'll also give you some *Kytta Salbe*. It contains *Wallwurz* – I think you call it comfrey. The salve also contains arnica, and will help with the healing.'

He gently moved my ankle in small circles. The pain wasn't so bad any more. And it was good to have shared some of my mental concerns. But it would only alleviate them for so long.

THE SMELL OF the salve the doctor had used on my ankle nauseated me. Each waft of menthol reminded me of my failed marathon. When I got home, I stepped into the shower and washed the aroma away. This was the only place in the house where I didn't feel so suffocated, despite the rapidly thickening steam. I kept hoping the needles of hot water would somehow wash all my troubles away.

I reflected how I had stopped answering phone calls. I couldn't face talking to Simon. And I couldn't face hearing any accusations or excuses from Kathy. I'd hurt her feelings by not supporting her in the hardest thing she'd probably ever done in her life, and I couldn't help thinking Matt's slip of the tongue about the photo in the restaurant was some kind of reverse karma. I deserved all this. And it was pathetic that the only person I could talk to was my Swiss family GP.

I stepped out of the shower, towelling my hair. Squeaking a space clear on the fogged-up mirror, I pulled my fingers through damp locks, and inspected my reflection. My mouth looked tight, and my eyes tired, with lines around them that hadn't been there at the beginning of the year. My hair was darkened with the dampness from the shower, but I knew there were strands of grey in there. Twisting the towel around my head, I exited the bathroom with a cloud of steam, and wandered into the bedroom. Coming to an abrupt halt, I gasped.

What the…?

Manfred stood in front of my open wardrobe, tentatively touching one of my long-unworn cocktail dresses.

Stunned, I remained rooted to the spot, mute with horror. Heat flooded my face as I remembered I was naked. I tugged the damp towel from my turbaned hair. Fumbling, I covered my torso. I hadn't heard him enter the house, but I was sure I had locked the door behind me. I hadn't heard the familiar creak on the fourth stair. He surely heard my heart pounding.

The silk of the skirt slipped through his fingers.

I could almost see the reflection of my own naked image burning in his eyes.

CHAPTER THIRTY-SIX

'*WHAT* THE FUCK are you doing here?' I shrilled.

Manfred jumped at my tone as he turned to fully face me. I found it hard to read his expression. Guilt? Wonder? Satisfaction? Certainly now confusion, as he heard the angst in my voice.

'I can explain. Don't panic so, Alice. You should know it's important for me to find something constant. Your life, it's so steady, so normal. It is something I strive for.'

'Jesus, Manfred! Riffling through my bloody wardrobe in my bedroom is hardly normal! Get out! Go downstairs! Get the fuck out of my bedroom. This is… this is… just go!'

My body went into a spasm of shivering. The sudden change of temperature from the steamy bathroom to the bedroom combined with the sickening realisation that Manfred wasn't at all stable. Thoughts battled in my mind. Even if he felt observing some domestic normality would help, this was totally unacceptable. *In my bedroom.*

Clutching the towel securely to my chest, my wide eyes willed him out of my space. I walked to the top of the stairs and scooped the air downwards. I swallowed as he slowly descended. The skin of his palm rasping down the banister was the only sound in the now-silent house apart from the blood beating in my head.

'Get out!' I shouted, and halfway down the stairs he turned to look at me.

I felt the cold chill of something out of control.

Because in that split-second Manfred's eyes had fallen on my body in my bedroom, I realised I'd seen something more than desperation in his eyes. There was a flicker of lust. And for the first time I wondered how far he intended to go to achieve his goal. How far would he go to have me?

As he reached the bottom of the stairs, he turned left down the hallway instead of right towards the front door, and my heart beat harder in my throat.

'No! No! No! You must leave!'

I rushed back to the bedroom and ran between the drawers and wardrobe. I quickly pulled on underwear, jeans and a sweatshirt. The skirt of the dress he had touched still protruded from the jumble of hangers at an angle. I felt sick. Tugging my wet hair roughly up through the neck of the shirt, I hobbled barefoot down the stairs, not wanting to leave Manfred alone for a moment longer in my home.

HE STOOD IN the living room, studying several photos of my boys on the shelf. He gave each picture frame the same amount of attention before moving to the next. He reached the photo of me and the boys I had put back in its place after visiting Gerry. Manfred raised his eyebrows and turned enquiringly towards me. I would not give him the satisfaction of learning how I had got it back.

I wanted his eyes off them all, wanted him to step away from my precious children, as though he would defile their images with his look. My feeling of charity for this man had long since worn off. Nervousness spread its gnawing fingers from the pit of my stomach.

My eyes flickered to the phone behind Manfred on the shelf. I didn't want to get anywhere close to him. I couldn't think where I'd left my mobile.

'You've got to leave now, Manfred. Please leave my home.'

He turned to look at me and held up one palm. He could see the sparking anxiety in my eyes.

'I'm so sorry, Alice. I'm so sorry for this misunderstanding. I don't know what happened to me. Look, I'm leaving. I see I've shocked you. Please don't…'

I made as though to dart past him, to get the phone from the shelf. He blocked me, must have known it was there, and we began a strange dance. He moved towards the door and I stepped aside so he would not have to come anywhere near me. I held my arms tightly to my sides so he couldn't see me shaking.

'I'll call you. When you have calmed down. I see you're not ready for this. But you will understand in the end. You'll see we are meant to be together.'

There was no desperation in his voice. But his menacing tone reaffirmed his absolute belief that we would be together.

'No, Manfred. There'll be no more calling. You must leave us alone now. Simon, my husband… I can't predict what he will do if you keep bothering me. You must stay away. You must seek medical help. Go. Now. Please.'

Manfred finally moved down the hallway towards the front door, opened it and exited. He stood momentarily on the landing outside our apartment before closing the door behind him. I heard his footsteps on the stairs leading to the building's main entrance. The familiar sound of the main door closing on its latch told me he was finally out of our home.

Heart still thumping, I leaned against the apartment door, turned the lock, and pressed my palms against the wood. I rushed to the lounge window and banged my head on the pane, trying to see where he was, then I ran to the kitchen, knocking over a chair on the way, to do the same there. Manfred walked along our driveway, making his way to the main road. He wasn't going back to his lookout post; he must have been going home. I breathed a shaky sigh of relief before looking frantically at the clock. It was okay. The boys would still be in school. I didn't want him passing them on the way.

He saw me naked in my bedroom!

I wondered what had been his true intention. How did he think he could make his belief a reality? I was sure I didn't want to know the answer. This was more than a reciprocal house visit. Our calling cards could not have been more different.

But I couldn't forget I had also barged into his home recently.

I could just imagine how that conversation with the police would go.

AS I TIDIED the clothes strewn around the bedroom and picked up the wet towel I had dropped on the floor, my glance fell on the half-open door of my wardrobe. The dress still protruded from among my clothes. When I closed my eyes I could see Manfred's fingers sifting the skirt between his fingers.

He saw me naked.

I ripped the offending article off its hanger with a clack. Bundling up the dress, I jogged downstairs to the basement, unlocking our apartment door on the way. I shoved the dress into the washing machine, and heaped an extra measure of detergent into the soap compartment. To cure it from the virus of his touch.

I knew I should tell Simon, but I couldn't face any more of his vitriol.

With a chill I realised I should have challenged Manfred about a key. Now I was sure he had been here, how had he gained access?

Voicing my stupidity to Simon about the way this whole thing had unravelled wouldn't take Manfred's fingerprints off my chiffon or cancel the memory of his eyes on my body.

CHAPTER THIRTY-SEVEN

BACK FROM WORK that evening, Simon slung his briefcase onto the bench, and shrugged out of his jacket. He had looked unusually smart in his suit that morning, worn specially for a business meeting. His life currently seemed to be one long string of meetings, hopping from one country to another. But this evening he looked dishevelled. He was breathing heavily, distraught.

'Well, I've had a good go at the bastard now. Let's hope he doesn't show his face around here again. I think the farmer thought I was off my rocker. He drove past me in his tractor as I was apparently yelling at a cow in the field. But I saw *him*, Alice.'

'He's always there, Simon,' I said miserably. 'He's like a sentry at that tree at the end of the track. You've just never seen him before. Perhaps it's because you're back earlier than usual. From what I've read about people with his psychological profile, though, we shouldn't be displaying anger or upsetting him in any way. He could be unpredictable.'

He saw me naked.

I stood at the sink, facing the window, and was surprised to feel Simon's arms slip around my waist, his body leaning into me. It felt strange after the asperity following our restaurant outing. I didn't know whether to melt into him or brace myself. The signals were confusing.

'I wish you were around more,' I heard myself whining again.

Simon had one hand around my waist, and put his chin on my shoulder. I glanced sideways at him. He was looking for Manfred through the window. I turned my head, followed his gaze, my eyes searching the twilight outside. Without thinking, I slapped his hand away.

'No, Alice, let him see. Why are you scared of showing that you don't belong to him?' Simon held me a little harder.

This new rancour, the jealousy I had picked up on at the bar in the Maldives, disturbed me. He was displaying emotions I did not recognise.

'I… I don't know, Simon. It just seems so sordid. Like some peep show or something.'

I wriggled free from his arms, slunk away from the sink in front of the window. Simon was becoming more waspish.

'Alice, if I didn't know any better, I'd say you're protecting him in some way. Do you like it? That he's always here for you? Is that what this is about?'

Simon's outburst at the bar on holiday seemed ready to repeat itself. Except this time he was sober.

'No! It's not that…' I was at a loss for words.

'Then what is it? This guy needs to be stopped. Please don't give him the satisfaction of thinking he's winning you over somehow. He's a creep. His focus is on you. He needs major help. But despite your qualifications, you're definitely not the one to give it.'

I shouldn't have been shocked that his frustration had finally manifested itself. But I was still reeling from the fact that he was hurting in his own way too. God knew what Simon would do if he found out Manfred had seen me coming out of the shower.

'I know that. I just…'

'Who's a creep, Mum? Who're you talking about?'

Oliver walked into the kitchen, throwing his football bag down into the doorway.

'What's for dinner?'

I was grateful Oliver didn't really require an answer to his first two questions. My gratefulness was short-lived, however, when Simon felt obliged to elaborate, making my head tingle.

'I saw the guy who's been stalking your mum,' he said.

My heart dropped. I knew I was in trouble now, as Oliver's eyes rounded in recognition.

'The weirdo? And *me*, Dad, he's been *stalking* me too!'

'*What?*' Simon was now furious. 'And how come no one told me about *this*? I thought a couple of kids just saw some guy outside the school.'

'Simon, I… I told Oli not to bother you with it. It wasn't a big deal. He talked to him on the way home from school one day. Please, don't get angry. You've been away so much, been so busy with the project.'

I put my hand on Oliver's shoulder to reassure him this outburst wasn't his fault.

'Oh, right, so now I'm not even permitted to be kept in the loop about my *kids*? Alice, these are my children too. I have every right to know what's going on. I'm now thinking this guy is a nutcase. You've got to take his instability more seriously. Look, I'm away again next week. I wish the project would hurry up and conclude, but the Copenhagen office has found a glitch on the legal side, so this thing could take months with so many parties involved. I don't want to be away. It's just as frustrating for me as it is for you. But I can't avoid it. Something must be done about this guy. You've got to *act*, dammit.'

Simon's anger was now unbridled.

I felt my mouth turn down involuntarily at the corners. A pounding welled behind my eyes. *Pull yourself together.* Once again I felt rebuked, and knew it was perfectly justified. But my actions couldn't be reversed. Simon's frustration was manifesting itself in a choleric reaction. I'd never seen him like this, and it was unnerving. I turned to the fridge. I hadn't a clue what to cook for the family for dinner. I hadn't a clue what to do, but knew I must somehow take control.

'Why do *I* have to act? Why can't *we* act? I've been to the police – twice – and the school has intervened and promised action. What more can I do on my own? Has it occurred to you I might need your help now too?'

The open fridge cooled my burning face. I turned back to face him.

'If you're so bloody uptight about the need for action, why can't you organise a time to come with me to the police station?

Back me up. You've seen him now. At least you can tell them I'm not hallucinating, or making up stories.'

'That's right. Shift the blame,' he said. 'Make it my problem now.'

'Oh, Jesus. Don't be so childish. You know I'm not blaming you! I know, I know. You don't have *time*. You are away a lot, and there's nothing we can do about that.' I took a breath to calm myself. 'I won't say it again, but you must know I regret the way things turned out. I won't say it's not my fault, and it was stupid of me not to have told the whole truth.'

I still hadn't told him everything. Simon's eyes blazed as he turned from me, wrenching his tie free from his collar, the sound of strained threads tearing in his shirt or his tie. He grabbed his jacket, keys falling to the floor, and left the kitchen. I picked up his keys, laid them gently on the table and stared at the static, crackling space in the doorway.

Oliver stood gaping at me. I pulled him towards me in a tight embrace.

'It's okay, Oli. It's not your fault. Everything will be okay,' I said without conviction.

As I listened to Simon's heavy footfalls on the stairs, and the ensuing thump of the bathroom door, I realised we weren't so different, he and I, running away from our responsibilities.

Later, I lay on my back in bed, eyelids closed but fluttering with the effort of feigning sleep. The only sound in the room was the occasional rustle, slide and flip of paper turning as Simon read another page of his novel. I wanted to stretch my leg out and circle my ankle, but continued to breathe deeply, hoping to convince Simon I was asleep, I reflected on this precarious new feeling I had when in close proximity to my husband. The silence between us buzzed in my head.

I had spent so long avoiding conversations and confrontations, I no longer knew how to start, like a girlfriend trying unsuccessfully to over-impress on the first date. The spaces around us were getting larger as we subconsciously avoided each other in the apartment. Tonight's display in the kitchen had been rare physical contact, and even that had ended badly.

He seemed oblivious to the fact that I felt almost constantly wretched. I ached to know his feelings, but knew disappointment in me must be high on his list. He didn't know about the childish gifts I continued to receive in the mailbox. He didn't know I had seen Manfred in our home. And he didn't know Manfred had seen me naked in our bedroom.

I wanted to spill the whole sorry truth, but feared his anger when he once again learned of the horror of the consequences of one fateful meeting. I could have kicked myself for my indecision and inaction. I wanted to touch him, but dared not disturb the static calm between us.

I was lying on eggshells.

'FUCK RIGHT OFF! Stop fucking calling, you creepy fuck!' Simon shouted into the mouthpiece of the handset before jabbing the cut-off button and slamming it down in its cradle. I imagined the hoarse, burning soreness of his larynx as he used a tone of voice I could only remember having heard at rugby matches.

The phone had rung in the dead of the night. Thinking to stop the ringing before it woke the whole household, I picked up the receiver and listened briefly to the silence before Simon leaned over and grabbed it from me.

I turned on the bedside light. The shock of the shouting and the language didn't quash my admiration for the many grammatical usages of the word 'fuck.' I held back the squawk of a laugh. Too late, he'd seen my face.

'It's not bloody funny. You ought to remember you got us into this weird mess,' he said.

I choked on the moment of hysteria, much like being told someone has died. The inappropriateness of laughter feeds the compulsion to giggle. Simon's retort stung harder than a slap to my cheek.

I almost wished he would hit me so I could have something to justify my pain.

CHAPTER THIRTY-EIGHT

I HAD NOT long seen the locksmith out of the house when my mobile rang.

'Alice, are you at home?' It was Simon. I told him yes. 'Then why didn't you answer the bloody phone? Listen, I need you to do me a favour.'

He sounded perturbed. I didn't tell him I rarely answered the house phone.

'Sure. What's up?'

'I'm at the garage. There was a bit of a problem with the brakes on the car. I've had a little accident. Had to swerve into a field on the way down to Zug.'

'Oh, my God, Simon, are you okay?'

You have got to be kidding me. Would Manfred go that far?

'Yes, yes, I'm fine. A little shocked, that's all. A fence post has done a fair amount of damage to my front wing. Thank God I wasn't anywhere near the gorge or on that flipping bridge. Can you believe it? On the one day of the week I take the car to work.'

'And thank God the boys weren't in the car with you.'

Would he?

'I need you to get me the insurance policy number for the Land Rover, and find out whether we're covered for marten damage – the mechanic says it's standard in this canton. It'll say *'Marderschade'* or something like that. But I need to make sure.'

'Okay. Hang on.'

I raced upstairs to our office and pulled out the file for household insurances. I thumbed through the policy, and picked up the extension.

'"*Marderschaden*". I think so, Simon. It looks like we're covered. But what does this mean?'

'The mechanic says the little bastards must have been in our garage. They've chewed through some cables and pierced the brake lines with their teeth, which means the fluid ran out. Jesus, I'm so bloody lucky.'

'Is he sure it was martens, Simon?'

'Of course! What else would it be?'

I couldn't air what else I was thinking at that moment.

WHEN I WENT to pick up the Land Rover a couple of days later, I asked the mechanic if he thought it could be anything other than martens that caused this damage.

'To be honest, I've never seen them biting through brake lines before, because most of the modern ones are braided metal. The critters usually attack electric cables or coolant hoses. But it's not unheard of, and these ones are old. They still have a bit of rubber tubing round the connection. So the damage was consistent with *Marder* damage, yes.'

He took out a file and showed me photos they'd taken of the damage for the insurance company. The images showed the lines were randomly pierced.

'The animals have very sharp teeth,' the mechanic continued. 'This old Land Rover has only two drum brakes. A modern car would have had the backup of a disk brake on each wheel. Your husband is a very lucky man. These cursed creatures are protected in our country, but they cause more headaches than anything else for everybody – drivers, us and the insurance companies.'

I stared at the photos. I so wanted to believe it was impossible for a human to have made these incisions with a sharp object. But my stomach was roiling.

CHAPTER THIRTY-NINE
NOVEMBER

I WALKED UP from the village, gazing distractedly at the lake, carrying a few provisions I'd bought at the Co-op. A fishing boat was trawling for perch on the calm water. A chevron of ripples widened off its stern.

A shout carried across the field, and my eyes darted towards the sound. Two figures were tussling on the grass verge next to the road a couple of hundred metres away, not far from the house. My first thought was that Leo and Oliver were having a fight. Limbs flew, clothing flapped, and the shouting grew louder. As I increased my pace and drew closer, I realised it was Manfred, and he was having a physical confrontation with... *Oh, my God, it's Oliver!*

I saw Oliver's leg kick out at Manfred. A raised fist arced towards his body. I heard a childlike squeal and Oliver stumbled away, bent double, before he tripped on a clump of grass, fell against a fence post, and tumbled to the verge.

'Oli! Oli!' I yelled, as I broke into a run towards them.

A sharp pain stabbed my ankle and the pack containing my shopping bounced against my back as I lumbered up the road. The chill air caught in my throat. I knew I should conserve my breath for running, but I was compelled to shout, depleting precious energy.

'Stop! Manfred, stop!' I yelled breathlessly.

And then I saw the unmistakable flash of a blade, and panic compounded my fear. With the realisation that Manfred had a knife, tears sprang to my eyes with the effort of running through my pain and the violent sense of self-reproach that I had misread this whole stalking thing from the start. Manfred stumbled towards Oliver lying on the verge.

I tried to run faster. It was like one of those dreams when one wasn't able to get away from an unseen threat. I couldn't get there quickly enough. I couldn't fathom what was happening. It didn't make sense. *He must not hurt my son!*

As I came closer, my strangled shouting finally registered, and Manfred looked up, a fistful of Oliver's T-shirt unravelling from his fingers. He saw me and his eyebrows shot up in what I could only think was shock, having been caught doing something by the one person he didn't want as a witness. I thought it must be guilt I saw flooding his face. He stared at the small knife in his hand and held both arms away from his body in a moment of comic surrender. I checked my pace briefly before continuing towards him.

He suddenly dropped the weapon, and it skittered along the pavement. I recognised the red plastic handle of a Swiss army knife.

'He means to harm me, Alice. He stops us being together,' Manfred shouted as he backed away. 'Nobody must stand between us. We are meant to be together. He is ruining everything. You must see this.'

'What?' I gasped. 'Get away from him. Get away from my son! This has nothing to do with him!'

He cast me one curious glance, a crooked smile on his face. Then he turned swiftly, and loped away towards the forest.

I finally arrived at the scene, and looked down at Oliver, my breath ragged. I was torn between chasing Manfred and bending to tend to my son. Oliver slowly stood up, his hand on his lower back. I reached down to pick up the Swiss army knife, and looked towards the trees in the direction Manfred had headed.

'You fucking monster!'

My energy now completely spent, the phrase came out as a strangled wheeze. Manfred was now too far away to chase, and had disappeared. I reached towards Oliver, smoothing my hand on his back.

'Mum. Don't. It's mine.'

'My God, Oli, what happened? What did he do? What did that man do to you?'

Oliver shook with sobs. He covered his face in the crook of his elbow to hide his tears.

'Oli, are you hurt? I'm so sorry I was a bit late. I thought I might catch you on the way home from school. Oli, please tell me what happened.'

I rubbed his back, feeling some tension ebb, the loosening of muscles.

'Mum, didn't you hear me? I said the knife is mine.' He sobbed again.

'This is *your* knife? What were you doing with it at *school*?' I asked in confusion.

'We had a project in the garden today. We're building a living shelter out of *Weide* branches. I think they're called willow in English. You know, like that story with Toad and Ratty.'

I shook my head.

'Oli. Please! It's okay. That's not really the issue here. What happened? With *him*?'

I nodded towards the forest, with the flashing image of the blade in my head. Learning the knife was Oliver's hadn't calmed my nerves. He took a deep breath.

'I saw him as I was walking home, and... Mum, I know you think he's a bit weird. I just wanted to... I wanted to scare him. I shouted at him. You know, after you and Dad had that argument. The knife was in my pocket from school. I felt somehow strong, protected, and held it in my hand. I don't want him to keep annoying you. I want him to go away. It was a stupid plan... I think it went wrong.'

He turned towards me, reached up to clasp his arms around my neck, and buried his face in my chest. My happy, funny preteen regressed alarmingly to a state of toddlerhood in utter confusion. He spoke into my sweater.

'He wanted to take the knife off me, and I did that feinting thing they do in the movies. He grabbed my arm and twisted. It hurt, so I let go, and he took it, and... and...'

He sobbed again, and we stood up together. I felt dampness on my jeans, and looked down. He'd wet himself. My heart went out to him. I felt ashamed with him, for him.

'Where are you hurt?' I repeated, and he shook his head.

'I... don't know. I'm... not sure,' he said, between his sobs.

Whatever physical damage had been wrought would be eclipsed by mental anguish at this point, but I couldn't shake the vision of Manfred holding the knife aloft.

Jesus.

If he hadn't heard my shout at that point, he might have used the weapon on my son. I had a sickening vision of the blade sinking into Oliver's chest.

CHAPTER FORTY

'WE HAVE TO get these trousers off. Come on. We need to get to the house. Let's get you to the bathroom, get you cleaned up.'

Oliver sobbed in gulps, great spasms of air heaving back into his lungs in threes, an involuntary reaction reminding me of him as a four-year-old with a grazed knee. Various scenarios ran through my head. He was either aware that he had escaped some horrific danger, or reacting to the humiliation of having wet himself.

We reached the bathroom upstairs in the house, and Oliver fumbled with the zip of his jeans. I was relieved to see the top button still fastened. Of all the nightmare scenarios still flashing in my mind, Manfred's transgression hadn't included *that*. I swallowed. Oliver stamped his jeans down to his feet, followed shortly by his underpants, adhering with dampness to his legs. I waited for him to speak, running the shower in the bathtub until the water warmed. His legs were shaking.

'I know you said I could never take the knife to school, but Herr Iten told us we could, because we were working outside and cutting the branches. We were allowed to take the knife, Mum. It's the one you and Dad gave me for my birthday last year.'

'It's okay, Oli. I'm just so sorry I was late home.'

'Herr Iten let us go early. Said it wasn't worth going back to the classroom for ten minutes. I was trying to protect you, Mum. I know he's been kind of interested in you, especially after the questions he asked last time. And I felt like it was wrong. I didn't want to hurt him. I just took it out and...'

I blanched, realising I should have warned him, warned both my children, about the unpredictability of Manfred. Another error of judgement.

He stopped speaking. I waited patiently, not making visual contact, fearing he would clam up if he saw my eyes. I busied myself helping him off with his clothes. The string of his sweatshirt had been pulled through on one side of the hood, which was half-torn from the collar. I wondered how long the fight had been going on before I noticed. Manfred had obviously used great force to be able to tear the cloth.

I tapped the side of the bath and Oliver climbed obediently in, shuddering as the hot shower hit his head and flattened his hair against his cheeks and neck. I glanced briefly over his body, making a rapid damage assessment. Everything looked normal front on. He stopped shivering, closed his eyes in the steam of the shower. I held his hand, and water ran up my arm as I crouched beside the bath, not wanting to let my baby go.

'What did he say while all this was going on?' I asked when Oliver seemed steady enough.

'He said he was sent to look after you. I didn't understand, Mum, but he said that one day we would all be a family. He said I was getting in the way. I think he's crazy. He kind of scares me now.'

Water spattered forward from his face as he spoke, eyes closed. I squeezed his hand, horrified at the thought of what might have happened if I hadn't turned up at that moment. Tears sprang to my eyes as I thought of Oliver trying to defend me, knowing he would have had no chance once the knife was in Manfred's hands.

'I realised the knife thing looked really bad. Then I tripped over some grass and fell against that post. I landed here.'

Oliver pointed to his side, an occasional inward sob the residue of his earlier trauma. I looked at the red scratches and a purple mark on the back of his hip. I sucked in my breath, a whistle across my teeth. Those wounds on his hip and back weren't just from a fence post. My head felt like it was about to explode. Manfred's hands had fallen on Oliver's body. But in the furore, I wondered whose story would be believed in an interrogation. I was too far away to have seen what was going on. And the wielded weapon was actually Oliver's knife.

'It's okay, Oli, it's going to be okay.'

I forced myself to sound calm for him, relieved he still had enough youthful innocence to talk about this, despite his humiliation. If it had been Leo, I might never have had such a detailed account of their conversation. I could not forget that look in Manfred's eyes. I asked myself again whether he would have used the knife. I realised I had been stupid to let this thing go on so long. A pyroclastic swelling of anger was now building in me. I had never felt such rage.

'Mum, why won't he go away? Is that what a stalker is? You know, when Dad and you were talking about it in the kitchen that day? I thought it was just someone who watches people.'

Oliver flung these questions at me. I reached for the towel on the rail as he turned off the shower.

'I didn't know this man would try to talk to you again, Oli. He has been following me, and yes, that's called "stalking", but usually a person who does this doesn't come so close. I'm so sorry I didn't do enough to prevent this happening. I'm so sorry.'

And as though the tables were turned, and I was the one who required attention, Oliver slipped his arms around my neck again, and I carefully wrapped the towel around his back. As I clung to him, the front of his body soaked my clothes from the shower. I had to control my anger to be able to feed Oliver my love.

It was nearing lunchtime. Leo still hadn't come back from school. I left Oliver sitting in front of a cartoon on television and marched outside the house, up towards the farm. I made my way towards the copse near the old plum tree. I couldn't see anybody. I walked towards the forest where I had last seen Manfred, and stopped before entering the trees.

'Where are you, you freak? Come here right now, come out and face me, you, you pervert. You *will* pay for this,' I yelled, rage making my voice hoarse and shaky. Spittle flew from between my teeth.

Manfred had made himself scarce, must have surely known that, this time, he had gone too far. I walked back down the road, stood in sight of the footpath leading up from the village and waited for Leo. Minutes passed, my heart rate calmed, and I tried to relax the muscles in my face, unclench my jaws. Manfred was nowhere to be seen.

Right on time, I watched Leo wandering up the road.

'Hey. What're you doing here? What's for lunch? I'm starved.'

The familiar questions. Back to normality.

'I was taking a walk, and thought I'd wait for you. All okay at school?'

I tried to make my voice sound normal. Leo continued towards the house.

'Uh, yeah, no problems.'

I walked next to him, and put my arm through his. He smiled at me uncertainly as my eyes searched the fields.

'What's your problem? You're acting a little strange.'

'Oh, it's nothing. I was late back this morning. There'll just be bread and cheese for lunch, nothing special planned.'

'I'm okay with that. Chill, Mum.'

He looked sideways at me, but didn't shrug away from my arm, and I squeezed him affectionately. We entered the house together. Leo dropped his schoolbag in the hallway and wandered towards the kitchen, but backtracked when he heard the TV in the living room.

'Hey, toe-rag, what're you doing home so early? You sick?' Leo asked Oliver.

I held my breath, wondering about Oliver's state of mind, wondering what he would say to his brother.

'Iten let us out early. We could come home if we wanted,' replied Oliver.

Nothing about what happened. He seemed okay. I smiled at him over Leo's shoulder. He shrugged and smiled back. It would stay between us, but that didn't mean I wasn't going to do anything about it.

CHAPTER FORTY-ONE

OLIVER AND LEO put their coats on after lunch to head back to school, and I grabbed my jacket. As I bent to tie my shoes, Oliver put his arms around me.

'Are you sure you're okay to go back to school?' I asked quietly.

He nodded hesitantly.

'I have to run a few errands in the village,' I lied. 'And I'll meet you after your last class. I'll give you a ride home as well, okay?'

'Come on, snotty,' Leo said humorously. 'Stop the soppy stuff, let's get to school.'

As we left the house together, Leo gave me a curious glance. I reversed the car out of the garage and the boys clambered in. Manfred was nowhere to be seen, but I didn't want to let the boys out of my sight.

I almost reached back and put my hand on Oliver's knee, but knew the unspoken etiquette between the two brothers would only elicit another comment from Leo. The boys chatted about a football tournament some of the classes were organising over lunchtimes in the playground the following week. I breathed a ragged sigh for Oliver. He seemed to have recovered from the encounter. He was at least talking normally to Leo, his arms rose briefly as he described something to his older brother. I dropped them at the entrance to the school playground, and when they had disappeared into the building, I drove home.

I sat down at the kitchen table and put my head in my hands, grinding the palms into my eye sockets.

What the hell had I been thinking all those months ago, trying to help this man? I couldn't cure him. That was so ridiculous. Did I think I could be the therapist, the practitioner? Was my life so empty that I had nothing better to do? Well, it hadn't worked. It wasn't as though I'd even been to medical school. I could hardly consider myself a doctor. All my decisions until now had been born out of stupidity. I felt like a fool, even down to becoming complacent to his presence, not realising the danger I was truly putting my family in.

I stood up abruptly, chair scraping on the floor tiles. I searched behind some pots and pans in the cupboard, and pulled out a bottle of white spirit I usually used to light the wick under the fondue burner. I took a couple of old newspapers out of the recycling bin, a box of matches and left the house without pausing to put on a jacket.

I limped up the driveway and along the road to the farm track. Balling up the sheets of newspaper, I scattered them on the ground near the old plum tree and sprinkled them with the entire contents of the bottle of fuel. Dropping first one match, then a second when the first one didn't light, the paper whooshed into flame, dead grass soon crackling.

I hoped this pyromaniac act would be cathartic, that it would help not only destroy the physical nest from where we were all being observed, but also destroy Manfred's notion that he had any control over our lives. But as I watched the flames licking around the bark of the tree, it occurred to me that this futile gesture wasn't going to put an end to the threat that now included my family. Simon and the boys. It wasn't going to put an end to the crux of the problem.

BACK IN THE house, I opened my handbag and rummaged through its chaotic mess. Lip balm, tissues, paper clips, credit card slips, and pens that no longer worked. At the bottom I found what I was looking for. Manfred's bipolar medication. I had never had the opportunity to try and persuade him to take it.

I stared at the box, studied the brand name, Quilonorm, and reflected on what Gerry had once said.

It would have been better for everyone if you had not been running in the Lorze Gorge that day.

From the kitchen window I could see smoke drifting out from behind the plum tree, and from time to time a lick of flames. The tree didn't go up like a torch, as I would have expected from something half-dead, but smouldered disappointingly for an hour or so, before a farm vehicle stopped on the track. Someone, the farmer or his wife or a farmhand, telephoned the fire brigade and they came to put out the fire. The stump of the tree still stood two metres high, blackened branches pointing accusatory fingers at the farm, the barn, our house, maybe Manfred.

I wanted desperately to talk to Simon, but he was in London on a two-day trip to finally secure and sign the contract he had been working towards for months. It was a pivotal moment for both the company and his career. I shouldn't disturb him. Anyway, he would have told me to call the police, and I knew I should do this, but the failure of my previous attempts to have Manfred stopped remained at the forefront of my mind. Would Police Officer Schmid still not believe 'the fantasies of an eleven-year-old boy'? Oliver was twelve now, had celebrated his birthday a month ago. Would that make him more likely to be believed? I didn't think so, especially as Schmid now thought he was a liar *and* a thief. And Oliver wouldn't want the whole sordid thing dragged up among strangers.

I had taken an incredible risk by burdening myself with Manfred. At the beginning I'd been too naive to see he wouldn't accept my help. And now he had displayed this dangerous behaviour, I couldn't risk his breaking in and casually picking up our breadknife in the kitchen. Or worse, fiddling with the car and putting all of us in danger. I finally admitted that his own son's original assessment of him must have been correct. He was beyond help. In addition to which it seemed he would stop at nothing to have me. Even at the expense of my family.

Adding the latest encounter with Oliver to the list of Manfred's offences had only enhanced his insanity. I must stop him before he ruined all our lives. I needed to be exonerated from my original error. He must go, and go for good. There was no getting rid of him for an hour, or a day, only to be a continual threat in our lives. This thing had to be permanent. I had the tools. Now it remained to be seen if I also had the power of persuasion.

CHAPTER FORTY-TWO

ONCE THE FIRE department had packed up and left the farm, I drove back down to the village. I sat on the wall outside the school and waited for Oliver and Leo to finish their last classes. We went back home together. Oliver seemed a little nervous, but bravely stoic. Leo made no comment about my presence, assuming I had run my errand in the village.

As we took off our jackets and hung them on the coat stand, Leo ran up the stairs to his room, and I quietly reassured Oliver this would never, ever happen again; that I was going to make sure that, after tomorrow, we would never see Manfred Guggenbuhl again.

I could not have known what was going through Oliver's mind. Perhaps he imagined I had the power to make the police or a doctor come and take that man away. I was his mum. He would assume I could do anything. He accepted my promise without asking how, and seemed more comfortable.

That evening I sat beside him for a while before he went to sleep. There were only so many times I could ask him if he was all right, whether he wanted to talk about what happened. He had closed in on himself, maybe realising that his openness with me earlier in the day had caused as much anguish for me as it had for him. As I sat next to him on the floor beside his bed, speaking of sledding and skiing, and plans for Christmas, he patted me gently on the head, and spoke as though our roles were reversed.

'It's okay, Mum, I'm pretty tired. You can go now. It's okay.'

I checked on him again before I went to bed. He made a couple of whimpering sounds in his sleep as I watched, and I wanted to climb under his duvet with him, hold him like I did when he was a small child. My chest tightened, remembering his wonder-filled eyes on the new-born calf in the field next to the house.

I went to my bedroom, sat on the edge of the bed and dialled Simon's mobile number. No answer. He must still be out to dinner, celebrating the deal perhaps. The ringing clicked over to his voicemail, and my mouth went dry. I ended the call before his message had finished. Despite being ready to tell him everything, there was always the thought that Simon, now more than ever, would still blame me for all this.

THE NEXT DAY was Tuesday. I woke up with gritty eyes. I felt like I hadn't slept more than a couple of hours. As I prepared breakfast for the boys, Simon called.

'Hey, Al, I saw you called last night. Sorry I didn't answer. We were in a loud restaurant, and by the time I saw your number, I thought it might be too late to call back.'

He knew if I had needed him urgently I would have left a message. I could hear him moving about his hotel room, clicking his briefcase, packing his things.

He called me 'Al.'

'It's okay. Did you sign the deal? Are you coming back today?'

'Yes, we signed the deal, at last, thank God. I just have a few things to clear up this morning and then I'm flying back at lunchtime.'

'Congratulations, Simon, I know how much effort's gone into this. You should be so proud of yourself.' I paused. 'I just wondered if you'd mind if I went for a hike this evening. I know you might want to celebrate, but the weather forecast is only good until tomorrow. My ankle feels better when I get a little exercise, and I'd planned to take a couple of photos before the season changes. The autumn colours are still so beautiful.'

'No problem. After all the stress, I'm absolutely knackered. We can wait for the weekend to celebrate.' He hesitated. 'Are you okay, Al? You sound out of sorts.'

'It's fine. I'll be fine. Well done on the deal, honey. Everything will be fine.'

I heard him stop what he was doing, to concentrate on our conversation, but knew he wasn't sure what to ask. If he could have seen my face... I took a silent breath, hating the remote neutrality of the phone. Before I could speak, he continued.

'Where are you going to hike?'

'Oh, above the farm, on this side of the lake. My usual. To see the sunset...'

I feared he might ask if he could join me. I'd had the feeling, over the past few weeks, that he wanted to talk to me properly, wanted to examine what was going on between us, but knew he could only initiate a conversation without the boys around. I wanted desperately to reconnect with Simon, but there was one thing I had to do before I could feel free. It was with relief, then, that he said he would pick up takeaway pizzas on the way home for himself and the boys. He re-emphasised that he was exhausted and needed a good night's sleep.

'Bye then, see you later on tonight,' I said.

'We can celebrate my success later. Hopefully I won't be going away for a while, sweetheart.'

It was the first time he had used an endearment in weeks.

It felt as blithe as a kiss.

CHAPTER FORTY-THREE

AS I WALKED the path next to the road leading around the lake, my senses buzzed. I kept my eyes mostly earthward, one moment afraid to see Manfred, the next afraid I wouldn't. But knowing without doubt that he would follow me.

Traffic was frequent at this time of day, people heading home from work. The sun was low in the sky. It skimmed the distant ridge of the *Zugerberg* to my rear. A cyclist passed me on the pavement, making me jump as I looked up. He called a jovial apology and pedalled on without looking back, his rear strobe light blinking along the path. The straps of my backpack dug into my shoulders, burning.

Two fishermen sat on a jetty by the lake, one smoking a *Krumme*, a twisted cheroot. Both men silently contemplated their motionless fishing lines. I smiled nervously as I passed and the non-smoker mumbled a gruff *'Grüezi.'* I followed the lane around the south of the lake, past the hamlet of Morgarten, and turned off the main road. Ten minutes' brisk walk heading west on the one-lane road, and I hadn't seen a soul. A breeze rattled the reeds at the lakeside and a moorhen chirped sharply, sending my heart fluttering to my throat.

The late autumn sun had already disappeared behind the hill as I climbed the steep, leaf-strewn trail up through the forest. I walked slowly, allowing for the fact that Manfred might not be wearing appropriate footwear. I was determined that tonight he would be able to follow me.

As I climbed higher into the forest, at each step I had to dig deep to keep hold of my courage. My brief thespian career was hanging in the balance. If I held the image of Oliver in my mind – not him sobbing in my arms, but his curious, light-hearted view of the world – I would pass my audition with flying colours.

But when I heard the faint swish of leaves and the rumble of a rolling stone underfoot somewhere behind me, I thought my head would burst.

I reached the high point of the path where a gap in the trees afforded a spectacular view across the Aegeri Lake. I stepped gingerly towards the edge, grabbing the rusted railing of the barrier erected to prevent the over-adventurous from losing their foothold and falling several hundred feet to a sure demise. The steep drop to the lake hundreds of metres below invoked the familiar sensation of wanting to jump. I released the rail to wipe the sheen of perspiration from my temple and breathed in the smell of the rusting iron on my fingers.

It reminded me of chain-links on park swings. The dangers of swinging as high as I could in the playgrounds of my youth rang a bizarre symmetry with flying high off cliffs and bridges in my mind. I continued up the trail, driven on by hearing Manfred trip on an exposed tree root behind me.

I traversed a summer alpine pasture long since deserted by cows, and arrived at a clearing in the trees. A wooden picnic table and a bench sat next to a fire pit. From our house across the valley I had sometimes seen a thin wisp of smoke rising from this very place and vowed one day to stop and set a fire.

I sat on the bench and waited.

It felt like an hour.

He was there. I could feel him. As dusk fell, my senses became sharper, and the occasional crunch of dry leaves told me he was edging closer to the picnic area. My breath vaporised about me, and I rubbed my arms in the chill.

'Will you help me light a fire?' I finally called.

My voice sounded too loud, echoing through the trees. It felt stupid talking to a blank space.

'We'll need a fire if we're to stay warm,' I said, the 'we' belying my uncertainty.

It was hard to control my trembling, a combination of nervousness, fear and deep, boiling rage. I placed my backpack carefully under the table, leaning it against the solid wooden legs.

A small pile of chopped wood was stacked neatly in a makeshift shelter at the edge of the clearing.

'We'll need some kindling. Can you help me look?'

As I began collecting small sticks and pieces of bark, I heard a footfall near me, and Manfred's curious voice.

'*Kinder... ling?*' he asked. My heart raced. It seemed apt that I'd uttered a word he didn't understand.

'Small sticks, dried twigs. Look. Kindling.'

I picked up a handful of dried wood from the undergrowth around the clearing, showing him I didn't mean I needed *Kinder* – children – to light the fire. It was as though he had walked beside me since the beginning of the hike. The fleeting look from the sticks in my hands to his manic eyes was as smooth as a well-spliced movie.

He came out from the shadow of the tree he had been standing behind, and delight shone from his face as he set about making himself useful. He looked back to me often, perhaps to make sure I wouldn't simply disappear in a moment of trickery. I could feel the intensity of his gaze burning into my back as I bent to collect more wood at the edge of the clearing.

Returning to the fire pit and scrunching a page of yesterday's newspaper I pulled from my pack, I placed it in the centre of the ring of rocks. The methodical Girl Guide task kept me busy, focused. Sprinkling a few twigs haphazardly on top, I lit the paper near the base with a lighter. The newspaper curled and fringed red, and ashy grey feathers floated upwards. As the twigs caught the flame with a popping and crackling, I breathed a sigh of relief.

As I loaded larger sticks onto the tiny pile of embers, the noisy combustion accompanied an ambient orange light, enclosing us in the small clearing, matching the colour of the autumn sky across the lake, but emphasising the falling dusk in the forest.

'You do this well. I like the fire. It will warm us both.'

Manfred's voice made me jump. I couldn't help thinking we had gone through some time warp. This man was now as close to me in proximity as a colleague or friend, and my hate for him eclipsed any feeling of sympathy I might have had in the past. It felt surreal.

Under the clear sky, a chill, dewy dampness was already forming in the thick autumn air. The heady smell of decaying leaves mingled with the sooty smell of the newly lit fire. I placed two split logs from the woodpile on top of a healthy bed of orange embers and finally rocked back on my heels. I sat on the bench next to Manfred, my heart pounding. He clasped his hands between his thighs like a small child.

Once the fire was roaring, I opened my backpack and retrieved a bottle of red wine, a rich Italian *Ripasso*. I pulled a corkscrew from a side pocket.

Manfred clapped his hands, making me jump.

'A *Fest*, a celebration,' he said with a childlike voice. I was startled by this new characteristic. As I turned to him, he pressed his hands together, touching his lips as though in prayer, and a worried frown appeared on his brow. The glint in his eye spoke of an excited child considering a forbidden act.

All I could think about was the wine.

CHAPTER FORTY-FOUR

AS I CENTRED the corkscrew over the middle of the cork, Manfred clapped again.

'I usually drink beer,' he said, and my heart dropped. 'I haven't drunk wine since I was at *Kaufmännische Schule*. This will be fun. Like my study years.'

I breathed out with relief, and hoped Manfred wouldn't insist on opening the bottle. My heartbeat quickened as the cork twisted within the neck of the bottle, the spiral screw only a centimetre in. I pulled gently. The weak pop sounded authentically like opening a good vintage at a dinner party.

It had been a while since we'd spoken. The sound and vision of the fire was soothingly mesmerising. He hadn't asked why I suddenly felt the need to celebrate our friendship, hadn't questioned this paradoxical decision to welcome him with open arms. I assumed, in his current manic phase, which might have been going on for months now, his had brain somehow filtered out the negative.

I cleared my throat, making me sound embarrassed. It was hard to know what to say to him.

Shaking two picnic beakers from their supermarket plastic wrapper, I indicated Manfred should take one. I poured wine into both our beakers.

'A toast!' I announced with forced jollity. I could hardly believe this was happening. A sickening contrast to what I was feeling in my heart.

'To us! Our friendship. Our future!'

Manfred's eyes shone.

'Yes, our future!'

He held the beaker of wine, and suddenly grabbed my other arm as I put the bottle down on the table, almost tipping it over.

My heart pounded. Before I knew what was happening, he planted an awkward and slightly misplaced kiss on my mouth, his soft lips imperceptibly open. I was so surprised I almost dropped my beaker, but was thankful I hadn't had time to react. I convinced myself that the taste of his lips was the taste of insanity. I raised my drink to my mouth, and made as though to swallow the first gulp of wine. My gaze held Manfred's, willing him silently to do the same.

As he took a tentative sip, an involuntary grimace passed over his face. He sipped again.

'I am not an expert, but this is not very good wine, Alice.'

I chewed my lip. He grinned, as though forgiving me for my poor taste.

'But it's okay, we must drink our celebration. Drink! *Zum Wohl!*'

Manfred laughed and took a larger sip as I smiled and made as though to take a gulp of wine, aware the liquid against my lips was as acrid as the smoke from the fire.

'It's getting chilly. Let's sit near the warmth,' I said as I took the bottle from the table.

Manfred spread his coat on the ground in front of a length of log, allowing both of us to sit with our backs leaning against the smooth bark. How far would I have to go to keep up this pantomime? As we sat, I discreetly poured the wine from my beaker onto the ground in the darkness.

I settled on the ubiquitous worldwide conversational topic of The Weather.

'It's been a beautiful autumn,' I volunteered.

'What did you think of my fine boy, Gerry?' Manfred asked without rancour.

Dispensing immediately with the banalities of weather, he seemed not to have heard my comment. His query must have been sitting so loudly in the forefront of his mind. I raised my eyebrows with a sharp intake of breath. *How did he know I had visited his son?*

'Mmm.' I tried to portray indifferent approval. I didn't want to talk about Gerry. He was my one weakness in this plan.

Manfred continued to sip his bitter vintage. I poured some more. He seemed to need it for courage, gulping the wine to loosen his tongue. *Yes!*

'I think you will be a better mother than Trudi. Certainly a better wife,' he said.

I wondered if he had convinced himself his wife was dead. Perhaps he thought he could replace her more easily that way, slot me into the role she'd once occupied in his life.

'Maybe when my Gerry knows you better he will also return to me… here.'

Manfred lightly thumped his chest near his heart twice with his closed fist.

'He has not understood me these last years. Did you like my fine son?'

'I… yes, Manfred, he is a nice boy.'

'Gerry spoke about us, yes? I am hoping he likes you too, Alice. He will know we are right for each other. And I will welcome your boys. I think your youngest son sees me as a good father figure. It was brave of him to show me his penknife. And now he knows how important you are to me.'

I bit my lip, controlled my breathing at the mention of Oliver, and realised Manfred could not possibly have heard me yelling in anguish as he ran away. Or he was choosing what to ignore and what to treasure.

I wondered how much Manfred knew of my conversation with Gerry, but couldn't ask, for fear of hearing something I didn't want to. I knew I must remain neutral, and never reveal the bitterness with which Gerry spoke of his father. I took a gamble, continued my act.

'Yes, Manfred, we talked about you. I think he would like to reconcile with you; he does love you. He just doesn't know how to show it. I think he liked me. I told him I had feelings for you, and he seemed to accept that.'

The thespian's finest hour.

'You did? Oh, Alice, that makes me so happy.'

I gritted my teeth behind a false smile. He had truly convinced himself his wife did not exist. I studied the fire as Manfred continued and felt bile rise in my throat.

'That is why I know our togetherness is for good reasons. We will all be together in the end,' he said as he took another sip of his wine, and I refilled both our beakers, blood roaring in my ears.

Yes, we will all be together in the end...

CHAPTER FORTY-FIVE

THERE WAS SOMETHING to be said about the old horse-to-water fable. In my case, I could take Manfred back to the bridge, but I could not make him jump. Suddenly so calculated, it had come to me after his abuse of Oliver, through my deep-red fury. To come full circle back to the beginning. A suicide all the same. Just not his choice.

This was my plan, but could I really carry it off? I had to be strong. Despite what we were constantly being spoon-fed through popular culture, the idea of taking another human life was abhorrent. The vast majority of us were never genetically predisposed to murder. How could I ever imagine I would be capable of committing such a crime?

But roaring visions kept flashing before me. My failed marathon, my teetering marriage and what had happened to Oliver, all making me even more determined to be rid of Manfred from my life. From our lives. The police would be of no help, I was sure of that now. There was no hope of healing him. The world would be better off without him. I had to believe I could do this thing.

ONCE I'D TAKEN the boys back to school after lunch that Tuesday afternoon, I stood in the kitchen, gripping the sink with nervous uncertainty. Grateful thoughts of my plan failing battled continuously in my mind with those of it actually working. I took a deep breath, rubbed my hands together and set to work.

Carefully removing the foil cap, I eased the cork out of a bottle of *Ripasso* with a newly purchased corkscrew. *A strong wine with the sweet undertones of the Amarone grape.* Out of habit, I sniffed the top of the open bottle to make sure it wasn't corked and stood it on the kitchen counter. I combed my hair back from my face with my fingers. Glancing out of the kitchen window with unease, I moved the bottle to the kitchen table, away from the afternoon light and prying eyes searching through the panes.

In a mortar and pestle usually reserved for the crushing of dried chillies or coriander seeds, I popped the remaining pills from Manfred's packet of Quilonorm medication.

An afternoon pharmaceutical lesson with Google had taught me that by mixing Manfred's lithium-based pills with alcohol I would be producing a potentially lethal cocktail. Throwing in a handful of anti-inflammatory tablets I still had from my injury – medication that could be obtained anywhere over the counter – would further strengthen the potion.

As I tipped a slurp of wine into the sink to make space, the aroma of red wine flooded the kitchen. I carefully funnelled half the powder into the bottle. It slid silently into the wine, the liquid rising steadily up the glass neck as I added more. Specks of white dust clung to the top of the bottle. I sniffed the opening, surprised I could still smell wine. Sacrilege to tamper with a stunningly good vintage. I wished I could share the irony with Simon, and chuckled nervously as a wave of hot anxiety washed over me. The drops I licked from my finger after I'd dipped it in the bottle left a bitterness on my tongue. I had transformed my bottle of vintage *Ripasso* into a dodgy, cheap plonk.

I leaned against the sink as a wave of remorse came over me. I kept repeating to myself that this was for the best. It was what he'd wanted that day back in April. It had been his decision.

Reaching for the cork, I lay it lengthways and sawed a thin line along its length with the breadknife. I then worked the cork back into the bottle, using the heel of my palm to push it flush to the lip. I carefully folded the foil wrapper over and around the top.

I glanced at the clock as I clicked my backpack closed. Almost 4.00 p.m. Simon would be getting ready to leave the office early tonight after his trip back from London. I didn't want to be around when my boys all came home.

I had no idea if this would work. For a start, I didn't know whether Manfred would drink any wine, doctored or not. What if he was a wine connoisseur? Imagine his retort:

'What are you trying to do, poison me?'

If Manfred had stayed around to witness my outburst outside the house the day before, he would sense a burning anger in me. If he had an iota of common sense, he couldn't possibly believe I would ever willingly have a relationship with him. But madness produces its own brand of irrationality.

I had to rely on him assuming that Oliver would be too proud, scared or embarrassed to say anything to me about his actions before I arrived on the scene the day before.

I willed all these advantages onto my side. This time I needed Manfred to follow me. I had to be strong. I had to overcome an entrenched loathsome repulsion regarding my own actions. I had to lure this monster, without creating suspicion, make him believe his intentions would bear fruit, without suspicion. This thing I was doing was more than my own personal justice. I must not falter from my path. I remained clear of head, silently begged for focus, swore it was right, believed it wholeheartedly.

But I was fully aware that the truth might contaminate me, rather than make me righteous.

Never get between a mother and her young, or there'll be big trouble.

CHAPTER FORTY-SIX

A TEEPEE OF glowing twigs and branches shifted and settled, sending a fan of dancing sparks up into the forest canopy. The fire collapsed into its own pile of suffocating ash. I wondered if anyone had seen the light of the flames from the village across the lake.

Manfred lay awkwardly against the log, leaning heavily into my body, his coat bunching up between us against my thigh. His hair was matted up around the sweatshirt he wore. His head dipped at an angle towards me. I pursed my lips and puffed gently through them, longing to blow not just a stray hair but this whole day a million miles away, to be carried on the sparks up into the heavens.

I dared not move any other part of my body. I couldn't see Manfred's face to know whether he was still watching the dying embers. The empty wine bottle lay on its side near the cinders. I pushed it away from the edge of the fire with my foot, scuffing my boots with white ash. Despite trying to remain still, the movement caused my upper body to shift slightly and Manfred's head slipped down to the crook of my right elbow. With a quickening heart I realised he was asleep. A stone wedged in my throat.

'Manfred?' I called quietly.

No movement, no sleep twitch or sudden arousal from slumber. I called again more loudly and moved my elbow twice up and down. His head bounced against my arm. He still didn't wake, but released a short snort of breath. I shuffled away from him and turned to lower his head onto his coat, gathering the material to create a makeshift cushion on the ground.

I put my hands to my mouth in a mixture of wonder and horror. His face was relaxed, almost angelic. His scruffy hair lay across his folded jacket and his square jaw was slack, giving the impression of fuller lips. His menace had flown, leaving the image of innocence. I reflected that the distance between what we want and what we fear is sometimes only the width of a pine needle. But I could never forget what he had done.

This was surely the beginning of the end. It all seemed so simple, so horribly facile to implement. And while the wait with Manfred beside the fire had seemed like an eternity, time now rushed in at me. I swallowed nervously. I thought I might be sick, took a series of deep breaths to calm myself, silently repeating a mantra: *This is the best thing for everybody.*

I had no idea whether this cocktail of pills would actually kill Manfred, but I knew from my experience with outdoor alpine activities that the cold was a sneaking, silent killer. Once the body's temperature lowered to a level where the anatomy no longer functioned, each part of it slipped into eternal slumber, eventually turning the brain off like a light going out. Dying in the cold was apparently the least painful or traumatic of all the ways to go. The pills should ensure that Manfred wouldn't wake up.

Standing away from him, I could barely see in the last glow of embers. His arm had flopped to his side. Two fingers lay inside the plastic picnic wine beaker, as though he would pick it up any moment and use it as a finger puppet to tell a joke. His hand looked uncomfortably bent, the fingers pressing cruelly on the rim of the plastic glass, but it didn't disturb him from his slumber.

He was beyond merely sleeping.

And finally, finally, I let a sense of victory lift my spirits. I had done this for the people I loved. There was nothing more important.

I would protect my family at all costs.

As the breeze dropped and the embers no longer reflected on the forest canopy, my eyes adjusted in the cold indigo shadows.

From the top pocket of my backpack, I pulled out a headlamp and put it around my forehead. I turned it on and immediately the jagged silhouettes of bare tree branches were chased away by the cold light of the bulb.

I avoided looking at Manfred's face and busied myself with new tasks – putting on a pair of gloves, taking out an empty bottle I had brought from our recycling box with the fingerprints carefully wiped clean. I pulled out the cork I had wedged only halfway in. I moved round to Manfred's other side and knelt beside him. Picking his arm up by his sleeve, I laid his hand over the top of the bottle, patting his fingers around the green glass, flopping like a ragdoll.

I still couldn't look at his face.

I laid the bottle near his feet. Wiping the corkscrew, I carefully fed the cork back onto the spiral, pressed his fingers onto the handle and placed it within his reach. Picking up the other empty *Ripasso* wine bottle, still vaguely warm from the fire, I put it carefully into my backpack.

I took out the empty blister sheets from the Quilonorm and Co-Dafalgan and slipped them into the pocket of Manfred's jacket. I couldn't reach Manfred's beaker without disturbing his body. I didn't think I had touched it, but I didn't want to touch his other arm to move it. I didn't want to touch him ever again. It was a risk, but I left it beside him. I tucked my own wine beaker into my backpack.

Finally, I took a last look at Manfred's sleeping face. My headlight flashed across his features. I thought I saw his eyes flicker, and drew in my breath. The beam shone into his face, its brightness casting a pale, waxy sheen on his skin. No movement. My eyes burned hot with tears, and I almost reached to shake him awake.

My old companion, guilt, had accompanied me every step of this journey and my constant uncertainty had made me want to backtrack at every corner. But on my shoulder sat the devil of determination to keep my family together, a simmering anger at this person lying on the ground who had stolen something precious from our lives and caused such anguish and pain. I blinked away the smarting tears as a last thin wisp of blue smoke seeped up from the fire pit and my throat caught on the acrid smell of cooling ash.

Hoisting the backpack onto my shoulders, I hiked carefully down the mountain. The descent in the dark was a little more treacherous, but less breathlessly demanding. Once I had left the clearing, I wanted to be away from Manfred as quickly as possible, but exercised caution. My ankle ached from keeping my balance on the steep, rolling pebbles and gravel in the dark, the limited light from my headlamp disorientating me. I wanted to run, but knew I risked an accident if I wasn't careful. I was aware of a dull ache in my injured ankle. The echo of my own footsteps on the path in the forest made me turn back constantly, thinking Manfred had awoken and was hurrying down the mountain after me.

When I reached the bottom of the steep hill, I turned off my headlamp as I came out from the cover of the trees. I stopped and waited for my breathing to steady, eyes and ears concentrated towards the forest, listening for the sound of following footsteps. The distant hoot of an owl carried to me on a hiss of wind through the pines.

The path took me round the back of a campground, closed now at the end of the season, before I reached the hardtop surface of the narrow asphalt road we had walked in on. It was a moonless night and my eyes ached with the strain of picking out the stony path. I kept my headlamp extinguished and allowed starlight and the ambient light from the streets and houses across the lake to guide my way back to the main road. Once onto the smooth black tarmac, my hiking boots felt cumbersome, cloddy. The walk home was never-ending.

I LAY DOWN in bed as carefully as possible so as not to wake Simon. It was late, but I didn't turn on the light to check the time. My eyes, gritty with fatigue, felt like they would superglue together the moment I closed them. A faint sooty smell drifted about my head. I thought the noise of folding back the down-filled duvet might disturb Simon from his slumber, but he lay still on his side, facing away from me as usual.

I lay on my back, my tired neck grateful for the coolness of the pillow beneath. It was a kernel of relief for my aching body to sink into nothingness. I calmed my breathing until all I could hear was the faint whir of a running tap in another of the apartments somewhere in the building.

Then a swish of the duvet, and Simon's hand found my palm lying downwards on the mattress. A pathway between two bodies, a bridge across the abyss. He squeezed my hand then patted it gently twice. In his semiconscious state, he wordlessly rolled back onto his side, returning to the comfort of sleep. The simple gesture caused my throat to close and my lips to press together involuntarily in the dark. I brought my hand to my face and clasped my mouth shut to prevent the threatened sob from escaping.

This signal of truce, of regained faith, of something saved. The simple gesture delivered a sliver of hope, a seed. I should grasp this, after weeks of feeling wretched and after a night of feeling the heaviness of evil taking over. This primeval thing I had calculatingly carried out to protect my family might eventually come back and haunt me. There were enough people who knew it could lead to this, even if they believed I wouldn't be capable of such a thing.

The Samaritan Alice.

CHAPTER FORTY-SEVEN

GLANCING IN THE mirror, I hurried anxiously to the door. The chiming of the bell still echoed in the hall. Several restless nights had taken their toll. Dark shadows pooled beneath my eyes. My left lower lid culminated in a puffy package, giving the impression I had been crying. I opened the door with a sharp intake of breath as I looked up into the face of Reto Schmid.

'Frau Reed, *guten Tag,*' he said. I thought he might click his heels. His use of High German was brusque. Instead he offered his hand in greeting. I tried to make my grip firm, belying my uncertainty. Chilly air blew up the stairwell from the main entrance, temporarily held open against a gust of wind. Snow was on its way. I could almost smell it. Nervousness I didn't want to convey sluiced through my body.

'*Grüezi*, Herr Schmid,' I said carefully, holding the edge of the door in my left hand, a barrier between the policeman and my home. He rubbed his hands together, hunching a little. He was alone.

'May I please come in?'

His voice was neutral, not unfriendly, not overly officious.

I led him to the kitchen, where an array of half-prepared lunch articles were scattered across the worktop, and pointed to a chair for him to sit.

'I hope you don't mind, I'm running a little late,' I said. 'My boys will be home soon. I can work while we talk.'

I needed the excuse to turn from him, to avoid eye contact. He mustn't read what was lurking in them. It was good to have my hands occupied. I thought I knew why he was here. But I mustn't show him I knew that.

'I'm sorry, I see you are busy,' he said.

Apologetic, that's a good sign. I picked up a carrot, reached for the peeler.

'I thought you would like to be informed about the death of Manfred Guggenbuhl,' he said.

My hand fled involuntarily to my mouth. Eyes now wide. Part of me wanted to think that Manfred was peacefully sleeping forever in the forest, caught in the comfortable illusion that he and I would be bound together forever. I felt sick, needed to sit down, but couldn't let this policeman see the guilt that flooded through me. I hoped he would read my reaction like anyone learning about the death of someone they knew. I tried to think of something appropriate to say.

'How? W… when?'

I was unsure of the emotion I should be displaying. My role as actress forgotten, I was horrified my terrible deed had worked, and had now been confirmed.

Alice the murderess.

My heart thumped, my face burned, and a new wave of guilt almost made me present my wrists to the man who now sat at my kitchen table. But the chattering of the boys coming home for lunch in the distance brought me abruptly back to my sense of duty. I could see them ambling down the driveway through the open kitchen window.

I did this terrible thing for them.

This silent justification, repeated as a mantra since returning home three nights ago. It was true; I would do *anything* to protect them. My eyes moistened and a twisted smile played on my lips as I watched the boys. Schmid cleared his throat.

'Yes, well, I should emphasise that this is a human tragedy, but I did not realise exactly how you would feel,' he said as I quickly packed away my smile.

The boys' voices were getting closer. They were arguing about something. I could hear Oliver clarifying a point in Swiss German while Leo answered him in English.

'It seems Herr Guggenbuhl has taken his own life,' he said.

My mouth opened to ask another question, but the policeman continued before I could speak.

'I cannot give you any details at this time. You should know that you may be questioned over the next week…'

My eyes widened and Schmid's hand came up in a calming gesture.

'…because you filed a, how do you say, *stalking* complaint about the victim some time ago.'

The boys were now in the porch downstairs. I pressed my lips together and looked pleadingly at the policeman, shaking my head to indicate I didn't want my sons to hear this conversation. He narrowed his eyes, but without explanation understood the silent entreaty not to reveal such horrors to the children. Standing up, he left the kitchen and walked down the hallway, pulling a card from his pocket like a door-to-door salesman.

'Are you all right, Frau Reed?' Schmid asked, gazing back at me curiously as he held out the card.

I could feel a flush at my throat, must have looked flustered.

'If you need to talk to me or any of my colleagues, this is the best number to use.'

I nodded as I took the card from him and slid it into the back pocket of my jeans. The boys were at the bottom of the steps. I couldn't face the curious teenage questions I knew I would have to answer with layers of lies, especially in front of him. Schmid hesitated.

'He will not be bothering you anymore. I think you will be relieved to know this.'

'Yes, thank you, of course. Goodbye,' I said hurriedly, shaking his hand briefly, wanting him to leave as quickly as possible.

I felt heady with both lightness and weight. The lightness because I was free, but all the same knowing I was bound to the weight of deception that might take months, years, to fade.

I watched the boys coming up the stairs. Oliver's mouth stretched to a letterbox rectangle, showing gritted teeth, and Leo gaped with open curiosity at the officer who threw them a jovial '*Hoi, Zäme*' as he passed them on the way out. Oliver cast a look over his shoulder as Schmid walked out of the door, remembering this wasn't the first time the policeman had been to our home.

'Whoa, Mum, what was he doing here? Someone been murdered in the neighbourhood?' Leo asked.

I blanched, swayed on the spot, and forced out a laugh.

'He was just making some inquiries,' I said, noting Oliver relax. The nightmare was truly over. But I was dizzy with the effort of thinking up another story. I walked to the counter in the kitchen, facing away from them, and drew my fingers across the perspiration on my cheek.

'I thought maybe toe-rag here got caught shoplifting again.' Leo turned to his brother as he sat at the table. '*Du bist so behindert.*'

'Leo!' My voice rang a little too loudly in the confines of our low-ceilinged kitchen. 'How many times have I told you not to say that? Do not call your brother, or anyone for that matter, retarded.'

I brandished a spoon, flicking pearls of salad dressing onto the floor tiles. My retort was ignored, and the fraternal bickering escalated. But Leo's teasing shifted the focus of the conversation, and rather than shutting down their argument, I let them continue, deciding only to intervene if the exchange became physical.

It did the trick. They were distracted enough that the memory of the policeman in our home was already buried in the backs of their minds.

I thought you would like to be informed of the death of Manfred Guggenbuhl.

The officer's announcement still echoed in my thoughts. The typical sterility of his speech gave no clue as to what was running through his mind. His steady look could have been one of concern, and he was likely gauging my reaction to his news. I had been glad of the arrival of the boys, which ensured his visit would be brief.

Only half-listening to the boys' conversation at the table evolving on both sides to Swiss German, I continued to prepare their lunch. I pulled a tray of *Chäs-chüechli* out of the oven and slid a carrot salad onto the table. As I opened the cupboard to fetch two plates for their meal, my gaze flickered to the window. At the end of the farm road in the distance I could see the dead limbs of the half-burned tree, and a flush crept up my throat.

'Hey, Mum, is it ready? Are you daydreaming or what?'

I turned. Both boys looked at me expectantly, Oliver's eyes on me, Leo's on the plate of food I was about to deliver.

'Sorry, here you go,' I said absently.

'Are you okay, Mum? Is it something that policeman said?' Oliver asked carefully.

I couldn't forget that his relationship with our local policeman was as precarious as my own. He hadn't forgotten then. I ignored his question.

'Bon appétit!' I said over-cheerfully as Leo cut his first morsel with the knife and fork, and Oliver picked up one of the little cheese quiches to eat with his hands.

'You mean *En guete!*' Leo stated before silencing conversation with a mouthful of food.

'Hey, they say a big snowstorm is coming this afternoon. Maybe you should wear your snow-boots to school after lunch. And you'll need hats. That wind is cold.'

I swallowed. Once again I relied on the indifference of a family routine, brighter on one side for the certain absence of a menace in our lives, darker on the other for the choking fibres of guilt that threatened to suffocate me.

'It was about *him*, wasn't it?' Oliver hissed as he put his plate in the sink after the meal.

The noise of the cutlery against the plate made me jump. I had expected him to rush off and look for his gloves, but should have known him better. I placed my hand on his shoulder as he waited for an answer.

'Oli, that man who was stalking me, who did those horrible things to you last week… he has died. He has committed suicide. He went into the forest and took too many pills… or something… He went to sleep and never woke up.'

I paused uneasily. The policeman hadn't given me the details of how Manfred had died. I turned away and methodically placed the dirty crockery in the dishwasher. Oliver's curiosity was understandable, but I'd already said too much for his young, fantasy-hungry mind.

'He won't be bothering us any more,' I said with finality, hoping he wouldn't ask any more details.

'Mum, you didn't tell Herr Schmid about what happened to me last week, did you?' he hissed theatrically. 'I thought we agreed you wouldn't do that.'

I held my hands up in mock surrender.

'No, Oli, I didn't tell the policeman. Your secret is safe with me.'

His shoulders dropped with relief.

'You must see if you can find your gloves as well, Oli. It's going to be really cold later.'

But he wouldn't let it go, and his eyes opened wide as he grabbed my arm.

'He committed... Mum, do you mean... Was it the same man you saved on the bridge in spring? Was it the same man who was following us? Was it *him*? Oh...'

'Yes, it was the same man. And I never told you, because I didn't want you to worry. You're too young to be concerned about things like that. I just wish... I wish he had taken his life earlier, before he hurt you,' I said wistfully.

'Mum – pills? What kind of pills? Do you think he did that because of me?'

'No, no, Oli. It wasn't your fault. You mustn't think he did this thing because of you, because of us. I don't know what pills he took. He was already a sick man. We talked about it in April, remember? Many people who attempt suicide will go on to try and do it again. He was terribly unhappy, and you mustn't ever blame yourself.'

'It's just that he didn't seem... sad. He was definitely angry, somehow, especially at me, but not sad. One thing's for sure, he was a freak. Maybe he should have seen a doctor,' Oliver mused. 'But freaks like that don't belong in our world, do they, Mum?'

'No, Oli, not if they don't want to be healed, they certainly don't,' I said as I bent down and slipped my hands around his waist.

I hugged him tightly, but he wriggled out of my grasp. I figured he was still feeling humiliated from his encounter with Manfred. The red marks on his back and hips had now turned to yellow bruises, but they were still a sulphuric reminder to me of the brutality.

'Some of the kids might talk about it at school, especially as the man lived in the village. Perhaps it's best you don't talk about it, in case people ask you about what happened to you last week, okay, Oli? Much of this story is best left untold, otherwise you might have to answer a lot of questions.'

Oliver nodded wisely, thinking about his own reputation.

CHAPTER FORTY-EIGHT

THE HOURS WAITING for Simon to come home that evening reminded me of the time I told him I was pregnant with Leo. That same nervous tension, no longer knowing if he approved of *anything* I told him now. Fifteen years ago, with the positive pregnancy test lying on the kitchen table, I had silently willed him to be excited. I was sure he would be thrilled, although we had said we would wait a few years before starting a family. I trusted his acceptance then, but there was always the underlying fear that the news would spur an unexpected reaction. This wasn't all that different. But why I thought news of Manfred's death would cause anything but relief, joy even, perplexed me. Perhaps it was because of the blurry confusion between fact and fiction building up in my head. But it felt good to finally be able to impart the news now Schmid had confirmed it. Simon had left for work that morning none the wiser.

He came home as I was taking a banana loaf Oliver had cooked out of the oven. The front door of the apartment closed firmly enough for me to wonder whether his day hadn't gone quite as planned. Simon rarely brought his frustrations home, but now the joint-venture deal had been agreed and signed, the post-achievement euphoria had rapidly diminished to an anti-climax as the monumental task of hard work needed to prove the company's worth increased. Family life went on, and we were still performing our same old duties at home. Although we were proud of his achievements, it was difficult to share in a business success the boys didn't wholly understand, despite Leo bravely listening to his father's explanations about mergers and acquisitions.

As Oliver carefully shimmied a knife around the edge of the loaf to remove it from the baking tin, Simon came into the kitchen, placed the palm of his hand between my shoulder blades, and kissed me on the cheek. I smiled at this unexpected display of affection and felt some of my tension ebb as Oliver beamed at the two of us. I hoped this meant it was as good a time as any to tell him. But before I could even think about formulating sentences, Oliver piped up.

'Hey, Dad. Good news today. You know the creepy guy, the stalker?'

Oliver's excitement masked the cloud that passed across Simon's face.

'Well, he's killed himself. He won't be around anymore to bother us… bother Mum.' Oliver looked at me pointedly, and placed a flour-dusted hand briefly on my arm.

My young protector. I wished he would stop. Stop stressing the 'us' part, knowing I still hadn't told Simon what Manfred had done to him.

Simon turned to his youngest son, brow raised.

'Wow, well, yes, I guess that gets rid of the problem. He *killed* himself, Oli? That's quite gruesome. When did this happen?'

Simon sniffed the banana loaf. I was surprised he didn't seem shocked. Oliver might just as well have told his dad he'd been a brave boy at the dentist. His reaction seemed too casual, too detached. Unless he was protecting his son from the horrors of death, trying to make light of an atrocity.

Oliver slapped at Simon's hand as he attempted to pick at a crusty corner of the loaf.

'You have to wait, Dad. It's for dessert,' he said with mock sternness, before answering Simon's question.

'It happened a few days ago, I guess. He took some pills, you know, like that Brad Renfro guy, like an *over*dose.'

I looked at Simon, his expression puzzled as our eyes met. I could tell he was thinking '*Who the hell is Brad Renfro?*' and I managed a smile.

My own curiosity focused on where on earth Oliver had learned the term 'overdose.' Simon turned back to him, paying more serious attention to his story. I saw consternation in his eyes that I hadn't read before and wondered how I had become so immune to my husband's signals. He probably thought *we* were treating this matter with too much apathy.

'That's quite some drama,' he said. 'How did you find out?'

'Mum told me. The police were here today. They told Mum, I guess because the guy has been following us – her, and all,' Oliver bowled on.

I suddenly felt a little out of control, reminding myself again that the policeman hadn't mentioned the details of Manfred's suicide.

LATER THAT EVENING, I climbed under the duvet, my feet seeking some warmth from Simon's side of the bed. With the change of season, the temperature was dropping outside and our ancient heating system hadn't yet fully kicked in with its winter schedule. A north wind was blowing hard enough to make the wooden shutters creak. I made a mental note to alter the thermostats on the radiators in the morning.

'Ouch!' Simon exclaimed with a smile as my chilly foot touched his leg.

He turned towards me on his side, gazing at me as I tucked the duvet under my chin. Stretching his right arm over me, he gathered me to him. I turned to him and smiled, but felt I was unable to hide the permanent creases etched into my face, still holding the strain of my locked-up thoughts. Simon mistook them for a frown.

'What?' he asked. 'Al, it's time to relax now. A menace has conveniently removed itself from our lives. This thing has been bugging all of us... well, mostly you... for months, and it's gone now. He's gone. Let him go.'

'I know, love, it's just been such a stress, and then the police again, what with Oliver's little adventure a while ago at the corner shop. Manfred's presence became a kind of intimidating habit. It feels weird. I can't quite believe he's... dead, gone.'

'Alice, you can't possibly imagine you could have done anything to save his sorry soul a second time. You sound like you're sympathising with him.'

'Simon, I…'

I felt myself spiralling, wanting to spill my emotions. But he silenced my dangerously repressed words with a kiss. The last thing I felt like doing was making love, but if I refused Simon now, months of rebuilding the delicate trust and love we had somehow lost might be ruined.

'I feel strange, Simon. Can you just hold me?' I whispered.

He pulled back to study my face and I forced my brow to smooth out and smiled at him. I waited for an irritated quip that didn't come. He pulled me towards him.

'Spoons?' he whispered. I nodded and turned on my side, back tucked into his chest, grateful for his sensitivity. Closing my eyes I pulled his arm towards me and pressed his hand to my heart, willing myself to turn the page in our lives and continue as if Manfred had never existed.

AFTER EVERYONE LEFT for work and school the following morning, snow-boots clopping on the disappointingly grey tarmac of the pavement, I decided to go for a gentle jog. It was my first in many weeks, as I was still carrying the injury. It was difficult to imagine I had been preparing for a marathon up until two months ago.

I figured a strenuous jog on a forest trail would help exhaust my demons. My ankle was surely ready for the test. Putting on an extra layer against the biting cold, I added gloves and a headband to my uniform. Clouds were thickening high over the valley, their grey bellies laden with the white jewels of winter.

I ran hard up the hill, throat burning with the effort in the cold. Wind hissed through the tops of the pine trees behind the farm. Every curve and landmark was so familiar to me on this hill trail, and I experienced unbridled euphoria in being able to gaze freely upon each object, each vista, and not fixedly earthwards to avoid the eyes that used to follow me everywhere. I ran up a gulley that fanned out onto open fields, affording a spectacular view of the Prealps from the ridge to the north of the Aegeri Valley.

The cold made my nose run and my ears ache as the breeze found the gaps at the side of my headband. But worse, my ankle started to ache, and I turned for home, slowing my jog to a stride. The first tentative snowflakes floated magically from the sky. Perfect tiny crystals settled on the hair spilling over my headband. I raised my face, blinking flakes off my eyelashes, and stuck out my tongue to childishly catch one on its tip.

As I came through the door at home, the phone was ringing. I answered as my heartbeat steadied, wondering when my angst would subside.

'Hi, Al. Oh, my God, I just read an article in *Twenty Minutes*,' Kathy said, referring to the local free newspaper.

The phone grew hot in my hand as she continued.

'I grabbed my dictionary straight away to get this one right. Listen to this: "The body of the man found dead on the Panorama Trail in the Aegerital last Friday has been identified as fifty-five-year-old Manfred Guggenbuhl. The events leading up to his death are still under investigation, but a witness at the scene said it appeared the victim had taken his own life. He leaves behind a wife and a son." It's *him*, Al.'

My heart leapt in my throat.

'A witness?' I asked weakly.

'I think they mean the guy who found him. A hunter came across him, apparently. The body was found on Friday afternoon. But they don't say when they reckon he died,' Kathy mused.

But *I* knew. He most likely died between midnight and dawn on Wednesday morning.

Three days.

I tried to imagine the state of his decaying body, although the cold might have preserved him. What would he have looked like? How long would it take for a body to start decomposing?

'Al? Alice? Are you okay? Surely you should be totally relieved. The nutter finally topped himself, finished what he wanted to do all those months ago when you saved him on that bridge. Good riddance is all I can say. What's up? You haven't said anything.'

'It just feels a little strange, Kath. Sorry, it's all so surreal.'

'Certainly a bizarre story, but Al, look, he won't be stalking you anymore. Surely you can be grateful for that...'

I wasn't ready to share Kathy's excitement. I wasn't ready to relive and rehash all those months of threat and uncertainty. I wasn't ready to embellish my lies. It felt too early to relax, let down my guard, risk making more errors in the way I handled everything.

I knew she wanted to share the juice of the story, but I couldn't even face her.

'Kath, I tried to run this morning, but my ankle's still not ready. We'll have to postpone our outings for a while, and now winter is coming, I'm not so sure about stability on the snow, even with crampons. I'll call you soon. We'll do something again before too long, I promise.'

Kathy was right. I should have been relieved. But I'd lived with broken expectations for so long, it was hard to believe even death could be final in his case.

CHAPTER FORTY-NINE

HANS MÜLLER ACCOMPANIED me from the front desk of the cantonal police headquarters near the appropriately named *Schutzengel*, Guardian Angel, quarter of Zug to an office at the back of the building. His card told me he worked for the KRIPO, the *Kriminalpolizei*.

I was surprised to see Schmid standing in the hallway near the reception area chatting to a colleague. He greeted me neutrally as I passed. I imagined him on a report-giving mission, occupying this space in the corridor because the excitement of a dead body found in bucolic Aegeri meant he had to spend time with the big boys in the big smoke. He seemed neither relieved nor suspicious as I returned his greeting, but I felt his eyes on my back as I passed.

Although the police officials didn't have specific titles – no DIs or DSs here – Müller exuded an air of higher authority, especially as he had a pleasant office with large windows. I called him *Detektiv* Müller in my mind, to give him a more senior role than *Offizier* Schmid.

A pot plant sat on top of a filing cabinet, and the screensaver on his computer was a photo of a small child playing with a Bernese mountain dog in a garden. I relaxed a little, having initially imagined I might be questioned in a windowless, dark interview room with only a table, two chairs and a police guard by the door. I'd seen too many detective movies.

As Müller settled at his desk and I took a seat opposite him, I could hear phones ringing in adjacent offices, the white-noise fuzz of a walkie-talkie moving down a corridor somewhere, and the regular mid-afternoon traffic rolling past the slightly open window. He offered me coffee, which I refused, and thought it might be too complicated to enquire whether they had any tea.

'Frau Reed, can you tell us what you were doing on the evening in question?'

I'd gone over this scenario so many times in my head. My pulse hardly changed, but I felt heat rise to my face, and hoped the detective read this as the absurdity of having to provide an alibi. I decided to stick as closely to what I'd told Simon as possible. He'd been my only other contact during that whole evening.

Müller loudly slurped his *Schale*, a large milky coffee, as he waited for my answer.

'I went for a hike. I usually walk or run most Tuesdays,' I said.

'Where did you hike that evening?'

He had the nervous habit of flicking his pencil between his index and middle finger, see-sawing it so the tip touched his notepad with an annoying pat-pat-pat. I found it hard to concentrate, trying to remember every detail I recounted in case I was asked again at a future date.

'I took the path up behind the farm near our house, followed the gully upstream and joined the Panorama Trail at the junction to the Raten Pass. It's a trail I've walked often over the past weeks.'

'Did you see anyone? Is there anyone who can verify your path that evening?'

'No, I didn't see anybody. I sometimes see people working at the farm as I hike past, but that evening I didn't see anyone.'

I had no intention of saying I'd seen Manfred that day. I wanted to scream at them that I was never alone, never for one minute. But by admitting that, I would merely have implicated myself.

'Can you tell me, please, exactly the times you went for your walk? What time did you leave the house, and what time did you come home?'

'I left the house at about 5.00 p.m. I'm not sure what time it was when I came home. It was dark. I stayed near the top of the pass to watch the sunset, waited until dusk. It was a clear night. Then I came home. I think it must have been between 9.00 and

10.00 p.m. My husband was already in bed, but I'm not sure he heard me come in.'

It had been late, I remembered. Simon had barely woken. He had turned slightly in his sleep, had laid that pacifying hand on mine, but we hadn't spoken, and he would have had no recollection of the time. My heart fluttered. In reality it had been closer to midnight.

'How long did you say the victim had been stalking you?'

I wished they wouldn't call him the victim. *I* was the victim, surely. And then I remembered again that Manfred was dead.

'He began stalking me the same day I stopped him jumping from the Tobel Bridge on the Sunday in April stated on the police report. He came back to the house after I had dropped him at the bus station. Then, later that day, the phone calls started. On my mobile and on our house phone. And went on for several months.'

'Did you have reason to believe Herr Guggenbuhl might still have suicidal tendencies?'

I forced my mind back to the days when I still thought I could help him.

'How can I answer that question? The man was *stalking* me. I had become his obsession. He seemed to think we belonged together in a normal life.'

My rising anger made me blab. I should have just said yes. I knew I shouldn't offer any more of my own opinions. I needed to let *them* do the psychology. I forced myself to calm down, and took a deep breath.

'He never told me he was thinking about suicide. But it's not easy to give an opinion about his mental state when I was the focus of his instability.'

This was beginning to feel like an interrogation. Herr Müller could see I was becoming agitated.

'I'm sorry, Frau Reed. I realise it would be difficult for you to answer that.'

I settled in my chair, heart gradually beating a little less hard.

'DO THEY SUSPECT you of something, Al? What's going on?'

Simon and I were in the kitchen after dinner that evening. The boys had left the table to go to their rooms. We were sharing the tasks of clearing away the dishes, rinsing saucepans, filling the dishwasher, the mundane jobs conveniently reducing our conversation to idle chitchat. I was happy to have my hands occupied.

'No, no, it's just that I don't have an alibi. I don't know what they're thinking. I guess they have to eliminate all possibilities. It's just that, can you remember what time you went to bed that night? Only I remember you vaguely acknowledged me when I came to bed, and I don't want us to have conflicting stories if they question you. The detective who interviewed me said there might be inconsistencies. I don't know what he means. I don't know if I would be implicated. Perhaps it was just an expression. But we need to get our details right, to avoid *any* suspicion.'

'Suspicion of what exactly? Crap, Al, I honestly can't remember. I know I was early to bed, not long after the boys. Ten maybe? I read a bit and then dozed off. I know you were there in the morning, but I must have crashed deeply into sleep. Jesus. Do they think you might have tried to chuck him off that bridge in the first place then? Don't they think you've been hassled enough?'

'I don't know. I was hoping we could all just forget about this whole thing. We do need a break.'

I put my hand out to place it on his shoulder as he reached down to close the door of the dishwasher. He didn't look up at me, but stared at the machine. I wondered what was going on in my husband's head. Surely this signalled a fresh start, especially after the softening of emotions the evening we'd found out Manfred was really dead. A new beginning without him in our lives.

Come back to me.

'I have to say it's mightily convenient that Manfred took his life. It does seem a little ironic,' he said.

He turned to face me, laid his hand briefly on my upper arm and squeezed. As he left the kitchen I raised my own hand to grab the empty space where he had slipped from my touch. I still had a lot of work ahead of me to regain his trust. To regain his love. I knew he must still be having a hard time dealing with the fact that I had lied to him from the beginning, hadn't told him the whole story.

CHAPTER FIFTY

'I'M SO SORRY we have to call you in again, Frau Reed. There are a few formalities we need to complete, and… I know how difficult this has been for you. I apologise for the stress this has caused you and your family.'

I breathed a sigh of relief. Müller smiled. This time, when an assistant offered me coffee, I enquired whether they had any tea, and he brought me a selection of herbal infusions and a glass of hot water. Not quite what I was expecting, but I was flattered by the attention. It felt like I was a guest, not a suspect, and I immediately relaxed.

The detective pulled a clear plastic zip-lock bag I hadn't noticed at the side of his desk towards him, then pushed it between us like a chess piece on a board.

'Do you know this article of clothing, Frau Reed?'

I was shocked. Hardly recognisable in its scrunched, vacuum-packed state was one of my favourite camisole tops. I suddenly felt ill at ease, wondering if it could implicate me. Where the hell had they found it?

Manfred must have taken it from the washing line in the summer that day he folded my clothes. Unless he'd somehow taken it from the drawer in my bedroom. I couldn't see how it could be linked to me. If it had been freshly laundered, it would no longer contain traces of my DNA, although there could always be a hair trapped in the lace, my fingerprint on a label as I folded it. Or *his*.

But I had to admit it was mine. My eyes had already revealed that much, which I was sure had been the detective's intention in the first place. To try and catch me off-guard, although I wasn't sure why it would make any difference. The article should have implicated Manfred, not me.

'Yes, that's my camisole top. I'm pretty sure Manfred – Mr Guggenbuhl – took it from my washing line a few months ago. He… folded my laundry once when it was raining.'

Müller cast me an incredulous look.

'When did you notice it was missing?'

'I've never really thought about it,' I said, shifting uncomfortably in my chair.

I remembered stuffing the clean folded laundry back into the washing machine to wash away the madness of his touch, but I hadn't realised anything was missing. Is that the sort of thing I should be remembering?

'No mention of the theft was made to us, Frau Reed. Stealing is a crime, although this is not a major theft. Perhaps you should have mentioned this to the police when you made your complaint.'

'But I didn't notice. Do you keep note of every piece of underwear you put into your washing machine, Mr Müller?'

My anger began to rise again, and I clenched my jaw to avoid making a scene. What kind of twisted society chased a perpetrator for a petty theft but did nothing about a stalker obsessed with a woman and her family?

I forced myself to smooth the lines of tension on my face, and sat stoically, waiting for the next questions. I was torn about voicing my frustrations. This was not the moment for that platform. I had to be careful. Who knew what error of speech would end up getting me thrown in jail?

'You refer to the victim by his first name as though he were an acquaintance of yours, Frau Reed.'

I stared at Müller, and could no longer hold my tongue.

'Do you realise how this crazy person, this mentally disturbed man, completely messed up our lives?'

He seemed to have no idea about the psyche of a stalker. I had more knowledge about the phenomenon from clicking through pages on the Internet than they had experience in the criminal department of the local police station.

'I think it's about time you guys got your act together and realised stalking is a criminal problem.'

I crossed my arms and leaned back. For a moment it seemed we had all forgotten we were talking about a dead man.

'The issue is being addressed, Frau Reed. Unfortunately, you are our first such case in the canton. It is not something we have had experience with before, outside domestic disputes and such problems between partners. Will you be walking again tomorrow evening, Frau Reed?'

The way he asked this made me blanch. It was as though he didn't believe there could have been such a coincidence. Going for a walk on the same evening as Manfred's suicide.

'Something is confusing to me. If you say you take a walk on many evenings, were you aware the victim was following you each time?'

'I... yes, once or twice I was aware, but he didn't approach me.'

'I find it strange that he chose that particular night to take his life, and did not follow you on your walk. We do not know his motivation because there was no note, no letter.'

I shrugged, unsure whether he was asking for my opinion again. From then on I decided only to answer direct questions. I'd already offered too many of my own impressions. My tea remained cold on Müller's desk, and I wanted to go home.

'When will we be finished here? I'd like to be at home when my children come back from school,' I said. 'They need to know they are now in a safe family environment. Things have been a little uncertain for them over the past few months, as you can imagine.'

'Of course, Frau Reed, yes, I'm sorry. This must be upsetting for you. Certainly you can go. If we need you again, we will contact you. If you don't mind...' Müller placed his hand proprietarily over the plastic bag. '...I would like to keep this until we have concluded our investigation.'

'That's okay, I don't want it back. You can keep it.' I hesitated. 'May I ask exactly what it is you are investigating? This man has committed suicide, hasn't he?'

I was hoping to hear an affirmative, but his next comment made the hair prickle on the back of my neck.

'There are many procedures we still need to follow before we can close this case, Frau Reed. We need to wait for the result of the victim's autopsy. The family has been contacted. There may be some inconsistencies. We are still searching his old home and apartment, his belongings. We would like you to remain available should we need to contact you again, yes?'

I nodded. *Inconsistencies?*

Müller rose from his chair and opened his office door for me. 'Can you remember the way out?'

I nodded, tucked my arm through the handles of my handbag and pulled it close to my shoulder like a shield, so he couldn't see my hands shake. I walked briskly out of the police station, a chill breeze gusting the last dead leaves high up into the air between the great glass edifices of the *Grafenau* buildings.

Instead of heading back to the bus station, I walked under a narrow railway bridge towards the lake and joined the path leading into the old town of Zug along the shore. The dark grey waters of the *Zugersee* were now unwelcomingly choppy with the wind, and I shivered.

I wondered what inconsistencies the policeman was referring to. Surely this was just a clear-cut case of suicide. Maybe they'd found a diary of Manfred's. A written record might have implicated me, although I wasn't sure how. Everyone knew he was stalking me.

Suicide was the natural explanation, the logical end to Manfred's story. What could possibly have presented itself as an *inconsistency?* I'd thought I would have felt better by then, safe, satisfied he was no longer a threat in our lives. But at that stage something was beginning to fray in my mind.

CHAPTER FIFTY-ONE
DECEMBER

I BARELY HEARD the doorbell over the sound of the boys thumping down the stairs with their schoolbags. Accompanying them into the main hallway of the building, I opened the door. My heart jumped in my throat.

'Gerry…' The hard 'G' of his name made me sound American.

As the boys rushed past me, Oliver yelled 'See ya, Mum!' and Leo muttered sarcastically under his breath '*Gary*,' imitating a cowboy drawl.

Despite the quip, they were not remotely interested in the newcomer. I watched the boys' backs until they disappeared around the corner. A chill wind pushed at the door, air whistling through the hinges and gaps. I wasn't sure whether to let Gerry in, couldn't read the expression on his face, so neutral, so closed. His eyes traced the doorframe, as if seeking the magic spell that would facilitate his entry into another dimension. I remained rooted to the spot in a panic of indecision.

'Come in,' I finally said, letting the door swing closed as I led him down the hallway into the living room. 'Please, sit down. Can I get you a coffee, a tea, something else to drink?'

'No, thank you, Mrs Reed – Alice.'

I hadn't heard my name on his lips before, and I felt a little uneasy with the familiarity. He sat confidently on the sofa, unzipped his crimson ski jacket, leaned back and crossed his legs. These messages confused me. It was as though he was making himself at home. Too at home in my house.

He was, after all, his father's son.

I perched on a tall-backed armchair and tilted my head, a silent encouragement to have him explain why he was there.

'Did you know my father is dead?' Gerry asked abruptly, dispensing with the exchanges of greeting and weather reports that usually eased vague acquaintances into conversation.

'I… Yes, the police came to see me. They say he… took his own life.'

I pulled the blouse together at my throat, thinking hives of nervousness might soon appear.

'I honestly didn't think he had the… how do you say – *guts* – to do this thing. He was so weak, so pathetic.'

Gerry shrugged out of his ski jacket, laid it next to him on the sofa, and patted it absently. He was wearing a plaited leather friendship bracelet clasped with a large brass stud, and I stared briefly at the knuckle of his wrist. The warmth of the room felt oppressively close and I regretted having cranked the heating up a few days before.

I couldn't tell whether Gerry was asking for sympathy or wanting to explore the reasons for Manfred's death with me. I thought he had cut off all contact with his father, thought he wouldn't care whether Manfred lived or died, but the very fact that he was here in my living room made me wonder if he had made a terrible mistake ostracising his own kin. Here was a man only a few years older than my own children. He couldn't be sure his opinions in life wouldn't alter. There was always time for forgiveness, for a change of heart.

If that was the case, it had come too late for Gerry. I detected a sort of frustrated sadness in the way he looked around our family living room. I followed his gaze. His eyes settled on the bookshelf, on the photo of me and the boys standing outside the Palace of Versailles.

'The photo sits well on your shelf. It's back in its rightful place. You must be happy now my father is no longer a threat to you and your family,' he said, eyes still on the photo.

He almost sounded jealous. I looked at the photo too, wishing I could magic myself back to that carefree visit to Paris over a year ago, to a time before all this happened.

With horror, I realised Gerry did have regrets about his father. Regrets existed where he had once told me he wouldn't miss him even if he'd thrown himself off the Tobel Bridge. Back then, he just didn't care.

The fact that he was sitting here on my couch meant he did care.

But it was too late now.

CHAPTER FIFTY-TWO

'GERRY, I'VE BEEN able to return to a normal life with my family. But I can't say I'm happy about what has happened. It would have been much better for everyone if your father had chosen to seek the help we all advised, if he had taken his medication, talked to a doctor or psychologist. Even checked into an institution. There are professionals who help people who've tried to take their lives, to avoid them returning to that dark place.'

I paused, watching Gerry run his fingers through the wave of hair hanging over his forehead. I could see him fighting a battle in his mind. I didn't want to see him suffer. We were all better off now Manfred had gone. But I could hardly voice this to his son.

This young man had so much ahead of him. Moving to sit beside him on the couch, I laid my hand on the top of his as it rested on his knee. It was supposed to be a motherly gesture, but when Gerry looked sharply at my fingers, I felt somehow that my touch had crossed a forbidden barrier.

'You mustn't blame yourself for what has happened, Gerry. If your father was still alive today, he'd probably have become ever more delusional, would have made all our lives more of a living hell. He's at peace now.'

'I didn't know when I came here how I would feel. I'm still not sure. I had to make sure you had nothing to do with his decision. To make sure you didn't somehow push him into it. I can see now I'm here that you wouldn't do that. You wouldn't be, how do you say, callous enough. But I can see why my father had this attraction, this obsession with you.'

I felt an involuntary heat rise from the base of my neck, and my pulse spiked. But contrary to logic, I didn't feel disgusted. He saw me flush, and hurriedly continued.

'What I mean is, I think you are a good person. I see goodness in you, and something else. I see you are fragile. People like us can still be broken.'

People like us?

'Gerry, I am so sorry this happened to your father. You seem like a good person too, and we can't be blamed for any mistakes we've made that might have brought about his death. Have you talked to your mother? You need each other to get through this.'

Gerry shook his head slowly.

'My mother... I didn't think we would see things the same way. At first she was a little more, how do you say, ruthless about what happened to my father. She seemed to want to shut that part of our history away and carry on as if nothing happened. She wanted to throw away all my father's things the day the police came to tell her he was dead, but they wouldn't let her. They've put tape around the storage room in our basement where some of my father's things still are. They've also put tape across the door of his apartment in the village here. I've just come from there. But, after all that, she still didn't seem to care.'

Gerry brushed his hand through his hair again, distracting me briefly.

'But then I couldn't believe it,' he continued. 'The morning after the police were in our house my mother came downstairs to go to work and she broke down. She went down to the basement and stood staring at the tape across the storage-room door as though she wanted to go in there, might find him sitting among his things. She was sobbing. She couldn't speak to me, kept shaking her head. I guess it was the same for me. It came to us both as a big surprise. Not just that my father died. It's the pointless loss of life that nature spent so much time creating in this complicated miracle of cells and chromosomes. You know, I'm studying science, and something so precious should not be discarded so easily... Life.'

Gerry looked away, glazed eyes not concentrating on the view out of the window, but looking into himself, at some unseen vision in his head. I discreetly studied his profile, then lowered my eyes as he turned to me and continued.

'But ultimately it made me angry, this show of misery. It made me angry that my father had once again upset my mother. I kept telling her he'd found a better place, like you said; that he'd made peace with himself. He didn't need *us* to find his way out. I think she was relieved then. She seemed to straighten herself up, brushed away the tears, and gave me a hug. She hasn't spoken about it since. But I don't know if that was it, the extent of her sadness, or if she's just hiding her emotions from me to make me think she's strong.'

Gerry shifted in his seat. A pinched look around his eyes gave me the impression he was holding back emotions he didn't want to show.

My eyes automatically filled with tears, and my chest constricted, knowing I was the one who had ultimately caused most of his pain. I kept the focus of our conversation on Gerry's mother.

'Maybe she needs more help than you think, Gerry. She *is* your mother.'

I could only put myself in Leo or Oliver's shoes at this point and hoped they wouldn't abandon me in a similar situation.

'I think she will be okay, but maybe you're right,' he continued. 'Maybe she is hiding that she is upset. She didn't even take a day off sick. She goes to work at the insurance company in Wohlen, comes home, does the things she has always done, a little embroidery, or reading. She even went to a *Jass* card game with her friends on Tuesday night, as if nothing had happened. She was always difficult to interpret. She seemed neither happy nor annoyed to see me when I visited her this week.'

'Gerry, it disturbs me that you sound so bitter. It sounds to me as if there is still a lot of conflict going on inside you.'

'Do you know there is an investigation going on?'

'Well, yes, apart from you telling me about the police tape just now, I was also questioned about his death.'

'*You?* I know I said I came here to make sure, but how could they possibly imagine you had anything to do with it?'

And just like that, I saw a cog of thought clicking in Gerry's mind. He'd been questioned too. Perhaps he thought they suspected *him* of some misdemeanour. I shouldn't have revealed I had been questioned. Gerry's eyes narrowed. He looked at me searchingly. We sat for a few moments in awkward silence, my gaze downcast to avoid eye contact at such close proximity.

'I feel better for having talked to you, Alice. Thank you for seeing me.'

He left his last thought about my police questioning unanswered, hopefully forgotten, some kind of rhetorical sympathy.

'That's okay, Gerry. I'm glad I could be of help.'

He searched my face, and it wasn't the first time I noticed his very green eyes, made brighter by his unshed tears. I felt a little tingle in my sternum. I cleared my throat and was about to speak again when he interjected.

'If I need to, you know, talk about it again, would it be okay if I called you? We can meet somewhere else if you like. I don't want to worry you by coming to your home. I know how strange it must feel, my father having been close by for so many months. But as you spent more time with him than anyone else, maybe I can try to sort out these... these feelings I can't yet identify. Can you do that for me?'

What could I say? I wanted to tell him I thought it would be better if we didn't see each other again. I should have told him that. Part of me couldn't believe how bold he was. It was time for me to forget about the horrors of the past few months. Time for me to put my house and my family back in order. On the other hand, I couldn't bring myself to quash his youthful hope that I could help him somehow. As though he was using me as a sounding board for something he should be asking his mother. I felt truly sorry for Gerry, for his conflict, for his unidentifiable emotions. So, without really knowing why, I said yes, he could contact me, and I gave him my mobile phone number.

'But Gerry, I think you should talk to a psychologist. A professional can help you more than I can. I'm not qualified to give advice.'

I remembered saying these very same words to his father some months before. The parallel made me shiver. I had to put the brakes on this association. I didn't need the complication of a new fellowship.

'Gerry, I need one thing. Just give me some time. A week or two to try and sort out my life again. I need a bit of distance to think. I don't want you to remind me of your father every time I see you. Do you understand that? Can you give me that space?'

He gathered himself, perhaps realising his own needs had triggered unpleasant memories for me. This had apparently not been his intention. He put his hand to his temple, mouth slightly open.

'Of course I can, Alice. I'm not going to start following you around like my father did. Please remember one thing. I am not my father. I am not like him at all. I do not want to be like him. I'm not that kind of person. I'm sorry... I should not have asked.'

He was so adamant, it was as though he was repeating a mantra to convince himself he would never become his father.

He dug into his pocket, pulled out a scrap of paper.

'And here is my mobile number, should you feel like calling about anything.'

He saw me pale with the unspoken obligation. I didn't want to take the paper from him. It was as though he had been prepared to give me the number before he even knocked at my door. Perhaps he would have left it in our mailbox if I hadn't been home. Most likely he simply wanted to talk about what had happened. And part of me thought perhaps I could assuage his guilt, in turn assuaging my own.

'It's okay. I'm just saying here is my number in case... You know, you have been through a lot as well with this whole thing with my father. I don't know. I realise you would probably want to move on from it all. I have not forgotten that you came to seek my help some months ago, and I turned you away. It means you have the option.'

That's something Simon might have said. Keep all your options open. He often mentioned it if I was wondering whether to take a rain jacket on a hike. I asked myself what options Gerry thought I had.

Feeling a little wary, I stood and led the way down the hallway to the door. As we shook hands, I smiled uncertainly. His palm was warm and dry, a strong handshake not unlike that of his father. Closing the door as he retreated down the stairway, my smile dropped away and I slapped my thigh.

What was I thinking, allowing this person to maybe contact me in the future? I wanted nothing more than to forget Manfred had ever existed. I put my hand to the back of my neck, massaging a tension I hadn't realised was there, and wiped dampness away with my palm. I stood for a few moments in the dimness, staring at the closed door, then turned to walk down the hallway to the kitchen. I screwed up the paper with his phone number and threw it into the recycling bag.

Through the window, I watched him walk down the road to the village. He pulled up the padded collar of his ski jacket and hunched into its warmth, as giant, fluffy snowflakes began falling thickly but silently past the windowpane, eventually obscuring my view.

CHAPTER FIFTY-THREE

APART FROM DURING the family holiday in autumn, Simon and I hadn't been on a date together for over a year. His company was throwing an extravagant evening out in Zürich for the management team, a thank you for the multimillion-dollar oil deal recently signed and sealed after many months of negotiation with a temperamental Russian conglomerate.

We were to attend a private performance of *La Bohème* at the *Opernhaus*, followed by a gourmet dinner above the city at the Dolder Grand Hotel.

I stood at the bathroom mirror, the bright neon light revealing fine creases of stress on my face that weren't there last spring. I smoothed a little foundation on, swept a layer of mascara onto my lashes, and pressed my lips together before pouting and grimacing with the unfamiliar taste of lipstick. My unruly curly hair was scraped back into a pleat and I tucked in a few wild strands, securing them with extra hairpins.

'Could you help me with my necklace?'

I held up a chain with an amethyst pendant as Simon came into the bathroom, fiddling with a cufflink. He secured the tiny clasp at the back of my neck, and gently pressed his lips to the curve leading to my shoulder.

'We brush up quite well for a couple of athletes creaking into middle age,' he said. 'You're still a beautiful woman, Al.'

I felt a thrill, the one that had made me yearn for him all those years ago. Warmth spread through my belly and I smiled at him in the mirror. We hadn't been like this together for months.

'Shame we don't have a little extra time… But I wouldn't want to crease your dress or muss up your hair-do,' he said with a playful grin.

With his hands on my hips we gazed at each other a moment longer, smiling shyly like a couple of lovestruck teenagers. Our history had held us together after almost a year of hell. A year of constant anxiety and uncertainty. We would rebuild what had crumbled over the next weeks. My eyes misted with gratitude that we hadn't lost the spark. Simon's hands fell away and he went back to the bedroom to fetch his tie.

I stayed in the bathroom a moment longer, staring at my face in the mirror. The make-up did make me look younger. I turned my head from side to side, my earrings catching the light with a spark. I supposed I was still quite attractive, once the faint, spider-thread lines had been covered with a little concealer. I might even have passed for someone five or six years younger.

I wondered how old Gerry thought I was. My brows creased. I felt instantly guilty, allowing someone other than the man who had just placed his hands on my hips to slip into my mind. I smoothed my skirt.

WE SAT IN the darkened theatre with stage lights glistening in our eyes. I felt as though the performers were watching us instead of the other way round. I guessed that's what came from having been observed for so long.

We were a group of thirty or so, clustered several rows back from the stage, the rest of the theatre a gaping universe of shadows and empty seats in the darkness. At some point during the evening, I had the uncomfortable feeling I was being watched. I looked over my shoulder to the darkness at the back of the theatre, then to my side as Simon caught my eye, and smiled reassuringly as he put a hand on my arm.

I brushed off my anxiety as a feeling I had grown used to over the past year. I figured it must be a combination of the novelty of a night out with a group of Simon's unfamiliar office colleagues, along with the eerie feeling the half-empty opera house evoked. But the sensation still lay like a stone in the pit of my stomach.

The private performance was in reality a dress rehearsal for the month-long production that would open to the public the following night in the *Opernhaus*. We'd been forewarned that one of the sopranos had contracted a cold, and sure enough, halfway through Musetta's Waltz in Act Two, her piercing voice cracked, and a coughing fit stopped her in the middle of the piece. The orchestra stumbled to a halt, their strings tripping over each other in their haste to silence, and the understudy had to be called before the performance could recommence.

The audience squirmed in their seats in embarrassment for the performers, and we all agreed how lucky it was for them that this happened at the dress rehearsal, making excuses for our presence. But the incident gelled the audience, a group of relative strangers, work colleagues and their partners who barely knew each other, and the anxiety I'd initially felt immediately dissipated.

After losing count of the glasses of champagne, we went on to enjoy a five-course gourmet meal at the restaurant. We were high on this rare social occasion, alcohol fogging our reality. Spilling into our pre-ordered taxi at the end of the evening, we snuggled like two young lovers in the back of the car while our chauffeur drove us home to an empty apartment. The boys had been farmed off to friends for the evening, allowing us the luxury of being alone for the whole night.

As we stepped through the door, Simon gently pulled one end of the shawl I was wearing and spun me around to face him in the hallway. He gathered me close, and kissed me deeply, the taste of a vintage Bordeaux on his mouth. I put my arms around his neck, and we waltzed comically into the living room where Simon closed the curtains with flourish. He lit two candles on the bookshelf, bathing the room in a cosy, sensual light, and pushed me gently back onto the sofa.

He knelt down to remove my shoes, and laid his head briefly on my lap, gently hugging my legs. He lifted my skirt, pulled my tights and knickers together down past my knees, and smoothed his palms down the inside of my thighs. The fervour in his eyes set me on fire and I knew we should satisfy this rare passion now, or it might never happen again. I began unbuttoning his trousers and tugged at his zip, the top halves of our bodies still fully clothed.

I turned to push him down onto the couch and he reached up to bury his hands in my hair, my French pleat long ago wild around my face. I straddled Simon, his hardness finding its own way into the familiarity of me, and we pressed into each other with a kind of desperation. One of his hands squeezed my breast, frustratingly constricted under the silk bodice of my evening dress.

'It's time to let go, Alice.' His voice was almost a shout, then cracked with hoarseness, his whole body on the verge of release.

I smiled, wondering if the neighbours could hear us, and leaned towards him, my hair whispering against his chest. He was close to losing control, and to keep me with him, pressed his fingers against me where our bodies joined, triggering the powerful climax I had been craving.

It had been months, so long. The power of sensations long forgotten brought tears to my eyes, either because of the months of missed opportunity or gratefulness for this moment. I laid my cheek against his chest as our breathing calmed.

Simon blew a lock of my hair out of his face and shifted slightly. I didn't know how many minutes we'd been lying there. I might even have fallen asleep, my ear pressed to his steadily slowing heartbeat. I was spent, suddenly exhausted. I felt Simon's hand shift from under us, his knuckles moving across the front of one of my legs as he grabbed at something under his back. I knelt upright as he held up the object he was lying on.

It was Gerry's plaited leather bracelet. My heart missed a beat.

'Yours?' Simon asked nonchalantly.

The leather friendship band hung from his outstretched index finger.

'No… It must belong to one of the boys,' I replied without hesitation.

It was so much easier than telling him Gerry had been in our home. I didn't want to risk his fury at finding out a stranger had been inside our house again, albeit under innocent circumstances.

Simon narrowed his eyes and looked at the bracelet sceptically. I forced a smile and plucked it from his hands. As I leaned in to kiss him, I lobbed it across the room, and it landed on the bookshelf out of his sight. But it burned there in my peripheral vision.

'Maybe Leo has a girlfriend,' I said jovially. 'It looks like one of those friendship bands all the kids are wearing at the moment. Perhaps he takes after his dad, and can't leave the ladies alone.'

I laughed, attempting to tease, and pulled up Simon's shirt to tickle him lightly on his stomach, making him laugh and wriggle.

As I tidied the cushions on the sofa and turned out the lights on our way to bed, I slid the bracelet off the shelf, folded it into my hand and tucked it into my handbag on the bench in the hallway. It continued to burn a hole there instead.

CHAPTER FIFTY-FOUR

THE POLICE CALLED again while I was shopping at the Co-op. As I was carefully selecting Braeburns from the apple boxes, I answered my mobile without checking. Only a handful of people had my number – Simon, the school, Kathy and a few women from the Chat Club. Manfred had it too, when he was alive. He would be the only person I truly didn't want to talk to. Since I knew he was dead, he wouldn't be calling me. I'd begun answering again without looking at the screen. But I'd forgotten I'd also given it to the police, and the unfamiliar Swiss-German voice immediately made me nervous.

It was unclear whether my presence at the station in Zug was absolutely required, but I obliged as soon as possible, and arranged a time the following day, before weighing my apples and sticking the price tag on the bag.

I felt self-conscious speaking on my mobile in the small village shop in English, and left without buying half the things on my list.

THIS TIME I talked to someone who introduced himself as Rudolf Meier – a police psychologist. He wasn't wearing a nametag or a uniform, and I sighed with the irritation of having to go through all the details again.

'I'm sorry you have had to come to Zug again, Frau Reed. We were hoping to visit you at home, but thought perhaps it was easier for you to talk somewhere neutral without the possibility of your children interrupting the… interview.'

For a moment I thought he was going to say *'interrogation'* and my mouth turned briefly upwards in a saccharine smile. Herr Meier continued.

'Now you have had time to digest the news and your conversations with Herren Schmid and Müller, we are wondering whether you have had any further reactions, emotionally, to the news that Herr Guggenbuhl has... passed away.'

I thought this was a delicate way of putting it, for someone for whom English was not his first language. He made it sound like Manfred died of old age after a long illness. I wondered what he was digging for. Were they being overly nosy, or was I simply being overly suspicious? For a police force that had paid no attention to Manfred when he was alive, they were certainly giving him a lot of airing now he was dead. The room seemed suddenly stuffy and I reached for the plastic cup left for me on the edge of Herr Meier's desk. The water tasted metallic.

'I'm not sure I understand your concern, or why I'm here, Herr Meier.'

'We wanted to make sure there had been no repercussions from his death. For you and your family. It is not always easy to learn of the untimely death of someone you have... who has been a part of your life for so long.'

I wished I knew how they expected me to react. He spoke as though I'd lost a beloved relative.

'How is your son?' he asked.

I stared at the psychologist. He shifted in his seat when I didn't answer.

'We were led to believe he had also been... affected by Herr Guggenbuhl. It is our duty to make sure that he does not require, how do you say, counselling. We ask you first to see if you think this would be the case.'

Something dark and slippery uncoiled within me, and before I could hold my tongue, I grabbed the seat of my chair and leaned towards my interviewer across his desk.

'Well, this is a fine time to be offering your damn help! After all those months of my family being persecuted! Why the fuck didn't you do something about it six months ago, when that man needed help, was obviously begging for it? Did you think you could save yourselves the hassle and have me do your dirty work for you? Or did you think if the pathetic little foreigner would just go away, then Manfred Guggenbuhl's problems would just go away too, and you wouldn't have an issue to deal with? Well, if I hadn't talked him off that damned bridge in the first place, you would have been dealing with a dead body much earlier in the year. Isn't it time you just left us alone? This whole thing disgusts me… You're more concerned with a fucking dead corpse than a human cry for help.'

My hand grabbed my mouth to stop myself, as if two parts of my body were fighting the reaction. Blood rushed to my face, and anger smarted my eyes.

Herr Meier leaned back, shocked by my outburst. It had been a long time since *anyone* had heard me speak like that, even my family and friends. I winced, put my head on one side and rubbed one eyebrow with the palm of my hand. Spinning shards of light kaleidoscoped before my eyes. The policeman's desk appeared to float, and the pens, paperclips and his coffee mug faded out and reappeared before me.

The last thing I should have done was lose control, draw attention to myself. The police knew Oliver had been followed home from school. It was me who had told them in the first place. I had been furious it wasn't until the school themselves made a complaint about Manfred that the police promised to patrol the village.

But what I hadn't told them was what that monster did to Oliver only hours before his death. My blood still boiled thinking about it. Thinking this could all have been avoided if the police had taken action earlier.

But I couldn't say anything more, in case coincidence and suspicion were to combine in the story they were now trying to piece together.

CHAPTER FIFTY-FIVE

'I'M DOING MY PhD at the ETH,' Gerry said.

I frowned.

'In biotechnology. It's the university, here in Zürich – just up the hill there, in fact.'

He pointed with his chin past the twin towers of the city's iconic *Grossmünster* church.

'Well, the main building is up there, but most of my lab work is done in *Hönggerberg*, a little further to the west.'

I still wasn't sure what my motivation had been for calling Gerry. I repeatedly saw the soft-plaited leather band in the inside pocket of my handbag where I kept my mobile phone. I occasionally pulled it out and held it in my hand, rubbing my thumb along the tightly woven suede to the brass stud at one end. I wondered if a girl had given it to him. He might have been sad to have lost it.

Gerry's mobile phone number took some time to find in the bag of paper destined for the recycling centre. I knew his family home number from researching their address some months before. But now I wouldn't dare call his home in Aargau where I knew he spent some of his weekends. His mother might answer. I should avoid talking to her at all costs.

Once I admitted I wanted to call Gerry, I panicked when I couldn't find the number, and tipped the recycling bag out onto the floor, spreading newspapers, magazines and various abandoned homework attempts across the kitchen tiles. The screwed-up scrap of paper was caught between the pages of a furniture catalogue. The fact that I had found it generated warm satisfaction. Like solving a child's puzzle. I laughed to myself. Not that I was really worried about losing Gerry's number. I didn't *have* to call him. I simply wanted some closure.

He met me off the train at Zürich *Hauptbahnhof*. The station was typically crowded, one of Europe's major rail hubs. Travellers rushed in all directions, dozens of different languages echoing against the high roof. In the great hall beyond the boards announcing the train departures, wooden huts were opening their shutters for the imminent Christmas market.

Gerry saw me first. I looked up to see him staring at me as I walked down the platform from my train, and a tiny frisson ran down my spine. This handsome young man was waiting for *me*. I brushed off my thrill as mere wistful remembrance of youth, the fleeting moment of feeling flattered by anybody's attentions allowing me not to think about why I was really here.

We skirted the top of the *Bahnhofstrasse*, avoiding shoppers ambling along the paths bordering some of the world's most expensive real estate and boutiques, and walked towards the Limmat River. Before reaching the *Fraumünster* church we crossed the river on the *Rudolf-Brun-Brücke*.

'Who was he?' I asked, reading the plaque on the pale stone bridge.

'The first self-appointed mayor of Zürich. In the fourteenth century.'

Not merely a scientist, I thought. Gerry knew his history too. I relaxed a little. It was so refreshing to be away from the domestic routine, to be talking about something other than football schedules and dirty laundry. I didn't often come to the city, and was enjoying the immersion in some urban culture. And I had to admit I was enjoying Gerry's easy company.

I wanted to reveal nothing of my own history. I was happy Gerry was content to talk about something neutral, be the tourist guide, and didn't have a hundred questions about his father, although I knew they would come. He was being discreet, would know I was nervous after his previous visit to my home.

'What do you do in the lab? What are you studying?' I asked when his short history lesson ceased.

'I'm a chemical engineer. Working on a sustainability project. We're looking at the conversion of plastics back to oil.'

'Oh! You should know I'm the recycling queen. It's about time someone came up with a solution for all that plastic waste and overexaggerated food packaging. Very admirable.'

He turned and reached out his hand towards me. I half-flinched.

'Even that fleece you're wearing was probably made from recycled PET soft-drink bottles,' he said, touching the brand label on my upper arm.

I presented my shoulder, and watched his fingers rest briefly on the embroidered edelweiss. The wind gusted up the river from the lake, whipping little white caps against the flow of the water. Seagulls steadied themselves on the air, and I pulled the zip of my fleece up to my neck.

'Let's get a coffee. There's the Grande Café over here. We can keep warm,' he said.

Gerry took my elbow. A neutral touch, avoiding my hand. He was so relaxed, showing none of the tension I expected. I knew the questions about his father would come, but he seemed grounded, unconcerned, and his demeanour contrasted with the turmoil going on in my head. I clamped my lips together with my teeth and nodded, pulling away a wisp of hair that had blown across my eyes.

I smiled at the waitress as she placed a cup of hot water in front of me. My rosehip teabag lay in a little porcelain dish on top of the cup. I tore the cover away from the bag on its dipping string, and dunked it into the water, watching crimson swirls mix like blood. Gerry looked at the heart-shaped pattern the waitress had created on the top of his cappuccino and stirred the frothy lines into a circle. I was inexplicably jealous of this tiny, endearing gesture the waitress had performed for Gerry. Waiting for my tea to cool, I twisted the wedding band on my finger.

'I'm just remembering the first conversation we had outside your house when I discovered my father had been stalking you,' said Gerry.

The sudden mention of his father made me swallow as though I had a crust stuck in my throat. I wished we were still talking about Zürich's architecture or plastic bottles.

'I remember saying I didn't believe I would feel remorse if he had thrown himself off the Tobel Bridge,' he continued. 'But the thing is, now I think I miss him. I regret some of the things I said. I guess time can do that to you. Soften the edges.'

My eyes widened as I stared at him across the table. It was as though he was deceiving me. Ten minutes previously, he had seemed a relaxed, happy-go-lucky young man, a dynamic student on a mission to make the world a better place. I would never have thought these ideas were going through his mind while he recounted snippets of the city of Zürich's history. When I didn't say anything, he continued.

'There's this thing going on inside me, Alice. I feel like my thoughts somehow led him to complete his suicide mission. I guess I'm trying to say I somehow feel guilty. Do you know what I mean?'

I looked at him sharply. He kept calling me Alice. It was unsettling. He should have been calling me Mrs Reed. But I couldn't tell him that.

'No… Yes… I'm not sure, Gerry. I'm not sure what you mean when you say you feel guilty. You shouldn't feel responsible. You shouldn't blame yourself.'

Although I'd thought I knew what I wanted to say if he brought up his father, all the scenarios I'd practised suddenly fled my memory.

'Scientists aren't religious people in general. In fact, relatively few Swiss people attend church. I guess we have nothing to fear. It's the people who have so little in life that tend to follow a God,' he said.

Gerry looked out of the café window and I followed his gaze to the spire of the *Fraumünster*, strangely bright turquoise against the greyness of the autumnal sky.

'You know when I told you I thought my father might have found peace by taking his life? Well, I may not be a religious person, but I keep thinking he might instead be locked in some kind of hell, a punishment for what he has done. People say God's law is that it's wrong to take one's own life, that you will never be accepted into heaven.' He paused. 'There I go, talking about God again. I never go to church either. The last time was a high-school theatre production.'

Gerry's voice was becoming agitated. I squirmed in my chair as he continued.

'I believe nature didn't intend for us to waste our precious lives. I believe we are only here on this earth one time and we should make the very best of things for ourselves and our families and the people around us. But those visions of eternal hellfire – I keep having these dreams…'

I put my hand out, drew it back, then put it out again and touched his arm. He expected comfort. I should be giving it. But I didn't trust myself to touch him. His green eyes glistened in the reflection of light from the window.

'Tell me about him. About how he almost ruined your life too,' he said.

I took a deep breath, moved my hand away and leaned back a little, smoothing both my palms down my thighs under the table.

'It started with the phone calls. In the night mostly. At first when he called he wouldn't say anything, there was only silence, but I sometimes heard an intake of breath or a shift in his body, his clothes making a whisper of movement. So I knew someone was there. I suspected it was your father because he sometimes left messages on my mobile phone, and little gifts in the mailbox. Once when I caught the flu he talked to me, wanting to come and look after me. He insisted he owed me something, because I had saved his life. It was like an honour code. I could understand that at first, but things quickly got out of control.'

I bit my lip, didn't want to say too much, and thought I'd given too much detail already. But when I looked down at the table, Gerry reached across and took my chin gently between his thumb and forefinger. He lifted my face up to look at him. His touch seared my skin, left me temporarily speechless, but I could see he wanted to hear more. I rambled on, thinking this was simply a gesture of innocent concern.

'He took to waiting for hours outside the house. He would appear in weird places while I was running. He worked out all my training routes. There was this one place he would frequent at the end of the farmer's driveway. A kind of copse next to an old plum tree. One day I went there to see where he spent most of his day, and I was totally blown away by the fact that I could see right into our kitchen from there, the working centre of our home, where we all spent more time together than anywhere else in the house.'

'Jesus, Alice, that's so frustrating. I'm surprised you didn't shove those pills down his throat yourself.'

The blood drained from my face, and I felt beads of sweat prickling at my forehead. My gaze sunk back down to the table between us. When I looked up again, Gerry was staring at me intently, his head slightly to one side with what I interpreted as sympathetic curiosity. As he saw my involuntary reaction, he looked at an invisible point over my shoulder and his hands pressed into the table. He smiled, leaned back, and changed the subject.

'A marathon runner. I remember you told me when I first met you. I'm impressed.'

I breathed more easily.

'I'm not sure what I'll do for sports once the snow arrives. In previous years I was happy to put crampons on my running shoes and brave the elements when there was snow on the ground, but my ankle is still bothering me from… an injury. It's weak, and I'm nervous about pacing on unsteady and slippery ground. Do you run?'

I was relieved our conversation had turned to a more neutral subject.

'Sometimes. If I have time. I used to play ice hockey when I was younger, and I like all winter sports. We are quite a sporting nation, the Swiss.'

'A friend in the village, Esther, said she wants to take me cross-country skiing when the snow arrives. She raves about it, says if I love running, then I will love *Langlauf*.'

'It will certainly keep you fit. It's a great sport. I hope we get good snow this winter.'

Gerry looked wistfully out of the window. His thoughts seemed to lie beyond the spires and neo-classical buildings lining the Limmat River, the modern glass blocks, and the web of tramlines strung across the city. His mind was on a distant, unseen mountain, and he suddenly appeared out of place in this urban environment.

He looked back at me, and caught my studious stare. Before I could react, he leaned across the table to place a straggle of hair behind my ear. I retracted as he did this. The movement was tender, reinforcing his earlier touch to my chin, a parent taking a moment to fuss over his child. I thought this an oddly tactile display from a Swiss person. I blushed and searched my handbag for my wallet to pay for the drinks. As I rummaged in the bag, the shiny stud on Gerry's leather friendship band caught my eye.

'Oh, I forgot! You left this at our house.'

I held up the braided bracelet and he took it with a smile and put it in his pocket.

CHAPTER FIFTY-SIX

WE LEFT THE café and waited for a tram to pass before crossing the road to the bank of the river. A little girl dressed in a pale-pink puffer jacket and fluffy bobble hat was throwing pieces of bread into the water. Ducks rushed back and forth on the swirling eddies for the morsels, and seagulls hovered above, hoping for more airborne crumbs. Their plaintive screeching seemed so out of place in this landlocked nation, thousands of miles from the ocean.

We laughed at the flurry of birds, and it was as though our tensions had been left behind in the café. It felt good to laugh, and I shook my hair in the wind, realising I hadn't felt so free for many months. Moving away from the birds, we crossed the bridge and leaned against the stone balustrade. We watched the grey waters emptying out of the *Zürisee*, mesmerised by the eddies. I experienced a brief compulsion to throw myself into the river.

'God, I just had that feeling I wanted to jump. Fling myself in,' I said.

As soon as I'd spoken, I put my hand to my mouth, remembering Gerry's father standing on the edge of a bridge. I searched Gerry's face. He combed his fingers through his hair in the breeze and threw his head back to laugh. I took my hand slowly away and, before I could react, Gerry clasped his hand round the back of my neck and brushed his lips against mine. I closed my eyes.

In a moment it was over. He released his fingers from my hair and was already looking across the river when I opened my eyes. My stomach turned to liquid fire, and blood rushed to my cheeks. I touched my lips with two fingers.

He kissed me!

'You shouldn't have done that.'

'No, I… *Entschuldigen*. Sorry,' he said.

He watched the water, some memory, perhaps not me, causing him to smile. Then he turned and took hold of my arm, lifted my hand. He carefully placed the friendship band around my wrist and clicked the brass stud closed. The touch of the leather and his fingers on the skin of my inner wrist sent a shiver up my arm. I wanted to snatch my hand away, afraid of the sensations my body was involuntarily experiencing.

'There,' he said. 'Friends.'

I pushed away from the railing, and shoved my hands deep in my pockets. Gerry companionably stuck an arm between my elbow and my side as I started walking, and the movement caused our bodies to bounce together. I stared ahead, knowing he was watching me. I concentrated on the path in front of me, and increased my pace towards the station. I finally took my hands from my pockets, if only to release his hold on my arm. *I should be getting home.* A chill wind whipped a crisp packet and an old tissue in a mini tornado in front of us.

'Not often you see rubbish on these streets,' I marvelled, knowing I had to speak, to break my mood.

'Alice, forget about the rubbish. I need to talk to you again. I need to see you.'

'Gerry, don't. I… I have to talk about the rubbish. It's keeping me grounded,' I whispered.

As my eyes inexplicably began to water in the wind, I smiled, and Gerry laughed.

'The rubbish it is. The rubbish of life!' he shouted rakishly, causing me to look around and see whether we had attracted any attention. My reaction confirmed that I was far from indifferent to his kiss.

'I rather like seeing it, the rubbish,' he continued. 'Like a statement of something free in our rather constipated society, don't you think? I sometimes have the compulsion to go out and join the secret graffiti artists along the sidings of the *Hauptbahnhof*. It's one of the only places you can still see an increase in what you would call vandalism. I think it's a beautiful statement, against all this stifled perfection.'

I frowned. This young man was so unpredictable. The kiss forgotten. Or perhaps not.

But it was imperative we both forget it.

'It's the very thing I have come to love about Switzerland,' I said. 'The cleanliness. Every time I visit my relatives and friends in England and see the chaotic traffic and struggling economy, the shabby houses and crumbling roads, I always breathe a sigh of relief when I step off that plane back in Zürich. It feels more like coming home each time.'

'Do you think you will stay here? I mean long-term?' he asked.

I had to believe this was all now small talk, that there wasn't any hidden wish or meaning in his chatter.

He kissed me!

'There's every possibility Simon will eventually be running the office in Zug. The boys are now pretty much fully integrated into the local school. Yes, I could see myself staying here. It's a good life we have.'

I didn't feel like talking about Simon and the boys. I wanted to keep them separate from the little bubble I'd put myself into this afternoon. It was my fault. I still couldn't forget Gerry was the son of Manfred, and having lived with his father's presence for so many months, I now wanted to put light years between my family and anything to do with him, and that included his son.

'I cannot tell you how much I appreciate your meeting me, Alice. I know you don't want to hear this, but it has helped me understand better my own emotions about my father. It has helped me to find some peace in the fact that we, my mother and I, didn't want to know anything about him. And yet, when we found out he had taken his life, we both felt a little of the guilt someone might experience in our situation, even though we knew we had done everything possible for him, tried to help him. He might one day have driven us mad with his own version of insanity.'

At the mention of the word 'guilt', my heart thudded and I quickened my pace towards the station. My throat was hot. As much as I was enjoying the company of this erudite young man, I knew I had to get away from him, aware his magnetism was proving dangerous. It was hard to focus. I was unsure whether the queasiness in my stomach was because he kept reminding me of Manfred, or because I might never see him again.

We walked into the station from the entrance facing the *Bahnhofquai*, and the bustle of the Christmas market greeted us through the tall doors. People meandered through the market, interspersed with those rushing for their trains, and I glanced at my watch. There were still twenty minutes before my train was due to leave.

'Do you have time to look?' Gerry asked, as though reading my thoughts.

I tipped my head to one side in uncertain assent, and he took my elbow, guiding me towards a stall selling spicy warm *Gluhwein*. The twinkling of a hundred thousand glass crystals on the Swarovski Christmas tree winked their reflections around the little wooden chalets of the market stalls.

'*Zum wohl.*'

Gerry clinked my plastic cup and for a horrible moment I remembered another time, another night, clinking plastic picnic cups, the ruby wine less sweet on our lips.

MY HEART CONTINUED to thud until the train pulled silently out of the station. I stared out of the window across the complex spaghetti network of dozens of railway tracks. The grand buildings of the insurance companies and banks, with their old Napoleonic architecture, were slotted between ultra-modern blocks of smoked glass. The train picked up speed and, as it descended into an underpass, Gerry's graffiti came into view, some freshly sprayed onto a recently poured concrete wall hemming in the tracks.

He kissed me.

I should have felt terrible. Surely it was just a young man's prank, a tease? All right, he kissed me, but I didn't kiss him back. Much.

I concentrated on Simon. I tried to remember our lovemaking on the night of the opera. I pictured Simon's faithful face and recalled the years we'd spent so comfortably with each other. I thought of the family we'd built together. I had no intention of destroying any of that. With Manfred a septic influence in our lives, I'd already come too close to the edge of sanity once.

And then I remembered how Simon had left me to deal with the whole stalking challenge by myself. Granted, he was busy with a massive project at work. But his reactions were far from sympathetic, especially the worse Manfred's obsession became. I thought of Simon telling me to sort myself out, to get it straight in my mind what was going on. That it was up to me.

But now there was this connection to Manfred's son. It was all too close to home.

He kissed me.

What did I think I was getting myself into?

CHAPTER FIFTY-SEVEN

I SIGNED FOR the box and warned the postman about the slippery patch of packed snow on the driveway. He smiled and told me not to worry. His post van's tyres were studded. The vehicle could navigate the slickest of hills. The most dangerous part of his journey was always walking between the post boxes and his vehicle. It made me think he could have made use of the running crampons I hadn't yet taken out of the cupboard. I glanced at the shovel in the corner of the porch and turned back to scrutinise my most un-Swiss shovelling handiwork in the driveway.

In the kitchen I unwrapped the package. It was a bottle of Swiss red wine, a Merlot from Ticino. I figured it must be from one of Simon's customers. Strange it was addressed to both of us, and had been sent to our home address. I picked out the padded packaging, and found a note in the bottom of the box.

To Alice and Simon,
I wish you a joyous Advent.
Best wishes,
Gerry Guggenbuhl

For a moment I thought I was going to be sick in the kitchen sink. I read only the name Guggenbuhl and irrationally thought the gift had come from Manfred. Gerry's name on the card caught up with me moments later and I let out a nervous laugh before taking a deep breath. This gesture was too close to the gifts his father used to leave. I hoped Gerry had no idea he'd mirrored an act of his father. I hoped his intention was an innocent gesture of gratitude.

Back outside later, I watched Simon drive towards the house, leaning against my shovel as I waited for him to park. I frowned at the sky, threatening to render my work invisible by later that evening. I'd cleared the snow from the door to the garage so he could drive straight in. He pecked me on the cheek as he joined me, and we walked into the house together.

I'd forgotten to clear away the bottle and its packaging from the kitchen counter. My hair crackled with static as I removed my bobble hat, and my jovial mood chilled when Simon picked up the note. The heat of the house suddenly overwhelmed me, and I tore off my ski jacket.

'You have got to be kidding me,' Simon said. 'Does he think he can take over where his arsehole father left off? Is he trying to step into his shoes?'

I bit my tongue, knowing that had also been my first thought. Simon's sarcasm made me immediately want to defend Gerry.

'Simon, he is not his father. He's probably as relieved as we are his father is gone.'

I sucked my lip. That sounded harsh. Simon looked at me curiously.

'I mean, this is either a peace offering or a kind of apology for all we've had to put up with.'

I was back-pedalling, trying to justify why the son of our stalker had sent us a Christmas gift. The last thing I wanted to do was tell him we'd met. Ordinarily that shouldn't have bothered Simon. But I knew he wanted to forget about the last few months as much as I did. He wanted to forget that his wife had made some bizarre and inexplicable decisions. He wanted to forget a stalker had almost destroyed our family. Almost. And he wanted to forget any memory of, or connection to, that awful person.

But Simon hadn't lived with it quite like I had. He hadn't had to deal with the uncertainty and confusion for those months. I'd had to do that alone. He'd only had to live with me. I, on the other hand, had had to live with them all.

'Probably a cheap, crap wine. We can always give it to someone else. You know, the dreaded bottle that gets passed around – taken to everyone's dinner parties.'

Simon looked at me pointedly before heading upstairs to change out of his work clothes.

We would not be drinking Gerry's wine.

I picked up the card and read it again, noting the haphazard cursive loop of the 'l' in 'Alice', hinting at his jauntiness. The card was neutral grey with no printed inscription. I touched the writing, drew my hand away and put the card down.

I stared at the bottle and rubbed my arms. This felt wrong. Too many messages to be misinterpreted. I stared out of the kitchen window at the snowflakes, blowing like cherry blossoms sideways in a bizarre reversal of seasons across the field beside the house.

WHILE SIMON SAT with Leo at the kitchen table after dinner practising algebra for a test, I went to the office and wrote a note to Gerry. The giving of gifts, the need for contact… these things should not start a trend. I refused to believe Gerry was displaying the same traits as his father. I recalled childish bouquets of wildflowers picked from the fields near the house in spring, a punnet of cherries bought at the summer fair, a handful of *Steinpilze* mushrooms from the forest with peaty earth still clinging to their papery stalks. Showers of gifts that had stopped just a few weeks ago.

Dear Gerry,

Simon and I thank you for the wine you so thoughtfully sent. However, we must insist that your generosity stops here. However grateful you have been for my counsel and help following the death of your father, I think it would now be wise for everybody concerned that we don't meet each other again. It is time for me to rebuild the blocks that have shifted in our family over the past months. I wish you and your mother a joyous Christmas and a prosperous New Year.

How to sign off? What the hell was I supposed to write? In the end I signed it simply *Alice*.

The trouble was, the rules had become distinctly murky in my mind. On a random day in spring, Gerry's father, Manfred, had misinterpreted my euphoric relief at saving him from suicide on that miserable bridge as budding affection.

I was sure Gerry had misinterpreted nothing.

I was sure, because I knew what he had seen in my eyes.

CHAPTER FIFTY-EIGHT

'IS THERE ANY way you'd ever consider moving back to England?'

I glanced at Simon as he lowered his book to his chest. We were lying side by side in bed waiting for the boys to fall asleep. Our plan was to sneak into their rooms and take the stockings off their beds to fill in the quiet of our own bedroom.

'I really miss Mum at this time of year,' I continued. 'Even though she's gone, I sometimes wonder if it wouldn't be best if we were closer to our relatives, sparse as they may be, scattered across the UK.'

Tears sprang inexplicably to my eyes.

'We're not enough for you, Al?'

Simon patted my arm paternally and a seed of resentment burned in the back of my throat. I knew he didn't mean to be callous, but my sudden desire to move away from all this, to get away from my unpredictable emotions, had been evoked by my meeting with Gerry. I knew we were on dangerous ground.

'I also feel like we should move far away from here after all the stuff that's happened this year.'

'Because some overgrown kid with a nutter for a father sends you a bottle of wine? Come on, Al, aren't you overreacting a bit?'

'I guess I'm just down on the whole Swiss thing at the moment. I can't get over how the police didn't do anything about Manfred when he was alive, but are spending so much time trying to work out what happened now he's gone. Don't they get it? It's making me hate the system. The system that's supposed to be so perfect and bound with red tape, where everything is examined with a fine-tooth comb, but then, when it comes to us, the measly foreigners in the equation, we're not given the slightest attention. That's what makes me want to move, Simon. And besides… this apartment. I know it's quaint and traditional, and every Swiss Family Robinson's dream, but it's suffocating me. I feel like there are too many bad memories. I can't shake them.'

'Seriously? I always thought you were positive enough to move on from it, Alice. You surprise me.'

Simon turned, leaned his head on his elbow. His hand closed gently around my wrist, and he hooked his little finger under the leather friendship band.

'You wearing that old thing you found? Does Leo know you're stealing his hippy fashion accessories?'

I shoved my arm under the duvet. It had been inevitable that Simon would mention it, but I'd never taken it off, and almost forgotten I still wore it. How stupid.

Simon traced his finger down the buttons on my nightshirt. I put my hand over his.

'If you don't want to move back to England, I think we should move house. Find a new apartment,' I said.

A seed of relief bloomed in the back of my mind, and I realised in my heart I hadn't really wanted to move back to England. The reason for my drastic suggestion was dead. His memory would surely fade. And Manfred *was* the only reason, I thought.

Simon feathered his fingers against my thigh. He wasn't taking me seriously. Before he could slip his hand under my nightie, I climbed out of bed and went down the hallway to fetch the empty stockings from the boys' beds.

Leo lay very still. I could hardly hear him breathing, which made me think he was still awake but feigning sleep. I recognised the tension in his body, reflecting my own skill over the past few months. Oliver's outward breath blew comical steady puffs through his lips, confirming without a doubt he was sleeping.

This childhood ritual was more for his benefit than Leo's. Both boys had long given up believing in Father Christmas, or the *Christkind*, as the secret bringer of gifts was known here. But I clung to the excitement Christmas afforded, especially as sporadic snow over the past week meant that, this year, our alpine Christmas would again be truly white. Who in their right mind would want to move back to England when they had this magic on their doorstep?

I returned to our bedroom and placed the stockings on our bed.

'Al, this apartment is great for us. It's just outside the village, with perfect access to the trails, and I love being immersed in nature here, so close to the forest. I don't want to move. Perhaps you should give yourself more time to think about this. You've hardly been in the most stable frame of mind over the past few months.'

I pulled out a shopping bag I had hidden behind the door earlier in the evening, and emptied the contents onto the bed.

'I can't seem to get over the fact that our space was violated by Manfred. Surely you can empathise with that emotion.' I tried not to sound petulant.

Simon's tongue sucked lightly against his teeth.

'Jesus, Al, the guy's dead,' he said loudly, making me jump. 'You don't believe in ghosts, do you? He's gone, not coming back. Can we move on, without moving out, so to speak? As I said, give it time!'

'Hush. You'll wake the boys. It's just me, I guess. That's how I feel. Surely my opinion counts for something? It's plaguing me. I assure you, I wish I could shake it.'

'And you think moving house is going to solve that? You didn't bring this up when he was alive.'

That had been sitting in the back of my own mind. I stared at the pile of gimmicky little gifts now spread on our bed. The sudden flash of anger in his voice was dangerously raw. It made me wonder who I wanted to run away from. Christmas Eve wasn't the time to be driving nails between us.

'If it's that important to you, Al, I guess we could consider a move. But we're approaching the middle of winter now, so there won't be any places advertised yet. No one moves during the snow season. It's too much hassle. It's even written into our contract we can only move three times a year: spring, summer and autumn.'

We began splitting the little gifts – mandarins, chocolates and nuts – between the two stockings.

'Aren't the boys a bit old for this malarkey, by the way?'

Simon picked up a wind-up toy – a pair of chattering dentures he'd chosen himself from a toy shop last week – and stuffed it into Oliver's stocking.

It was time to make peace. I didn't want to end the conversation on a fractious note and experience yet another restless night worrying about our delicate relationship.

'I guess you're right. About the move. It's the one disadvantage of living in a mountain community. We can realistically only move during the snow-free months. We're in the midst of that famous dead-rental period.'

'If it's that important to you, Al, we can revisit this in spring. But you know I'm really happy where we live, and the boys love it here.'

As we each took a stocking to place on the end of the boys' beds, I made a mental note to study the local papers, contact the estate agents and look on the noticeboard at the village Co-op.

Carefully closing their door, we reunited in the hallway and Simon, knowing the spirit of Christmas shouldn't be ruined over the next few days, took my hand as we tiptoed back to our room.

We lay in bed and Simon pulled me towards him affectionately. I tucked my head into the crook of his shoulder, my heart still beating with the tension of our conversation. Listening to the blanketed silence beyond our windows, interrupted only by the ticking of a radiator, I blinked hard in the dark. My head rose and fell gently as Simon's breath deepened. His heart beat steadily against my ear and I finally fell into a fitful sleep, wondering whether moving house would solve any of my own internal issues.

I AM SPRAWLED on a satin swirl of cool bed sheets, my legs intertwined with the muscular thighs of an unfamiliar body. The man in whose arms I lie has a wavy shock of brown hair. The tendons in his shoulders flex as he shifts away from me and moves down my body. His kisses flutter like moths on my skin. My heart thumps in my chest. I'm filled with a longing need. I want him to be part of me. This is wrong. It's not Simon. But I can't stop myself. He's touching me, touching me. The agony of the ecstasy. I look up, into the smoky green eyes of Gerry.

Where is Simon? How did I get here? What am I doing? I panic. How can I be cheating on Simon? I resist, but so want this feeling to continue. Passion is singing through my veins. I am out of control. This feels so right. But it's wrong. Oh, oh, oh. It's a dream.

I woke up breathing heavily. My legs moved over each other in the bed. My heart continued to beat hard, and there was a slight throbbing sensation between my thighs, my lower abdomen tight. I was lying on my side, and squeezed my legs together to try and calm the feeling in my stomach. As I brought my knees into a foetal position my legs swished under the duvet.

'Baby?' Simon murmured. 'Are you awake?'

'Yes, I… I had a strange dream. I…'

Before I could continue, Simon moved towards me and pressed himself into my back. He was hard. His hand reached around my arm and grazed my nipple. I gasped, and a shudder ran through me. He parted my thighs from behind and slipped into me.

'Honey, I…' Simon silenced me with a deep thrust.

I wanted to tell him I didn't want this. I wanted my emotions about moving house acknowledged. That issue couldn't be resolved with sex. When we'd made love last time, after the company evening out, I didn't know when Simon would touch me again. Why did he suddenly want me now?

As the memory of my dream bloomed hot in my head, an animal need now eclipsed any mental solution I might have been seeking in the dark. Simon moved rhythmically. I reached behind me to grasp his hip, encouraging him.

Waking in the middle of the night and simultaneously rising to passion had filled me with a sense of feral fascination. It was blocking all other feelings, my compulsive need for an almost violent act overwhelming. It was as though my dream, which had left me crying out for release, had awoken an equal and inexplicable passion in Simon, my pheromones dragging him from his own slumber.

Suddenly he was thrusting harder into me. He had never possessed me like this. This was not making love, it was... I didn't know. He pushed again and again. I felt his teeth against my shoulder. He pinched my nipple between his thumb and forefinger. The pain was exquisite. I closed my eyes. My hips pressed backwards to meet his, our movements now urgent. I wanted to cry out. Simon put his hand over my mouth, perhaps afraid I would wake the children.

The tumultuous relief I had been craving was ready to split open. The pleasure. The pain. And with eyes clenched tightly closed, the vision of Gerry swam before me, and I was riding the wave of a pulsing climax, on fire. As much as I tried to eliminate his face from my mind, it was Gerry whose sinuous body was tucked behind me, Gerry who had given me release.

I lay with the crumpled duvet twisted around my lower legs, lungs heaving and a swathe of perspiration cooling the space between my breasts. Our unresolved conversation was forgotten, forced into oblivion by the lasting, horrifying vision of someone else in my marital bed.

Deeply disturbed by a rising self-loathing, I opened my eyes and tried to turn to gaze at Simon's face. But he was a shadow in the dark, and I could not eliminate the feeling that it was Gerry's hot body entangled with mine.

My beating heart calmed and I imagined there was a logical explanation for thoughts of Gerry creeping in beside those of the husband I so desperately wanted to reconnect with.

Should either of these men discover my secret, it would manifest a drastically different reaction in each of them. The revelation to one would destroy my family, the other, my freedom. And like all good, well-kept secrets, it had become a simmering infection in my mind. The deceptions piled in, one on top of the other now, creating an avalanche of shame.

It was only my confused exhaustion that stopped me experiencing my mental adultery with alarming clarity.

CHAPTER FIFTY-NINE
JANUARY

AN INFANTILE SQUEAL of frustration escaped my mouth as my legs slid out from under me and I collapsed onto the snow. An initial flash of anger at myself simmered down to a bout of giggling as I looked over to Esther, who had a gloved hand in front of her mouth to stifle her own laughter.

'Oh, my God. It's so hard. These skis are so skinny,' I screeched, still laughing.

She sidestepped towards me and took my arm to pull me up.

'Here, use your stick to push against the ground.'

I did as Esther instructed, trying not to put too much weight on the delicate and seemingly fragile pole, and together with her help managed to stand upright. I teetered on the thin skis, gathered my balance and brushed the snow from my backside.

It was a beautiful day. Above us a cloudless, cornflower-blue sky stretched to the snow-laden peaks of the Glarner Alps. There was a hint of warmth from the sun on our faces on an otherwise sub-zero morning with no wind. The temperature had rendered the snow squeaky, but kept it soft. The corrugation of the groomed *Loipe* stretched its ribbed lines to a stark point of perspective in the distance, a geometrical juxtaposition to our natural alpine surroundings. There were barely any traces on the loop at this time of the morning, with few skiers having yet arrived.

'Come on, Alice. This is what you'd call payback time for all the help you've given us in the Chat Club.'

Four of us had driven the short distance over the saddle at the end of the Aegeri Valley, our skis jumbled into the rear of my Land Rover, with the backseat down. Esther had already tried to allay my doubts about the day's venture. We were taking

249

time out from English lessons and taking a lesson in something completely different. Esther, an avid cross-country skier, was curious to see whether I wanted to learn her sport.

'I'm sure this will be healthier for you than all that long-distance running.'

'I'm definitely open to finding an alternative way to keep fit over the winter. And to be perfectly honest, I've grown tired of alpine skiing – though please don't tell the boys. I can't stand all that lugging heavy equipment around and waiting for hours in lift queues.'

'You'll find the calmness of the *Langlaufloipe* far more agreeable,' she said.

'That's all very well for you to say, you're an expert.'

I hoped my beginner's performance wouldn't hinder the girls.

'Esther grew up on skis,' said one of the other women. 'She will be your best teacher. It runs in the family.'

'My father comes from this village, Rothenthurm. Generations of us have grown up on skis. In his twenties, he won the local *Volksskilauf*, People's Ski Race, several times. We may see a few racers training today. The annual event will take place in two weeks' time. If you're a natural, we shall register you for the race by the end of the day.'

I spluttered, but knew she was joking.

I realised it had been a long time since I'd been in the company of a handful of women, discussing something other than the construction of the English language, or the perils of being stalked. I relaxed, enjoying this moment of sisterly camaraderie.

The other two women waited patiently at the start of the ski loop while Esther made sure I was steady on my feet.

'Maybe I should have started out with the classic style first. Isn't that easier?'

'I think, in the end, you will enjoy skating more. Although it takes more energy here...' She tapped her thigh with her hand. 'You will have less pain in your ankle.'

'They're so narrow, compared to alpine skis.'

'And lighter. Not so much for the *lugging around*.' Esther smiled.

The sensation of free heels on the skis was unfamiliar. I had assumed my experience on alpine skis might help, but had been a little shocked to find myself floundering with a different set of equipment.

Esther patiently showed me, with very slow, exaggerated movements, how to push off, first with one ski and then the other in a sweeping skating movement. She made it look so easy, so graceful. She told me to practise back and forth on the first two-hundred-metre section of the loop, which was flat and wide, easy to navigate.

'Take a little time here to get accustomed to the movement on the skis. I come back and check on you in a little while. That's good.'

Esther left me with her encouraging words and joined the other two women to ski a quick loop on the short training circuit.

I watched them skate gracefully away, envying them their experience, and continued to practise. My attempt at skating felt more like plodding on the snow, and I was unsure what to do with my poles. Beginning to wobble, I accidentally caught the basket of my pole underneath my right ski and ended up on the ground again, sprawling inelegantly on the snow. Resting a moment before expending the effort to get back on my feet, I felt truly incapable.

'*Gaht's, da?*' asked a voice above me. '*Hier, nimm mini Hand.*'

I huffed, looked up, and squinted at a person offering his hand to help me, face silhouetted against the morning sun.

'*Danke!*' I said as I grabbed the hand. The man's strong grip pulled me easily to my feet as his own skis blocked mine from sliding forward. I stood up, untangled my hand from the straps of the pole grip, and began slapping the snow from the side of my thigh.

'Hello, Alice. I thought I recognised you,' said the voice of my rescuer.

My heart jumped as I turned to see Gerry, a ski hat pulled tightly over his normally abundant wavy hair, eyes hidden behind almond-shaped sunglasses.

'Gerry! What are you doing here?'

I was embarrassed *he* had had to scoop me off the ground. My belly clenched. I blushed furiously, thinking my statement might have sounded rude.

'I mean, of course you're skiing, but I didn't know you were a cross-country skier. You come here to skate?'

He didn't have to justify why he was there. These were questions I had no business asking. He had a right to be there, just like any other skier. I made it sound like he was intruding on my territory somehow. As though this was more than just a coincidence. That couldn't be. He was not his father. I was angry with myself for feeling so defensive, giving away undefined emotions. My overreaction implied that the coincidence might be of my making, and I regretted asking. I was behaving like a star struck teenager.

Gerry laughed.

'I think there are a few of us in this country who put a pair of skis on our feet from time to time,' he said mockingly, but with a smile. 'And I even know a few runners who exchange their shoes for skis in winter. But I can see you might need a little time to adjust.'

My cheeks burned, and I hoped the crispness of the morning would cover my self-consciousness.

Gerry turned to his two companions and said something to them in Swiss German. They waved, and skated away. I assumed he would catch up with them in a minute, part of me hoping he would go soon, but another part of me hoping inexplicably that he would stay a moment longer.

'My friend Esther has been showing me a few basic moves, but I've yet to master them efficiently. You all make it look so easy,' I said, exasperated.

'Come, skate with me for a few metres,' he offered.

I looked round to see whether Esther and her friends were close to completing the training loop. They were still far off in the distance, on the outer edge of the circuit. I recognised Esther's pink hat and turquoise sport pants.

'Okay,' I said tentatively. Gerry stepped over to stand beside me.

'Look at your hands,' he said. 'Keep them always in front, but plant your pole beside your foot here. If it's too far forward you will hurt your shoulders. And when you skate off, point your nose in the direction of the ski, not straight ahead. It is a diagonal, side-to-side movement, like a pendulum. Like this…'

Gerry pushed off on one ski in a long glide, then moved his body to the other side in a graceful, sweeping movement, his poles pushing behind him in perfect synchrony. I tried not to watch the muscles above his knee tense and knot, his athletic thighs straining against his black winter Lycra.

After a few skating movements, Gerry stopped about thirty metres along the flat trail. I gathered myself, pushed off, and tried to copy his style. My pace was less efficient than his and my balance was still shaky, but I understood the pendulum metaphor and exaggerated it to increase my glide. I was pleased with myself; I was finally getting it. I stopped in front of Gerry, laughing with delight.

'That's it!' he said. 'You should practise that up and down this flat part a few times before going any distance. Try to stay on each ski for as long as possible to get used to the balance. It's also good to practise with your poles tucked under your arms like this, to improve your steadiness on your skis. Then you won't worry about getting the poles caught under your skis and tripping. I think you will do well. You're a natural.'

'Pah! You're overgenerous,' I said with a laugh.

I could see Esther skating over a small incline to reach the end of the training loop.

Gerry hadn't mentioned the letter I sent. Perhaps I should have said something. It was almost as though he hadn't received it. But he hadn't called me either after our meeting in Zürich. It had been almost a month. And in between we'd celebrated a family Christmas and set ourselves New Year's resolutions. Perhaps he was sensible enough to have moved on from it all.

No need to ask any more questions about his father. And hopefully he didn't feel the need for us to see each other.

But now he was there, I realised it wasn't like I didn't think about it at least once a day. Memories of that dream still made me blush.

I worried he might mention something about his father. It was still our only thin connection. He'd seemed so desperate for me to help him with some answers a few weeks previously in Zürich. Under different circumstances, I would have been flattered by his attention.

'I should join my friends,' I said hastily. 'Thanks so much for the tips, Gerry.'

'It's a pleasure, Alice. Maybe I'll see you around. I often come here on Tuesday or Thursday lunchtimes with my friends. On those days my courses at the university don't start until 3.00 p.m. *Tschüss!*' he shouted jovially, and turned to leave.

He was doing exactly what my head had wanted him to seconds before, but a part of my heart wished I wasn't watching him skate away. I studied his professional style and lithe legs. I laughed inside. I would never do anything to jeopardise my relationship with Simon, however fragile it was at the moment. But I was allowed to admire a handsome body when I saw one. Gerry must have known I was watching. I had no control over the messages my body was giving out. But despite his attractiveness, it didn't make sense. His father's son.

I vowed never to see him again.

'You are making some friends,' said Esther as she skied up to me, making me jump.

'I already knew him. He's the son of...'

I was about to tell Esther that he was the son of the stalker, but something made me hesitate. The chapter of our lives involving Manfred Guggenbuhl was over. I wanted to move on. Esther had been part of that story, but there was no harm in lying about Gerry's identity. It would avoid any awkward questions. It felt good to pretend he was just a handsome young lad who had rescued me from a fall. I could live with that fantasy.

'He's the son of someone Simon knows at work,' I lied smoothly.

'He skis well. Is he training for the race?' asked Esther, following my gaze. I shook my head, more to clear my thoughts than to answer Esther's question.

'I don't know,' I said vaguely, then more determined, 'Okay, Esti, let's crack this thing.'

I followed her back onto the training loop, waddling as though I had a pair of diving flippers on my feet. The two other women skated off to find a longer circuit, and Esther stayed with me for another hour or so, until my marked improvement once again deteriorated with increased fatigue.

Casting a brief backwards glance to the *Loipe*, we loaded the car up with our skis and made our way home.

CHAPTER SIXTY
MARCH

'I NEED TO TALK to you,' Gerry pleaded.

My heart raced. I couldn't control the reaction, although it had been weeks since we had seen each other on the *Langlaufloipe*. He called me on my mobile as I was driving, and although I answered on the hands-free system, I had to pull into a layby because I couldn't concentrate.

'The police have contacted me,' he said.

My stomach lurched, and I was glad I'd stopped driving.

'Isn't the case closed? Why do they keep hassling you?' I asked carefully.

'Some final loose ends to tie up, I guess. It's horrible, though, Alice. They still have his body in the morgue. They haven't been able to release it yet because of their... investigation. I wish this thing could be finished. It has been weeks. We need to bury him.'

Indeed we do, I thought. We needed to bury this whole affair.

'I thought... you didn't care what happened to his body. Are you planning a memorial service?' I bit my lip.

'I cannot believe it is taking so long. It is confusing.'

'Don't they think you've been through enough?'

I wondered if he still needed reassurance that he had done nothing wrong, or if he simply needed to hear the sound of my voice.

'Can I see you, Alice? I need to ask you something.'

'I've told you I think it's better we don't see each other. You... I... There are some feelings it would be a good idea not to encourage.'

'So you admit you have some feelings for me?'

'That's not what I'm saying. I mean *your* feelings for *me*.'

My head felt hot, and a dull ache developed in my belly.

'It's dangerous for us to see each other.'

'Not for me, Alice. I have nothing to be scared of. Do you have something to be scared of?'

'Stop digging, Gerry. You know why. I'm married with a family. A family that needs and loves me.'

I thought of Simon, of his reluctance to share my enjoyment on the cross-country trail. He'd given it a go a couple of weeks ago and said it wasn't for him. I was trying to find something we could do together as a couple, something to help us reconnect. I was frightened of what I couldn't control.

'Alice, it is not about my physical attraction to you…'

The phrase 'physical attraction' sent an electric current through me. I could no longer trust my body when I heard Gerry's voice. What the hell was happening to me? Just because of some stupid dream and memories of a brief kiss? It was insane to be entertaining any thought of an attachment to this… this boy. Keeping a line of communication open was only tempting fate.

But his next words stopped me in my tracks.

'The police have some questions about the substances found in my father's blood at the autopsy. And something you asked me some months ago, about the medication my father was taking, jogged my memory. I need to talk to you, to settle my own mind. Not on the phone.'

I swallowed, the lump in my throat so hard I was sure he could hear. The last thing I now wanted to do was meet him face to face. I knew I would unravel.

'The thing is, Gerry, I just can't see you.'

I heard him draw in a breath. Perhaps he assumed I couldn't trust myself with him. This was true, certainly, but the real reason was that people's suspicions were making me nervous.

'Alice, please, I must see you.'

His voice was pleading, and my head began to spin. I made myself think of Simon, the last time he had looked at me so lovingly in the bathroom mirror, months ago. I thought of the boys and their craving for independence. Their attempts to make us think they didn't need us any more, while still secretly enjoying the attention bestowed upon them during events such as holidays and Christmas.

But it was no good. His plea sucked me up.

'All right. I'll meet you. But I can't promise you much time. Things around here have become somewhat... hectic.'

'Alice, have you not told your husband we have met?'

I flushed. The question was loaded with innuendo. I couldn't lie. If I told him the truth, which was no, it would confirm to Gerry that my feelings might not be completely platonic. Yet if I told him yes, that Simon knew all about him, I feared a petulant reaction might trigger something else, something floating on a wave of jealousy. Instead of answering I said:

'We'll meet in Allenwinden. I'll park near the post office. We can walk if we want; it's not far to the Wildenburg ruins. I can meet you after lunch on Tuesday or Thursday. Then you won't miss class.'

'You remembered! Tuesday is good.'

Yes, I remembered. Not just when Gerry had classes. I also remembered he was almost young enough to be my own son.

'Goodbye, Gerry.' I rang off before he replied.

It wasn't until I was about to start the engine that I realised I'd parked near the road leading to the Tobel Bridge. I changed my mind, pulled the key out of the ignition and got out of the car.

As I walked towards the bridge, something was different, although it had been months since I was last there, in another season. Rising from the walls of the bridge on either side were panels of reinforced glass, fixed to the top of the concrete wall with solid steel brackets. The glass glinted in the daylight. I pressed my hands against the panes, leaned my forehead against their frosty coolness and stared at the gorge below, distorted through the thick glass.

I hadn't heard people talking about this installation. Wouldn't Kathy have said something? Simon maybe? I reached up to the top of a panel, my arm stretched almost to its full extent, fingers folding over the top. The strength it would have taken to pull myself up and topple over the lip would have been too much.

And although Manfred was taller than me, he could never have made the extra effort to haul himself over the top of this barrier. For Manfred, and for me, this addition had come too late.

My fingers remained hooked over the top of the panel, and I leaned into the wall, my eyes closed. I reflected on the fantasy I had briefly conjured. That none of it had ever happened. That I had never seen Manfred that day on the bridge.

A car beeped its horn as it drove past, making me jump. I turned to look. The driver's mouth formed an 'O', his passenger craning back to watch me, wondering what I was doing on the bridge.

CHAPTER SIXTY-ONE

THE FOLLOWING TUESDAY, I drove to Allenwinden and parked in the middle of the village. Gerry was already there, sitting on a wall outside the village shop. His jean-clad legs were stretched casually out in front of him. He was watching me as I pulled up in the Land Rover. He combed his hair with his fingers before standing, and I tore my gaze away to manoeuvre the car into a parking space. As I pulled the key from the ignition, I glanced in the rear-view mirror and tucked a ringlet of hair behind my ear. I caught Gerry smiling at me and pressed my lips together, knowing he'd seen me check myself in the mirror.

'Hello, Alice, it's good to see you again.'

Before I could react, he was holding both my arms and kissing me three times on the cheeks in the traditional Swiss greeting. My heart was still beating from his approach. I thought he was going to kiss me on the lips and I turned my head slightly towards him. The result was our noses bumped a little awkwardly before his lips brushed my cheek, and I felt foolish.

'Let's walk. There's a footpath out towards the forest over here. The exercise will do us both good,' I said more casually than I felt.

I shoved my hands deep into my jacket pockets as we wandered through the school grounds towards the trailhead

'I've been stuck inside the lab all morning, and I'm sick of the smell of sulphuric acid,' Gerry said. 'I hope I don't smell of chemicals.'

Apples, balsam, laundry detergent, I wanted to tell him. I wondered if his mother still laundered his clothes.

The path took us around the edge of a sports field where a game of soccer was taking place. The occasional shouts from the kids drifted to us across the grass and I felt somehow safer with young children in the proximity.

'You mentioned the police had contacted you again,' I said.

'They asked me about the medication my father was taking at the time of his suicide.'

'Mmm?'

My heart hammered, but I remained outwardly calm.

'And I remembered I'd given it to you from our medicine cabinet. I didn't say anything, but wondered if you still had it.'

My mouth went dry. If they had done an autopsy on Manfred, they would certainly have identified the Quilonorm in his system.

'I went to visit your father in his new apartment once,' I said carefully. 'I thought there was a vague chance I could try to get him to continue taking his medicine, to see if it would neutralise his... mania. Our conversation took a different turn at the time, and we never even broached the subject of his medication. But I left the box of Quilonorm with him. Is there a problem?'

'No, no problem... The latest questions by the police reminded me I had given them to you, that's all...'

I swallowed. I couldn't imagine what was going through his mind.

'The thing is, they didn't just find lithium in his body. They found other stuff.'

My stomach knotted.

'Something that can only be obtained with a prescription. And I have no idea how he might have obtained it. The police have asked our family doctor and my father's psychologist. But he hadn't seen either of them for many months before his death, and neither of them had prescribed this drug. They are curious to know where he would have obtained it. That's all.'

That's all? I swallowed and shivered, pulling my jacket around my chest. I had been careful not to use something that couldn't be obtained over the counter. I was thankful I hadn't accepted my own GP's offer of a sedative, otherwise that might have found its way into Manfred's lethal cocktail. I was nevertheless uneasy about Gerry's comments. He must have been mistaken about the prescription drugs. I shrugged.

In the distance, someone scored a goal, and the joyous roar from the young team allowed me the opportunity to stop, turn away from Gerry and concentrate on the celebration on the field. A group of boys gathered round the goal scorer, jumping up and down and administering high fives. I chewed my lip.

'I'm not sure why you think this is significant enough to have to meet me, Gerry. What is it you think you will learn from me?'

'I'm not sure.'

He looked sad now, and I felt sorry for him.

'It was because of that connection with his medication. I guess it's a bit late to be searching for answers, isn't it? You already tried to help my father all those months ago, and I'm now sorry I didn't help you more. I am sorry, Alice, really.'

I looked at him. He seemed genuinely upset. It felt like the most natural thing in the world to place my arms around him and give him a comforting hug. But as he lowered his head and buried it against my shoulder, it was too late. Touching him could have been the undoing of both of us. I heard the intake of his breath against my ear, and the hair on the back of my neck stood up.

'Gerry, I… No.'

I pushed gently at his arms.

'Alice, Alice. I need to see you. Please don't push me away.'

'Gerry, I'm so sorry. I think you've misunderstood. I cannot reciprocate your feelings. I'm not even sure I understand what is going on here. But I am a married woman. I have a family. Whatever fantasy you are building, it cannot happen.'

He looked at me with forlorn eyes, then stood straight and replaced his wistful look with an uneven smile.

'I know how I make you feel, Alice. Wisdom may be on your side, but I am youthfully aware of what constitutes attraction. *That* kind of attraction. I am attracted to you. It's as simple as that. And I know you feel something too.'

'I know you are, Gerry. And I'm not denying you are an attractive young man. You just need to know that I would not…'

Gerry's hand wound itself in my hair and, with his other hand on my shoulder, he pulled me towards him, placing his exquisitely soft mouth on mine. He tasted minty. Toothpaste, not chewing gum. As if he had been planning this. A real kiss.

I was horrified to find myself kissing him back, my breath whipped from my throat, my knees suddenly weak and my belly on fire. As my head began to spin, I pushed him away.

'No… please, Gerry. Don't do this. You have to respect my wishes. I don't want to destroy my family, let down my husband.'

'He will never know.' Gerry smiled strangely, and placed his finger gently on my lips. 'Shh.'

It was as though the roles were reversed. I was now the innocent young maiden and he the lover with many years' experience. I was helpless. I couldn't let him kiss me again, no matter how much I wanted him to.

We never even reached the trailhead. I thought we might walk to the Wildenburg ruins on the edge of the Lorze Gorge, but now I knew I needed to get away as quickly as possible.

'I have to go. Gerry, we cannot meet again. It will destroy both of us. I'm sorry. I have a lot more to lose than you.'

The football game came to an end with a triple shrill of the referee's whistle. I turned to watch the teams jogging towards the centre of the pitch, forming a line with their backs to us to congratulate each other on the game. I wondered absently who had won. Team blue or team red. I had to think about something other than the sweet burning sensation on my lips. I turned to walk back to the post office parking lot, fists still deep in my pockets so Gerry couldn't hold my hand.

As we reached the car, I pressed the key to unlock it, and he gallantly held the door open for me. He took my hand as I shifted into the seat, the confines of the car protecting me from his touch. He turned my wrist, looked at my other arm.

'You took it off. The friendship band.'

I kicked myself mentally for not having returned the bracelet. I didn't want to be beholden to him for anything. It was in my bedside drawer, but now I vowed to throw it out.

'But we are still friends, yes?'

'Yes, Gerry. Of course we are still friends. You are a fine young man.'

It was hard to know how to finish this conversation. It was difficult enough tearing myself away, regret now flooding in on my guilt. But something inside me knew I shouldn't anger him. A breeze ruffled Gerry's hair, and I leaned over to pull the door closed.

'You must have a string of women after you,' I said. 'You shouldn't be occupying yourself with someone like me. I'm just about old enough to be your mother.'

I winced at the age-old cliché, but wanted to try and shock him into accepting the truth of our incompatibility, without enraging him with my rejection. At the same time I was a little sad. The excitement of a first attraction I would never again be allowed to experience. He tried not to look hurt.

The door clunked shut and I opened the window halfway. I didn't offer to drop him anywhere, and I didn't ask how he'd arrived there in the first place. I turned the key in the ignition, and the Land Rover coughed into life. I wished I could hold on to that feeling of excited devotion. There was a certain exhilaration – made to feel young, the energy, the goodness. Wanted.

'There's one more thing, Alice.' Gerry hesitated, and my ears rang with the change in his voice. 'I can't help feeling there might be something you are not telling me. About the day my father died.'

I went cold. And just like that I knew he suspected.

'Alice, if you change your mind about seeing me, you have my number.'

He spoke through the rectangle of space, his voice now monotone.

'You can always call or text me. I'll be around, and if you think of anything significant you need to tell me, I'm here. I'm here for you.'

A cold wind momentarily roared through the gap in the window, making my eyes smart as he turned to go. Initially grateful he had kept me sane by not constantly dragging me back to the memory of Manfred, I now imagined this was all a ruse to disarm me, make me talk.

I drove away, eyes flicking to the rear-view mirror as Gerry diminished in my vision. The warm glow I had felt half an hour before was now a cold brick in my stomach.

ALTHOUGH I HAD performed the mundane domestic task of the weekly shop on the way home, I was still wavering between worry and betrayal as I walked through the apartment door. I carried my bags to the kitchen.

'Hey, hey! What's going on?' I exclaimed as I shrugged out of my jacket.

The fridge door was wide open, and an empty chocolate wrapper lay torn on the kitchen table. School and sport bags were piled up in the doorway.

'Don't you have any homework? Have you showered already? How was training?'

I closed the fridge door.

Oliver dragged his schoolbag over to the table.

'We didn't have training tonight. We had an away game. The first of the season. The other team couldn't play on Saturday. There was a change at the last minute.'

His voice was tight.

'Let me go and start the laundry, and I'll be right back to prepare dinner, and you can tell me all about it.'

'Mum... you...'

'I'll be right back. Kit in here?'

I didn't wait for an answer and left the kitchen.

'You don't care that I scored a goal then!' he yelled angrily after me.

He was in a bad mood, provoked by finding his brother had eaten all his chocolate, and wasn't yet home to argue about it. It was pointless talking about it if Leo wasn't there to defend himself. I bit my tongue and shook my head as I walked down the hallway. I would give him five minutes to calm down. Down in the laundry room I stuffed Oliver's football gear into the machine. Red jersey. Their home jersey was white. *The red strip…* It was their away strip. *They played away.*

Fear clutched at my throat. The blood drained from my face, and panic kept me rooted to the spot as I listened to water trickling into the machine and the first whir of the turning drum.

CHAPTER SIXTY-TWO

'MUM, DON'T YOU even care that I scored a goal? It's the first time they put me on as a forward. I've always been in defence. This is huge for me.'

'Of course I care, Oli. I think it's fantastic. I'm so proud of you!'

'You don't care, Mum. I saw you there, schmoozing with that bloke.'

My stomach dropped. I grabbed the back of a chair.

'Who *was* that?' Oliver continued. 'I thought I recognised him, but couldn't see from across the pitch. Didn't I see him here one time? Isn't that the kind of stuff married people aren't supposed to do? I never saw you kiss Dad like that.'

My heart raced and my mouth went dry. My whole future was in danger of splintering into a thousand sharp pieces. I added raw fear to the cocktail of emotions I was now experiencing.

'Oli, that man you saw me with today, he was just a friend, he needed comforting, he was…'

The front door slammed and Simon strode down the hallway, pulling his tie away from his collar as he came into the kitchen.

No! I need more time!

I was still in shock and didn't have time to hide the worry on my face.

'What?' Simon came to a halt, and I shook my head, forcing my mouth into a smile.

I drifted towards him and put my arms around his neck. I hugged Simon and glared at Oliver over his shoulder, silently willing him not to say any more. But Oliver's anger was still coming off him in hormone-enraged waves. He was hurt, wrongly assuming I had made the effort to go and watch his game, but missed the one defining moment of his pre-adolescent football career.

'Mum was snogging some guy at the football match today. She didn't give a stuff about my game.'

Simon burst out laughing, gently pushed me away, and fetched a beer from the fridge. I put my hand to my forehead.

'I didn't know you had a match, young fellow. How did you do?' Simon asked, popping the cap off a *Baarer Bier*.

'At least *you* care,' Oli said, pouting. 'She couldn't even get her mouth off his face.' Simon's smile faltered. He lowered the beer.

'Whoa, hold on there. What are you on about? What are you accusing your mother of? Why the anger, Oli? Did you guys lose?'

Simon's gaze flickered to my face, and he stood straighter, registering my glossy eyes. He put the beer bottle on the counter and wiped a fleck of froth from his lip.

'No, Dad, we won, and I scored a goal. The winning goal.'

Oliver placed the palms of his hands on the table and stood up. His chair screeched on the floor tiles as he pushed it away with the back of his legs, then stamped out of the kitchen and up the stairs. My mouth hung open. I was stunned. This was the last thing I'd expected – and it was all down to some incredibly bad timing.

'What guy?' Simon looked at me curiously.

My teeth clicked as I closed my mouth. Sweat pricked at the sides of my nose.

'What guy, Al? Hello, Alice? What guy? He's got some story mixed up here. Let me go and talk to him.'

I had to say something, but didn't have time to think. Another lie would have been the more sensible option.

'It was Gerry. Gerry Guggenbuhl.'

'Wha…? The stalker's son? You've got to be shitting me, Alice. You went to a football match with the son of your stalker? What the fuck?'

I sucked in my lower lip. My eyes felt white-hot.

'I didn't know Oli was playing a match. It was a coincidence.'
Oh. That sounded bad.

I couldn't think straight. I usually had time to devise the scenarios that were making up my whole life of lies, but the suddenness of Simon's entrance had messed up my lines. I hadn't had time to rehearse.

'So, let me get this right. You're meeting this kid in secret? What the hell were you doing?'

'Not secret, Simon. I just hadn't told you yet.'

'And that's not the same as keeping it secret?' He raised his eyebrows.

I wasn't sure whether I preferred his sarcasm or his heated bewilderment. He turned and left the kitchen, took the stairs two at a time, and I heard the clunk of his shoes down the hallway to Oliver's room. My mind went blank. All I could think about was that Simon hadn't taken his shoes off. We didn't do that. We all took our shoes off before going upstairs.

Seconds later, I raced after him. The last thing I wanted was for Oliver to become involved in some whodunit game of finding out what Mum had been doing during her clandestine meetings with someone Dad thought had completely disappeared from all our lives.

In the short time it took me to run up the ten stairs, I had a massive decision to make. There were secrets upon secrets it hurt to keep inside. I felt my guts rotting with the weight of them. Sometimes I wasn't even sure what was truth and what was fiction any more. I had become as much of a pathological liar as the man who had stalked me for half a year. I wanted to lance the boil, spill the whole putrid truth in front of Simon. I wanted to be absolved of my wrongdoing.

But if I told him the whole truth, I would implicate him in my actions to protect my family. I loved Simon enough to want to avoid doing that at all costs. He must never know the whole truth. Someone had to be around to look after the boys in case this whole thing went belly up.

But how I was going to explain myself to Simon, right then, escaped me.

Simon was too angry to acknowledge that Oliver shouldn't be made to rat on his mother. Oliver had enough burdens to deal with. Things Simon didn't know. We already had too many secrets between us. I guessed that's why Oliver was feeling so betrayed by me. To see me with a strange man, barely more than a boy. That might not ordinarily strike a chord with him, but he'd seen me kissing him. And I couldn't forget I'd kissed him back.

'Are you saying you saw Mum *kissing* this man? Are you sure you saw right? I mean, you were busy scoring a fantastic goal. Don't you think it's possible you could have made a mistake?'

Simon's voice was urgent, wanting it all to be a mistake.

A sob caught in my chest, and something unravelled.

'It was the guy who was here once. I saw him leaving the house. I'm sure it was the same guy.'

My palm clapped to my chest in a futile gesture, to keep my heart from pounding.

No, Oli!

I could feel the rainbow of Simon's emotions from where I stood at the door. Confusion, betrayal, disappointment and, lastly, searing anger. He could no longer speak, and I imagined the rage that had now caught his tongue. He stood up and brushed past me where I was leaning on the doorjamb, knocking into my shoulder. I steadied myself and locked eyes with Oliver as we listened to Simon walk down the hall and shut himself in the bathroom.

Oliver's angry face had calmed. He looked at me warily, worry pitting his chin, and his lip trembled. I wanted to hold him.

'It's not what you think, Oli. He's...'

I wanted to tell him the truth. I wanted to tell him that Gerry was the son of the man who'd been menacing us. But to explain everything would take too long and become too complicated. There were things I would need to miss out of that explanation. That I had kissed that young man would disgust Oliver all the more. And telling him only part of the story would make everything sound worse.

It was Simon I needed to talk to first. Simon who needed straightening out.

I knocked softly at the bathroom door. 'Can I come in? I need to talk to you.'

Silence.

I went to our bedroom, sat on the edge of the bed and pressed my palm over the duvet, smoothing out non-existent creases.

Simon took an age. I imagined him looking in the bathroom mirror, wondering what had possessed his deranged wife. He would be giving himself a pep talk, as he might do before facing the crowds at a conference. I heard Oliver in his room playing with the battery-operated Transformer he'd received for Christmas, and I knew he had already moved on.

The front door of the apartment slammed, and for a brief moment I thought Simon had gone quietly down the stairs and left the house.

'Mu-um! They didn't have any hot dogs at the club.'

Leo must have been dropped off by another parent. He dumped his bags in the hallway and I heard him searching for us in the rooms downstairs.

'Power was out,' he continued. 'I haven't had anything to eat. Is there any dinner left?'

Oh, I forgot the dinner!

'I'll be down in a minute, Leo,' I called. 'We haven't eaten yet. Can you press the "off" button on the oven, please?'

The lasagne I had prepared that morning would have been ready long ago, with help from the oven timer. I heard him mumble something about 'having to do everything round here' as he went into the kitchen.

'Blimey, Mum. The lasagne looks a bit burned,' he shouted back. 'Can I have a shower first? There was no hot water either.'

He started up the stairs and the bathroom door opened. Simon must have heard Leo come in and his subsequent requests.

'Uh. Hi, Dad.'

'Did you have a good day? How's the karate coming? Learn any good moves?' Simon's voice sounded so normal, I marvelled at his control.

'It was cool,' Leo answered. 'Same as always. I'm just going to shower.'

I heard Leo's clothes being shed outside the bathroom door. The floorboards creaked as Simon appeared through the bedroom door. His eyes were red, but not from tears. He was angry. Very angry. He pushed the door closed.

'I'm not sure what's going on with you, Alice. But the biggest mistake you've made here is in somehow involving one of our boys.'

And I thought: *God, you don't know the half of it.*

CHAPTER SIXTY-THREE

'WHATEVER OLIVER SAW, and whatever you will shortly tell me it was that Oliver saw, he already has some kind of predetermined picture in his head of something his mother has done wrong.'

I opened my mouth, began to rise from the bed, but Simon put out a hand.

'I haven't finished.'

He spoke as though he was addressing one of the boys. I was no more than his child right then.

'I know Oli is not yet a teen, and has to deal with all the temptations of deceit that come with hiding stuff from his parents, but I trust his judgement, probably more than yours at the moment, and… Jesus Christ, Alice, what were you thinking?'

'You're not even going to let me tell my side of the story?'

'Alice, the main issue here is you shouldn't be having anything to do with that arsehole's son in the first place. If this is all just an innocent meeting that went horribly wrong, I'm willing to give you the benefit of the doubt. But Oliver said it's the same guy he's seen here, in this house. In our home! He's not lying, is he?'

I sucked in my lower lip. My confused mind still hadn't had time to think up a valid excuse.

'Is he?' Simon yelled, making me jump.

Through the narrow gap in the door, the mechanical toy buzzing in Oliver's room ceased and, in the heavy space between our words, I heard Leo run the shower in the bathroom. Socked footsteps padded along the hallway. Oliver pushed open our door.

'Did you call, Dad? I'm hungry. Is dinner ready yet? At this rate it'll soon be bedtime.'

Oliver looked innocently between us, hunger eclipsing any registration of tension. Adolescent priorities.

'Simon, we'll talk about this later,' I whispered.

'Don't bother serving me, I won't be down to eat,' said Simon as he kicked off his shoes and stamped on the legs of his trousers to take them off.

He sat on the bed and turned on his bedside light. With his back to me, his shoulders slumped, his body language was suddenly weary.

I laid a hand on his shoulder, and he flinched, shunning my touch. I took a breath to tell him I loved him, but clamped my mouth closed, thinking it might sound pathetic. I hoped my gesture of physical contact conveyed my regret. I took my silence down to the kitchen to serve burned lasagne to the boys.

Oliver was unaware his anger had caused a rift. As I dished up a steaming plate of food, it occurred to me that my maternal role as the provider of meals, clean laundry, tidy beds and refilled shampoo bottles superseded the concept that I was someone who could potentially destroy his family. His ego was bruised. Analysis of why his mother was at or near his football game in the first place didn't enter into it. The kissing thing probably disgusted him on a more infantile level than understanding the implications of my betrayal. The fact was, although he hadn't known I was going to be at his game, I was there anyway, but missed him scoring that goal. He was the one betrayed, not Simon.

He now had a voracious appetite, and all other thoughts were obliterated as he satisfied this fundamental human need.

'Where's Dad?' Leo asked absently between mouthfuls, wet hair plastering his neck.

'Dad's not hungry,' I said. 'He's not feeling well.'

'I like it crunchy like this on top, Mum. Good stuff,' he continued, my answer ultimately of little importance to him.

After pushing the blackened cheesy crust to the side of my plate, I couldn't face eating either, and sat quietly listening to the boys' chatting away in Swiss German at the table. Their fluency in the language, and my exclusion from their banter, made me feel all the more isolated. As soon as their cutlery clattered to their plates, I cleared away the dinner things and went back upstairs to the bedroom.

Simon was lying on top of the covers in his boxer shorts, his shirt open to the waist, socked ankles crossed. I was sure he wasn't reading a word of the book he was holding. I gently closed the bedroom door so the boys couldn't hear our discussion. Simon spoke first.

'He *has* been here, hasn't he?'

I pressed my lips together, and silence confirmed my guilt.

'I thought so. That stupid leather bracelet. It was his, wasn't it? Jesus, Al, did you fuck him on the sofa where we made love that night? How could you?'

'No! No, Simon we didn't... we haven't. Nothing like that has happened. How can you say that when you don't even know what's happened? We haven't had sex!'

At the mention of sex, I recalled the dream I'd had about Gerry on Christmas Eve. Simon narrowed his eyes. For him, the expression I could not prevent appearing on my face said it all.

'Wanting to is almost as bad as actually doing it, Alice.'

He stood up abruptly, his creased shirttails comical against his thighs.

'Well, I know one thing. You're the one who wanted to leave this house. Now would be as good a time as any to make your choices without the rest of us. It seems to me that's what you want, isn't it?'

'This has all got way out of control, Simon. Please, you have to believe me. There is nothing going on between Gerry and I. I swear. Are you telling me you think I should leave? Isn't that a bit harsh? We need to talk this through.'

'Alice, my patience has been tried for the past six months. You've become progressively more uncommunicative with me, your partner, your husband. And, for God's sake, your behaviour has become completely irrational. You've made some decisions not even a child would make.'

My breath came in puffs and I bit my lips together. He stopped, realised he'd gone too far. It was pointless for me to try and justify my actions, when the chemical synapses that produced Simon's vitriol had themselves been triggered by irrationality.

'I can tell you this. You're not sharing my bed tonight. And it's not me who's going to stoop to the pull-out in the office. You can make your own bed and sleep in it. Excuse the metaphor, *Mrs* Reed.'

Without speaking, I gathered my nightshirt, bathrobe, and a book I knew I wouldn't be able to read, and headed to the office, pulling a set of sheets from the hall cupboard on the way. As I smoothed the bottom sheet over the concertinaed mattress of the sofa bed, Leo poked his head around the door.

'What's going on, Mum? Dad sounds really pissed off. Are you sleeping in here?'

I bit back a quip about Leo's coarse language.

'It's just one of those marriage things. We can't get on all the time, I guess. Relationships have their ups and downs, Leo. We'll be all right in the morning.'

I couldn't speak any more. A sob blocked my throat. My hair swung around my downturned face as I concentrated on smoothing the sheet onto the mattress again and again. Leo wandered off to his room. I took a shaky breath, and went to check on Oliver. He was lying on his bed with headphones on, head bobbing gently from side to side, oblivious of the chaos he had created.

CHAPTER SIXTY-FOUR

'WHY, MUM? THIS is so extreme. Why can't you "work things out" here, in our home?'

Leo's voice wobbled, and I put down the sweater I had been folding and hugged him. I was surprised when he hugged me back, hard. Of both the boys, I'd thought Oliver would be the one who would be more upset about the temporary separation.

'It won't be for long. Your dad and I have talked it through, and it's for the best. Sometimes it's easier to talk about things when there's distance in between. Anyway, you guys are going off on a fantastic ski trip soon.'

Simon was adamant about having the break. If I hadn't gone on about wanting to move out of our apartment in the New Year, he probably wouldn't have insisted on the separation. He thought this break would prove to me that my negative sentiments about where we lived were unfounded, and that I'd find a way to sort out the confusion in my head about what had happened.

I'd rented a studio room on the ground floor of a row of houses directly on the lake, not far from the centre of the village. A small part of me was thrilled to be so close to the water, a sentiment shared by Oliver, who hoped I would still be there in the summer so he could enjoy swimming directly from the garden area in front of the building. I told him it would probably only be for a few weeks at most, and he sulked for an entire afternoon.

The boys would come to me for lunch every day, but would continue to live at home. They could call me whenever they wanted, and we would be free to go on outings at the weekend. For the moment, Simon and I would perform these duties on an alternating basis, and would see very little of each other. I also thought he'd insisted on taking on all this extra work as a kind of test for me. He wanted to know how far he could truly trust me to keep my word.

Easter was approaching and Simon wanted to take the boys on a skiing trip to Zermatt. They would be staying in a stunning hotel on the edge of the ski slopes and I had to fight the jealousy in my gut. I wouldn't have downhill-skied, as my ankle was still pestering me after many months, but I knew it would be a fantastic experience for the boys, and I petulantly wished I could be part of their memories.

Instead I thought I might take the bus to Rothenthurm if the days were clear and have the last skate ski of the season.

WHEN SIMON AND the boys left, there was a strange emptiness. Everyone had gone. A part of me wondered if I would even have been happy to see Manfred around the corner in the village.

I awoke on Saturday to a beautiful spring day, and knew the last of the snow would soon be gone from the pre-alpine cross-country trails, so I dressed early and left for the *Langlaufloipe* without breakfast. I'd skated a few times over the winter, thrilled to find that the sport put no pressure on my ankle, and I'd gradually improved over the season.

As I tapped my boots free of snow so I could put the bindings in and close the Velcro around the pole straps at my wrist, I looked up at the flags flapping next to the trail. A warm *Föhn* wind had begun to blow from the south. They said it carried the capacity for lunacy and irritability, but that morning I felt good, and there was something secretly divine about playing hooky from my family.

I'd skated a full ten kilometres before I realised I'd forgotten to fill the water bottle in my belt. The sun was blazing, and the hot wind that had been blissfully at my back as I headed along the valley now blew into my face as I rounded the loop to head into the blazing sun. My energy was sapped, and I started to feel weak with hunger. The sunlight glistened pale yellow in the traces left by the other skiers ahead of me. The snow was softening, and in some places water was beginning to gather in the tracks. I was amazed at how quickly conditions had changed, although, with spring on the way, I should have expected this.

My skis were no longer gliding smoothly. The melting snow gripped them, and I began to struggle up the slightest of slopes. I saw a chalet in the distance, the *Steinstübli*, where they served drinks. I had some change in my pocket and knew I must stop before I dehydrated. I ordered a mineral water from the outside bar and walked around to the east side of the chalet to sit in the shade. My face was hot, and my head began to ache dully.

'*Endlich.* I find you here, and on such a beautiful day!'

My body was too exhausted to react to Gerry's greeting, and I smiled flatly. I'd known there was a possibility he would be on the *Loipe*, but thought it unlikely we would meet. Now I wondered whether our running into each other had somehow been manipulated. He peeled the Velcro pole straps from his bare hands and pushed his sleeves up his arms. His head was bare, his hair shining in the sun.

'You look a bit hot. Here, take some of my magic potion. Pure water doesn't always do the trick in these conditions.'

He handed me the bottle from his ski belt, and I gratefully took a sip. Although it was lukewarm, it tasted of lemon and was slightly salty, and I couldn't help myself. I gulped the liquid once I realised it contained the energy my body needed.

'Are you okay?'

Gerry knelt down beside me, and my eyes involuntarily filled with tears. I couldn't work out why. Was it because I missed Simon and the boys so much, that I was just happy to see someone I knew, or was it that, deep down, I was always hoping I might see him? Heat exhaustion was blinding my logic.

'I need a coffee. I'll be right back,' he said.

I looked around and realised he was on his own. He walked to the bar. His muscular legs in the tight Lycra ski gear still made the heat rise to my already flushed face, in turn making my temple throb. He returned to sit by my side, leaning against the warm wood of the chalet wall, and we surveyed the snow-covered moorland.

'They say beavers may return to live here. I love the wilderness.' He sipped his coffee. 'I think this will be the last ski day this season. You see how quickly the snow can melt? I think we should not stay long, otherwise we will not make it back to the start of the *Loipe*. You're alone?'

I nodded.

'Thanks for the drink, Gerry. I'm already feeling better. It was stupid of me to go without breakfast this morning. You're right. I'd better make a move. I'm not very competent on this sticky snow.'

'I'll come with you. Here.'

Gerry put out his hand and I reached out to take it. A little static shock connected us as he pulled me to my feet, and he hung on to my hand a moment longer than necessary.

When we arrived back at the start of the loop, I was exhausted. Gerry greeted a couple of skiers, friends of his packing their equipment into their ski bags, and I half-hoped he would be persuaded to go with them for a beer or a meal. But that half-hope turned to an inexplicable feeling of gratitude as he came back to me instead.

'Do you have your car?'

'No... I came by bus.'

'Then I can take you home. It's no trouble for me. It's on my way. I often drive through Aegeri. There's always a chance I might see you.'

He smiled and a chill went through me. It was still there, his desire.

'Gerry, I...'

'It's all right. Come on... lighten up. I'll drop you at home, okay?'

My legs were tired, and I was grateful not to have to walk to the bus stop. Instead we made our way to a red hatchback in the parking lot. Gerry opened the back and changed his boots, placing them neatly in a sports bag. For a young man, I thought he had so much confidence, and hoped it wouldn't be long before my own boys displayed this type of self-sufficiency. He pulled out a dry T-shirt, and I felt my own shirt, damp at the small of my back. He pulled his ski top off, and a tiny cloud of steam drifted from his torso. My gaze was transfixed by the sinewy muscles in his arms and shoulders, tapering to a slim waist. As he hauled the dry shirt over his head, my knees went weak.

It was my undoing.

CHAPTER SIXTY-FIVE

THE DISTANT, PERSISTENT quacking of a restless duck at the lakeside woke me, ever the light sleeper. An almost full moon shone through the open window, lighting Gerry's chest. The window creaked slightly with the warm breeze that still blew across the lake.

Lunacy and irrationality.

My temples pounded and the cloying aroma of wine swam about my head.

The cover had slipped off Gerry's body, half-turned towards me. His arm reached unconsciously across the mattress, causing my heartbeat to quicken. Those hands, so soft on my body only hours before. His tongue, opening me like a delicate flower for the first time. Bringing me to pleasure for so long, tears flowed at the exquisiteness of it, before he filled me, claiming a deep part of me I was sure no one else had ever touched, not even Simon.

The moon cast an ethereal glow on his skin, its colour-leaching pall accentuating the creamy smoothness of youth. I wanted to reach out and touch the taut, muscular stomach, but I was afraid to wake him. It was as though I was hallucinating. The smugness of some teenage reverie.

But this was not a dream.

He was like a young god, in the confidence of youth. I could not have known what he had experienced before me, but his passion made me weak, thinking about it. This fleeting time was an indulgence, to be studying him so unabashedly without him being aware. My fingers hovered above the strong deltoid muscle of his shoulder. With alcohol still swimming minnows through my brain, I refused to allow guilt to ruin this moment, this privilege.

My hand stopped mid-air. This had been the test. The test of resistance. And I had failed miserably. I reluctantly pulled my thoughts back to Simon, and rolled onto my back. There were so many things Simon must never know.

It was crazy to think that anything long-term could endure with Gerry.

When we had stopped outside my studio earlier, I'd automatically invited him in. My thirst still raged, but instead of the water my body needed, we drank wine, first one bottle of Chablis from my fridge, and then a Spanish Rioja Gerry had rolling around in his car. On an empty stomach, and with the fundamental need for nurturing and attention, I sipped from his cup. Enough of it for me to lose any sense of judgement.

THE BREEZE CAUSED the window to swing wide and then thud gently into its frame. Gerry stirred. He placed a hand on my thigh and I thought how adult the gesture seemed. Something Simon might have done. It was hard to believe this young man was only a dozen years older than Leo.

'Hey, beautiful.'

Gerry propped himself up on his elbow and drew circles with the tip of his finger on my abdomen, sending delicious shivers down my body.

'Alice, what is that word you use to describe something said that you don't mean, or something that happens that is not as it seems, and is the opposite of what you expect? In science we use the word *paradox*.'

'We use that word too. Are you thinking of irony? What do you find ironic, Gerry?'

I wasn't sure I wanted to hear.

'That my father wanted you all that time, but could never have you. And that he would never really have known you, never have had you so completely in this way. I have done this for him. It's like a legacy. What I have done for him.'

I swallowed and shivered as the breeze grazed my skin. He had done this *for* him? He must have meant he had done this *instead* of him. I remained silent and he continued.

'This is so pure, this thing. We are standing on the precipice of truth, Alice. I have at last possessed what my father never could. And I know there is a part of his journey that you have also been on. I know you have been there. It is a journey I hope never to take, under your loving guidance. But you must believe me when I say I will not let you fall.'

I wondered what journey he was talking about. To the bridge?

How naive I had been to think that sleeping with this young man, securing a place in his heart, would quash the suspicions and uncertainty in his mind. I was terrified he meant his father's final journey into the forest. I wasn't sure whether he had doubts, or whether there was an alternative agenda.

That we both stood on the precipice of truth was evident. I was now too close to the edge to shout out loud, for fear of losing my balance and falling. As long as I did what he wanted, I was sure Gerry would save me. By giving myself so completely to him, I was sure my family would be safe.

But when I woke in the morning, the enormity of what I had done pounded on my conscience as painfully as my hangover. Hot tears pressed at my eyes, and scant relief came from their spilling onto the pillow as I held my head.

I couldn't stop crying, although I knew I must. I couldn't let Gerry think I regretted this. I needed him on my side more than ever.

CHAPTER SIXTY-SIX
APRIL

THEY CAME TO my studio, two of them in a car, and politely insisted that 'immediately' would be a good time to go to the police station in Zug to discuss some issues. I was confused, but I still believed Gerry would save me. He knew now, more than anyone, even Simon, how his father had made my life a wretched hell. It was almost a year ago to the day that I had talked Manfred off the Tobel Bridge.

I initially thought it was ridiculous that I was being arrested. Manfred's death was a clear-cut case of suicide. He'd finally achieved what he set out to do that Sunday last spring. His son, Gerry, would be my character reference and my alibi. He would be my life support. I even believed he would lie for me.

In the cantonal police administration block I was made to wait in a room that looked like any other office. I couldn't run away now. We were four floors up, but the windows were closed. The only way out was through the reception into the stairwell. The automatic glass door leading there required the swiping of a key card to open it. It was a far cry from Müller's office downstairs.

When they asked me to put my hair in a ponytail, I complied with puzzlement. I thought they were going to perform some test on my eyes, or take a DNA swab. They asked me to step into the office next door, where a large-bellied man sat in an office chair, swivelling from side to side. He didn't look like a lab assistant. He was dressed in green camouflage trousers and wore a multipocketed jacket. I was sure I'd never seen him before. But as he nodded first at me and then at another policeman near the desk, he said gruffly '*S'isch ihr*' – *It's her* – and I realised this had been an informal identity parade. If I'd put a colleague next to him with a thin, tatty cigar in his mouth, I'd have known immediately it was the fisherman who'd said hello to me by the lake on that last hike.

I waited another hour before a tall, thin man carrying a bike helmet was led into the room and did the same thing. He walked behind me, looked at my distinctive wild curls clutched back into the ponytail, and said the same thing as the fisherman.

Shortly afterwards they asked me to remove the band from my hair and a woman came in I didn't recognise. Until the officer ushered her out and I heard a faint '*Danke, Frau Steinmann...*' in the corridor.

This confirmed the first of my many lies to the police. That I hadn't been where I said I was hiking on the afternoon of Manfred's death. And they now knew I'd been in his apartment.

THE COURTROOM WAS a benign, pale-grey space. Nothing like the wooden-clad, opulently historic chambers of English films and TV programmes. A judge asked for Gerry to be present. This was an unusual digression from the norm. The Swiss system was not the same as in the UK. Witness reports were usually already incorporated into the public prosecutor's report, and it was up to the judges to discuss the case and come up with their verdict. In effect, they were much like a jury themselves.

I turned to my court-appointed lawyer, Herr Blattmann, with silent curiosity. He shrugged his shoulders.

'They must need to reconfirm or discuss something they have seen in their report. It happens sometimes.'

Despite this alteration to the programme, their request for Gerry to be present was delivered in a kind of bored monotone. He must have been somewhere in the vicinity of the courtroom, perhaps waiting in the hallway, and he sauntered in as though late to a lecture. I was almost relieved to see him, sure his contribution to the interviews as a witness had cleared me of any suspicion. He'd promised me he 'would not let me fall'. He sat on a plastic tube chair like the ones we were all sitting on, placed like an afterthought a short distance from where the judges were sitting. A jug of water and a glass were on the table within arm's reach.

Although my heart was now racing, there was an understated lack of drama surrounding this unusual case of *Tötungsdelikt* – homicide.

Blattmann stretched his neck out of the collar of his shirt, as though he was unaccustomed to wearing a tie, and glanced sideways at me with a nervous smile. I thought he'd done a pretty good job so far, but how would I really have known? I'd only understood half of what was going on. And I mustn't forget I had blatantly lied to him as well. Everyone had had a veritable dose of my deceit.

Every now and then one of the five judges at the table asked me in broken English if I was able to follow the proceedings, as though this was not about me, but someone I had accompanied here. Blattmann instructed me to nod and say yes. It wouldn't go down well if they had to constantly clarify everything to me.

Gerry took his seat and leaned back, crossing one ankle over his other leg. He glanced around the room and perhaps realising the casualness of his pose, planted his feet firmly back on the floor. As his gaze fixed on me, my heartbeat increased and I awarded him the slightest of smiles. A smile I hoped conveyed positive – yes, even loving – thoughts to him. I knew Simon was sitting at the back of the courtroom, but he could not see my face.

I felt the blood rush to my face, though, as I realised Simon would be able to see the intense stare Gerry now gave me. Gerry's look still flipped my stomach, and I was ashamed of the sensation in the public courtroom.

I knew Simon didn't realise it was Gerry who would save me. Having him witness the intensity of Gerry's gaze was a small price to pay for the protection I'd afforded my husband and the boys.

This was crunch time. I knew Gerry would save me, if he believed we would be together. Whatever happened, after this trial, things would never be the same.

One of the judges asked Gerry a question, and he replied in a laconic voice. I reflected he might be a university professor one day, and pride inexplicably bloomed in my chest.

I was a little confused that he didn't speak High German for my benefit; he knew I would find it easier to follow. I was suddenly finding it difficult to understand him, and as he continued to recount his version of events and answer the judges' questions, Blattmann began to fidget beside me. Gerry said something the lawyer was uncomfortable with, and I wasn't sure what. Once or twice Blattmann raised his pencil, cleared his throat, and then looked at me with blatant disbelief, his lower jaw hanging, lip caught on his teeth.

My head went cold, panic set in and I strained harder to understand what Gerry was saying. I saw everything happening from the end of a long tunnel, and my breath came in little pants. Two of the judges stared at me with frowns, while the three others stared at Gerry with raised eyebrows. It was then that I realised he was not following the script.

He was no longer looking at me and began to speak faster, as though he should get it all out before he lost confidence. Although I thought it was unlikely he would lose confidence at all. At that moment he was the most self-assured young man I had ever seen.

And I suddenly realised I'd been getting all the messages wrong.

CHAPTER SIXTY-SEVEN

I WANTED TO yell, 'What the hell are you doing? What do you think you are saying?'

Instead, a panicked 'No, no, no…' tumbled out of my mouth.

Herr Blattmann put a hand on my arm. I wasn't sure whether I would be held in contempt of court, whether contempt even existed in a court of law that looked more like a corporate conference room in the middle of the safest country in Europe.

Before I knew it, Gerry was ushered out, with the instruction that he should stay in the building. He would most likely be required again to give evidence. To give evidence? What were they saying? To give evidence against *me*?

The public prosecutor was instructing the judges to refer to their reports on certain pages. I saw clipped articles of evidence and coloured photos of bags, including my favourite coffee-coloured camisole top, which, somehow, had both Manfred's and my DNA woven into it. I heard the word '*Sperma*' and it made me sick to wonder what he had done with the article of clothing. It was then clear that Manfred hadn't taken it from my washing line, but must have taken it from my dirty laundry basket with evidence of me all over it. And they had found it in Manfred's apartment, along with one of my hair scrunchies and my fingerprints, which were all over his door handles and kitchen furniture.

They did end up taking a DNA swab from me later that day in the police station, to support not only the match on the camisole, but also some hairs found on Manfred's shirt. At the time I'd thought it was routine. As things began to unravel before me, I realised no one was interested in the fact that Manfred had been in my home, had sat in my car, had sought access to me for many months, and would have potentially touched many of my things with traces of my DNA.

If only I'd known, I should have declared that camisole stolen many months ago as Schmid originally suggested. It might have protected me. Except for what came next.

I kept thinking, thank God I hadn't ended up agreeing to the sedatives my GP wanted to prescribe. I wasn't that stupid. There was a pharmacy report. But it wasn't from my doctor. It was from the medics' organisation at the Lausanne marathon. A volunteer remembered giving me a box of Co-Dafalgan. I was the last person seen for medical intervention after the race. But what I hadn't realised was that the 'Co' stood for Codeine, and that this was a medication not available over the counter in Switzerland. But it had been in my bathroom cabinet in my studio.

It was one of those things anyone might keep in case of the occasional headache or menstrual cramps. And the only person who had been in there apart from me was Gerry. I swallowed. According to the evidence report, two of the blister packs were missing from the box. Doses and reports were compared. A pharmacist's report revealed it was possibly the Codeine keeping Manfred asleep, rather than the mixture of lithium and alcohol, that had killed him. The cold probably claimed him in the end, after all.

Back in November, I hadn't counted on such a detailed autopsy. But then again I hadn't thought I'd used anything requiring a prescription. Perhaps I'd concentrated too hard on other things, a result of too many old detective movies where fingerprints were the most damning evidence. Of course, a warrant to look through my studio would have quickly revealed the medication. They had already seized a number of items from the farmhouse.

But I also hadn't counted on Gerry staying with me, hadn't counted on him going through my bathroom cabinet.

It felt strange to learn he was playing detective all along, in order to seek the truth about his father's death. His suspicions had grown despite my attempts to allay his fears. I almost felt sorry for him. He must surely have been tormented. He could not have made love to me like that, looked at me like that, without some regret about his final decision. He must always have known, deep down, our relationship could never go anywhere. Or was it that, once he'd learned I'd been in his father's apartment, he thought we might have slept together? It tied in with another witness report from a waitress at the Lido Café stating that Manfred and I had been seen drinking coffee together the year before. Had jealousy triggered the madness?

Although my heart ached with the betrayal, I could hardly ignore the irony.

CHAPTER SIXTY-EIGHT

WHILE MY HEAD was lowered, there was a commotion in the corridor, voices raised to an angry level. My eyes had been focused on my hands in my lap, twisting the wedding ring on my finger, and I lifted my head to see two journalists rushing to the door. I looked behind me to where Simon had been sitting and saw his empty chair. He must have taken a break to go to the bathroom or get some air. The thought that the strain for him had long since started to take effect made my chest ache.

Gerry's voice punctuated the open door, unseen in the hallway.

'But she killed my father!' he yelled, and I blanched, as though my guilt had only just been precisely identified, as though he was the presiding judge in my trial.

'So you twist her mind, her heart – what for? To make her confess? If you knew it all along, why did you continue such a farce? Don't you think she's been through enough torture at the hands of your sick father? You're a bigger liar than she is. Such deceitful tactics. You are despicable.'

My eyebrows creased and my mouth turned down at the corners with a fleeting smile. Simon was sticking up for me, in his own way. If *I* couldn't explain to him what had possessed me to allow my emotions to be so manipulated by Gerry, then perhaps Gerry could tell him.

I looked up sharply as Gerry appeared, backing through the door into the room, accompanied by a court official who stood aside to let him cross the threshold. He was on his way back to the witness chair when Simon rushed into the room and grabbed him by the shoulders. My hands flew to my mouth. There was a scuffle and fists started to swipe, but it was a comical parody of a fight, every flailing arm missing its mark, like toddlers in the playground. I heard an involuntary 'oof' and couldn't tell whether it came from Simon or Gerry. The searing brightness of a camera flash galvanised the court officials into action. I was sure they'd never seen anything like this in a Swiss courtroom before.

Simon drew back his fist to try and place another punch, but a security guard, sent for when the commotion started, grabbed his arm to detain him. Simon was led out of the room and I felt a deep, welling sadness that he wouldn't be there to support me in his own silent way for the remainder of the hearing.

But I wouldn't be there for much longer anyway. They'd already made up their minds. I could see it on their faces, and I could play this game of deceit no more.

There were no jury deliberations, and even if there were, there was no longer a case to argue.

In my head, as loud as a shout, I pleaded guilty.

AS I WAS led out of the courtroom to return to the holding cells, I passed Gerry sitting in the hallway with his head in his hands. His dishevelled hair sprouted like silky dark snakes between his fingers.

The guard holding me firmly by the elbow hesitated as I halted in front of Gerry. Perhaps he had witnessed what happened in the courtroom and felt sorry for me to the extent that I was allowed this one last glance at my Judas.

Gerry looked up slowly, and I was at a loss to describe what I saw in his red-rimmed eyes. Something between raw anger and hopeless sadness.

'Why Gerry? Why?' I asked quietly, and he shook his head. 'After all you told me about letting things take their course. How your father would never be well. How you never wanted to see him again. Why?'

'You, more than anyone, should know that family is the most important thing. I have been torn. He was my father, Alice. Blood is thicker, and all that. You need to be made to answer for what you have done. But that's not all. My father had a piece of you, and I realise I never can. You will never be mine. I realised after we spent the night together I could never completely possess you.' He paused. 'But if I can't, no one else will either.'

I stared at Gerry open-mouthed and couldn't speak for the madness of it. I wondered if, after everything – after convincing myself he was the key to my freedom – he'd known better than me all along.

'YOU HAVE TO believe me, Simon, I was only *with* him because I was afraid he would reveal my secret. I could never be sure, but I often suspected he had guessed the truth. And then when we were together and I realised he had… fallen for me… the things he was saying. He didn't say outright, but I misread his devotion to me, thought he would cover for me whatever. I can't believe I got it so wrong.'

'Why didn't you tell me, Alice? That's the one thing that eats me up. I can't believe you didn't trust me enough to confide in me at the beginning. You heard the defending lawyer. It was a crime of passion. If you had come clean at the start, things wouldn't have gone this far. Now we have to deal with the perjury and contempt of court. Why, Alice, why?'

'I don't know. I wanted to protect you,' I whispered, tears catching in my throat.

We were sitting in a holding area in the courthouse while they decided on my sentence. As my husband, Simon had been allowed some private time with me, and all I wanted to do was cling to him. My rock. My knight. I couldn't believe I had been so stupid, since the very beginning. But he wouldn't touch me.

I couldn't believe my infatuation with Gerry had led to such an error of judgement. I felt despair hiding behind a wave of incomprehensible emotion, but forced it down while I was in the company of Simon. I would wait until I was alone to open the floodgates.

'I didn't want to implicate you,' I said once my trembling voice had recovered. 'I know my deed can never be excused. But I can't turn back the clock. What would be the point of going over all the mistakes I've made over the past year? What good would that do? I don't have the answers you're looking for. And for that, and all the other shit, I am so, so sorry. I don't know how many times I can say that. I feel truly horrible.

'The thing I feel most terrible about is losing the ability to trust you,' he said. 'And… maybe losing your love.'

'Never my love, Simon. Never my love.'

At this point, neither of us could speak any more.

CHAPTER SIXTY-NINE

AFTER MY SENTENCING they moved me to the all-female Hindelbank Prison near Bern. I was given five years for manslaughter – *Totschlag* – but not for murder. The judges decreed I was an offender under serious distress, provoked by the victim, and under indeterminate serious threat. This constituted a crime of passion, and I might be considered for parole in as little as a year, although as a foreigner I wondered if I would get to apply for it at all.

The biggest issue the court had was with the magnitude of my deceit and therefore my perjury while being questioned originally as a witness. It was one thing to be driven to murder someone. It was another to try and cover all my tracks, apparently. All my sorry mistakes meant that someone, namely Simon, would have to cough up some massive police and court administrative fees to the federal and cantonal governments.

I didn't know whether I would have Simon's support when the time came for me to fight for parole. I was only allowed one phone call a week. We weren't allowed mobile phones. There was one phone booth on each floor of the cellblock, but I had to fight for my place in line each time with a sorry bunch of women who were mostly drug smugglers, and spoke only Spanish or an array of Asian languages. When I did get through to Simon and the boys at home, those behind me in the line kept up a constant barrage of caterwauling or arguing among themselves, so it was hard to have any kind of coherent conversation.

I was only allowed visitors once a month, which I found the hardest of all. Simon chose to visit with the boys after I'd settled. It was very hard for me not to cry when they all piled into the visitors' room. Oliver did all the crying for both of us anyway.

After a genuine hug from Leo, he spent the time shuffling his shoes on the floor under his seat and craning his neck to observe all the cool stuff he could tell his friends about the inside of a prison. I didn't think it was good for them to be there.

In the end, I told Simon not to bring them again, until we all had an idea of how life was going to be in the future. I didn't know whether it was worse to have to say goodbye to them at the end of a visit or not see them at all, and I was too humiliated by my environment to be sure they would keep my memory fresh in their minds. Perhaps it was better for them to forget their mother was a convicted killer. Although how could they forget that? They said the kids at school were okay with them, but I wondered how long it would be until some parent forbade their children to associate with the sons of a murderess. So in the end I chose not to see them, as though by cutting them off from me would protect them from the hostility of their peers.

I could tell Simon was reluctant to visit after that. He was having a hard time dealing with the whole thing. The report of the farce at the trial had been in the paper. I imagined everyone in the village and at school would be horrified. Perhaps Esther might have a grain of sympathy, knowing I had been concerned from the beginning. But I think even Kathy was shocked. She didn't write to me, and if she had tried to get a message to me through Simon, he didn't pass it on.

'You can't imagine the shit I've had to face at work. Jenkins seems to think I had a hand in it somehow. Your "misdemeanour," as he put it. The flipping cheek of it as it was him who sent me all over the place to support the Russian deal last summer. If I'd been around more, and had seen how much that creep was affecting your life, perhaps I'd have paid more attention. There's always a part of me that will take a little blame.'

My eyes watered at his words, and my brows creased.

'But don't go thinking I'm condoning your actions,' he finished.

The tiny moment of compassion had passed. And I knew he was now thinking about Gerry and I as lovers. I wondered how long it would take for Simon to not feel disgusted every time he looked at me. I think he only dragged himself to the prison for a visit so he could bring news of the boys. I was still their mother, after all.

Their overprotective mother. Not the Samaritan they used to think, but a criminal. A killer.

CHAPTER SEVENTY
JUNE

SIMON VISITED ME on the first day of June, when the rows of regimented maize plants in the fields had grown to form a low corridor on either side of the road leading from the Hindelbank village.

He brought a coloured pencil sketch from Oliver, and a short letter from Leo. Oliver's creation showed our home surrounded by animals, not just the farmer's cows, but cats, dogs and birds too. In the foreground, two adults sat at a round table, on the terrace in front of the house. Two kids – Oliver and Leo – swung on ropes in the trees to the side of the building. The drawing spoke of the yearning to have his family back together. Every time I looked at it, a lump wedged in my throat. I tacked it to my cell wall afterwards.

I wanted to save Leo's letter for later, but with conversation not exactly flowing between us, as though Simon was visiting a relative in hospital with a terminal disease, I kept my hands and eyes occupied by unfolding the paper, and silently read my eldest son's short missive.

I could almost hear the distaste in Leo's words – his spidery, cursive skipping impatiently across the paper. He wrote about getting a green belt in karate, how he'd managed to get a five in geography, a brief 'I hope you are well,' forced out by his sense of obligation. I could feel his reluctance not only to put pen to paper, but to communicate with his mother at all. The love between us was of a delicate complexity. I was probably an embarrassment to him, to his social circle. Nothing cool at all about my actions any more. Thank God.

My heart ached for them, all of them. I missed them so.

As Simon stood up to leave, he uncharacteristically gave me a hug, holding me silently. I could tell he was fighting emotions. I allowed my tears to flow unabashedly. There were only so many times I could say I was sorry. Sorry didn't make anyone feel better. Oh, this wretched mess we had found ourselves in. My follies had piled up one after the other. I'd been grateful for my incarceration in one respect. It would give me time to try and work out a plan to make amends for all the hurt. Of course, we could not go back to the way we were. There was too much collateral damage. But I hoped I could patch things up somehow, pull my needle through the threads of the emotions I knew were still there, and sew us all together in a different kind of patchwork.

The thing that saddened me most was that I knew Simon completely understood why I'd done it, why I'd committed murder to protect my family. I think he even understood the reasons behind my relationship with Gerry. He believed it had been born out of a misreading of his own rejection on one hand, and the need to keep the secret of Manfred's murder on the other. He believed Gerry had tricked me through some kind of emotional blackmail without my really knowing.

Simon kept saying he had his own guilt to deal with. A guilt that had him kicking himself for not asking more questions all those months ago about what was going on in my head and heart. Our new open communication gave me a grain of hope for us. But I couldn't forget that his guilt was featherweight compared to mine.

I didn't think I'd be in this place for long, despite my lies, my deception and then my attempt to cover up the atrocity. Stalking had recently become a more recognised crime in Switzerland with the public exposure of my case. My court-appointed attorney, Herr Blattmann, promised to work towards having my sentence drastically reduced, and told me I might realistically be out in as little as a year.

IN THE MEANTIME, I wrote to Simon and the boys every day. I had plenty of time to perfect my drafts. I had nothing to talk about other than how sorry I was. It became a continual penitence, and I told Simon to throw the letters away if he thought I was repeating myself too often. I didn't want this to appear to be obsessive behaviour. I had been to the edge of that too many times in the past two years, from both sides of the abyss.

I often picked up the photo I treasured, of the boys and me standing outside the gates of Versailles two years previously. I remembered Simon taking the photo. The wind had blown my hair across my face, and I had just shaken my head to rid myself of all but a strand, which lay across my cheek. The boys were innocent, one just a teenager, the other gangling between childhood and puberty. Both were smiling at Simon, who held the camera, and made some quip about posing with their mother. The photo frame was made of simple, unvarnished pine, stained grubby by the many hands that had held it.

I imagined the skin of the fingertips that had touched the wood. Manfred, who possessed the photo for weeks. Gerry's prints were there too, on the glass.

It was as though he was my first teenage love. The memory of him still sweet but bewildering. Between a fanciful crush on me and a morbid curiosity to find out if his father was truly suicidal, he would now be writhing in his own torment. He did not contact me, and I was sure he knew it would be futile to try, after all he had done. The fact that I was here, because of him.

The last hands to touch this picture were my own, fingers feathering across the glass each day, wishing I could return to a time before my Samaritan deed, my charity, my crime and my incarceration.

ACKNOWLEDGEMENTS

Bouncing the seeds of an idea back and forth some years ago as we ran the trail in the shadow of the magnificent *Lorzentöbelbrücke*, Carolyn Forsyth was intrinsic to the conception of *Strangers on a Bridge*. She is also one of the members of the multinational book club who became my first beta readers.

To others who have given feedback at various stages: Nicola Upson, Robert Peett, Andy Stafford, Alison Baillie, Louise Buckley, Kathryn Taussig, Vicky Newham and Antony Dunford. To my editor, Hannah Smith, for her enthusiasm and perspicacity.

For technical and legal stalking issues I thank Sargent Totti Karpela, CEO and former President of the Association of European Threat Assessment Professionals (AETAP). Many thanks also to Hansjürg 'Johnny' Baumann, Dienstchef, *Zuger Polizei* and Thomas Rein, Staatsanwalt, Zug.

To my husband, Chris, for his feedback and continued support, and to our two sons, Max and Finn, for the hours I spend ignoring their laundry and hogging one side of our dining-room table. And lastly, to the spectacular landscape surrounding the Aegeri Valley in the Swiss canton of Zug, which continues to inspire me with the desire to write.

ABOUT THE AUTHOR

Louise Mangos writes novels, short stories and flash fiction, which have won prizes, placed on shortlists, and have been read out on BBC radio. Her short fiction appears in more than twenty print anthologies. She holds an MA in crime writing from UEA for which *The Beaten Track* formed her dissertation.

You can connect with Louise on Facebook — /LouiseMangosBooks, or Twitter @LouiseMangos, and Instagram as @louisemangos, or visit her website www.louisemangos.com where there are links to some of her short fiction.

Louise lives in the Aegeri Valley where the novel is set, with her Kiwi husband and two sons.

Lightning Source UK Ltd.
Milton Keynes UK
UKHW011116210422
401839UK00001B/49

9 781915 433138